FOURTH ESTATE

DOUBLE BLIND Book 4

DAN ALATORRE

FOURTH ESTATE *DOUBLE BLIND Book 4*
© 2023 Dan Alatorre. © This eBook is licensed for your personal use only. This eBook may not be re-sold or given away to other people. Thank you for respecting the hard work of this author. © No part of this book may be reproduced, stored in a retrieval system or transmitted by any means without the written permission of the author. Copyright © 2023 Dan Alatorre. All rights reserved. This is a work of fiction. Names, characters, places, and incidents either are the product of the author's imagination or are used fictitiously, and any resemblance to actual persons, living or dead, businesses, companies, events or locales, is entirely coincidental.

OTHER THRILLERS BY DAN ALATORRE

NOVELS

Jett Thacker Mysteries
Tiffany Lynn Is Missing, *a psychological thriller*
Killer In The Dark, *Jett Thacker book 2*

The Gamma Sequence Medical Thriller Series
The Gamma Sequence, *a medical thriller*
Rogue Elements, *The Gamma Sequence, book 2*
Terminal Sequence, *The Gamma Sequence, book 3*
The Keepers, *The Gamma Sequence, book 4*
Dark Hour, *The Gamma Sequence, book 5*

Double Blind Murder Mystery Series
Double Blind, *a murder mystery*
Primary Target, *Double Blind book 2*
Third Degree, *Double Blind book 3*
Fourth Estate, *Double Blind book 4*

A Place Of Shadows, *a paranormal mystery*
The Navigators, *a time travel thriller*

CONTENTS

Acknowledgements

FOURTH ESTATE

A Note From The Author
About The Author
Other Books By Dan Alatorre

ACKNOWLEDGMENTS

This book is the result of a lot of help from a lot of people – readers who share their thoughts; writers that I haven't spoken to in years but whose patient input very early on in my authorish endeavor is still heard in my ear as I toil away at the keyboard today. I appreciate what they did for me way back then, and what those memories still do for me now.

Certain information on weaponry and explosive devices is intentionally vague or exaggerated so if some kid picks up this book, they won't learn enough to do the things described in the story. Such inaccuracies may be irritating to a trained eye, but I hope you can appreciate my rationale.

CHAPTER 1

As Kaliope Hernandez glanced up from her small desk, a sense of apprehension rushed over her.

Something is wrong with that man.

Warm Florida sunlight beamed into the lobby of the Stafford-Love law firm, glancing off the white-tile floor and casting the morning's first visitor in a near-silhouette. The African-American man was more or less average height, but with an awkward kind of stocky build under his red windbreaker. His torso was lumpy, like little kids up north who put on too many layers of clothing to go play in the snow. The visitor wore a paper medical mask across his face—a rare sight but not altogether uncommon these days, even in Tampa—and dark sunglasses, topped off with a blue baseball cap.

But it was the man's blue jeans that caught Kali's eye. His skinny legs didn't seem to match the apparent bulkiness of his torso.

That, and the fact that he had entered the law office without saying a word and now stood just inside the door, silent and still, facing her.

The sunglasses hid the stranger's eyes from Kali's sight, and his stiff, overly rigid posture came off as... odd. And threatening.

As the glass entry door glided shut behind him, the lobby's large, decorative wall clock ticked off the seconds. The visitor's hands slipped into the front pockets of his bulky red windbreaker, but otherwise he didn't move.

A shiver ran up the petite clerk's spine.

Not exactly how a prospective client usually enters this office, but he's not dressed too differently from what some people seeking legal counsel from this firm wear.

Could be drugs...

Forcing her uneasy feelings aside, Kali closed the invoice software on her computer. She took a deep breath and managed a smile. "Good morning. May I help you?"

This guy is probably just down on his luck or something, that's all. Tanny Stafford has certainly been known to occasionally take on an oddball client from time to time.

I hope he's not dangerous.

The man took a step towards her, then stopped.

Kali glanced at the doorway to the adjacent corridor. It separated the lobby area from the lawyers' offices. One of the small firm's two female partners was just around the corner from Kali's workspace, engaged in a phone conversation with a client, as was the practice's sole male associate.

At least Francie and Benjamin are here, so nothing bad is going to happen.

Just chill out, Kaliope.

She gave a quick peek to the corner of the lobby ceiling—and the tiny security camera mounted there.

It should have reassured her, but the odd feeling wouldn't leave. A knot forming in her stomach, Kali returned her gaze to the visitor. "Did you have an appointment, sir?"

The stranger finally moved from the entry, approaching Kali's desk as he glanced toward the hallway door. "Tanny Stafford."

His words were low and gruff, an unexpected combination. Even considering his size and build, Kali expected a more normal voice.

Is he disguising his voice for some reason?

Frowning, she shook her head, preparing to open the office appointment calendar. Her boss was offsite, filming another of the firm's many TV commercials. Tanny Stafford was attractive by any measure, with long dark hair, high cheek bones, and sparkling hazel eyes—and TV viewers agreed, making her commercials very popular. Lately, she had expanded from conventional commercials to short, instructive clips for use on YouTube and TikTok, as well as Instagram, Facebook, Twitter, Rumble, and a host of other, newer social media sites, driving calls to the law firm substantially higher. Tanny's regular videographer had a job cancel at the last minute, so he had phoned the office early, and Tanny agreed to go film something fast, before the day got too hot and ruined her makeup.

"I'm sorry," Kaliope said. "Ms. Stafford is not in the office this morning. Did you say you had an appointment?"

The stranger's hands fumbled with something inside the windbreaker pockets.

"Sir?" Kali slid her mouse across the screen of her computer, engaging the calendar's scheduling tab. "Would you like to make an appointment with Ms. Stafford? Or can I take a message?"

"Uh…" Glancing over both shoulders, the stranger's hands shuffling again inside the bright red windbreaker.

Kali clutched her mouse.

What's he got in there?

He inched forward, turning his head toward the hallway. The conversations of the law firm's other members carried into the reception area.

Another twinge of apprehension washed over Kali.

There is definitely something wrong with this guy.

The knot in her stomach grew. She swallowed hard and forced herself to maintain her professionalism. "Sir?"

The stranger took a half step forward and turned his face back toward Kali, looming over her small workspace.

She held back a shudder. "Did… you want to leave a message?" The credenza behind her held several trophies—one for a girls' softball team that the firm sponsored, and two were legal awards that the founder had won during each of the two fledgling years she had spent running her own business.

In a pinch, any of the trophies would be heavy enough to use as a makeshift weapon.

"Tanny Stafford." Nodding slowly, the stranger maintained his awkward, rough manner of speaking. "She's my lawyer."

"Of course," Kali said.

It's like he's intentionally deepening his voice, the way a woman or child tries to imitate an adult man.

What a weirdo. Why would he do that?

But the paper mask and sunglasses, the baseball cap—it all worked to hide the client's identity in an extremely amateurish—but effective—way.

For a few more seconds, anyway. This guy will have to give me his name and phone number if he wants Tanny to call him back.

And if he's really a client, I bet she will have some wild story about him!

Kali opened a new message tab on her laptop, preparing to scroll through the firm's client list.

The stranger's hands again groped with something in the windbreaker pocket. His breathing became audible and heavy, making the hairs on the back of Kali's neck stand on end. Resisting the urge to shudder, she made herself focus on the computer screen.

The quicker I get you out of here, the better.

"And your message for Ms. Stafford, sir?"

A tiny bead of sweat glided past the stranger's ear and down the side of his cheek. Kali halted her mouse, her heart racing.

He's nervous? Why would he be nervous?

"Sir?" She shifted on her chair and cleared her throat. "Sir, are you—are you... okay?"

Glancing over both shoulders again, the stranger's hands fidgeted inside the windbreaker pockets.

"Sir?"

The man breathed faster, his face directed at hers. He took a step closer to Kali's desk.

She instinctively leaned away.

Down the hall, Benjamin Freed ended the call with his client. "Kali?" His voice bounced into the little lobby. "Can you please pull the Great Oak file? I think I'm going to have to take them to lunch today."

The stranger's head turned toward the sound of the male associate's voice.

"Of course, Benjamin." Kali allowed her neck muscles to relax, a small sigh escaping her lips.

This weirdo finally realizes I'm not alone.

Leave your message and get out of here, creep!

Benjamin's desk chair creaked. His leather dress shoes clopped over the tile floor as he walked toward the lobby.

Kali put a hand to her abdomen.

Yes, please. Come out here.

Sitting up straighter in her chair, she addressed the client, her pulse racing. "Sir..." Kali's voice wavered. Her trembling fingers gripped the mouse tighter. "What... message may I give to... to Ms. Stafford for you?"

The visitor looked toward her, barely an inch from the front of her desk, his shoulders swelling with each rapid breath. He glanced back toward the hallway door. Benjamin's footsteps grew louder as he neared the reception desk.

The stranger's hand pressed outward against the thin material of the red windbreaker, slowly coming out of the pocket. "Yeah," he said. "I have a message for Tanny Stafford. You bet I do."

Nodding, Kali inhaled deeply and prepared to take the client's message. Her shoulders eased, the tightness exiting her chest and neck.

Finally.

The stranger's bulky arm swung upward, pointing a large handgun directly at the clerk's face. "You can tell her this for me."

Kali's jaw dropped. Gasping, she clenched her eyes shut and raised her arms over her head.

A blast exploded from the killer's weapon, the noise of the gunshot filling the air.

Kali's body slammed backwards into her credenza, splattering the firm's awards in thick, red droplets. Her arms dropped to her sides and her head sagged, then she slumped over and crashed face-first onto the tile floor.

As screams came from the offices around the corridor, Kaliope Hernandez's murderer walked forward and turned her body over, putting his weapon to her forehead and pulling the trigger until the gun clicked empty.

DAN ALATORRE

CHAPTER 2

Detective Sergio Martin hugged the lacy, lavender-colored pillow under his head, pulling it up and over his eyes in a failing attempt to keep the morning sun from fully waking him.

Reaching across the bed, he felt for what he knew wouldn't be there—the beautiful woman whose bed he'd shared the prior evening. The mattress and sheets on that side of the bed were cold.

Frowning, Sergio lifted his chin from his partner's soft pastel pillow and squinted to block out the intrusive sunlight, a clump of hair sticking up from the back of his head.

Couldn't Carly skip her morning run just one time when I sleep over?

He sighed, rising from the bed. Scratching his firm, naked rear end with one hand, he gave a quick tap to his phone screen on the nightstand. The device lit up, indicating the time: eight seventeen A. M.

Okay. Plenty of time to drive home and change clothes before the meeting.

But... not enough time for any fun with Carly before I go.

The detective plodded to the semi-dark bathroom and pushed open the door, stepping onto the cold, hard floor tiles. The sound of Carly's voice caught his ear, emanating from somewhere out in her living room.

Or maybe we do have time.

Smiling, he turned around and reached for the bedroom doorknob—but halted, looking down at his nakedness.

It might not be a bad idea to put on some pants, just in case she's out there talking to the newspaper delivery kid who stopped by to make his collections for the week.

Sergio glanced around. His blue jeans had once again been neatly folded on the corner chair. His sneakers rested side-by side on the carpet next to the chair, and his shirt had been draped over the chair back.

Chuckling, he reached for his jeans.

Carly's such a mom.

He slid himself into his jeans and eased open the bedroom door to peek out.

His beautiful partner was sitting on the far end of her living room sofa, facing away from him, with her phone pressed to her ear. Carly was still wearing her running gear, but a light ring of sweat around the collar told Sergio she'd already completed the mini marathon she ran each day before work.

He gazed at Detective Sanderson's shapely figure, admiring her toned back and long legs. Carly had gathered her dark hair into a ponytail for her run, and now it swayed back and forth, brushing the nape of her slender neck as she spoke. On the coffee table next to her rested a cluttered array of papers, her laptop computer, and an enormous, slightly lopsided ceramic cup, adorned with a hand-painted rainbow and equally colorful letters that spelled out "World's Best Mom."

Sergio tiptoed across the living room, trying to make his presence known to his partner without also making it known to whoever was on the other end of the call. He crossed to stand in front of Carly, giving her a small wave.

Her face was drawn and tight. A slight smile came to the corners of her mouth when she looked at Sergio, and she reached out and took his hand, pulling him toward her.

The soft fullness of Carly's lips sent a warm surge through Detective Martin, but he didn't let that take away from the perception that whoever Carly was talking to, they were giving her some kind of unpleasant news. Her lips lingered on his, the breath from her nostrils hot on his unshaven skin. Her hand released his and slid up his arm to the back of his neck, caressing his hair.

When Carly eased her face away from his, her unhappy expression returned.

A slight unease rippled across Sergio's abdomen.

I hope her mom didn't have another health scare.

Carly cupped her hand over her phone, looking at him, her voice a whisper. "I need a minute, Marty."

Nodding, Sergio righted himself. Carly rarely referred to him as Marty outside of when she needed to make a point he wasn't grasping or when she was being personal and playful. This was obviously neither. As Sergio commenced his retreat, he leaned to one side, mouthing the words, "Is everything okay?"

Carly's reply was to close her eyes and put a hand to her forehead, lifting the phone back to her chin. "All right, well... I can't really talk right now. I'm swamped with status report reviews, and I have to get to a meeting downtown, so I need to get going."

Sergio moved as far away as his curiosity would let him, pausing to lean against the door frame of Carly's bedroom.

She nodded a few times, her hair bobbing at every move of her head. Straightening her posture, she sat upright on the arm of the couch. "Okay. Bye."

As she ended the call, Carly dropped her hands to her lap. Her shoulders slouched and she let out a long, deep breath. Then she turned toward Sergio and looked at him with her big, beautiful eyes.

She looked tired—unusual for her, especially right after her run.

He shrugged, hooking his thumbs into the waist of his jeans as he sauntered over to her. "Anything I can help with, gorgeous?"

"No." Shaking her head, Carly got up and wrapped her arms around Sergio's naked torso. She kissed his chest.

He enjoyed the warmth of her body against him, her long hair tickling his exposed skin as they hugged.

"It's just…" she said, "some more unfinished business."

The phrase "unfinished business" had become code words for anything to do with her pending divorce. Sergio had never been divorced—and had never come close to getting married, for that matter—but he had seen a friend or two go through the emotional woodchipper that masqueraded under the wildly inaccurate misnomer of "family law." In their work, Detectives Martin and Sanderson had witnessed the divorce process push normal people to the limits of their sanity—and occasionally beyond that point, sometimes with ugly and homicidal results. Even the divorces that ended amicably tended to leave lasting scars on all involved, especially the kids—which is why, in his present romantic arrangement, Sergio did his best to defer to any and all of Carly's wishes whenever her two sons were involved.

He squeezed his partner, lowering his nose to enjoy the fragrant scent of her long, soft hair. "Whatever you need, dude. I've got your back."

"Mmm." Nodding, she peered up at him and took another deep breath. "You always do, don't you?" She put her cheek back to his chest. "That's why I—"

He leaned back, grinning at her and putting a finger under her chin. "That's why you... What, exactly?"

Carly's eyes twinkled in the morning light. She swallowed hard and opened her mouth, looking at him—but she didn't speak.

A pickup truck rumbled by on the street outside, music thumping from its stereo. The sounds faded as the vehicle continued on its journey. As silence returned to the house, Carly's words still hung in the air.

"That's why I—"

Detective Sanderson cleared her throat. "That's—that's why... uh..." Carly looked away. "That's why I... count on you so much—of course." She twisted away from him and scurried to the kitchen, her hands going to her reddening cheeks. She stopped next to the refrigerator and grabbed the handle, tugging the door open and disappearing behind it. "For example, car shopping." Carly peeked over the door at him. "You *do* still owe me a car, and it's been months…"

"No, not that!" Throwing his arms out, Sergio collapsed backwards onto the sofa. "Please, not that. Not again."

"You promised."

"To *buy* a car." He propped himself up on his elbows, viewing her over the back of the couch. His legs dangled over the armrest. "I didn't promise to *shop* for a car forever. It's cruel and unusual punishment, except it's becoming not too unusual."

FOURTH ESTATE

Carly pulled a container of flavored creamer from the fridge. "If you hadn't wrecked my car, you wouldn't be in this mess."

"Yes. Guilty as charged." Grabbing the back of the couch, Sergio pulled himself into a sitting position. "And I'm ready to pay for your new ride, using the reward money I got from Mrs. Dilger when I was suspended and working for Tyree. Just decide on a car, and it's yours."

"Yeah, well… It's not that easy."

"Really, it is," Sergio said. "Four wheels and an engine? Check. Some doors? Check. Done."

Detective Sanderson opened a cabinet and took out a can of coffee and a mug, setting them on the counter. "My car also needs to be able to fit two growing boys, their friends, a pile of baseball and soccer equipment that seems to get bigger each week, and enough groceries to feed all of the above. Plus, it has to be able to fit a big cooler for their field trips and sports events—as well as enough additional provisions for the ever-hungry sleepover companion that the mother of the house occasionally allows to spend the night."

"What can I say?" Sergio shrugged. "I like eating here. You're a way better cook than me. And, as I stated, I'm happy to pay restitution for destroying that rolling orange nightmare you used to drive—"

"That you also loved driving."

"—that I also loved driving. But may I ask this? The former vehicle in question, Halloween float that it may have been, was a lovely gift from your deceased father… but it was also a freaking Chevy Camaro. I mean, that's totally not the kind of vehicle you're talking about now, you know? A Camaro isn't a minivan, and it's not an SUV. It wasn't very fuel efficient. It would fit your two kids in it, but not much else. It barely had a trunk the size of a six-pack."

Carly huffed, leaning on the counter and narrowing her eyes. "And your point is?"

"That you loved that car. Seems to me the smart move would be to just replace the wrecked Camaro with another Camaro. You already know how they drive, so you don't even have to go for a test ride in the new one."

"It's not that simple." She pulled the plastic top off the coffee can and deposited a scoop of the granulated mix into her coffee maker. "There were two cars in the family at that point. I could swap mine out for Kyle's SUV anytime I needed to."

"Aha." Sergio wagged a finger at her. "So, if I hear you correctly, Kyle's SUV was an appropriate-sized vehicle that accommodated all of your needs. Why don't you just get another of those?"

She reached over and slowly lowered the lid on the coffee maker. Carly then dropped the plastic scooper back into the coffee can and replaced the lid, quietly returning it to the cupboard. She put a hand on either side of the coffee maker as it commenced gurgling.

Her head sagged.

"Because…" Carly's words were barely audible over the little machine. "When I walk out to my garage, I don't want to see Kyle's car there, okay? I don't need that daily reminder in my life. Not right now."

Sergio let the weight of her words sink in.

"Yeah, okay." He scrunched up his face. "That's… that's fair."

"So, will you come with me tonight and help me car shop?"

"Yes. Absolutely." He nodded his head. "We'll meet up after I hit the gym. We'll go look for a version of Kyle's SUV that's *not* the same make or model, so it *doesn't* remind you of him every time you go to the garage—but one that has all the same accoutrements."

"Exactly. Thank you."

Sergio got up from the couch.

Yeah, that won't be too impossible.

He glanced at his partner. "I should at least get some sort of credit for time already served though, Your Honor."

"Oh, is that right?" Taking a coffee cup from the cupboard, Carly filled it. She cradled the mug with two hands as she carried it to Sergio. "Remember who caused all this car shopping to be necessary at all."

"Fair enough." He took the cup from her. "But I have looked at and test-driven every variety of motor vehicle with you. Twice, probably. Tonight, it's time for you to pull the trigger."

"Hmm." She folded her arms, smiling. "You think so, huh?"

"Oh, I know so. Let's buy the red Ford Explorer you liked. Or the gray Chevy Trailblazer. Or the Dodge SUV, with the cool back seats that fold down electronically. They're all pretty much the same, and you've driven each of them a zillion times."

"I only—wait, what did you say?"

"Huh?" Sergio raised the coffee cup to his lips. "What? What did I say?"

Carly slipped a finger into the waistline of her partner's jeans, the backs of her fingers gently brushing against his firm lower torso. "You said 'Let's' buy."

Sergio blinked a few times, his coffee cup still in midair. "Yeah…"

"That's 'let's.' As in, 'let us.' Are you planning on being part of this vehicle purchase?" She wrapped her arms around him. "Part of the ownership of the vehicle in question? Are you planning on becoming a part of the household in which this new automobile will reside?"

Sergio set his coffee on the counter. "I'm… I think I'm just footing the bill to replace the car I totaled. Unless you have other ideas."

"Actually, I do have an idea." She nuzzled his neck, whispering as her soft lips caressed his skin. "Come car shopping with me again tonight and I promise to narrow the list down to three top contenders."

Sergio grimaced. "Oh, I have died and gone to Hell. Three? You probably really mean five. Or, knowing you, ten."

"Come on." Carly leaned back, smiling. She gazed into his eyes. "I'm really close. The insurance stops paying for the rental at the end of the week, so I need to decide, but it's not as easy for me to buy a car as it would be for you. Car salespeople try to take advantage of women."

Shaking his head, Sergio put his hands on his partner's arms. "What a load of crap. Nobody ever took advantage of you in your life, lady. Besides, you carry a gun. Let the sales rep know that. It might speed things up. Right now, the car dealers run away when they see you pull into their parking lot."

"Just come with me." She held firm to her man, swaying back and forth. "If you do, I won't ask you to take the boys to baseball practice on Saturday."

"I like taking them to baseball practice. It's soccer I don't like. Whatever genius thought that youth league soccer in the Florida heat would be a good idea, they should be brought up on child abuse charges."

"Then I'll let you take them to baseball practice," she said. "Twice."

"We do need to work on our infield drills…" He pursed his lips, bobbing his head back and forth. "Wait, no! It's time for you to stop delaying and make a serious decision, Carly."

His partner raised an eyebrow. "Oh, is it, now?"

"Yes. By now, you know what you want. Just take the next step. Don't be afraid."

A wide grin stretched across her lips. "Are we still talking about cars?"

"Uh…" Sergio looked down at her. "Maybe."

Carly's phone rang from its location on the top of the coffee table. The word "Mom" appeared on the screen. She scrunched her face up, releasing her man and reaching for the phone. "Saved by the bell."

"Who was, me or you?" Plucking his coffee mug from the counter, Sergio headed to the bedroom.

As he dressed, he tapped his phone screen again to check the time.

Okay, let's see...

I can still make my meeting, but now there's not enough room in the schedule to get all the way to my place and change clothes first.

Frowning, he glanced at the clothes on the bedroom chair.

Guess last night's clothes will have to do. Sorry about that, Lieutenant.

He plopped down on the edge of the bed and put on his shoes.

By the time Sergio was finished dressing, Carly sounded as if she was wrapping up her call.

She appeared in the bedroom doorway, with her phone still to her ear. "I gotta run, Mom. Thanks again for watching the boys last night. I'll be able to pick them up from school today. Love you. Bye." She strolled to the closet and took out a smart-looking white blouse, glancing at Sergio as she did. "So, big fella—what's your day look like?"

He shrugged. "Meet with Satan—I mean, Lieutenant Davis—and then chase down leads for some open cases." Looking up at Carly, he smiled. "By the way, I appreciate you letting me sleep late. Can't say I like having a morning meeting with the Antichrist, but the side perks are nice. I get to spend the night over here with you."

"Yeah, that was nice." Carly laid a skirt on the bed. "And Mom's been great. The way they keep rescheduling my final interviews for promotion to Sergeant, it has really messed with the boys' usual routine. But they sure don't mind spending the night at Grandma's. She seems to forget what a vegetable is when they're over there. It's pretty much a nonstop diet of Oreos." She placed the blouse next to the skirt and adjusted its silky sleeves. "I miss having lunch with you, though. After my interviews, I'm free. What do you say? Wanna hit Café Cubano?"

"Sure." He grinned. "We can shop for cars afterward."

Carly's eyes widened. "Ooh!"

"No, no, no. I'm kidding." Holding his hands up, Sergio recoiled and fell into the bedroom chair. "I'll die first. Honest. Doing any more car shopping may be hazardous to my long-term health."

Carly resumed her foraging through the closet, pulling out a pair of dark blue flats. "Stop being a baby."

"No. And you can't make me." He stuck his tongue out.

Exaggerating a sigh, she put her hand on her hip. "Lover, I already have two children. Please don't use every opportunity to act like a third."

Sergio stood up and tucked his wrinkled shirt into his jeans. "Okay, I'm off. I'd wish you good luck with your interviews, but you don't need it. Everybody knows you're the best candidate. Wish me luck with my meeting with Lucifer, though. I'll try to get the odor of sulfur off before lunchtime."

Carly winced. "You're... going to your meeting with Lieutenant Davis dressed like that?"

Stopping in the doorway, Sergio turned around to face her. "Something tells me the answer to that question is 'no.'"

"Marty, it's a meeting with your boss. You need to look professional. Wear a suit—and take a shower. You have time."

He shook his head. "I don't. Wearing a suit means I'd have to go home and *get* a suit, and there isn't enough time for that."

"Yes, there is—you have a suit here and a clean shirt. From the other night." Carly walked back to the closet, shoving aside a thick mass of hanging clothes. "I had them cleaned for you. They're here, in the back of my closet with my nice dresses." She withdrew a charcoal gray suit in a plastic drycleaners bag, and a bright white dress shirt.

"Sneaky." Sergio took the freshly pressed garments in his hands. "Am I going to shave as well?"

"No," Carly said. "The stubble is sexy."

"Do... I need to look sexy for the lieutenant?"

"No, but after your meeting, you're mine again." She leaned forward and kissed him. "And I like the stubble."

He grinned. "I like the sound of that. I can't wait for you to get promoted. I'm so excited for you."

"Thank you." Carly peeled off the rest of her attire as she headed toward her bathroom. "You can use the boys' shower while I use this one."

"We can't shower together?" Sergio asked, following her.

"There's definitely not enough time for that." She gave him a wink and eased the bathroom door shut between them. "Now go."

DAN ALATORRE

CHAPTER 3

The small staff of NewsAction Inc. filed into the company's tiny conference room, seating themselves around the former surfboard that served as a meeting table—and the large collection of internet cameras that protruded from its center. The company's wiry-haired CEO entered the conference room last, his shirt sleeves rolled up and his necktie askew, a half-eaten bagel in one hand and a large Starbucks cup in the other.

As he made his way to the pointier end of the surfboard, Jasper Menendez-Holswain glanced at his blue jeans and t-shirt-clad staff, and smiled. "Okay, gang. Ready to give the monster its morning feeding?"

His employees roared with enthusiasm, settling into beanbag chairs, the worn leather wingback, the purple sofa, or simply leaning against one of the orange, red, or purple walls. The conference room was just one of the interoffice locations that NewsAction used for their wild, three-times-a-day internet sessions, and each area was adorned with whatever random and festive ornamentation the young team members could find and hang up. A green mannequin in a Che Guevarra t-shirt stood next to a poster of The Rolling Stones in concert. Rusty, discarded road signs hung next to shiny, new political posters. A tie-dye painted bust of Mozart grew a leafy, green herb from a hole in the top of its head.

The attire of the staff members was essentially the same eclectic mix. Today's warm, springtime air had most of them in blue jeans and t-shirts, but on hotter days the teammates would show up in shorts and flip flops. Jersey Targo was known for his hibiscus-print bolo shirts and ever-present vape pen; McSwain Tannenbaum occasionally showed up wearing nothing but a string bikini and sunglasses, fresh from the beach. Whatever style each member of the NewsAction team deemed appropriate was fine with their boss. All that mattered to Jasper Menendez-Holswain was the constant stream of content and clicks that came as a result of the frenetic, live internet sessions NewsAction held with their rivals—the reporters from various other news agencies that would be attending online.

Menendez-Holswain prided himself on Tampa-based NewsAction being first with any breaking report in national politics, professional sports, or Hollywood. His detractors tended to agree that NewsAction might get stories first, but often via unfounded political rumors and unsourced gossip about Tinseltown that rarely panned out under close scrutiny.

Nonetheless, NewsAction got ratings. Its website was updated no less than hourly, all day, every day, with fresh fodder for the bottomless social media machine—where Menendez-Holswain's staff delivered fiery, outrageous stories with aplomb for immediate regurgitation by their competitors. And the entire NewsAction staff appeared on the live sessions, gathering in the conference room or one of the other sets while streaming to any and all social media services.

It was this last feature that made NewsAction its name. The reporters, almost all of them under the age of thirty, lived and breathed their stories, 24/7. Only Menendez-Holswain himself had actually celebrated more than three decades of life, coming up on fifty but barely looking thirty-nine, and Anne Ferrol, a gray-haired holdover allegedly from the pre-internet, pre-computer era when news stories were typed on IBM Selectric typewriters and on-air reporters like Anne did their own hair and makeup.

"McSwain," the CEO said. "Lights, please."

A slender woman with face tattoos and a barrage of piercings reached to a console on the surfboard and flipped some switches, bathing the entire staff in bright light. Her skinny, multicolored arms displayed inky images of skulls, spiderwebs and mermaids as she maneuvered the buttons and levers of her mixing board, bringing tiny LED lights to life on top of the cameras aimed at her colleagues.

Across the room, on a rusty-looking ironing board, rested a small wall of high-definition video monitors with the faces of NewsAction's friends and foes. Each showed a "muted" icon as the respective news person waited for the chance to get a fresh round of gossip or prepared to wage war on the most recent NewsAction website update's incorrect and slanderous stories.

Allegedly.

Because those news outlets fed at the same trough as Menendez-Holswain's team did. NewsAction just did it better, faster, and with more pizazz. The near-constant live sessions NewsAction provided were a chance to attack and be attacked, to rebut accusations or provide background details in stories that had gone viral in the news world.

And NewsAction almost always went viral, in part because their competitors—when they would launch a misguided attack or even when they were correct in their allegations—could rarely debate on the level of the NewsAction team. Jasper's reporters were voracious in their verbal sparring, on and off camera, just as he was. The takedowns of competing reporters were legendary and brutal, and witnessed in real time—and millions of fans tuned in to see it happen.

McSwain adjusted the ring light facing her boss. "Ten seconds, Jasper."

Nodding, the CEO took a deep breath and sat upright in his chair. He gave his sleeves one last adjustment and placed his hands flat on the conference room table.

FOURTH ESTATE

"Five…" The tattooed audio-video technician held up her ring-filled fingers, counting down the seconds. "Four… Three…"

The last two seconds were silent, only McSwain's slender hand wafting up and down to acknowledge the passing of the last moments until airtime.

A thumbs up indicated her boss was live.

"Welcome to NewsAction!" The CEO beamed. "I'm Jasper Menendez-Holswain, founder of the internet's hottest site for news. Let's get straight to what everyone will be talking about tomorrow. Janielle Shepherd has a story with Hollywood's latest star-crossed lovers, Diamond and her rapper beau, Terrence Big Time."

McSwain cut to a youthful African-American reporter across the room from her boss.

"That's alleged Hollywood lovers, Jasper." The reporter smiled, leaning forward in a yellow bean bag chair. "And my sources tell me the indiscreet couple is flying to Cabo San Lucas so they can get hitched, because… get this. Diamond is preggers!"

The screen became a two-shot, with Jasper on one side and Janielle on the other.

"Wow." The NewsAction CEO shook his head. "I bet professional screenwriters couldn't come up with a plot twist like that. The ink on their divorces from their prior spouses isn't dry yet. How far along is the bride-to-be?"

"According to someone close to the source, breakout singing sensation Diamond Darrow, a.k.a Candice Wendfield, made a trip to her Rodeo Drive gynecologist yesterday—and an unnamed staffer there says she is almost at twelve weeks."

On the wall of video monitors, raised hand emojis littered the screens of the muted rival reporters.

"Pardon my math," Jason said, "but doesn't that mean the baby isn't Terrence's? We reported that they only started dating about two months ago."

McSwain lowered a lever, bringing Janielle's camera up to fill the whole main screen.

"That's right, boss. Looks like there'll be fireworks in ol' Mexico when the top-ten rapper finds out he ain't the baby daddy."

Jasper stood up, walking toward a big screen TV in the corner. McSwain waved to a heavyset man in a striped t-shirt with a mobile camera in his hand. He aimed it at Jasper as McSwain dropped the shot into the main feed.

"Luckily for us," Jasper said, "we were able to sneak a reporter on their flight. NewsAction's own Lessica Kumar is holed up outside the plush resort where Diamond and Terrence Big Time are staying, and she plans to drop the bomb as soon as they step outside. Lessica, any updates?"

The reporter held a microphone in front of her, speaking in a loud whisper. "I'm here in Cabo San Lucas, at the poshest five-star real estate that a stack of greenbacks can get you. And just across the parking lot is the majestic suite that rapper Terrence Big Time procured as his getaway love nest. But it might not be champagne and roses for long, based on our reporting."

FOURTH ESTATE

To the right of the NewsAction live feed monitors was a set of security screens, each displaying its targeted NewsAction location: the tiny front lobby, the sidewalk view on the outside of the entry door, the office's two hallways, and the rooms used for live feeds. A wide-angle camera displayed the middle section of the office, where the reporters had—but rarely used—their own cubicles and desks.

On the security monitor at the top of the rack, a large man in a blue baseball cap appeared on the sidewalk, wearing a bulky red windbreaker. He pulled open the NewsAction front door and stepped inside, the lobby camera showing his skinny legs and bulky upper body. Sunglasses shielding his eyes from view, and a paper mask hid the rest of his face.

He entered the lobby, walking with a stiffness, his hands stuffed inside the pockets of the red windbreaker. The third security monitor showed the man continue down the hallway, coming to a stop just outside of the conference room where the livestream was happening.

Muting her headset microphone, McSwain leaned over to Jersey Targo. "Looks like a fan got into the lobby again. Somebody must've forgotten to lock the door. Go ask them to leave, would you?"

Targo shook his head as he chewed on his vape pen. "My segment's coming up."

"You have another five minutes, at least. My Insta report says we are hitting it big with the Diamond and Terrence story, so Jasper will want to milk it. Go."

Grumbling, Targo slipped his vape into his shirt pocket and stood up. As he exited the room, McSwain caught his image on the security monitors.

The stranger stood in the hallway, not moving as Targo approached. Stopping a few feet away, the NewsAction reporter held his hand up and pointed toward the lobby exit. Targo shrugged and held his hands out, gesturing to the exit again, but the stranger didn't seem to react at all.

The reporter took a step toward the uninvited visitor.

As McSwain glanced back and forth between her boss and Lessica Kumar on the live feed, she glimpsed the stranger push past Targo and head toward the conference room.

He pulled his hand from his windbreaker pocket, displaying a large handgun.

McSwain jumped up, adrenaline rippling through her insides. She waved at Janielle Shepherd as she scrambled to get to the conference room entrance. "Close the door! He's got a gun!"

Janielle looked up just as the stranger stepped inside the room.

Jasper Menendez-Holswain interrupted his banter with his on-location reporter, his eyes going to the African-American man with the weapon standing on the other side of the surfboard conference table. His reporters scurried away from the stranger, screaming or gasping as they saw the gun. McSwain backed away, her heart pounding, holding her hands up as she inched toward her seat.

FOURTH ESTATE

"Everybody, be cool." Jasper swallowed hard. "Just be cool." He looked at the intruder. "Hey, friend…"

The man in the red windbreaker faced the NewsAction CEO, stone-faced and rigid.

"You… you want something, right?" Jasper held a hand out, palm up, like he might have wanted to try to shake the stranger's hand. "Okay. Uh… Tell me what you want, and I'll see if I can get it for you. How's that sound?"

The stranger didn't respond.

Behind the intruder, outside the conference room, Targo crouched behind a desk and tapped the number screen of his cell phone.

"Tell me what you want." Jasper took a step toward the conference table, his voice wavering. "I—I can help you. I have lots of friends—powerful friends, you know? People with influence."

Next to Jasper, the heavyset man in the striped t-shirt pointed his mobile camera at his boss, then moved it to get the stranger on screen. Half a second later, the wall of NewsAction video monitors became filled with the image of Jasper, then the intruder.

"Are we—are we streaming this?" Jasper's trembling words were the only sound in the room. "McSwain, are we—"

"Yes." The technician shoved a lever forward on the console. "We're streaming this live, Jasper."

"See?" The CEO raised his eyebrows, his voice breaking. "We can get you help. Or, or, or… whatever you need. You don't need to…" His gaze went to the large weapon in the intruder's hand. "...to hurt anyone."

Frozen and unmoving, the stranger simply continued to stare at the shaking NewsAction CEO.

"Please." Jasper shook his head, his words closer to a prayer than to speaking. "Please, don't. You—you don't have to hurt any of us. These... these are... they're fine people. They—"

"Yes." The stranger lifted his chin, his gaze still on the NewsAction CEO. "I want something."

"Good. Good!" Jasper let out a breath. "Okay. Just—just tell me, and I'll get it for you." Panting, he leaned forward and placed one hand on the conference table, the other going to his chest. "What do you want?"

"Just this."

The stranger lifted his gun and pointed it directly at Jasper Menendez-Holswain's mouth, pulling the trigger. As Jasper careened over backwards, his murderer leaned across the table and emptied the gun into the gaping jaws of his victim.

CHAPTER 4

OFFICER MARK HARRIMAN RUSHED DOWN THE corridor of the second floor Tampa PD offices, stopping at the vacant desk of his sergeant. Not five minutes ago, the desk's current occupant, Sergeant Deshawn Marshall, had instructed Harriman that he was not to be disturbed.

Pursing his lips, Harriman looked around. "Sergeant Marshall? I have an urgent message."

No reply came.

Harriman raised his voice. "Deshawn?"

Sergeant Patterson trudged out of the break room, carrying a gigantic stainless steel travel mug against his round belly. He slumped into his desk behind a stack of file folders, his shoulders slouching and his eyes baggy.

"Sergeant," Harriman said. "Have you seen Lieutenant Davis?"

Patterson grunted, not looking up. "He's busy."

"What about Sergeant Marshall? Do you know where he is?"

"Also busy." Sighing, the elder sergeant raised his eyes. "What can I help you with, Officer?"

Harriman clutched the report. "We just received word of a homicide and I thought they should know about it. Apparently, the receptionist at the Stafford-Love law offices was gunned down in cold blood. I figured Lieutenant Davis should be made aware so he can assign it."

Nodding, Patterson returned his gaze to his stack of folders. "Leave it with me. I'll get it assigned."

"It's… in the lieutenant's sector, sir."

"The lieutenant's been pulled away from assigning cases this morning," Patterson said. "Some BS about needing to do the final round of interviews to fill Sergeant Marshall's old position. Deshawn's in the can, putting on a suit so he can help assess the candidates. Half our cops are out sick and everybody else is deployed. So, leave your report with me and I'll see that it gets handled."

Harriman shifted his weight from one foot to the other. "Sir—"

"Officer…" Running a hand over his face, Patterson leaned forward. He put a hand on his knee and scowled at Harriman. "I just came off working twelve straight hours, and I'd like to get home and see my wife sometime before she heads to the hospital to start her shift. Leave the report."

FOURTH ESTATE

"Yes, sir." Harriman walked toward the stacks of folders on Patterson's desk. "Uh... you know, Sergeant Patterson, I've been the second-in-charge on quite a few of Detective Sanderson and Detective Martin's homicide cases..."

"Uh-huh." Patterson snatched the paper from Harriman's hand and dropped it to the desk. "Good for you." He returned to his file folders.

"I'm just saying..." Harriman held his hands out at his sides. "I mean, sir, if we're understaffed..."

"You want to be the lead on this one? Officer..." He narrowed his eyes, looking toward Harriman's name badge. "...Harriman?"

Harriman shrugged. "We could ask someone from the night shift to work O.T."

"We could." Patterson turned toward the young officer, pushing his wrinkled tie away from his belly. "But then you'd miss out on a chance to show your ungrateful higher ups what you can do."

A smile stretched across Harriman's face.

"What do you think, Officer Harriman?" Patterson leaned back in his chair. "You get a plumb assignment and one of your poor, tired co-workers gets to go home at a reasonable hour."

"I think that sounds pretty good to me, sir. I won't let you down."

"Yeah. Don't." He handed the report back to Harriman and turned once again to his folders. "The interviews should be over by noon, so you can direct any questions to Sergeant Marshall or Lieutenant Davis at that time. Expect a detective to take over for you, but until one does, if you've been second-in-charge on homicide cases with Carly and Sergio, then you should know what to do. We'll get some support over to you when we can."

"I appreciate this opportunity, Sergeant." Harriman held his hand out.

The sergeant frowned, staring at Harriman's outstretched hand for a moment before finally reaching over and shaking it. "Don't screw it up, kid."

CHAPTER 5

Carly's rental car crawled along through the morning traffic into downtown Tampa. Behind the wheel, she sat with the ends of her earbuds protruding from her ears and her jaw hanging open. As her phone conversation wrapped up, she uttered an incoherent mumble and ended the call. The phone screen went dark, and the device slipped through her fingers, dropping onto the passenger seat next to her overstuffed computer bag and her purse.

I can't believe it.

Vehicles on the crowded interstate inched out of one congested lane and into another, apparently searching for the fastest route to their destination, but Carly's sedan stayed in its lane. The unexpected phone call from her soon-to-be ex-husband had thrown her into a daze.

She gripped the steering wheel with both hands and shook her head, trying to clear the haze of their conversation from between her ears, but it wouldn't go away.

I just can't believe it.

Echoes of Kyle's words floated around in her head—scraps of comments, pieces of dialogue... They swirled and swelled until the main point of his call came rushing up to the top of the churning cauldron, his stark request cutting through the fog like a laser-lit diamond.

The detective clenched her jaw and slammed her palm into the steering wheel.

I can't believe it!

Putting a hand to her forehead, she rested her elbow on the windowsill of the driver's door.

Now what do I do?

The urge to punch the passenger seat a few times was followed by the urge to pull over and close her eyes, followed by a wave of relief and memories of old times. Happier times.

Followed by another wave of anger.

Sighing, she yanked the earbuds from her ears and dropped them into the cupholder. As if on cue, the phone rang again.

Her head whipped around to read the screen. The word "Mom" lit up the device, over an image of her mother hugging Carly's two sons. Groaning, Carly picked up an earbud and jostled it into her ear canal as she tapped the screen to answer the call.

The earbud dropped away, bouncing off Carly's thigh and disappearing between the driver's seat and the center console.

"Crap. Hold on a sec, Mom." Carly picked up her phone and pressed the speaker option. "Hey, sorry about that. What's up?"

"I forgot to mention before, you asked me to keep tabs on that rash on Isaac's back."

"Oh, right." Carly steered with one hand and dragged her other hand along the carpet at the base of her seat in an attempt to locate the fallen earbud. "Yeah, how'd it look this morning?"

In front of her, traffic moved slower and slower; but in her head, the conversation with Kyle came back, flying at her faster and faster, again and again.

I really cannot believe it.
And I especially can't believe he said that!

"I put some skin cream on him last night," her mother said. "And I had him sleep in a clean t-shirt after he took a nice, long shower. The rash had pretty much cleared up by this morning."

"Uh-huh." Carly nodded, her thoughts racing.

After all this time—weeks, turning into months—to then suddenly come out of the blue and say... that, of all things!

"...gets through school today without another flare up, he's good to go."

The sound of her mother's voice yanked Carly back to the conversation at hand. She sat upright, trying to focus. "Okay. And, hey—did that red spot on Isaac's back go away overnight? The rash?"

The silence on the other end of the phone indicated Carly had just made an error of some sort.

"Mom?"

"Dear, I just told you." Her mother huffed. "I put some cream on Isaac's back last night and the rash pretty much went away."

Carly winced. "I'm… sorry. I'm—I've got another round of interviews this morning and I guess I'm distracted."

"You? Distracted by an interview? I don't believe that."

"Well…" The detective glanced at the report-laden computer bag resting on the seat beside her. "I also had a bunch of updates I had to file. I was up super early finishing them."

"Oh, come on."

Her mother's tone was the same as when Carly was twelve years old and stayed up late during a sleepover, then tried to deny it the next day at breakfast as she almost fell asleep in her cereal. Her mother gently admonished her for the youthful deception, noting that she had gone into her daughter's bedroom at two in the morning because the lights were still on, and found Carly's guest sound asleep, but Carly herself sat with her eyes halfway closed and one of her books open in front of her on the mattress.

"You're forgetting who you're talking to," her mother said. "What's really bothering you? It certainly isn't some silly reports or an interview. Not you."

There was no point in dodging the question any longer.

FOURTH ESTATE

Mom's going to find out sooner or later. Besides, she might have a few ideas on what to do about the situation.

"Mom, it's..." Carly bit her lip. "Kyle called. He—I was on the phone with him right before you."

"Did you have a fight?"

"No. No." Carly peered through the windshield, searching the sky for the words. "We were fine. Things have gone really well, all things considered, but... Mom, it's like we're two people who know each other so well, but we've also somehow become these awkward, half-strangers that are walking on eggshells as we try to avoid hurting each other's feelings while we rip each other's hearts apart."

The car ahead of her inched forward. Carly eased her foot off the brake and let her sedan move to occupy the vacant space.

"He called earlier, too," Carly said. "This morning, after I had finished my run. I was pressed for time, so I told him we could speak while I drove to work. And he did. He called. And he... he said..."

Words. They're just words.

Say them.

"Mom, Kyle said he wanted to come back. To... come home. He asked if he could move back in with me and the boys, to try to work things out."

Carly gripped the steering wheel with sweaty hands. Her heart pounded, and she didn't know why.

The conversation with Kyle had been mostly one-way, with him obviously working up the nerve to say the one important thing he wanted to say. Carly had held her breath for what seemed forever, imagining her husband was about to announce he'd found someone else.

The raven-haired detective's dreams were occasionally filled with frustrating images of Kyle and some young blonde associate from his firm, laughing and drinking wine before spending the night together—even though he'd given her no reason to think anything of the kind had been occurring. Kyle hadn't left for another woman. He'd simply left.

But the way he was speaking on the phone—the awkward manner, the hesitant words—made it seem as if the imaginary blonde floozy was draped around Kyle's shoulders when he made the call.

He's found someone else.
He's calling to tell me he's in love.

Instead, Kyle's words took a while to register. He'd asked the thing Carly had wanted him to ask for weeks and weeks. Just moments ago, the conversation with her soon-to-be ex-husband had almost seemed surreal. Now, forcing herself to repeat it out loud to her mother, the words were almost too real.

"What did you tell him, honey?" her mother asked.

"I—I didn't know what to tell him. It took me by surprise. He said he missed me and the boys, and I know he was sincere..." Carly raised a finger to her lips, gnawing the nail. "But, Mom, I never asked Kyle to go. He was the one who said he was unhappy. He was the one who said things weren't working. So, we did the counseling thing... and when they said to try a temporary separation, I was shocked when he said yes. And now, to say he isn't happy being apart, and that he thinks he made a big mistake... Part of me is overjoyed, but part of me... I just don't know. It hurt so much, when he left, I don't want to be stupid and take him back and open up all those feelings again only to have it turn into *my* big mistake."

"You're a little scared." Her mother's voice was gentle and comforting. "That's understandable. But, dear, it hasn't been that long..."

"Well, that's the thing. It has." Taking another deep breath, Carly let the words and feelings spill out of her. "For a long time, we were drifting apart. It was an eternity of opportunities to fix something—anything, small or large... but neither of us tried to fix it. When Kyle suggested going to counseling, I felt like my world was going down the drain. And when he finally announced that he was leaving, it was almost a technicality. He'd already been gone for a long time by then. He was just formalizing what we both knew. So, I understood that he wasn't coming back, and I grieved—for the loss of the man I loved, for the marriage we shared, for the time our sons would lose with their father... I cried when I thought about all of us being under one roof and happy, the way we used to be. But I grieved a year ago, because that's when it all died."

Her mother's voice stayed calm and even. "Do you want him back?"

"I never wanted him to leave in the first place."

"But he did. And now the question is, do you want him back?"

Carly extended her arms as far as they could go, pushing against the steering wheel and forcing her shoulders into the back of the seat. "I…"

The detective stared out into the haze of traffic.

I don't know.

I spent so much time trying to move on because I thought I had to, the idea of going back seems like a foreign concept.

And what do I tell Sergio?

"Mom, I'm not sure I can just take Kyle back. This decision… it's harder than that. There are a lot of things to consider."

"I'm sure it wasn't an easy decision for him, either. Marriage is hard. Making it work is hard."

Carly's abdomen clenched into a throbbing knot. "But he left, Mom. He said we had schedules that were too full—but he meant that I had a schedule that was too full. He said we never saw each other except on vacations, and even then, my mind was on my work. He said those things, and then he left." The waves of emotion returned. Anger, sadness, fear… and embarrassment over a failed marriage she felt was ultimately her fault. Yes, their schedules were busy, but hers was unpredictable. Kyle was dutiful; he still called to talk to the boys all the time, and took them on the weekends, continued to take them hiking and camping… Carly fell asleep looking at pictures of homicide victims. He always tried to leave his work at the office; hers came home in files and folders and thumb drives, rarely leaving her thoughts until the case was closed.

He drifted away, and I let him drift. Maybe I drifted, too.

"People can say a lot of things over fourteen years," her mother said. "And now he's saying he wants to come back."

Carly nodded, her stomach a churning mess. "And I... I'm not sure I can do that. It was too hard. Too tough. I can't just... I can't forget that it happened."

"What Kyle said and did, how you felt during the split..." Her mother lowered her voice. "Is that the only reason you're hesitating?"

Her mother's words hit Carly like a slap to the face, but the implication was clear: Sergio. It was only a matter of time before her mother brought him into the conversation.

Carly tapped her fingernails on the steering wheel.

But if I was going to ask anyone what to do, it'd be my mom, and we'd get around to talking about Sergio's role in this debacle at some point.

"Honey, your heart is... You did something to get through a tough situation. Now, you have a chance to put your life back together—the way you first wanted it to be." She sighed. "I like Sergio well enough, but deep down, he probably knew this... this little *arrangement* the two of you had, that it wasn't going to last."

"I... don't know." Carly's shoulders slumped. "Maybe you're right."

"And if Sergio thinks he has future plans with you, it's best to correct him right now. Bad news doesn't get better with time."

"Mom, it's not that easy."

"Isn't it?" Her mother's tone became more rigid. "Which man stood next to you at the front of the church, as you promised to stay married to him until death do you part? I don't recall Sergio being at the altar."

Heat rose to Carly's cheeks. She jutted her jaw out. "Mom…"

"Honey, you have to at least tell Sergio the situation. It's going to be painful for him—and for you. But… do it like a bandage. Be direct, and be fast. Don't drag it out."

Carly considered her mother's advice.

Am I always going to wonder if Kyle will leave again? Will each disagreement and petty dispute be laced with the worry that if it goes too far, he'll walk out? He did it once.

"Kyle's the one who left, Mom."

"Is scorekeeping what's important now?" her mother asked. "You two have children. Kyle has realized he made a mistake. He's not the one who jumped into bed with a co-worker."

Carly grimaced. "Ouch."

"You can't tell him about that, either, Honey. Men… don't react well to such things. But Kyle is still your husband. You have to try your best to make the right decision."

"What if I don't know what the right thing is?" Carly shrugged. "Even if I get this promotion, I still work where I work. The hours aren't going to change much."

FOURTH ESTATE

"Is staying with Sergio the right thing? You were with Kyle for over a decade. You've been with Sergio for, what? A month? Two?"

Carly shook her head. "Sergio and I have known each other almost five years, and he has—"

"You've known him that long as a co-worker, not as a committed partner in a marriage. It's different. You know that."

Carly opened her mouth to reply, but stopped herself. Her mother was right. It was different.

The situations were completely different problems.

Sergio was her friend for so long—a best friend, really—but he grew to be more than that, too. An off-hours drink became spending time with her family during the weekend, playing backyard volleyball with the kids and attending parties in the evenings. Sergio was a fairly constant fixture at her house, and he and Kyle got along well. They were actually alike in some ways.

Detectives spend long hours at work together, and it can build a bond between partners. Days at work with Sergio could be intense and dramatic, but they were fun, too—in ways that were very different from what she had at home with her husband. She had always liked Sergio's sense of humor and his courage. He was smart, despite his joking nature. And he'd been there for her when others weren't, more than once.

It wasn't difficult to kiss Sergio that first time after Kyle left, because she'd already thought about it. From that story he told her when they were out for an after-work drink.

Carly hadn't felt butterflies like that since she'd been in high school, and she let herself recall the story and the moment on occasion. But she never acted on it, because she was happily married.

Until she wasn't.

Until Kyle left.

Then, when her good friend and work partner learned of her situation, he came over to console her and help her through a rough time. Sergio was there for her again. He had her back, like always. She was the one who asked Sergio to stay with her on that lonely, rainy evening.

At present, Sergio didn't sleep under her roof every night; only when the boys were already scheduled to be at their grandmother's. When the kids were around and Sergio came over, he and Carly behaved platonically in front of them. He could go home when things got tricky, or Carly could ask him to go stay at his place.

And Kyle?

Kyle had always worked to resolve things—until lately. He didn't run off with another woman, he just needed to take a break to see if he wanted to spend the next forty years the way he'd spent the last ten, with a workaholic wife who was gone more and more.

That's what he said. Those were his words when he left.

And it ripped open her heart. Her happy home had taken on a dark and empty aura, with a growing pain and sorrow. Loneliness, despite laying down each night next to her husband. Fear about the future, as he seemed less and less engaged in conversations.

And mostly the knowledge that the man she'd committed herself to... could actually leave the arrangement. That hadn't occurred to her before. Not like it did when he left. Then, it was all too real.

And Sergio had filled that gap. The pain endured but Sergio snuffed out a lot of the embers. She was building something new and different with Sergio, but still interacted with Kyle as they spent hours talking about the new responsibilities their separation required. Many times, those conversations had descended into angry arguments, but just as often they drifted into lonely tears for both of them. They also brought back memories of happy times—so many happy times—and the possibility of future happy times together. It always lingered on the edges.

But as soon as she let herself imagine a future with Kyle, the memory of him walking out came rushing back.

And that pain was still much fresher and deeper than the happiness of any fond memories. The scales tipped heavily in one direction.

She had learned that lesson in grade school and seen it reinforced many times since. People break up for a reason, and that reason inevitably comes back and breaks them up again. She witnessed it in school and at work, with friends and with relatives.

Some things, once broken, don't reattach stronger.

Is Kyle the exception?

The traffic loosened up, the cars ahead of her increasing their speed and heading to their destinations. Carly looked at her phone, where her mother still waited for answers to her questions, but none were forthcoming.

"Mom, I gotta go."

Her mother said goodbye and Carly ended the call, pushing aside all issues about Kyle and Sergio. She had an interview to prepare for—an important one.

But the two men in her heart came rushing back into her head.

If I tell Kyle to come back, I'll break Sergio's heart.

If I tell Kyle not to come back, I'll break Kyle's heart.

What do I do? I don't want to hurt anyone. But I have to try to save my marriage, don't I? Isn't that what I wanted for a whole year?

Groaning, she put a hand to her forehead.

Sergio at least deserves to know what's happened. You owe him that. Tell him, but do it quickly, like ripping off a bandage. It'll hurt, but he deserves to know the truth.

And the truth is… what, exactly?

Shaking her head, Carly accelerated the sedan and once again tried to focus on her pending interview.

CHAPTER 6

Sergio pulled his car into the Tampa PD overflow lot, glancing across the river of traffic on Kennedy Boulevard and the station entrance beyond. Taking out his cell phone, he checked the time.

Made it with a few minutes to spare—but just a few.

Sliding a thumb upward on the screen, Sergio woke his phone up and tapped the Favorites icon. He selected the name Big Brass. After only one ring, Lavonte answered.

"Hey, five-oh," Big Brass said. "Gotta keep this line clear. I'm expecting an important call."

Sergio located an empty parking spot and aimed his vehicle toward it. "What, is a big drug deal going down—I mean, a big vitamin sale going down? I thought you quit that life."

"Not funny, and I got no time for jokes, my man. And I *did* quit the drug life. Now, whatcha need?"

Easing his car between two SUVs, Sergio put the transmission in park and turned off the engine. "Can you feed Marcus Aurelius this morning?"

"Again? Man, I done told you, I ain't no cat sitter."

"It's the last time, I swear." Sergio opened his door and climbed out of the car, clipping his police ID to the front of his belt. A warm breeze pushed his hair into his eyes. "Alejandro comes home tomorrow."

Lavonte huffed. "And you can't do this because…"

"Because…" Sergio chuckled. "I kinda had to stay out late attending to a work-related matter." He slipped his keys into his suitcoat and hurried to the corner. "Just go by and put some food in the bowl on the front porch. And make sure he has fresh water. That's it."

"Work-related matters." Big Brass' tone was as icy as the frozen food section at the Winn Dixie. "You ain't foolin' nobody. That's code for spending the night at your lady cop's house again, expecting me to pick up the slack for your horny butt. Bro, Alejandro's crib is all the way over on the east side. I can't make it. I'm busy."

"Yeah, I guess you're right." When the light changed, Sergio jogged across the traffic-laden street. "I'm pretty busy, too. In fact, I think I'm way too busy to keep feeding leads to the private detective agency you work for."

Big Brass huffed again. "Man, you as cold as an ice cube."

"Look, you know I'd do it—I've been feeding Marcus Aurelius all week—but today I have a meeting I have to get to. Now, Alejandro and his mom will be home tomorrow. You're off the hook after that—and you'll have my eternal thanks."

"Okay. But you owe me, Sergio."

"You're a good guy, Lavonte—no matter what anybody says." Sergio approached the Tampa PD headquarters and a small cluster of people outside. "Oh, and slip fifty bucks under the food dish for me, would you? Alejandro's mom starts her new job tomorrow, but it'll be at least a week before she gets a paycheck."

"Fifty bucks!" Big Brass yelled. "Fifty American dollars? Am I the black Easter bunny? Tell me, am I? Because last time I checked, I ain't been hopping around, hiding painted eggs! This here is blatant exploitation of a righteous African-American man by a tyrannical government through their systemically racist police force, and I'm—"

A crackle of static came over the phone line.

"Sergio?

The detective recognized the voice of his female attorney friend. "Hi, Abbie."

"We'll make sure Alejandro's cat gets fed." Abbie's voice almost drowned out the frantic ravings of Big Brass in the background. "And we'll make sure Alejandro's mom gets fifty bucks."

"Woman, you ain't got no right…" Lavonte's voice still came over the line, but quieter, as if Abbie had taken his phone and walked to a different room.

"Don't be pledging my funds to any charity other than the Big Brass Home For Righteous Individuals. You a lawyer. How 'bout doing some representing of me here?"

Sergio held back a laugh. "I should make it a hundred. Is he gonna be okay?"

"Probably," Abbie said. "He's apparently stressing about some big meeting he's trying to schedule, and that's got him wired up. I'm only here to get a copy of a contract for Mrs. Dilger or I'd stay and watch him flame out."

Down the street, almost directly in front of the Tampa PD entrance, a man in a khaki vest broke away from the group, shouting obscenities at two uniformed police officers as they exited the building. The man had a Go Pro camera strapped to his head and a phone in one hand, holding it up as he yelled at the officers. One of his companions repeated the taunts through a megaphone.

Sergio frowned, eyeing the men. "Well, I appreciate your help, Abbie."

"You can thank me by taking me to dinner sometime. I'm free tonight, by the way."

"Sorry." Sergio smiled. "I have to go car shopping."

"You'd rather do that than spend an evening with me?"

He could practically see her pouting over the phone—the big lower lip, pushed out, as she batted her big green eyes. It would have worked on him, too—a few months ago. Abbie was beautiful and smart. Any man would be lucky to be with her, and he'd told Abbie that more than once.

FOURTH ESTATE

Just not me. Not anymore.

"I'd rather do almost anything than go car shopping again," Sergio hustled toward the ranting citizen. "But dinner with you is out of the question. I'm a one-woman kind of guy these days, and Carly's my 'one woman.' I'm trying to be a good boy."

"Carly's a lucky lady."

He smiled again. "I like to think I'm the lucky one."

"Well… Call me if you change your mind?"

The man with the Go Pro went back to his two friends. They huddled together for a few seconds, then spread out, cell phones aimed at Sergio as he approached the station doors.

"Gotta run, amigo." Sergio quickened his pace. "Thanks in advance for feeding the cat. Tell whiny butt I'll see him at the gym tonight. I'll give him his fifty bucks then."

"Hmm." Abbie breathed softly into the phone. "Maybe I'll come pick it up for him instead."

Chuckling, Sergio ended the call and headed toward the front entrance of the police station. The wind picked up, sending the bottom of his suit coat flapping.

"Hey!" the Go Pro man shouted, glaring at Sergio. "Check out the fancy threads on this pig. And look—he's trying to hide his badge under his jacket. But I see it. Wearing a badge with a suit, you must be the Chief of Police." The man stepped in front of Sergio, blocking his way into the station. "How many innocent people of color did you kill today, tyrant?"

The two others lined up about ten feet away on either side, their phones at arm's length. The one with the megaphone chanted, "Pigs in a blanket! Fry 'em like bacon!"

Sergio took a deep breath and forced a warm grin, peering at the stranger in front of him. "What can I help you with, friend?"

The man shook his head. "I'm not your friend, you ugly pig."

The stranger's demeanor was rude but calm, like he wanted to antagonize Sergio without appearing to do so.

And it was working.

But Sergio knew the game. He'd seen videos on social media of people like this, starting some sort of confrontation in the hopes that the officer being videoed would react poorly—thereby creating a video that the instigator could edit and post online. The clips tended to be one-sided, usually without context, and appeared to have been edited to only show the police in a poor light, regardless of what the initial instigator had done to get a reaction. The resulting videos ended up gaining thousands of views, sometimes tens of thousands, and occasionally an expensive monetary settlement for the instigator.

The department had informed all officers to direct any media inquiries—and the man with the Go Pro on his head would almost certainly insist he was a member of the media—to the head of Public Relations, ensuring that any ambushed officers would escape the trap unscathed.

"Pigs in blankets." The instigator's friend continued, megaphone blaring. "Fry 'em like bacon."

FOURTH ESTATE

"Well..." Sergio checked the time on his phone. *I need to get going or I'll be late.* "I'm on my way to a meeting, so, if you'll excuse me..."

He reached for the door.

The stranger leaned into Sergio's arm, dropping to the ground and letting out a sharp howl. "He hit me! That's assault! Freaking tyrant!"

Sergio's jaw dropped, heat rising to the back of his neck. "Buddy, I didn't hit you." He clenched his teeth and pointed to the stranger's friends. "Your own cameras recorded us the whole time."

They want a scene. A bad reaction. Don't give it to them.

Pushing his anger aside, Sergio extended a hand to the man on the sidewalk. "Let me help you up."

"You assaulted me." The man slapped Sergio's hand away.

"Technically," Sergio growled, "striking an officer's hand could be considered assault. A cop who's not as nice as me could really ruin your day now."

A few uniformed officers came outside, surrounding Sergio and the others.

"He assaulted me," the Go Pro man said.

"Sure he did." One of the uniformed officers approached the man on the ground. "How about you guys stop filming us before we run you all in?"

"For what?" The man recoiled. "Exerting the freedoms guaranteed to me by the Constitution?" A few feet away, his cohorts filmed every word and gesture. "I'm a sovereign citizen," he shouted. "I know my rights. You can't stop us from recording you in a public place. You're public servants. You guys work for me, pig."

Sergio scowled, clenching his fists.

How many times have I heard that one? Every lowlife I ever arrested, every criminal I booked...

The man on the ground looked at Sergio. "Look at him, in the suit. He wants to punch me so bad, he can taste it. He can't wait 'til the moment I'm in handcuffs and defenseless, and then he'll let loose with some police brutality—but you'll all make sure it takes place out of sight, so no one can hold you accountable. That's how you do it. Fascists!"

Reaching for his handcuffs, the uniformed officer's voice grew stern. "Mister, are you gonna get up and leave, or am I going to lock you up?"

"I'm going to file charges against that pig." The man pointed at Sergio. "He assaulted me. Don't try to cover up for your fellow tyrant. We got it recorded."

"So did we." Sergio waved a finger at the front doors of the police station. A video camera was mounted above each door, and one more was mounted on each side of the building, at the corners. They were all aimed at the group in front of the station. "It's gonna show your flop act and everything else." He extended his hand again. "Why don't you let me help you up?"

The stranger narrowed his eyes, staring at Sergio's hand.

The detective maintained eye contact with the stranger, keeping his voice firm and even. "I know. It's blatant exploitation of a righteous man by

FOURTH ESTATE

a tyrannical government through their systemically racist and brutal police force. But..." He took a breath, letting some of his anger subside. "Maybe we're not the suppression arm of tyrants. Maybe we're just trying to keep the streets safe. Either way, let's at least help get you up off the ground, okay?"

Sighing, the man grasped Sergio's hand and got up from the sidewalk.

The detective glanced at the other two instigators. "What were you hoping to accomplish today, guys?"

"We do First Amendment audits," the man with the Go Pro said. "We're members of the free press—the Fourth Estate. Socially conscious media keeping the government honest."

"Yeah?" Sergio put his hands in his pockets. It was a stunt, as he suspected, and it had failed. "Well, gotta keep that tyrannical government in line."

"That's right, pig." The man scowled. "We're sovereign citizens of the—"

"Yeah, yeah. I got that already." Sergio reached for the station door again. "And as much as I'd love to stay and listen to what I'm sure would be a fascinating dissertation on the United States Constitution, I already passed seventh grade Civics—and I'm going to be late for a meeting."

He pulled the door open and stepped inside; the three strangers followed.

And the uniformed officers followed them.

Upon entering the building, the leader of the pack raised his camera again.

"Hey!" An officer at the duty desk waved his hand. "There's no recording in here."

"No?" The instigator turned his camera to the desk officer. "This is a public space, so I can record all I want, tyrant."

The uniformed officers swarmed around the Go Pro man again.

He yelled out, his voice echoing off the lobby walls. "Are you gonna tell us there's no video recording allowed in here, pigs? A public space? I'm a taxpayer. You and your 'back the blue' accomplices are all violating my civil rights!"

Grimacing, Sergio walked back to the group. "Guys, he's allowed to record in public spaces. That would include this lobby." He faced the man. "But check with the head of Public Relations. They can tell you where you can film."

The man with the megaphone gritted his teeth, stepping up to Sergio. "How many people of color will you kill today, you stinking pig?"

"Stinking? I just took a shower." Sergio rubbed his chin. "Actually… I did send a black man into hysterics a few minutes ago on my way in." He looked at the auditors, their faces falling slack jawed. "He may have died. But that was over the phone so I'm not sure. Would that count?"

The Go Pro man's accomplice did not appear amused. "You think you're funny?"

"I think you guys are much funnier." He checked the time on his phone again, and winced.

Now I'm going to be late.

FOURTH ESTATE

Turning to head to the elevators, Sergio gave the radical videographers a wave. "Well, fellow sovereign citizens, farewell until we meet again."

The Go Pro man pulled a business card from his khaki vest and pressed it into Sergio's chest. "We're independent journalists, exercising the rights guaranteed to us under the Constitution and its amendments—tyrant. We plead our side in court, not on the field. You haven't heard the last of us yet."

Sergio plucked the card from the man's dirty fingertips and shoved it into his suitcoat pocket. "I haven't heard of you at all." Turning away, he rushed to the elevators.

DAN ALATORRE

CHAPTER 7

Sergio tapped his foot, staring at the elevator console and taking deep breaths to shake off the aggravation from his confrontation with the first amendment auditors. He rolled his shoulders, working to get his pulse under control.

Let that crap go, man. You need to be calm and cool for this mystery meeting with the lieutenant.

The elevator doors finally opened on the second floor. As Sergio stepped out and hurried toward Lieutenant Davis' office, his phone rang in his pocket. He glanced at the screen as Carly's name appeared, sending a smile across his face.

Nice. She'll calm me down.

He answered the call and kept walking, grinning as he put the phone to his ear. "I knew you'd call, Dude. You forgot to wish me good luck at your house, so you're doing it now."

"Sergio, I—I wish I had some good luck to give you." Carly's voice was tense. "But I don't." She exhaled, her words coming slow and soft. "In fact, I have some bad news. Not *bad* news, really, but… news I don't think you're going to like."

Sergio stopped in the corridor. He glanced around, lowering his voice. "What's up? What happened?"

It must be her mom. Another health scare.

Whatever it is, Carly needs you. Keep cool and walk her through it.

But do it quickly. The meeting is about to start.

He held his breath, his phone mashed against his ear.

"It's… Kyle." Carly took a deep breath and let it out slowly. "He wants to come home. He… wants to come back."

The words hit Sergio like a punch to the gut. He stood rigid, frozen in the hallway, letting the words sink in. Swallowing hard, he managed to speak. "He, uh… forgot his JetSki, right? I knew he'd eventually remember that and come back for it."

"He just called and… and I thought I should tell you what he said. I guess… I mean, he's the father of my children. I have to consider giving him another chance, don't I?"

Sergio's stomach jolted.

"That… uh, I…" His head reeled, knots forming in his abdomen. "I mean… wow, that's some news all right." Cringing, he put a hand to his forehead. "Geez, dude."

Carly exhaled into the phone. "I'm so sorry."

"No, it's... it's—it's—it's..." His gaze went up and down the police station walls, looking for a word or phrase—anything to break the nausea building inside him. His eyes landed on an empty wooden bench in the corridor. Head humming, he made his way to it. "It's probably, it's probably... geez."

"I'm so sorry, Marty. I... don't know what else to say."

"Yeah. Me, either." The breath went out of him. He lowered himself onto the bench, putting an elbow on one knee and propping his head up with his free hand. "I guess there's really nothing else to say."

"I didn't tell him yes," Carly said. "I didn't tell him anything. I said I'd think about it. He wants to meet me for dinner tonight and talk about things. I... said I would."

Sergio nodded.

If you were going to tell Kyle no, you wouldn't be calling to tell me this.

He recalled her statement a month ago, in Georgia, at the Fire Marshal's house, when he'd almost gotten killed.

"You're important to me," she said. "You thought I was getting back with Kyle—which I wasn't, and I won't..."

Sergio pursed his lips, staring at the floor.

What changed?

It wasn't a question he could ask. Not right now. His partner was on the phone with a problem.

But it wasn't his partner that was on the phone. It was the woman he cared about more than anyone else in the world.

This is Carly. She's not trying to hurt you. She's obviously torn about the phone call she got, and she needs you to be a friend.

To do the right thing. To have her back.

Wincing, he cleared his throat, an emptiness hollowing out his insides.

That's what she needs. That's why she called.

"Dude, it's..." He shook his head slowly, making sure his voice didn't break as he spoke. "It sucks, but I—I get it. Kyle's your husband. Something like this was bound to happen. And I get out of car shopping, so there's that."

She half laughed, half sniffled.

"But let me tell you something." He sat upright on the bench, pointing his finger and jabbing the air. "The last month or two... being with you..." He smiled, forcing himself to keep going. "It was a dream come true for me, Carly. And whatever happens tonight, just... I guess I just want you to know that." He blinked a few times, his energy fading. "It was absolutely a dream come true."

Carly's voice was a whisper. "I never meant to hurt you, Marty."

He bit his lip.

And yet you did.

"Listen, Dude..." He swallowed again. "I... I—I gotta go."

"Sergio—"

"No, really, I gotta go. I gotta go."

"*Marty...*"

He stood, brushing a hand over his suitcoat. "Don't worry, we'll—we'll talk, you know, tomorrow. Okay?"

"Are you okay?"

He winced. *No.* "I'm fine," he said. "I'm fine, but I really gotta go."

"Okay…"

"Okay." He nodded. "Bye."

He hung up, the emptiness now washing over him like a tidal wave. His phone screen turned dark, and he lowered it to his side, staring down the corridor at nothing.

Goodbye, Carly.

"Detective Martin?" Officer Mellish, the lieutenant's assistant, waved at Sergio from a conference room doorway near the end of the hall. "We'll be meeting in here this morning."

Sergio nodded, barely aware of what Mellish had said. He slipped his phone into his pocket and trudged toward the meeting room.

DAN ALATORRE

CHAPTER 8

Lieutenant Davis stood at the conference room window, his hands clasped behind his back and his face to the glass. On the other side of the window, the tall buildings of downtown Tampa loomed in the early springtime sunlight.

Sergio took a seat near the head of the table, his mind still humming from Carly's news. In front of the chair next to him, a yellow legal pad and a pen were neatly placed alongside a condensation-laden steel pitcher brimming with ice water, and a large, empty glass.

That's obviously Satan's seat.

Davis glanced at his wristwatch, then re-clasped his hands behind his back again. "Thank you so much for almost being on time, Detective."

He turned, sneering at Sergio.

"Yes, sir." Sergio lowered his head. "I apologize for that. There was a group out front that was—"

"Jordan..." Lieutenant Davis waved at Officer Mellish. "Ask the others to join us."

Sergio squirmed in his seat.

Others? Is this another meeting with HR? Am I in trouble?

A thin, middle-aged man in a dark gray suit entered the room, followed by a short-haired blonde woman. They sat at the far end of the table, as far away from Sergio as possible.

That can't be good.

The man took out a pen from inside his suitcoat and opened a folder, making some notes. The woman leaned back in her chair, crossing her legs as she adjusted the collar of her blouse.

As Officer Mellish stepped outside the conference room, he pulled the doors shut behind him.

Who are these people?

Why would he not introduce them already?

The woman was pretty. She had nice skin and a good figure, but an expression that Sergio couldn't make out—was she stern, or was she keeping a poker face? The man was overly tan, like the retirees from the Midwest that buy a condo on the beach and then spend all their waking hours out in sunshine. He had a good hairline for his age—thick, dark hair, combed straight back, with a hint of gray around the temples—but had the same unreadable look on his face as his associate.

FOURTH ESTATE

Whoever they were, they were here about him. That much was certain.

And if Lieutenant Davis is involved, I know I won't like whatever this is about.

"Detective..." Davis turned away from the window. "How would you assess the Department's standing in the community?"

Sergio chewed his lip. The wrong answer could land him in hot water.

If I say it's good, he'll remind me of when I drove Carly's Camaro through town in a high-speed chase before it went into the Bay.

If I say it's bad, he'll say I'm the reason.

So... what do I say?

"It's not a trick question, Sergio." The Lieutenant chuckled, walking to the head of the table. "You can answer honestly."

Sergio nodded.

Answer honestly? I bet. What's he up to?

He took a breath and tried to let the accumulating stress out of his system.

Just... do what Carly would tell you to do— shut up and take whatever the lieutenant's dishing out, and don't get tangled up along the way.

"Uh, well, Lieutenant..." Sergio cleared his throat. "I'd say Tampa PD enjoys a pretty solid reputation within the community, but we could always improve."

How's that?

Grinning, Sergio viewed the two strangers. His face fell.

The man in the suit wrote on his notepad, his face just as unreadable as before. The woman leaned back in her chair, interlocking her fingers around her knee and eyeing Sergio, her face still expressionless.

What is he writing?
Why is she looking at me like that?
Who are these people?

"Solid... solid... Hmm..." The lieutenant picked up his pen and clicked it half a dozen times. "Solid is an interesting choice of words. Would you say solidly good or solidly bad, Detective?"

Crap.

"Good sir." Sergio wiped his hands on his suit pants. "Solidly good."

Davis stared at his notepad. "Mm-hmm."

"But..." Swallowing hard, the detective reached up and tugged at his collar. "Like I said, there's always room for improvement."

"Improvement. Yes." The lieutenant's gaze remained on his yellow legal pad. "And what would be some areas in which we could manifest some improvements, Detective Martin? Any ideas?" Holding up his pen, Davis swirled it around in a circle. "Any improvement thoughts swimming around in your head at the moment?"

Under the table, Sergio massaged his hands.

Geez, what is he driving at?
And who are these people?

The police detective shifted in his chair again. "Well, Lieutenant, I don't exactly have any suggestions at the moment, but I'm sure if you gave me some time, I could come up with some."

"Aha." Davis nodded. "If I gave you some time."

FOURTH ESTATE

Sergio tried to take a deep breath without appearing to do so.

Why are you repeating everything I say?

"Why don't you take a little time right now, Detective?" Davis pulled out his chair and sat down. "After all, I've asked these nice people to sit in on our meeting. Let's not waste their time. The Tampa PD has given itself a series of black eyes over the past year or so. I've decided to let an outside party assist us in removing those black eyes." He gestured to the man and woman at the far end of the table. "These are consultants from the public relations firm of Sonntag, Fox and Associates. I retained them to help spruce up the department's image a little. Maybe you'd be good enough to help us—ah—to help them."

Sergio glanced at the expressionless consultants and forced a grin. "Well, getting the bad guys is always a good start."

"Detective," Davis said, "would you say racing an orange Camaro through the streets of town helped the image of the Tampa Police Department? Or would you say it hindered our efforts to improve the department's reputation in the community?"

Sitting upright in the chair, Sergio clenched his jaw.

I figured we'd get around to that.

First, some crazy First Amendment "auditors" try to start crap with me out front on the sidewalk, then Carly says her husband's trying to get back into the picture, and now this.

Terrific.

My day is starting out great.

The back of Sergio's neck grew hot. He looked the Lieutenant directly in the eye. "I'd say apprehending a murderer and drug dealer was helpful to the department." Sergio's gaze moved to the consultants. "Detective Sanderson and I also apprehended the Seminole Heights serial killer a few weeks before that, when everybody in town was afraid to come out of their houses at Christmas. That was kind of a big deal. Maybe the Lieutenant forgot to mention that to you, but it was the top story on all the news services. And then there was—"

"I don't think there's any call to get defensive, Detective." The lieutenant clicked his pen, idly looking over the notes on his yellow pad.

"I don't get defensive." Sergio gritted his teeth. "What I do is, I *confront* people like that serial killer. We're talking about an armed man who had murdered several people, but Carly and I had to go toe-to-toe with him, right upstairs in this very building. People with desk jobs might not understand this, but we had to physically tackle that maniac as he was actively shooting into a room full of cops. Then I got to wrestle with him in the staircase, where he stabbed me and threw me down a flight of concrete steps. But that's the job—and we got him."

"You got him?" Davis raised his eyes, glaring at Sergio. "I believe that suspect died—isn't that correct?"

Sergio nodded, his pulse pounding. "That's correct. It may sound trite now, in the safe confines of a clean and quiet conference room, but when a big guy in a stairwell is strangling you and stabbing you—actively trying to kill you—it's all a little different. I'm here now to talk about it, but in the moment, you can't know how a situation like that is going to end."

"It ended with a dead suspect, without due process or a trial." Raising his eyebrows, Davis returned to his legal pad, making a note. "No one alive to give his side of the story."

"Are you kidding me?" Sergio gripped the sides of his chair. "Are you for real?"

"Sergio—"

"Yeah, he died." The detective's cheeks were on fire now. He extended his index finger and pounded the tabletop with it. "That was his choice. That psycho killed a bunch of people, and when he tried to kill some more, a few cops like me and my partner Carly took control of the situation and stopped him. And, yeah, he died in the process. That's regrettable. But he died as a direct result of his own actions. You go shooting into a room full of armed police officers, you can't expect to walk out again."

"I'm just saying…" Davis stroked his chin. "Perhaps there was more to the story."

"There is." Sergio glared at the lieutenant. "Like how a nut job like that was allowed to transfer here from another police force in the first place. Maybe some better screening would have helped raise our public image—maybe a lot. It definitely would have saved a few lives."

Lieutenant Davis' eyes narrowed. "That's enough, Sergio."

"Look, Lieutenant." Sergio threw his hands out. "Since we're all being so open and candid, why don't you tell me what's going on?" He pointed at the consultants. "Because I don't need some middle-aged pencil pusher like that guy telling me how to do my job."

"I said that's enough."

"I've had enough, too." Sergio stood up.

Lieutenant Davis slammed his hand on the conference table. "Sit down, Detective Martin!"

Pursing his lips, Sergio took a breath and placed his hands on the edge of the table.

Get it together, Sergio! You were supposed to shut up and take whatever the lieutenant's dishing out, and not get tangled up along the way—right?

You're not doing that. Not even close.

He exhaled slowly, looking at the lieutenant and softening his tone. "Sir, you're the expert on public relations, not me. You do all the department interviews with the press. You know the first names of all the local reporters, and that's to your credit. But that's not me." He hooked a thumb toward the middle-aged man. "Don't saddle me with this guy. He's just going to get in my way and slow me down. It hasn't been that long since you were in the field. It's not a place for… you know—guys like him." He turned to the male consultant. "No offense, pal. Really."

A thin smile crept across the face of the middle-aged man. "None taken, Detective."

"And we have rules about this stuff," Sergio said. "Protocols. If he's not up to speed physically, he could get hurt." He glanced toward the man a second time. "Again, no offense."

FOURTH ESTATE

"Of course," the man said. "And again, no offense taken."

Facing his superior officer, Sergio shrugged. "So, let the two of them do a duty tour of the station and talk to some uniformed officers. Let them conduct a poll, if they want. But don't make me be part of it."

"Too late." The lieutenant clipped his pen onto the notepad. "You're already part of it." Davis stood up, gathered his belongings, and walked to the door. "I've assigned consultant Fox to work with you for the next forty-eight hours, side by side. Field rides, duty tours, the works. Where you go, the consultant goes, like you're glued together at the hip. Is that clear?"

Sergio shook his head. "Sir—"

"Is that clear, Detective?"

"Sir, protocol says—"

"Protocol?" The lieutenant wheeled around. "Like the protocol that says don't conduct a high-speed chase through the streets of Tampa chasing a drug dealer?" His face turned red. "Or like the protocol that says direct all media inquiries—not some, *all*—to the department's head of Public Relations and to *not* engage with reporters like those idiot First Amendment *frauditors* on the sidewalk in front of headquarters, on camera? Protocols like those? Or do you need another unpaid suspension to remind you of just how thin the ice is under your feet, Detective?"

Sergio lowered his head, his shoulders slumping.

He must've seen it on the interoffice monitors, or somebody told him. But they sure were quick. There wasn't five minutes between me talking to those bozos and getting up here to sit down with Davis.

A jolt went through Sergio's insides.

Could Davis have set me up? Could he have arranged for those so-called auditors to be out front when I got here, just to confront me? And I walked right into the trap?

"We're spending a lot of money to improve our image—an image you helped mess up, Detective." Lieutenant Davis pointed at Sergio. "Now, you *will* take this PR consultant with you, and you *will* engage in honest discussions about the department while you conduct yourself in the execution of your assigned duties. Is that clear?"

"Yes, sir." Sergio nodded.

Stay focused. If Davis wanted to use the reporters to burn you, this meeting would already be over. If there's a trap, that wasn't it. Get your head back in the game.

Sergio squared his shoulders, peering at the middle-aged man seated across the conference room table. "I hope you brought some strong coffee with you, pal, because from here I've got an appointment at the shooting range, followed by a whole day of follow-up interviews. It's police work, but it's the kind that has been known to induce a coma in the uninitiated."

"Change of plans," Davis said, folding his arms across his chest. "Keep your scheduled time at the shooting range, then come back and do a tour of each department, to explain how they assist you as a detective. The departments heads are expecting you."

"But I have to do the follow-up interviews for my case work. There are—"

"Not anymore." The lieutenant smiled. "This is your schedule now—and you'd better stick to it. Now go."

Placing his finger on his suit coat lapels, Sergio tugged at the material. "I'll at least need time to go home and change out of this suit before heading to the gun range."

"It's safe to say I didn't anticipate that," Davis said. "But here we are. Get to the range. You can expense the drycleaning bill."

"Sir, I really—"

"There must be some miscommunication." The lieutenant took a step toward Sergio. "I believe I oversee departmental assignments, and I just explained your schedule for the day." He leaned forward, looking his detective in the eye. "Any further questions?"

"Nope." Sergio sighed. "Let's go, fella. Bring some coffee. You'll need it."

"I believe there's been another miscommunication." The woman got up from her chair and smoothed the wrinkles from her suit. "I'll be going with you today, Detective Martin."

"What?" Sergio's jaw dropped. "No." He looked at Davis. "Lieutenant…"

The smile on the lieutenant's face grew larger. "Detective Sergio Martin, meet Ms. Avarie

Fox, of the Public Relations firm of Sonntag, Fox and Associates."

Sergio took a step backward, eyeing the slender blonde. "You're… the 'Fox' in Sonntag and Fox?"

She nodded. "You catch on quick."

"Not quick enough." Sergio grimaced. "But don't expect special treatment just because you're…"

"Because I'm a woman?"

"Be…cause… you're short," Sergio said. "Bad guys look to take down the easiest target, and a short person can draw that kind of attention from them, ma'am."

She raised an eyebrow. "Will we be running into a lot of bad guys at the shooting range, Detective? Or in the follow-up interviews that are so difficult to stay awake in?"

He swallowed hard. "Bad guys can be anywhere."

"Lucky for me I'll have a big strong detective along to protect me."

Sergio turned to his lieutenant. "May I speak with you privately, please?"

"Sergio, we hired these consultants to help us." Exhaling sharply, Davis waved his hand. "To do that, they need access to more than what they can read in the press. They need to see what happens behind the scenes. I've opened the entire department up to Sonntag and Fox. They have a full-access pass. Now…" He straightened his suitcoat, peering down his nose at his detective. "Whatever you want to say to me, you can say in front of them."

"Okay. Well…" Sergio glanced downward and took a breath. "This is a bad idea, Lieutenant. There's no telling what type of calls could come in. It's kinda dangerous."

"Then I expect you'll protect our guest like she was your little sister." Lieutenant Davis turned to the exit. "You two are glued at the hip now—and nothing happens to her or it's your ass. Time to play by the rules for once, Sergio. If you can't handle that, maybe being a detective isn't for you."

"But, sir—"

"I believe I've made myself quite clear, Detective Martin." Davis opened the door and stood in the threshold. "Now—you've got a reservation at the shooting range? Get going. And then get right back here for that duty tour." Davis left the room, heading in the direction of his office.

"Yes, sir." Sergio glanced over his shoulder at the slender blonde consultant. "Let's go, little sister."

DAN ALATORRE

CHAPTER 9

Officer Mellish stood next to Lieutenant Davis' desk, laying out some file folders. As the door opened and the lieutenant stepped inside, Mellish moved to one side. "How'd the meeting go, sir?"

Davis chuckled, plopping his legal pad onto the desk and sitting down. "It went well. Very well. I don't think when Sergio came to work this morning, he thought he'd be leaving with a watchdog strapped to his side. You should have seen his face, Jordan." He rubbed his hands together. "It's going perfectly. Absolutely perfectly. Avarie Fox is going to hang Sergio out to dry."

Mellish clutched the remaining folders to his chest. "She agreed to that—to help you get rid of Sergio?"

"Fox doesn't know anything about it. She's an overrated desk clerk with a college degree and a nice ass." Davis leaned back in his chair, folding his hands behind his head. "Her report will create a full accounting of whatever Sergio does this week—impartial, and fact based. That's all I'm going to need. He was already as hot as a pepper when I left the meeting. He might not get to the parking garage without blowing up."

"A week?" Mellish said. "Sir, I thought Ms. Fox was only going to be observing Sergio for one or two days. The schedule you had me file with the Chief said as much."

"Yes. That was the initial schedule." The lieutenant propped his feet up on his desk, a broad smile stretching across his face. "But I'll make up an excuse to amend the schedule, and that curvy little blonde spy will be with Sergio for as long as I deem necessary. Mister Serial Killer Catcher might be able to maintain his party manners around a consultant for a day or so, but a week? No chance. At some point he'll let his guard down. He'll become his hot shot self again, and he'll screw up—in front of Avarie Fox. She'll have no other option than to record that mistake in her supporting data. And I'll have no issue using that information to bounce Sergio out of here."

Mellish nodded. "It'll be her unbiased findings, so your hands will be clean. It won't look personal. The Chief will see it that way, too." The junior officer rubbed his chin. "We need Sergio gone that bad?"

"Oh, absolutely. In fact, Sergio said it himself, in the meeting. I wrote it down." Davis sat forward, flipping through the pages of the yellow legal pad. "Here. He was talking about the Seminole Heights serial killer. Sergio said, 'He died as a direct result of his own actions.' That's exactly what Sergio will do." Davis dropped the pages back down over the pad. "Detective Martin's blatant disregard for the rules will be his own demise. He is a cancer in the department. We can't let his reckless actions encourage others to behave the same way, or the defiance will spread. I'm not having that." He picked up the legal pad and opened a drawer, dropping the pad inside. "That's why he's got to go, Jordan. It's for the good of the entire organization. The fact that I'll enjoy Sergio's departure is merely a happy side benefit."

"Of course, Lieutenant," Mellish said. "But what if he doesn't screw up? What if Sergio manages to keep it together while the consultant is with him?"

"That's a calculated risk, sure. But Detective Martin has a track record. He's shown time and time again that he can't hold back."

"Yes, sir." Jordan shifted his weight from one foot to the other. "But again... what if he does manage to color within the lines while Ms. Fox is with him?"

"If Sergio somehow manages to defy the odds and not break departmental rules for a whole week, then I'll get credit for putting him with that stupid PR rep and helping rein him in. It's a win-win for me. And the department, of course."

"Of course."

"We have rules for a reason. Everybody needs to follow them, with no exceptions." Davis eased one foot onto the corner of his desk and raised the other foot to rest on top of it. "The fact that Sergio Martin can't seem to follow the rules... Well, that's not my problem. Not for much longer, anyway."

CHAPTER 10

As the consultant clipped the seatbelt over her hips on the passenger side of Sergio's car, the detective frowned and reached for the ignition key. The sedan's engine rumbled to life, and Sergio maneuvered it out of the parking lot.

He drove neither fast nor slow, but with an abundance of caution, aware of every movement he made—and fearing that it was all somehow being recorded by the PR rep in the seat next to him. Avarie Fox sat in silence, her purse and computer bag at her feet, as Sergio gripped the steering wheel and headed to the shooting range.

As he drove, the morning's events came rushing back to him, tightening his neck muscles and heating his cheeks.

I have to do my job with a freaking overseer watching my every move? And meanwhile, Kyle is trying to move back in with Carly, and I can't do anything about it. Then there's that idiot First Amendment auditor, who might be filing a BS complaint against me right now or posting an edited version of this morning's footage to make me look like an abusive psycho, which would be the excuse Lieutenant Davis needs to put my butt in a sling...

Stifling a groan, he clenched his teeth.

Could this day get any worse?

If I could talk to Carly, I could see where her head is at with this Kyle stuff, but I sure can't make that phone call with my personal spy listening in.

Crap, what if this PR rep knows about me and Carly, and that's why she's really here? We never filed that HR paperwork about co-workers dating...

A jolt of unease rippled through his insides. He glanced at his passenger.

No. She's not out to get you. She's just doing her job.

Nodding, he scanned the roadway, observing traffic as he took a deep breath. The tension in his neck eased.

But what if she's a friend of Lieutenant Davis? What if she was secretly hired just to ride along with me and catch me making some penny-ante mistake so he can make a big deal out of it?

The tension came rushing back to his neck. Wincing, Sergio tried to peer at the consultant out of the corner of his eye.

She's pretty. Is that part of the ruse? Davis sends an attractive woman to spend forty-eight hours with me, writing down everything I do, and hoping

FOURTH ESTATE

I'll be distracted and mess up in front of her. That's his scam. That has to be it.

"Detective, are we going a bit fast?" Avarie Fox put her hand on the dashboard. "I think I saw a sign back there that said the speed limit is forty-five."

Sergio squeezed the steering wheel with sweaty hands.

That's Lieutenant Satan's plan. He wants an outside observer to watch me mess up so he can fire me.

So… I can't screw up. That should be easy enough. I can do that.

"Detective Martin?" Fox pressed herself backwards into her seat. "Should you slow down? You're going nearly sixty."

Sergio recalled the smugness on the Lieutenant's face during their morning meeting.

That desk jockey, trying to set me up from the get-go. It's all a trap. Even the part where he didn't tell me who the consultants were, so I'd sit there wondering, all nervous. He's trying to get me off balance and keep me off balance.

Sergio shook his head.

Well, if that little jerk thinks he can snare me that easily, he'd better think again. I'm not going to walk into his little—"

"Detective!"

Sergio glanced at the consultant. Her jaw hung open, her face pale. She held onto the dashboard with one hand and the armrest with the other, nearly rising out of her seat.

Sergio looked out the windshield. Traffic had come to a stop in front of them.

And his car was still moving fast.

He swerved the sedan into the emergency lane on the right side of the road and took his foot from the gas pedal, putting it onto the brake and slowing his car. Loose road gravel and bits of discarded tire bounced off the asphalt and went flying upward into the wheel wells, making a clatter of small banging noises. To his left, a row of cars that was at a standstill; to his right, a long stretch of concrete dividers that were much too close.

Ahead, a dump truck blocked the emergency lane, backing up as it raised its payload bed. A small avalanche of dirt rolled down onto the side of the road, directly in Sergio's path.

A road worker in an orange safety vest stepped in front of the dump truck. Sergio slammed on the brakes, screeching his tires.

The worker scowled, waving his hands and yelling obscenities.

Sergio waved back, sliding down in his seat. As the angry road worker approached, Sergio reached for the police ID on his belt, unclipping it. He held it up and put down the window. "Sorry. Police business. I'm trying to get through and I thought this lane was clear."

"Well, it's not!" the worker shouted.

"Yeah, I see that now. My bad."

Scowling, the worker held up a hand to keep the line of stopped cars from moving and waved Sergio through.

"Thank you." Sergio waved. As they passed, he glanced in the rearview mirror. The worker was flipping him off. "And thanks for that, too," Sergio said, waving again, his cheeks hot with embarrassment.

Keeping his eyes on the road, Sergio maneuvered around the construction and back onto the road.

Next to him, in the passenger seat, Avarie Fox let out a loud sigh. "I know you're not happy about me riding with you, Detective, but there's no need to kill me, is there?"

Sergio slunk lower in his seat. "I'm sorry about that ma'am. Totally my mistake. My mind was… elsewhere."

She adjusted her seat belt. "Do you think you can stay focused the rest of the way to the shooting range or should I get an Uber?"

"I promise, you'll be fine, Ms. Fox." Frowning, he clenched his jaw.

Nice going, Sergio—you idiot.

DAN ALATORRE

CHAPTER 11

EARBUDS DELIVERING HER LATEST AUDIO BOOK, Kerri Milner walked past a white Mercedes SUV as it rolled to a stop in front of her place of employment. The car's engine cut off as the reporter tucked a small paper bag under her arm and pulled open the door of Instant News Network. Inside, the newsroom swarmed with ringing phones and loud conversations.

Kerri slid her computer satchel off her shoulder and pulled the earbuds from her ears, dropping them inside the bag. As she viewed the bustling newsroom, her fingers found the edge of a paper bag, and she pulled its contents out—her breakfast, a cold apple pastry. One of her male colleagues rushed into the room, not pausing to say good morning to the shapely twentysomething. As he dug through the debris lining the shelves of the supply closet, Milner pushed her short brown locks from her eyes and glanced around the office. "Looks like I missed something."

"You sure did," he said. "Jasper Menendez-Holswain was murdered this morning."

She eyed the TVs in the newsroom, taking a bite of her breakfast. Each screen was filled with digitally-blurred images of the NewsAction boss being shot to death in front of his staff during their morning livestream.

"Wow." Milner chewed her pastry. "Sucks to be him today." She walked to her desk and dropped off her gear. "What was the beef? Some disgruntled employee?"

"No one knows yet." Her male colleague pulled a phone charging cord from the cabinet and slammed the door, racing into the next room. "Suarez has everyone working it."

Nodding, Milner strolled to her Editor-In-Chief's office, leaning on the door frame and idly rolling the front hem of her black Rolling Stones t-shirt as she waited for Miranda Suarez to wrap up a call. On the TV in the private space, the blurred video of the murder was replaying on a local TV station.

"Right. Keep me posted." Miranda tossed her cell phone to her desk. Groaning, the middle-aged woman leaned back and dragged her manicured fingers through her long, curly brown locks. "Kerri, please tell me you have an angle on the Menendez-Holswain murder."

Milner shrugged, shaking her head. "Nope. I just heard about it now."

FOURTH ESTATE

"Now?" Standing, her boss cursed as she went to her office door. "How can you be in the news business and not watch the news?" She leaned into the newsroom, clapping her hands. Her staff members stopped what they were doing and looked at their boss. "Everybody!" Suarez shouted. "None of my sources at NewsAction knows why the killer gunned down Jasper. That means you need to work your second and third leads for info. Squeeze them all until they squeak!"

A young woman lowered her phone from her ear. "We are, boss, but everybody over at NewsAction is getting inundated with calls. All the local TV stations, plus CNN, Fox... McSwain says it's chaos."

"That's why we have to keep pressing them. We're local, so we should have the advantage. Get over there. Maybe she'll give you more in person." The news boss glanced over her shoulder at the reporter standing in her office. "Kerri, didn't you used to date someone from there? That guy who always wore those stupid flowery shirts?"

Swallowing a bit of pastry, Milner nodded. "Jersey Targo." She brushed a crumb from her lip. "But we didn't exactly end things on speaking terms."

"Call him."

"He walked in on me with another guy, so I'm guessing he won't answer."

"Try." Suarez grabbed a remote from her desk and flipped channels on the TV. Each local station displayed the same scenes from the

NewsAction killing. "Maybe if he thinks he's got a second chance, he'll open up."

Milner winced. "Miranda..."

"I'm serious." She placed her hands on her hips. "Whatever news agency gets the inside scoop on this is gonna rule the ratings for the next two weeks. I need that to be us. Now, get over there. And wear something sexy."

"Uh, no."

"Here." Suarez went to a closet in the rear of her office, yanking it open. She took out a black lace bra and a sheer white crop-top t-shirt. "Take this. You can change on the way." She thrust the clothes into the reporter's hand.

Holding the t-shirt up to the overhead office lights, Milner shook her head. The ceiling tiles were almost completely visible through the material. "Seriously?"

"Seriously. Since FRT got aggressive a few months ago, we've been hemorrhaging cash. This story could put us in the black."

Kerri held the t-shirt up to her thin torso, the wispy white material extending well past the shoulders of her black Rolling Stones shirt. "Boss... it's not going to fit."

Her editor picked up her phone and tapped the screen. "Then tie a knot in the t-shirt and skip the bra. And get over there before the police wear them down—and before Jasper's lawyers show up."

"Yes, ma'am." Sighing, the reporter sauntered out of the office. She dropped her half-eaten pastry into a trash can, followed by the t-shirt and bra, and headed for the exit.

FOURTH ESTATE

Her videographer waved at her from across the newsroom. "Kerri, are you going on site at NewsAction?"

She nodded. "Looks like it."

"Want me to tag along and do a remote shot?"

"Nah." She picked up her gear bag. "That'll be every local clown's move. I'm supposed to get inside."

"How?" The videographer scrunched up his face, recoiling. "Not... With Jersey?"

"Yeah." Kerri raised her eyebrows, slinging her bag onto her shoulder as she walked out of the room. "Wish me luck."

As she reached the building exit, she extended her hand to push open the door. Instead, the door swung outward without her touching it, almost causing Kerri to lose her balance.

An African-American man in a red windbreaker filled the doorway.

"Sorry." Kerri stepped back, looking at him. "I kinda didn't see you there."

The man lumbered inside, his hands in his pockets. Sunglasses covered his eyes, and a baseball cap covered his head. His face was obscured by a paper surgical mask.

He turned his head as if to inspect the newsroom and everything visible from the front door, but said nothing. He simply stood there.

"Hey," Kerri said. "Uh... can I get by you?" She tucked a strand of her short brown hair behind her ear. "I kinda need to get to an assignment."

The stranger remained in the doorway, blocking her exit. He breathed at a shallow, rapid pace, like he'd been exercising.

Kerri looked him over a second time. The man's legs appeared too skinny for the rest of his body.

Odd.

"Mister?" She cleared her throat. "I need to leave. Would you mind…"

He turned his face to her. A drop of sweat descended from the hair at his temple, running slowly down across his cheek.

Kerri gestured toward the exit. "I have to go. Would you mind…" She looked past him to the door.

He remained silent, turning his face back to the bustling newsroom, his hands jostling inside the pockets of his windbreaker.

Stepping back, the reporter stuck her hip out. "Who are you here to see? We're all pretty busy this morning."

Miranda burst into the room. "Oh, good, Kerri. You're still here." She held up a slip of paper from a pink memo pad. "Madison just hung up with McSwain Tannenbaum at NewsAction. She and Jersey Targo have agreed to talk to you—if you hurry."

"Okay." Kerri took the memo and glanced at it, then pulled her phone from her hip pocket to check the time. "Thanks, Miranda. I can be there in about five minutes."

The stranger moved his head. "Miranda?"

FOURTH ESTATE

Kerri looked up. The man's voice sounded strange, as if he was trying to speak an octave lower than his natural pitch.

Her boss didn't bother to look at the man standing next to them. Instead, she turned her back to him, facing the newsroom—and scowling. "That's right. Who are you? We're very busy this morning."

He took a step toward her.

Miranda frowned, giving the stranger a half glance from over her shoulder. "Who are you here to see? I don't have time for games."

"You are… Miranda Suarez?"

"That's right." The Editor-In-Chief of Instant News Network huffed. "And who are you? I need to get back to a major news story. Jasper Menendez-Holswain was killed this morning. So, unless you have some hot, unreported information related to that, I really need to get back to my desk."

He took another step. "I know about that story."

Kerri Milner cocked her head.

That's definitely a fake voice.

"Do you, now?" Miranda leaned forward, peering toward the newsroom TVs. "You know about the murder at NewsAction, huh? And what insights might you share?"

An odd feeling swarmed inside Kerri's abdomen. She backed away from the stranger, reaching out for Miranda's arm. "Hey, boss… How about you come with me on that assignment?"

Suarez's gaze stayed on her newsroom TV. "Crap, we are blowing this. We need more—"

"Miranda." Kerri kept her eyes on the stranger as her fingers latched onto Miranda's forearm. "Come on. We'll be late."

"What?" Suarez turned back around. "What are you talking about?" Her eyes went to the visitor, catching his hands moving inside the pockets of his red windbreaker.

The front of the jacket was splattered with dark red spots.

Miranda's jaw dropped. She recoiled as the man withdrew his hands from his pockets and held up a large gun, pointing it directly at her face.

CHAPTER 12

As they continued the drive toward west Tampa and the outdoor shooting range, Sergio observed every speed change—and stayed at least three miles under the limit. Narrow streets turned wider as the car moved away from downtown. The deep valleys created by concrete and steel skyscrapers became strip malls, then sprawling warehouses north of the airport, eventually yielding to the grassy residential neighborhoods of the Town N Country area. Between the latter two, large swaths of land had been designated for use by industries like paver manufacturers and marble importers—businesses that didn't mind the loud noise that came with being located in the international airport's takeoff and landing paths.

"You know, I read your file," Fox said. "You seem to bounce between hero and screwup." She turned to face her driver. "Why is that?"

Sergio shook his head, keeping his eyes on the road. "I wouldn't categorize my time with the department in that manner, ma'am."

"No, I suppose you wouldn't. Tell me this, then. Why did you want to become a police officer, Detective Martin?"

He rolled his eyes. "Why, to serve and protect my community, of course." Taking a turn onto a mostly-gravel road, Sergio glared at his passenger. "Why'd you want to become a public relations consultant? Because lying for a living seemed fun?"

The consultant turned to the window. "I don't lie for a living."

"And I didn't bounce from hero to screwup." Sergio shrugged. "I guess we're both just misunderstood, which is odd, for one of us."

He stopped the car in a gravel parking lot, in front of a long, warehouse-looking structure with a wooden fence and a sign that read Tampa Police Shooting Range—Authorized Access Only.

As Sergio exited the vehicle and walked to the trunk, Fox stepped out and put her hands on her hips. Rapid popping sounds filled the air in the distance, interspersed by occasional loud bangs and brief moments of silence.

"What's that comment supposed to mean?" she asked. "Odd for who? Me?"

Sergio shook his head. "I'm just saying, if a PR firm is viewed as a bunch of hired liars… maybe they have a public relations problem."

"Oh, I see." She nodded.

He popped the trunk. Inside the messy space lay two Kevlar vests, a pair of muddy work boots, a man's navy-blue sweatshirt, assorted soccer gear, and a bucket full of very worn baseballs.

Avarie shut her car door and took a step, then stopped and looked at her hand. A thick layer of road dust coated her fingertips. As she wiped the mess away, she stopped at the cluttered trunk of the car and peered inside. "Nice to see your car is as clean in the inside as it is on the outside."

Scowling, Sergio rummaged through the piles and took out a black container the size of a large shoe box with rounded corners.

Avarie shook her head. "Are you always this cordial to your guests, Detective?"

"See?" Sergio said. "Again, we disagree. You're not my guest. You might be a babysitter, or you might be a spy, but you're definitely not a guest. The Lieutenant assigned you to ride with me, over my protests, remember?" He slammed the trunk and placed the box on top, staring at her.

"So..." Fox scrunched up her face. "That justifies you taking me on a near-death excursion in your car? What, are you five years old?"

Sergio's anger immediately turned to awkwardness. "That was—well, that... I have a lot of stuff on my mind this morning, and I was distracted. That was a mistake."

"I agree." She kept her eyes on his. "The question is, what were you so distracted about that, when riding with a woman your boss wants you to work with, you almost scare her to death?"

DAN ALATORRE

Sergio pursed his lips, nodding. The consultant didn't seem angry—at least, not completely. And she wasn't asserting her authority, insisting that his bosses hired her and so he needed to comply.

She is... doing what, exactly?

Fox tilted her chin upwards and narrowed her eyes. "You don't trust me, do you, Detective?"

"Don't feel bad about it," Sergio said. "We just met."

His companion took a deep breath and let it out slowly, kicking a pebble with the toe of her shiny, expensive-looking shoe. "It's going to be a long couple of days if we continue going the way we've been so far." She peered up at him. "How about we make a deal?"

"Sure." Sergio folded his arms across his chest. "You go back to your office, and I go back to doing my job?"

"Yes. I'll do exactly that. If..." Fox looked toward the shooting range door. "...if you can score better than me on the shooting range."

Grinning, Sergio eyed the petite blonde. "You must want to go home pretty bad. I do this for a living. I'm a good shot."

"You talk a pretty good game," she said. "What do you say? If you win, I go back to the office and leave you alone. But if I win, you stop acting like a jerk and let me do my job. Deal?"

The wind picked up scattered bits of paper and pushed them across the gravel lot. Muted pops and bangs came from somewhere behind the building.

Smiling, Sergio yanked his metal box from the lid of his trunk. "Little sister, I'd take that deal and even order you an Uber for your trip back to headquarters." He moved to walk past her. "But Lieutenant Davis will be awfully upset if you go back early."

"I'll handle the lieutenant." She stepped into his path, her hands on her hips. "I lie for a living, right? I'll say I got sick or something. Now, do we have a deal?"

The slender consultant held her hand out, the wind tugging at her hair.

"Okay, sure. We have a deal." Frowning, Sergio shook hands with her. "Let's go. This oughta be fun."

Inside the range office, Sergio procured shooting glasses and ear protection for himself and the consultant, then headed out to a vacant stall in the open-air section of the shooting range. Torso targets—plates of steel, cut in the shape of an adult's upper body—had been placed at varying distances on the short grass. A tall wall of dirt rose up at the far end of the shooting area, spanning close to fifty feet high, to stop any stray shots. Each of the covered, three-sided stalls on the range contained a short wooden bench and a small table for rifle use. Next to that, a thin shelf protruded from the front wall, above a section of concrete floor that had been painted to designate where the user should stand while discharging weapons from an upright position. Coffee cans had been nailed to the walls to collect discarded shells; signs had been hung to remind customers about gun safety protocols, using eye and ear protection, and not walking out to inspect a target during live fire.

Sergio slipped out of his suitcoat, draping it over the short table and rolling up his sleeves. He opened the metal box and removed his auxiliary service weapon, a black Smith & Wesson handgun, then pulled his beige Sig Sauer service gun from his holster. Placing both weapons on the wooden table, he stepped back and looked at the consultant. "Okay, little sister. Which do you want to use?"

As Sergio opened a box of ammunition, Fox inched toward the table, leaning over and looking at the weapons, but not touching either gun. She held her hands close to the base of her throat. "They look alike. What's the difference?"

Smiling, Sergio picked up the black gun, released the magazine, and checked the chamber to ensure the weapon was completely unloaded. "I use this one for—"

"That looks like a little girl's gun." The consultant stuck her lower lip out and poked a finger at the weapon. "It's a bit on the tiny side."

Sighing, Sergio set down the black gun and picked up the beige one. "The department likes this one, and so does the Army. It's a Sig Sauer P-320. Not exactly a little girl's gun."

"Hmm." Fox tapped her chin with her index finger. "The little black one goes better with my outfit. I'll try that. Who's going to shoot first?"

"You can have first honors, little sister." Sergio swept his hand over the weapons. "Let me load it for you, and—"

FOURTH ESTATE

The slender blonde grabbed a handful of bullets from the box, slid them into the magazine, slapped it into the handle of the Smith & Wesson, and pointed the gun at a target twenty-five yards away. "Say when." She held the gun at arm's length, cupping her left hand around her right hand and dropping her eye toward her shoulder.

His jaw hanging open, Sergio took a step backward. "Fire a—"

Six blasts sounded in rapid succession, the black gun jumping in Avarie Fox's hand. Empty shells streamed over her right arm and clattered to the concrete floor.

Twenty-five yards away, the steel torso target pinged six times.

"—way," Sergio said.

The consultant popped the magazine from the weapon and opened the slide, then placed the empty gun on the table.

"Six hits in under two seconds—if anybody was keeping time." She wiped her hands on her skirt as she moved behind the detective. "Beat that."

Sergio stood with his hands at his sides, blinking. "Yeah, okay." He shook his head, his jaw hanging open. "Uh... Good shooting."

Strolling to the front of the stall, Sergio loaded the beige handgun. He raised the weapon and fired off six rounds in an almost unending volley, hitting the steel target each time.

Stepping back from the wall, Sergio checked the weapon to ensure it was empty again. "I don't know how fast that was, but it was fast."

"At least as fast as me." Fox nodded. "Probably faster."

He leaned against a wooden support post. "Why do I feel like I was set up? You're a good shot, Ms. Fox."

"Call me Avarie." She slid her protective eyeglasses to the top of her head and removed her ear protection. "And I'll call you Sergio—okay?"

"Okay." Sergio took his hard plastic earmuffs off and laid them on the table. "So, what gives? You didn't learn how to do that from watching YouTube videos on your way to Lieutenant Davis' office. What's your story?"

"Don't try to change the subject. I believe it's time to collect my prize."

"Actually…" Sergio glanced toward the exit. "I was thinking about taking a lunch break."

"What?" She frowned and took her phone from the little table, checking the time. "It's a little early, isn't it?"

"A detective's schedule is unpredictable." He pushed himself off the support post and collected his belongings, sliding his service weapon into his holster. "We might get a call and end up working all night, so we eat when we can. Do you prefer tacos or hamburgers?"

"I can probably get a vegan salad easier at a taco place."

"Then, hamburgers it is—for me." Picking up his gun box, the detective walked down the row of stalls. "Enjoy your taco salad, little sister. I'll see you back here in an hour. I'm sure you have the Uber app on your phone. Have the driver take you to Enrique's. It's just around the corner."

Avarie chased after him and cut him off, blocking his path. "No dice. I won fair and square, so we stick together. Your boss said where you go, I go."

"Yeah?" Sergio gave her a wry smile. "Eventually I'm gonna have to go to the bathroom. Are you coming in there with me, too?"

"So tempting, but no, I think I'll skip that." She extended her finger and poked him in the chest. "But look, for everything else, if it's part of your life, having me along is going to increase my ability to help your department. And you *do* want to help your department, don't you?"

Another muted volley of gunshots rang out from the other side of the range. Sergio stepped back, looking at the consultant. Nodding, he answered her with the truth. "Yes, I want to help the department."

"So, let's be straight with one another," Avarie said. She gave her head a toss, sending her short blonde locks over her shoulder. "Anyone can see you're bugged about something, but whatever it is, I didn't cause it. I understand that you don't want me here, but—"

"Lieutenant Davis is trying to bait me. He's using you to help fire me."

She opened her mouth but halted, studying his face. "Let's say that's the case, and he is trying to bait you. Then just… don't screw up. Is that so hard?" Her tone eased, a softness coming to her eyes. "I know what it's like to feel as if everyone's digging the ground out from under your feet. You have skills.

Use them to outperform the situation. Don't just be defiant. Maybe I can help you there. I mean, if you're a screwup, you shouldn't be working here anyway, right? But as I said, I saw your file." A gentle breeze lifted a strand of her golden hair and laid it over her eyes. "There is hero material in there, and not just one instance of it. I don't see that in every police department I go to."

She gazed at him, the noise of the shooting range drifting away as he took her in.

She's a little firecracker, this one. What happened to make you that way, so full of passion? You sure don't take any crap—at least, not from me.

But you still might be part of a trap.

Sergio held his gun box in front of himself and leaned back, clasping his right hand with his left. "But there's screwup stuff in that file, too, right?"

"Some." She peered into his eyes, not blinking and not looking away. "Why is that?"

"Sometimes you have to bend the rules." He shrugged. "The desk jockeys and Human Resources clerks who make those rules call that screwing up."

"Bend the rules? Or break them?"

He looked over at the shooting field, the steel targets shining in the morning sun. "I respect the rules, but sometimes a dumb rule can hamstring you. Then the bad guys get away. Nobody benefits from that." He turned to face her. "Not even the people who write the dumb rules. They want their kids safe to play in the park, too."

"I'm not naïve," she said. "A piss-poor attitude isn't going to help you do your job or help me do mine. Besides, aside from all that, we had a deal. Did I outshoot you?"

Sergio cocked his head. "I'd... say it was a tie."

"Ties go to the runner, Detective." Avarie smiled. "So, are you going to stop acting like a jerk and let me do my job? What's it going to be?"

He sighed. "I'll... stop being a jerk."

"Thank you."

"Let's get something to eat." He tucked his case under his arm and waved toward the exit. "I skipped breakfast. It's never a good idea to meet with the antichrist on a full stomach."

"Antichrist? The lieutenant?" Avarie walked alongside him. "Is he that bad?"

"I'll tell you after breakfast. I can't discuss him on an empty stomach, either. Just... tell me you were joking about that vegan stuff. Because Enrique will—"

"I was joking." She chuckled.

"Oh, what a relief." Sergio leaned against the exit doors and pushed them open, holding the heavy steel door for Avarie as she passed. "I think I dislike you less already."

She rolled her eyes. "I was *so* worried about that, too."

As they walked to his car, Sergio dug his keys out of his pocket. "So, come on—where'd you learn to shoot like that?"

Fox trudged over the gravel lot. "What, a girl can't learn to shoot?"

"It's not uncommon, but it's not exactly something I see every day, either. Not like that. You had a pro stance and got off six quick rounds, hitting the target each time—and in a tight grouping. Not a lot of people can do that."

She stopped, glancing over her shoulder at the shooting range, then turned back to Sergio, squinting in the bright morning sunlight. "My grandfather was a cop. My uncle was a cop, too, and my older brother… So maybe you could cut me some slack and consider I'm not out to burn you, and that maybe I'm actually trying to help you and the Tampa PD."

"That's a lot of cops in the family—but not your dad? Was he the black sheep of the bunch?"

"My parents divorced when I was little. All the cops are on my mother's side. But to answer your question, I learned to shoot at the police academy in Orlando, okay? But I found out policework wasn't for me."

"No?" Sergio's phone buzzed in his pocket. "Why not?"

He pulled the phone out, a text from his sister Mina's phone appearing on the screen. Sergio tapped the phone to open the message.

Come to Tampa General ASAP. Mama is trouble.

"Oh, man." He stopped and looked at the consultant. "Avarie, hey, I'm sorry—I need to go. My sister is texting me from the hospital. Something's wrong with my mom. Can I drop you somewhere? Or, why don't you stay here and grab an Uber?"

"Is it serious?"

"Mina says it is."

Avarie rushed to the car. "I'll ride with you to the hospital and get an Uber from there. Seeing some behind-the-scenes insights will help with my work about making cops relatable. I won't pry, I promise."

He pursed his lips, looking at her.

"Sergio, I'm not going to embarrass you. Especially now that you're starting to trust me. Even Lieutenant Antichrist couldn't have arranged that text about your mother." She opened the passenger door and climbed inside the vehicle. "For the next forty-eight hours, where you go, I go—so, let's move. We're wasting time."

Growling, Sergio jumped into his car and started the ignition, racing the engine as he sped out of the parking lot.

DAN ALATORRE

CHAPTER 13

As Sergeant Deshawn Marshall approached the conference rooms, a uniformed officer appeared at the other end of the hallway, carrying a sheet of paper. The sergeant raised his hand and waved at the officer.

Name... Name... Terley? Terlinney?

As the woman came nearer, the sergeant was able to make out her name badge. Ternihey.

That's right— Kristia Ternihey. Came to us from the Broward County Sheriff's Office last fall. Her mom works in City Planning.

"What have you got there, Kristia?"

"Another murder, Sergeant." She handed Deshawn the preliminary findings report. "Just outside of downtown. The offices of that internet gossip rag—NewsAction, Inc."

"Who's the vic?"

"The deceased is the owner, Jasper Menendez-Holswain." Ternihey's gaze went to the PFR as the sergeant reviewed it. "The killer walked in and shot him point-blank during a livestream event. It's all over the internet. His whole staff was there, but Menendez-Holswain was the only casualty." Ternihey exhaled sharply. "The freaking guy just popped him and walked out."

Deshawn nodded. "We have uniforms on scene?"

"Yes, sir, but no detective has been assigned yet." She hooked a thumb at the conference room door. "I was about to interrupt the interviews to see who Lieutenant Davis wants on the case. The murder was in his sector."

"I'll tell him." Deshawn handed the report back to the officer. "Do me a favor. We had a shooting earlier this morning, so we're stretched pretty thin. Get downstairs and see what detectives are still available to handle this one. Come on into the interview room when you have the info. We might have to call some of the night shift to come back in."

"Two murders in one day." Ternihey shook her head. "Must be a full moon."

"Then let's hope for an eclipse." Deshawn moved to the door of the interview room, putting his hand on the knob. "And see where Carlos Fuentes is. He's handled the secondary duties on a few of these. Maybe he can run the NewsAction scene until the cavalry arrives. I know you're new here, but you're not new to law enforcement. I want you prepared to assist Fuentes in the field if necessary."

FOURTH ESTATE

The young officer's eyes lit up. "Yes, sir."

"We're looking to promote quality people around here, Kristia." Deshawn nodded, opening the door to the interviews. "Be one of them."

* * * * *

In the conference room adjacent to the one where the interviews were being conducted, Carly sat at the table. A dozen chairs surrounded her, each one being vacated by the respective applicant as their name was called. Now, it was just Carly and one other interviewee in the room—Mona Schmerz, a long-time detective with the St. Petersburg police department. Carly had spotted Schmerz's red hair and stocky build upon entering the waiting room, opting to sit as far away from the elder detective as possible. Their paths had crossed a few times in the field and in training, but for whatever reason there always seemed to be some simmering contentiousness between them.

Carly peered at her open laptop as a coffee pot sputtered on a small counter in the corner. She had been sipping coffee and staring at the same page of the same report update for an hour, unable to focus enough to actually update it.

You'll do fine. Davis said you were a sure bet for the job.

Some of the rival candidates for the position of Sergeant had seemed to be in their interview forever; others came and went in less than five minutes. Carly recognized most as inside applicants—fellow officers from the Tampa PD, looking to move up; a few were from outside agencies, like Schmerz.

As the final two candidates awaited their interviews, Carly glanced in the St. Petersburg detective's general direction. The fiery redhead glared back at her.

"You know…" Schmerz tipped her head back, peering down her nose at Carly. "Some of us are here because we've earned the right to apply for a promotion like this. Unlike you, Sanderson."

"What?" Carly sat upright, butterflies swarming through her abdomen. "What's that supposed to mean?"

Schmerz shrugged. "I heard you think you're a sure thing to get this promotion." She looked at Carly out of the corner of her eye. "Tell me—rumor has it that you slept with Lieutenant Davis like you slept with your partner. Is that why you're so confident the promotion will be yours?"

Carly's jaw dropped. "What!"

"You heard me." The redhead turned away and primped her graying hair.

Gasping, Carly clutched her stomach.

Do people think that?

They couldn't. Could they?

The conference room door opened and a uniformed officer stuck his head in. "Detective Schmerz, the interview panel will see you now."

Schmerz stood, gathering her things. "You aren't fooling anyone, Sanderson. I'm getting this job—without resorting to any cheap tactics."

Carly's cheeks burned, her thoughts a jumble. "I—I didn't sleep with the Lieutenant."

"Of course you didn't." Schmerz narrowed her eyes, deepening the crows' feet etched around

FOURTH ESTATE

them. "Well, hey—then may the most qualified candidate win. Which is me, by a mile." She walked to the conference room door and stopped, glancing over her shoulder. "And when I become your sergeant, I won't be a jerk to you when it comes to scheduling assignments. Probably."

The door shut behind Schmerz.

Carly lifted a finger to her mouth, biting the fingernail for the dozenth time. Butterflies filled her insides.

Is that what people are thinking? They can't be.

She shook her head, working to regain her composure.

Schmerz was just trying to get me off balance. She wants me to screw up in my interview, so she dropped that bomb at the last minute. That's all it was. A trick.

Nodding, Carly wiped her palms across her thighs.

It was a trick, because she can't get the job unless she can make the other candidates appear lesser, somehow.

Well, I worked hard to be here. I earned the right to be considered for this promotion, and no stupid trick is going to get in my way.

Sitting upright, Carly straightened her jacket and reviewed her interview notes again—big cases she'd closed, how she had improved the image of the department through her role as a detective, strong relationships she'd forged with the panel members.

She checked the time on her computer, then stared at the conference room door, the sputtering coffee pot making the only sound in the room.

Geez, this is torturous. I hate going last!

She hadn't expected so many applicants for the final round of interviews. Deshawn had indicated there would only be a few, and that the process would practically be a formality. Even Lieutenant Davis said that Carly was a shoo-in—and she believed him, because she believed she'd earned the job, despite what Schmerz indicated.

But the lieutenant had been known to be duplicitous on occasion.

Maybe he told a lot of people they were a sure bet for the job so there'd be a ton of candidates. That probably makes him look good to the Chief somehow.

She opened a file on her computer and quickly shut it again, her nerves rising.

I hate interviews. It's like giving a speech about yourself. I hate giving speeches.

I especially hate talking about myself to small groups.

Or large groups.

She sighed, rolling her shoulders and moving her head back and forth. It didn't work; the stress refused to exit her body.

"Just... be yourself," she whispered. "You know what to say. You've been helping Deshawn with Sergeant duties for a while, and you've kicked butt on all of it."

She dropped her hands to her lap, sliding them across the material again.

You got this.

FOURTH ESTATE

The idea of becoming a sergeant had both positive points and negative ones. There was a raise, which would help with her new status as a single mom of two kids, and the hours would be more flexible. She could spend more time with her boys, but she'd be doing more office work.

She'd be working with Deshawn and Lieutenant Davis more, doing more recruiting and training, more scheduling, more oversight…

And spending less time with Sergio. A lot less.

She'd enjoyed her time with her partner. They'd worked together as detectives for almost five years, and ninety percent of it had been good. The other ten percent—the stuff she enjoyed much less—had almost nothing to do with Sergio and almost everything to do with the hours. It was difficult to make soccer practice when a victim had been thrown from a fourth story window and splattered across Kennedy Boulevard. Play dates with her sons' friends at the lake got missed because a dead body showed up in the Hillsborough River. Being a chaperone for beach field trips got fobbed off on Grandma.

It was a never-ending stream of rescheduling, apologizing, and promising to make it up to her boys. To everyone. Her mother, her friends, the teachers, the coaches. Everyone always said they understood, but it never felt good to do it the next time. The guilt lingered—and built.

That will change if I get this promotion. Some of it, anyway.

She shook her head.

Not if. When.
When you get the promotion.
You're prepared. You've done the homework. You have the skills.

She took a deep breath and squared her shoulders.

You got this, girl.

The door opened, sending a jolt through Carly's abdomen.

The administrative officer who had poked his head inside the door almost a dozen times before, was now entering again—and looking at her. "They're ready for you now, Detective Sanderson."

Carly stood, shutting her laptop and sliding it into her bag. Picking up her purse, she righted herself and walked toward the door.

The officer gave her a wink as she passed by, whispering. "You're the best of the bunch, Detective Sanderson, and everybody knows it. Good luck."

Carly moved briskly across the short distance between the entry door and the vacant chair in the middle of the interview room, her stomach in a knot. The space was well-lit and familiar; she'd attended meetings and briefings countless times in it over the years. Today, it was more foreboding. On one side of the room, behind a long, oval conference table, sat four senior members of the department staff—Lieutenant Don Davis, Sergeant Deshawn Marshall, the head of Human Resources, Felicia Canding, and the head of the Legal Department, Lois Martinez. Next to her sat Doctor Ita Stevens, a forensic psychologist who worked with the department on occasion. They were all known to Carly; she interacted with most of them on an almost daily basis and saw the others very frequently in her work. And yet the importance of the assembly—and the layout of the room—was intimidating.

The lone chair, off by itself, as if it were under a spotlight for an interrogation, awaited her.

She seated herself and placed her bag on the floor at the base of the chair, voicing a general greeting to the members of the final interview board.

"Good morning, Detective Sanderson." Lieutenant Davis opened a leather portfolio resting in front of him, displaying a yellow legal pad. He picked up a pen, clicking the top as he leafed through the pages of his pad. "I believe you know everyone."

"Yes, Lieutenant. Good morning, everyone."

Her insides jumped.

You already said good morning to them!

Davis stifled a laugh and leafed through his yellow legal pad. "I'm sorry we had to reschedule your interview so many times. The recent budget cuts have had us all jumping through hoops."

"That's not a problem, sir." Carly managed a smile.

Yeah, you delayed it three times in two months, probably just to show how much money you could save and make yourself look good to the Chief.

But at least we're finally doing it now.

She put her hands in her lap, massaging one with the other. "All of us in the field have been busy. I'm sure it's been no different for the other departments."

"Indeed." As he continued to click the pen, his eyes wandered over his notes. "Sergeant Marshall has been serving as Acting Lieutenant for that same time, basically pulling double duty." The lieutenant cleared his throat and sat upright, releasing his note pages and letting them fall back to the pad. "Let's get started, shall we?"

There was a knock at the door.

"Come in," Sergeant Marshall said. The Lieutenant turned to him, frowning. Deshawn leaned over and whispered into Lieutenant Davis' ear as Officers Ternihey and Mellish approached the conference table. Leaning back, Davis nodded.

The lieutenant rubbed his chin, then put his hands on the table and looked at Carly. "Change of plans, Detective."

Carly winced.

Don't tell me he's rescheduling again!

"We need to postpone this interview." Davis stood up, adjusting his suitcoat. "Contact Mellish to reschedule."

Carly stared at him, blinking.

I can't believe it. It's almost like he doesn't want me to get this job.

Maybe he doesn't.

What do I do about it? Insist he continue with the interview?

"Urgent business." Davis gestured to his counterparts at the table. "I'm sorry, I have to go. My office will contact you to see when all of our schedules can align again. We'll continue the interview at that time."

The panel of participants stood up.

Mellish raised his hand. "I'm happy to look at your schedules, at your convenience."

FOURTH ESTATE

"Hmm. That could be a while." Doctor Stevens gathered her notes into her briefcase. "Tomorrow, I'm heading to France to oversee a week-long psychological study, and then I'm in Norway for two weeks—it's the Alliance of Forensic Psychologists annual conference, and I'm co-chairing the event."

Carly shifted on her chair, the knot in her abdomen surging.

"That..." Felicia Canding picked up her phone and studied the screen. "...would put your return right at the start of annual reviews."

Stifling a groan, Carly kneaded her hands.
Can you reschedule them?

"Can you reschedule those?" Doctor Stevens asked.

"It's almost a thousand employees." Canding shook her head. "No, we can't reschedule those." The HR head looked at Carly. "I'm sorry, Detective Sanderson."

The Head of the Legal Department delivered the next blow. "That puts us to almost spring break. We'll have lots of employees on vacation from Legal. Not a good time for me."

"Well, I'll get it figured out," Mellish said.

Lieutenant Davis moved toward the door, taking out his phone. "Again, thank you all for coming."

Sergeant Marshall followed the lieutenant, signaling to Carly to come with them.

"What's that?" Davis pressed his phone to his ear. "Do you have an image? Send it to me." He ended the call and looked at Deshawn. "We need to get to a computer, fast."

The sergeant pointed down the hallway, toward a mass of cubicles. "HR is closest."

Davis glanced at Canding. "Felicia?"

"Use any one you like, or mine's available, since I'm here."

The group followed her to her office, Carly trailing. Davis slid behind the desk and accessed the keypad as the others gathered around.

Sergeant Marshall lowered his voice, looking at Mellish. "Get the door please, Jordan."

As the door closed, an image appeared on the computer screen.

"Okay, Deshawn.' Lieutenant Davis leaned toward the screen. "You've been coordinating this. Tell me what I'm looking at."

On the left side of the screen, a man in a red windbreaker was walking through the lobby of a business with brightly-colored walls. On the right side of the screen, the same man appeared to be talking to two women in a different workplace.

Davis' eyes moved back and forth between the images. "These are both from today, but different locations? That's got to be the same guy."

"Sir, look here." Deshawn lifted his finger to the time and date stamp embedded in the first image, then moved it across the screen to the second image, where a young lady was looking at the time on her cell phone. "These homicides took place less than forty minutes apart."

Davis sagged back in the chair, his hands falling to his sides. "Holy crap."

FOURTH ESTATE

"Holy crap is right," Deshawn said. "That makes three."

"Three?" Davis looked up at him.

"Yes, sir. There was another homicide this morning."

Nodding, Davis pointed to the computer. "We need to see if that one is related to these—but we need to do it quietly. We don't need to send the public into a panic." He glanced at Mellish. "Who do we have available?"

Jordan shrugged. "Carly is here, and Sergio has the PR consultant with him. The rest of the detectives are assigned."

"We'll need to redeploy some of them." Davis got up from the desk. "But while we do, we need some people steering this. Carly, find out who's on each location and get out there. But tell them to keep all radio talk to a minimum. Reporters listen to our frequency, and the story will get out before we're ready. Sergio can keep his schedule. We don't need the PR consultant seeing this today. Not before it's under control."

"Sir…" Mellish approached the Lieutenant, taking a pink notepad and a pen from the desk. "May I make a suggestion?"

"Make it quickly."

"Since Sergio's already in the field with the consultant, it might be better to let him coordinate the information between the two homicide scenes we know are connected—but from the field. All the preliminary information will be coming here to the station. If he's not here, he'll only have the information you send him, and the rep will only see that." Mellish scribbled on the notepad and tore off the note, folding it in half before handing it to the lieutenant. "It's much more controlled that way, sir."

The lieutenant glanced at the note, then refolded it, his mouth opening and his gaze going to the window.

Carly cleared her throat. "Uh, sir, I can handle the incoming. It'd be messy trying to do that from the field."

"And it'd be a good test of her abilities," Deshawn said. "A sergeant has to juggle multiple investigation scenes all the time. Doctor Stevens and the department heads can see her in action, as a candidate for the job. That's better than an interview."

Davis rubbed his chin, glancing at the pink note again. He folded the paper and slipped it into his pocket. "What? Fine." Nodding, he headed for the exit. "Carly, you coordinate. Deshawn, you oversee the operation." Stopping in the hallway, he looked over his shoulder at the group. "And keep me posted on every aspect of this. No detail is too small—do you understand? I'm on this twenty-four seven until it's resolved."

Officer Ternihey and Mellish followed Lieutenant Davis from the room, heading toward the elevators. As Carly went to leave, Deshawn tapped her on the shoulder and nodded his head toward the opposite end of the corridor, where the stairwell was located.

She followed him in silence. The Sergeant opened the heavy steel door and stepped onto the stairwell landing, holding the door open for Carly and easing it shut behind her.

"What do you think was in that note?" he whispered.

Carly sighed, walking to the railing and leaning on the top bar. "I don't know. Jordan isn't a snake, but Lieutenant Davis…"

"Mellish and Davis. Could be anything." Looking down, Deshawn put his hands on his hips and pursed his lips. "Be careful, then, Carly."

DAN ALATORRE

CHAPTER 14

Red-faced, Lieutenant Davis stormed into his office and immediately wheeled around. Mellish, following, almost ran into him.

The lieutenant brandished the pink note, growling at his assistant. "What's the meaning of this?"

"Sir, don't you see?" Turning around, Mellish closed the Lieutenant's office door. "It's exactly what you wanted."

Davis went to his desk and sat down, frowning as he peered once again at the pink slip of paper.

Sergio runs investigation & rep stays w/him.
Big pressure = big mistake potential.

Mellish stepped forward, lowering his voice. "Lieutenant, you said you needed Sergio to screw up in front of the consultant. Where is that more likely to happen? Taking a consultant on a duty tour of the station and chatting with department heads? Whereas, in the field…" A smile crept across the officer's face. "Haven't you said that's where Sergio always gets ahead of himself? Laying out two homicides, perpetrated by the same killer—that certainly has a lot of exciting possibilities. It might be too much for Sergio to resist. Isn't he more likely to try something bold in that situation? And Ms. Fox will be there to see whatever happens. I'd say that scenario has a lot of potential, sir."

Davis took a long, slow breath and tapped his fingers on the desk. "Yes… it has possibilities. But what if Fox gets hurt? Then it'll be my butt in a sling."

"Ask her to pull off. In fact, call her from here, on a land line so it'll be recorded, and tell her she has to come back to the station. She'll beg you to let her stay with Sergio because that's where she thinks she'll do the most good. Then, the liability is off of you and onto her. She knows a duty tour won't yield anything she really wants to see, and you'll have recorded proof that you requested she come in."

"She'd probably give me immunity over the phone." Davis nodded. "I like it." He grinned at his assistant. "You're becoming pretty sneaky, Jordan."

"I learned from the best, sir," Mellish said. "Within forty-eight hours, Detective Martin will do what he always does—and you'll have an impartial witness there to see it."

CHAPTER 15

Carly sat down at her desk in the detectives' station, running her hand along the faded wooden edge. Phones rang from down the hall as the department staff went about their regular duties.

When I left here yesterday, I thought it might be one of the last times I sat here. Today, it looks like I might be sitting here quite a while longer.

She sighed, reaching for one of the dozen or so file folders on her desk.

Taking on some of the duties of sergeant was a gift from Deshawn; a way of letting her see what was required in the job, and letting others—like the Chief and Lieutenant Davis—see her performing the role and doing it well. While it wasn't the same as being a full-fledged sergeant, acting as a sergeant was different from her daily work as a detective. Actual police sergeants were first-line supervisors who were almost as visible as their uniformed officers in the field. They handled complaints about cops when someone in the public felt wronged. They often decided which officers would be assigned to go to a good or a bad assignment. They planned work rosters and evaluated the men and women who did the work.

They performed all the duties of a police officer as well as a lot of other things, both inside and outside their department.

And what will it be like when I'm doing that full time, if I get promoted?

She caught herself again.

Not if, Carly. When.

When I get promoted.

Manifest it.

What will it be like when I get promoted and I'm doing that stuff full time?

The money would be better. The potential pension would increase. There would be more opportunities to move up in the department.

She had watched Deshawn and others in the role over the years. Some flourished, others floundered. The latter always seemed like fish out of water in the role, unable to gain the trust and respect of those they were responsible for.

Will that be me?

The new sergeants that did well always seemed to remember where they came from—that they, too, were once uniformed officers, drawing assignments in rough neighborhoods. They had spent hours doing paperwork for a run-of-the-mill B&E. They had pulled an overdosed child from a dumpster.

FOURTH ESTATE

Those sergeants were there when bad news got delivered to a grieving mother or distraught father. They stood next to their uniformed officers and saw the tears of the victim's siblings as the look of recognition came over their young faces.

She saw the good times, too.

Deshawn celebrating with Officer Jasmine Rhodes when she announced she was pregnant. He was best man at Officer Marco Stanzmore's wedding. He went to the hospital when Harriman was sick with cancer.

He cared about his people.

Carly smiled.

I can do that. I already do that.

The long nights of being a detective might come to a close—a lot of them, anyway. Deshawn had stayed out late with Carly and Sergio plenty of times, working a case when the situation required it. But the overall better hours and the raise in pay would help a lot at the Sanderson homestead.

Mom will be happy. She'd never admit it, but the boys drive her almost as crazy as they drive me sometimes.

Kyle would have been happy, too, I think. About the money, sure. About the hours... well, that was the real problem, wasn't it?

She drew a deep breath.

Kyle...

The dinner tonight would be awkward. That, she was certain of. He would say what he wanted to say, and he would quietly wait for her answer.

And what do I tell him?
What do I want?

She looked at the time on her computer.

Only a few hours before I go home, change, and drive to the restaurant to meet him.

She envisioned Kyle in a suit and tie, waiting at the table, smiling like he was on a first date.

Nervousness rippled through her, settling in her abdomen and tightening around her stomach.

So many questions.

How soon would he want to move back in? Will he step up more with the kids? Will my new hours be enough, if I get the promotion? And what if I don't get the job? Then what?

And what about Sergio?

The pain on his face when I tell him.

If I tell him.

I can still say no to Kyle.

Right?

Suppressing a groan, she put a hand to her waist, a knot forming in her stomach.

I can't think about all that now. It'll happen soon enough, and there's work to be done. Concentrate on something else.

If you're distracted by all that crap, you'll end up not getting the job, so focus!

She picked up a report that needed to be reviewed and evaluated—her one hundredth for the week.

Deshawn approached her desk.

"Good news." He smiled. "I got you assigned to a murder. You'll oversee everything in the investigation from here, like a sergeant. What do you think?"

FOURTH ESTATE

Carly sat upright in her chair. "I think it'll be weird to not be out in the field tracking down the killer."

"Yeah, but you'll be updated every step of the way, without getting your shoes muddy. Let's go."

"Uh..." Carly looked around. "Where?"

"To the sergeant's desk." Deshawn hooked a thumb over his shoulder. "You've been doing a good job of reviewing field reports. Time to dive into the real stuff." He leaned over, whispering. "There'll be a lot more visibility if you're closer to the lieutenant and the chief while you're spearheading this case."

Carly nodded, putting a hand to her chin. "Seems a little unfair to the other candidates."

"What a shame." Deshawn stood. "Well, I can give the assignment to Judith Renner. She applied, too."

"No, no. I trust your judgement in this matter." She pushed the stack of file folders to the edge of her desk, shut off her computer, and picked up her purse.

"Thought so," the sergeant said. "Hand those reports off and grab your gear. It's the vacant desk next to mine. I'll see you there in ten minutes."

"Okay." As he turned to go, Carly stood up. "Deshawn... thank you."

"I should be thanking you." Grinning, Deshawn walked back toward her desk. "Do this right and get the promotion, Carly. We need a few more competent sergeants around here so I can stop being an acting lieutenant and start being a real one."

DAN ALATORRE

CHAPTER 16

Sergio tried to call Mina as he sped toward downtown and Tampa General hospital. "My sister's not answering." Frowning, he ended the call and tried again. Avarie held onto the dashboard with one hand and her door's armrest with the other, bouncing back and forth as the car careened down the street.

The sedan jerked to the right as Sergio looked up from the phone screen and swerved to get back onto the road, plastering Avarie into the passenger door.

"Here, give me that." She yanked his phone from his hand. "You just drive."

"Hey!" He reached for his phone.

Avarie held it away from him. "You almost killed me once in this car today. That was enough."

DAN ALATORRE

She hit redial and put the phone on speaker. After six rings, it went to Mina's voicemail.

Sergio clutched the wheel with sweaty hands, racing through traffic. "Try again."

"How about I text her?" Avarie said, holding the phone with both hands. "Tell me what to say."

"Just say…" Raising his upper arm to the side of his face, Sergio wiped his brow. "Uh, say 'Call me ASAP.' And tell her I'm on the way."

Avarie typed on the screen. "Done. I'll call her again, too."

The speakerphone rang, but Mina didn't answer.

"Come on, Mina." Sergio huffed. "What's going on?"

His sister's recorded voice played over the speakerphone. "Hi! You've reached Mina. Please leave a message."

Groaning, Sergio pounded the wheel. "Send another text."

"Same message?"

"Yeah." He nodded. "Just keep sending them. We can get to Tampa General in about fifteen minutes, maybe twenty, depending on how bad traffic is."

He chewed his lip.

I wish she'd answer.

Avarie moved her fingers over the phone screen. "You know, maybe she can't answer right now. Hospitals don't usually allow phones in places like the Intensive Care Unit, so…"

A jolt went through Sergio's insides.

FOURTH ESTATE

Mom might be in the Intensive Care Unit? Crap!

He mashed the gas pedal.

Grimacing, Avarie looked at Sergio. "Sorry. I didn't mean your mom's probably in the ICU. Hospitals also don't let people use phones in the X-Ray area. Or... well, lots of places, really. And it's hard to get a signal in a hospital because of all the machines."

Panting, Sergio kept his eyes on the road.

"I'll... I'll just keep calling and texting, okay?" Avarie typed on the screen again. "I'm sure your sister will answer. She's probably... Hospital doctors always ask a million questions, and they aren't keen on phones ringing when they're trying to talk to a patient—even if the person only got a splinter in their finger. Mina probably put her phone on mute and forgot."

"Yeah." Sergio frowned. "Or Mom's in the ICU. Or the cardiac unit. Or the X-Ray area. Lots of possibilities."

Avarie hunched over, blushing as she typed on the phone screen. "I'll keep dialing."

As Sergio maneuvered his car through a parade of slower-moving vehicles, the skyscrapers of Tampa's downtown appeared in the distance. To the south of downtown—and its narrow streets packed with never-ending congestion—rested Tampa General Hospital on the little plot of land known as Davis Island, which was reachable only by bridge.

As Sergio's vehicle slowed, Avarie glanced up at the windshield. A thickening wall of cars gathered in front of them.

Sergio grimaced, clutching the wheel. "Just so you know… Mina told me that Mom was complaining about chest pains the other day—after they had been on the phone for an hour. The next day, Mina said Mom didn't remember half the stuff they talked about. That's why I'm a little bugged about that text."

"That's understandable," Avarie said. "It's your mother, and it sounds like she could have been having a cardiac event. How old is she?"

"Old enough to have chest pains." He leaned closer to the wheel. "Mom's version of a healthy diet consists mainly of Spanish food like rice and beans, fried okra, and fried shrimp—and watching Oprah. Not exactly conducive to longevity, you know?"

"Well, if your sister took her to the hospital, your mother is in the best hands."

Sergio's phone rang. The words Tampa PD Main Line appeared on the screen.

"It's the office," Avarie said.

"Here." He took the phone and pressed it to his ear. "This is Detective Martin."

Deshawn Marshall's voice came over the line. "Sergio, we need you to check out a homicide investigation near downtown, and another one by the University of Tampa."

Sergio winced.

That'll make it harder to get ahold of Mina and find out what happened to Mom.

"Okay." He bit his lip. "What do you want me to do with Satan's PR rep while I do that?"

"I'll send a black and white for Ms. Fox," Deshawn said. "She's here to do PR work. She doesn't need to see a couple of messy murder scenes. When you get to the first location, have her stay in your car. Someone will be there soon to bring her back. You just make contact with the officer in charge ASAP."

"Okay."

"Ternihey is sending you the first address now," Deshawn said. "And Sergio… Keep radio silence on all this while you await further—"

Sergio's phone beeped. He held it away from his ear and looked at the screen.

Tampa PD Main Line.

"Sarge, I'm getting another call from the station. Let me grab it and I'll be right back."

"Take that call and get to the crime scene." Static came over the line, crackling as the sergeant spoke. "We'll contact you there if we need to."

Ending his call, Sergio clicked over to the other one. "This is Detective Martin."

"Sergio." The stern voice of Lieutenant Davis boomed through the phone. "We have a situation. Did Sergeant Marshall contact you yet?"

"We just hung up. I'm on my way to the murder scene."

"Good. We're going to have Ms. Fox disengage from her field ride with you. Have you told her yet?"

"There wasn't time," Sergio said. "Like I was saying, I hung up with the Sergeant to take your call."

"If you'll give her the phone, I'll inform her myself."

"Yes, sir." Sergio lowered the phone and looked at Avarie. "It's Lieutenant Davis. He wants to talk to you."

She took Sergio's phone and put it to her ear. "Hello, Avarie Fox speaking."

"Ms. Fox, we've had an incident, and the department is running on scarce resources. We need Sergio to go to the site of an active homicide investigation, so I'm afraid I'll have to pull you off the field ride for now. A uniformed officer in a patrol car will pick you up at the crime scene and take you on your scheduled tour of the departments."

"An active crime scene?" she said. "Sounds like just the kind of thing I should see, sir. May I stay with Detective Martin? It would give valuable insights into what the members of Tampa PD do for the public."

"I think that might be too risky, Ms. Fox. Your safety is paramount with the department—and with me. I couldn't ask you to do it."

She shook her head. "You aren't asking me. I'm asking you. I'll take full responsibility, Lieutenant."

"Ms. Fox..."

"I'll be with one of your detectives, won't I? That sounds pretty safe to me. And you said I'd be glued to his side for forty-eight hours. I agreed to that, sir. I understood the risks."

The Lieutenant exhaled a long, slow breath into the phone. "You're sure?"

"Absolutely sure." Avarie grinned.

"Well… if you think it'll really help you gain insights into what our fine officers go through on a daily basis…"

"It will, Lieutenant." Her head bobbed enthusiastically. "I'm positive about that."

"Then… okay. You can stay on task, just as before. And keep careful notes. We'll need all the details for your assessments."

"I will, Lieutenant. Thank you."

Davis cleared his throat. "Let me talk to my detective again, please."

Avarie handed the phone back to Sergio. "Your turn."

Sergio took the device.

"Change of plans," Davis said. "The consultant will stay on her field ride with you, Detective."

"What!" Sergio's jaw dropped. "No!"

"Yes. Nothing has changed in that regard. Conduct your investigation without putting her in harm's way, but keep her with you. She'll be able to see firsthand the responsible way the men and women of Tampa PD respond to a crisis, and help put us back in a positive light. We could use that right now."

Sergio grimaced. "Lieutenant… It's not safe, and it's going to slow me down."

"Slowing down is probably what you need, Detective." A steeliness formed in the lieutenant's words. "Keep Ms. Fox with you, and keep her safe. Act like your job depends on it. Because it does."

CHAPTER 17

Carly lowered herself into the desk next to Deshawn's as the sergeant stood next to her.

"Here's the situation so far." He leaned over, pointing to the two open report screens displayed on the computer in front of her. "It shouldn't be unfamiliar territory, you're just seeing a lot of it from the other side. We have two murder scenes. You'll oversee one, I'll handle the other."

Carly nodded. "Okay."

"First is Jasper Menendez-Holswain." Deshawn's finger moved to the left side of the screen. "He was the owner and editor-in-chief at NewsAction, Inc., and he was murdered on camera during a livestream event this morning. It's kind of a staff meeting with live updates from reporters on their stories. Fuentes is handling it, with Ternihey assisting from here."

"Carlos Fuentes is good," Carly said. "I've worked with him. He knows the drill."

The sergeant moved his hand to the right side of the screen. "Miranda Suarez was murdered next. She was the owner and editor of Instant News Network. We had Sergio take that one over."

Carly nodded.

"Since we're a little light on staff, both investigations will be run from here. According to Lieutenant Davis, that will allow us to maximize our resources in the field. You'll see all the regular details as they get uploaded for each case." Deshawn looked at Carly. "So, if you want to read twenty witness interviews, you can. If you want to skip that and just call out to the officer on the scene and ask which witnesses are the best ones to follow up with, you can call them or direct someone else to do it. That'll be very important now—delegating. A sergeant uses the field personnel for what he or she wants done. You don't do it yourself. You can send them whatever questions you have, or you can watch their body camera here and ask questions as the interview is happening—but I advise against that, because it can turn into a time vacuum. My suggestion is, you direct the questioning and let the officers on site carry out your instructions and file a report."

"And that's what we want, anyway." Lieutenant Davis walked toward them. "Direction from here, so the best brains are working the case and using the field officers as our eyes and ears."

FOURTH ESTATE

Carly tried hard not to bristle at his comment. "I'd say we have some pretty good brains out in the field, too, sir."

"Of course we do." Davis folded his arms across his chest, looking around the room with his chin up. "But from here, we can see everything in real time. We can maximize our capabilities."

"Yes, sir," Carly said.

Sounds like a lot of double talk to justify more budget cuts.

"And," Deshawn said, "we can still go into the field if necessary. We aren't chained to these desks."

"That reminds me..." Davis glanced over his shoulder. "Sergeant, may I speak with you in private for a moment?" He nodded toward the break room.

Deshawn nodded. "Sure, Lieutenant."

Davis walked away from Carly's temporary workstation, with the Sergeant following.

* * * * *

In the break room, Lieutenant Davis picked up a coffee cup from the drying rack by the sink. He sauntered to the coffee pot and poured a cup for himself. "What would you think of having Detective Sanderson oversee both murder investigations?"

Deshawn folded his arms, chewing his lip. "She can handle it, if that's what you're asking. But it seems unnecessary."

"Ah." The lieutenant looked out the doorway, toward the windows and the Tampa skyline. "We're almost running on a skeleton crew. Carly's run a murder investigation—she could do it in her sleep.

Really, it's just a matter of adjusting to doing it from here, in the office."

"Sure." Deshawn frowned. "But like I said, it seems unnecessary."

"Hmm. Well..." Davis took a sip of his coffee and headed for the door. "I'll decide what's necessary, Sergeant."

* * * * *

Carly moved the mouse over the computer screen, absently rolling a pencil back and forth across the desk. The number of field interviews increased—slowly—for each murder investigation. Comments from the detectives for each case were entered, their confidential "work product" musings on the killer or killers, and the possible motives, ranging wildly.

Suarez hired a killer to murder her ex and couldn't pay him. The INN news outlet has been on hard times. Maybe her name was still on his insurance policy. Maybe she wanted to get rid of a competitor.

One of the reporters did it. Grudge/revenge murder. Which employees worked for both places?

One of the people they did a hatchet job on got angry and took them out.

The last one made Carly sit back. Both news agencies specialized in scandals and gossip. Anyone they embarrassed in the last year or two could be a suspect—and that would include the mayor, the chief of police, several city council members, some county commissioners, the governor, the Florida Senate, the House, and any and all celebrities from Key West to Nome Alaska, especially Hollywood stars and rappers. NewsAction practically made their living off of terrorizing celebrities. INN was almost as bad.

The number of prominent Tampa citizens the two companies had tried to ruin was extensive. No recognizable name was safe from the NewsAction and INN scandal-hungry spotlights, innocent or not. More lawsuits were filed in Florida against NewsAction than any other company for the past three years, and NewsAction seemed to have only survived because the owner had a legal degree. Jasper delayed, obscured, stalled, and postponed every motion and hearing for months at a time, wearing down the wounded party or emptying their pockets as they tried to pay the never-ending legal fees for their defense. Most of the parties attacked by NewsAction simply settled or gave up completely, finding Jasper's process of legal maneuvers kept their scandal in the headlines—so Jasper appeared to emerge victorious, and was right back at it with a new victim the next day.

As Carly read the other speculations about motive and suspects, Sergeant Marshall came back to the desk. "How's it going, Detective? Getting a feel for the screens?"

She shifted in her seat. "Yeah, but… It's going to be weird, running a murder investigation this way. I feel like I'm missing something."

"You are. Your partner."

"Yeah, I guess that's it." Carly picked up the pencil and clutched it with both hands. "Somebody to bounce ideas off of. Sergio's thinking was always so different from mine."

"Yin and yang." Deshawn nodded. "You worked side by side for years, so it feels odd going solo. But by now you can probably guess what he would say in a given situation. Almost like he's right there on your shoulder, speaking into your ear."

"Yeah." She set the pencil down, looking away. "Yeah, I guess so."

"Then you still have that," Deshawn said. "Use it. And trust yourself. You'll be fine."

* * * * *

An alert on his computer screen caught the eye of Officer Mellish. He clicked the alert and read the reporting status change.

"UPDATE: Det. C. Sanderson changed to oversight status, Case 2023-576671. Replacing Sgt. D Marshall."

Mellish scrolled through his reports. Carly was also the lead oversight on case 2023-576622.

He clicked each report file. One was Miranda Suarez, the other was Jasper Menendez-Holswain.

Mellish frowned.

Nobody's replacing Carly as lead oversight on the first murder? She's running both?

That's got to be a mistake.

He got up from his chair as Lieutenant Davis was coming down the hallway. "Sir, I think there's been some sort of clerical error." Mellish followed Davis into the office. "Carly's been added to a second murder, but she's still assigned to the first one. She's overseeing both now."

The lieutenant shook his head. "It's not a mistake."

"But sir…"

Davis strolled past his assistant and walked to his desk. "Get the door."

As Mellish made the office private, the lieutenant sat down behind his desk.

"Carly Sanderson is a top-notch detective," Davis said. "She'll make a great sergeant. And as such, she will be reviewing the performance of those under her. Officers, administrative staff, detectives…" The lieutenant raised his hands in front of himself, tapping his fingertips together. "She'll need to act impartially in the execution of her duties."

"Yes, sir…" Mellish shifted his weight from one foot to the other.

"So," the lieutenant said, "as you stated so eloquently, Sergio will mess up somewhere along the line. I'm merely raising the pressure—and the odds of Sergio making an error. Carly's run an investigation with multiple murders before. That's basically what this is. But with her supervising both investigations, she'll likely allow Sergio more flexibility. And when he screws up…"

"She'll be the one having to do the disciplinary action." Mellish's mouth hung open. "Why sir, it's absolutely ingenious."

Nodding, the lieutenant turned to the window. "I agree."

"But what if she doesn't?"

"She will." Davis placed a finger on the blinds, lifting them to allow the Tampa skyline to become more visible. "Carly will be forced to take disciplinary action against Sergio. If she doesn't, she loses out on being promoted—and does so in full sight of the Chief." He turned to Mellish, a wide grin stretching across his face. "A second disciplinary action so soon after a suspension will require HR to recommend Sergio's termination—and my hands are clean all the way through."

Mellish shook his head. "Amazing."

"Yes. Now all we have to do is sit back and wait." Davis turned back to the view from his window. "Sergio gets his head taken off at the chopping block, and the executioner's axe is wielded by his partner. It's absolutely perfect."

CHAPTER 18

THE AMBULANCES WERE STILL PRESENT at the offices of Instant News Network when Sergio drove past, as was the coroner's van. The sidewalk outside the building teemed with crime scene investigators and first responders, but not any news crews.

Not yet, anyway. They'll be here soon enough. They always are.

He parked half a block away and shut off the engine, propped his left elbow on top of the steering wheel as he turned to Avarie. "Look, I know you want to see how we do things, and I appreciate that, but... a murder scene isn't the place for the uninitiated. I want you to stay in the car until I check things out."

"I've been on crime scenes before." Avarie reached for her bag. "And I've seen some pretty gruesome stuff online. I think I can handle it."

"Maybe you can, and maybe you can't." Sergio glanced down the block at the first responders. "The text I received said that the victim took multiple point-blank shots to the head and face. That means there could be clumps of brain all over the floor. She could be lying there with the top of her skull missing and one of her eyeballs popped out. The sudden impact of a bullet can do some nasty stuff."

Avarie let out a nervous laugh. "Detective, are you trying to scare me?"

Taking a deep breath, Sergio ran a hand across his face. "I'm just saying, there's going to be a lot of blood over there—and not TV blood, but the thick, sticky, real stuff. It's not online, where you're seeing it through a screen, either. It has viscosity and an odor, and it takes a few minutes to wash it off your fancy shoes when you accidentally step in the wrong place. You don't need to see that to do your job."

"If I can't handle it, then neither can the general public—and maybe that's the problem. Maybe we should let them see the stuff you have to deal with to keep them safe."

Leaning back, Sergio chewed his lip. "I'm not saying you won't get on scene. Can you just stay in the car until I check it out?"

She clutched her bag to her abdomen and reached for the door handle. "I can't do my job from the car."

FOURTH ESTATE

Sergio put his hand gently on her forearm. "Please?"

He said it softly, without anger, and without malice. He said it with genuine, heartfelt concern. He'd been that eager young rookie, fresh from the academy, who helped investigate a few robbed convenience stores and one junkie's overdose when the body was bloated and covered with flies, thinking he could handle the real stuff.

And when he did, he reacted how a lot of fresh, new cops do. He threw up.

His training officer took him to a murder scene where a man had killed his wife and baby. An African-American woman lay dead in the middle of the small living room, her worn brown carpet now stained with her blood. The summer heat had baked the room to over a hundred degrees, and the smell of rotting death crept into Sergio's nostrils and wouldn't leave. The woman's bruised body was motionless on the floor of the low-rent apartment, the back of her shirt dotted with three holes and stained with blood.

He never forgot the way the redness had seeped into the material of her blouse. She was in a server's uniform—a waitress at a coffee shop or restaurant—but with a few changes here and there it could have been a nurse's uniform or dental assistant's. The blood saturated the cloth, stretching outward in dark blotches and turning dark brown at the edges, rimmed by a watery-looking yellow ring around the perimeter. The uniform looked how butcher paper looks when the meat is taken out after a few days, or the way a week-old bandage covering a cut finger looks when it finally gets replaced. It was too wet in some spots; too dry in others.

That same uniform, had it been worn by a nurse or dental assistant that day, seemed like it wouldn't be on a dead woman lying on the floor of a crappy apartment.

The woman's husband ended his life in their bathtub, apparently by inserting the murder weapon into his mouth and pulling the trigger. Red splatter coated the tile walls, his body slumped over in the corner. A handgun lay on the bottom of the tub, a slow trickle of blood crawling past it and dripping down over the rusty drain.

All that, Sergio was able to manage—but just barely. He stood in the hot bathroom, trying not to breathe too much of the stale air that reeked of the man's blood and urine and feces—the latter two merely an involuntary reaction to the loss of muscle control upon death—but Sergio was keeping it together.

Until his training officer cried out from the living room.

"Oh, no. Oh, no, no, no."

His supervisor's voice broke as he said it. The words of the veteran cop, fifteen years on the force, were warped and clogged with emotion that Sergio hadn't witnessed in their months together.

When he turned around, Sergio saw that the responding officers had turned the woman over to inspect the front of the body.

And there, they discovered the baby.
Still. Quiet. Unmoving.

Probably not even three months old, the tiny infant's eyes were open and drying, blood seeping from the corners of his small, gaping mouth. The back of his head had been ripped away by one of the bullets that pierced his mother's torso.

The emotion washed over Sergio like a tidal wave, filling his eyes with tears and his gut with sadness. She was protecting him. With her life.

But the bullets were too powerful.

And the man in the bathtub may have regretted it, but by then it was too late. Anger or drugs or insanity had taken over and ended three lives.

One that had barely gotten started.

As the pain overwhelmed him, Sergio ran for the door, tears streaming down his face. He made it to the hallway before dropping to his knees and vomiting, not wanting any of what he'd seen inside to be part of him anymore. Not the air, not the smells, not the sights. He choked and cried in the hallway, embarrassed as the more experienced officers laughed, or turned their heads and walked away, or patted him on the back and told him *we all go through it.*

It never went away. Not really. The images faded with time, but sometimes in the middle of the night, Sergio still found himself standing in the crappy apartment with its dark brown carpet. Then, the woman was laying in the corner of his bedroom, thick red puddles congealing around her in the dark. The memories of what he witnessed that day drifted away after each visit, but never left him—and on some level he didn't want it to. He wanted to keep it with him, to remind him of what his job was ultimately all about—and what was possible, in the starkest of terms, if he and people like him didn't stop the bad guys.

Sergio gazed into the eyes of the pretty, young consultant sitting in the passenger seat of his car, hoping to help her avoid such a nightmare. He lowered his chin and peered up at her, his voice falling to a whisper. "I'm asking you, stay in the car. Please."

Avarie swallowed hard, the urgency leaving her. "Just until you check it out?"

"That's right." Sergio nodded.

She turned to face the window. "Okay. How will I know when that is?"

"I'll send someone over." He put his hand on the door release. "Until then, just… sit tight. Maybe you could call my sister from your phone a few times for me, too."

Avarie sighed, turning to him and putting her hand out. "Sure. Give me the number."

CHAPTER 19

DESHAWN GOT UP FROM HIS DESK AND went to the break room, returning with two coffee cups. He handed one to Carly. "The hardest transition is remembering to think like a sergeant now. Delegate tasks to people, don't try to do it all yourself. It's not your job and there isn't time."

"I know," she said, "but... sitting behind a computer feels so limited. I need to see things at the scene, to investigate things."

"What would you look at if you were there?"

"I'd scour the videos, for sure." Carly stared at the computer screen. Her checklist had gotten substantially bigger since being assigned the second murder case. "I'd be all over them. Videos always catch something we miss with the naked eye. Then, I'd use that and the witness statements to help me figure out what evidence was left behind that might match up with the other crime scenes."

"Good. Tell people to do that. Then what?"

"Have someone start pulling cell phone traffic from the INN site and the NewsAction site. Odds are, only the killer's phone was at both places. That'll narrow things down. If I was on scene, I'd take bullets from the dead bodies and have Ballistics match them against the ones fired into the walls at the third location. Maybe the killer used the gun in a prior crime. I'd look for video cameras in that last office and its surrounding areas, that might have caught the killer coming and going. Request a warrant and send it to the car manufacturer so we can get the black box data and see where the car's been…"

"Perfect." Deshawn smiled. "You'd spend two days doing that yourself, or you can have ten people get it done in a few hours. What's top priority?"

Carly pursed her lips. "I'd say tracking the car, but getting that request through will be slow. So… figuring out the location of that video would be my top priority."

"Okay. Maybe that one, you take for yourself."

She nodded, her eyes on the screen and her stomach knotting.

Two murder cases today, and a dinner with Kyle tonight. Mom will have to pick up the boys—again. I've left Sergio halfway twisting in the wind about Kyle…

And meanwhile, I'm operating under a microscope in a day-long interview, twenty feet from Lieutenant Davis' office and thirty feet from the Chief's.

Could this day get more stressful?

She swallowed hard, massaging her abdomen.

Deshawn leaned over and nudged her on the arm. "Hey. You seem a little distracted, Carly. Is everything okay?" He pointed to the screen. "You'll get used to assigning people from here, the same way you did in the field."

"It's not that, it's…" She shrugged, setting the mug on the desk. "I'm having dinner tonight… with Kyle."

"You've had dinners with him since he moved out," Deshawn said. "What's different about this one? You're acting squirrelly."

"He…" Carly took a deep breath and let it out slowly, turning her eyes to her sergeant. "Kyle said he wants to come back. To move back in. We're meeting tonight to discuss it."

"Whoa, that's big." Deshawn sat down on the edge of her desk. "No wonder you're squirrelly, girl."

Carly sighed. "Yeah, well, when I woke up this morning, my plan was to ace my interview and go car shopping tonight. Things have changed a little since then."

"I'd say so." Deshawn rubbed his chin. "Well, one thing for sure—even though we sergeants can work around the clock, it's not always a requirement. This case won't wrap up today. I'll let the lieutenant know you need to leave at a decent hour." Deshawn got up. "Maybe he'll pull you off double duty."

Carly winced, putting her hand on Deshawn's arm. "Let's not tell him right now. I'm in an interview, right? Maybe I could call Kyle…"

"We don't have to tell Davis at all." He sat back down. "But if your man got all the way to wanting to come home, that's a dinner you shouldn't postpone."

"No, I know." She lowered her eyes. "But…"

The sergeant leaned down and peered up at her, his voice softening. "But Sergio, right?"

She nodded again. "Among other things."

"Oof. You sure got your foot in it now, don't you?" He sat up, taking a sip from his coffee cup. "Well, don't worry too much about it. Like I said, this case isn't going to wrap itself up today, so odds are you'll be able to leave at a reasonable time and make your dinner date. I'll help keep an eye on the time."

Carly exhaled. "Good."

"But," Deshawn said, rising. "You have to call me after the dinner with Kyle and tell me what happened."

CHAPTER 20

After jotting down Mina's contact information for Avarie, Sergio exited his vehicle. He squinted in the brightness outside, the sunlight heating the sidewalk and bouncing off the shop windows. As he approached the office of INN, sweat gathered on his shirt collar, making it stick to his neck.

Sergio lifted a yellow ribbon of police tape and stepped underneath to observe the scene.

To his right, a half dozen police cars filled the street in front of the INN office, lights flashing, as uniformed officers kept the gathering onlookers from getting too close. To his left, two CSIs stood over a dead woman on the office floor, placing their plastic evidence markers for the crime scene photographer. They were already up to number twenty-one.

Other officers corralled the group of people that were probably the office staff, ostensibly conducting preliminary interviews with them.

Sergio exhaled, rubbing the back of his neck. The scene could quickly descend into chaos if it wasn't managed properly, and a lot of valuable information would get lost if it did.

An attractive young woman walked away from the office with the assistance of an EMT, carrying a blood-splattered computer bag over her arm. Her eyes were red and swollen, her mascara smeared across her cheeks.

"Is that a witness?" Sergio rushed forward. "Hold on. I want to speak with all the witnesses before they're released."

The EMT turned to him. "Everyone's still here, Detective. We're just taking her to the truck to get cleaned up."

"Then I'll come with you."

"Detective." A uniformed officer ran over to Sergio, handing him a tablet computer.

Sergio glanced at the man's nametag.

Delveccio.

"We're logging samples of everything," the officer said. "I've got more than twenty witnesses for you so far." He nodded at the young woman. "This is Kerri Milner, an INN reporter. According to her preliminary statement, the deceased woman was her boss, Miranda Suarez, the owner of INN. Ms. Milner was standing right next to Suarez when the murder happened."

"Please let me leave." Clutching the yellow copy of her police interview form, Kerri choked on her words, her gaze going from Sergio to Officer Delveccio and back again. "If you want my computer bag, take it. I don't think I'll be using it again, ever."

Sergio took the bag from her and set it on the ground, noting the little red droplets all over it—and on the face and clothes of the bag's young owner. "Let's talk, okay? Can you do that? I'm Detective Sergio Martin, Tampa PD. You were right there. Can you tell me what happened?"

She sniffled, her thin body wilting. "I already told the other officer everything. I just want to go home."

"I know this has been difficult." Sergio invoked a soft tone, the way he'd seen Carly do with a key witness so many times after a tragic event, and with great effectiveness. "We'll get you home as soon as possible, I promise. Is there someone we can call to stay with you? Being alone isn't probably the best thing for you right now."

Kerri nodded. "My roommate Lasya. She's at work but she can get away."

"Okay. Let me have one of my guys call Lasya for you, and you tell me what you remember." Sergio put his hands on Kerri's shoulders, guiding her to sit on the back bumper of the ambulance. "Just take your time. There's no rush."

The EMT opened a cleanup kit and handed Kerri a towel. The reporter shrugged, wiping the cloth across her face. When she pulled it away, it was smeared with blood.

"Oh, no." She dropped her hands to her sides, squeezing her eyes shut and tilting her face to the sky. "Oh, Miranda."

Sergio's heart ached for the young reporter as a tear rolled down her cheek. He cleared his throat, leaning close. "I know that was a hard thing to see, Kerri, but can you help me, so we can find the guy who did this to Miranda?" Squatting, he locked his eyes on hers. "You're a reporter, so you're trained to notice details—things that can help us stop him before he hurts anyone else."

Kerri lowered her head. "This big creepy guy came in and shot Miranda. That's all I know."

"This guy?" Sergio took out his phone. The screen displayed the image that officer Ternihey had sent to him from downtown—a split screen image of a man in a red windbreaker.

"Yeah." Kerri nodded. "That's him. That's the guy who killed Miranda."

"Did he say why he wanted her dead?"

"No. Like I told the other officers, he barely said anything. He was just creepy looking, standing there staring at the newsroom."

Sergio nodded, looking at the phone. "He's got a weird appearance, I'll give you that. Was there anything distinctive about him?"

She shook her head. "He was wearing one of those paper hospital face masks and sunglasses... a baseball cap... so I couldn't see much. I'm sorry."

"No, you're doing fine, Kerri." Sergio kept his tone soft. "You said he barely said anything—so he said something? What did he say?"

To Kerri's side, Delveccio took out a small notepad and unclipped a pencil from his pocket, making notes.

"I don't remember." She blinked away another tear and looked down the street. "He was creepy because he just stood there, blocking the door. He just said Miranda's name when she came out… and then he shot her."

"He said her name?" Sergio leaned forward. "Did he act like he knew her? Or did she seem to know him?"

"She didn't seem to know him, and he acted like he didn't know who she was until… until I said, 'Thank you, Miranda.' Then he started shooting."

Sergio nodded. "Nothing distinguishing about him, though."

"Well… He spoke funny." Kerri wiped her cheek with the back of her hand. "When he saw her and found out who she was, I noticed his voice."

"Funny?" The detective cocked his head. "Like he had an accent?"

"No, like he…" She dropped her hands to her lap, balling up the towel and unballing it again. "I listen to a lot of audiobooks, you know? And sometimes you have a female narrator, but she's got to do male voices for the story, and she'll make her voice sound artificially deep. It was like that. Like a kid trying to sound like an older guy, or a woman trying to. Maybe even an adult guy with a higher voice. They just overdo it, and it sounds… fake. Forced. Not natural."

"Yeah. That's what I mean—you reporters notice things." He smiled at her. "Why don't you go ahead and clean yourself up here with the EMT, but hang around, okay? I'm gonna need to talk to you some more." He took out one of his business cards

DAN ALATORRE

and handed it to her. "And later on, whether it's tonight, or tomorrow, or next week—if you think of anything else, any other details, you call me, okay?"

"Detective," the EMT said, "I don't want to be out of line here, but I overhead some of your guys talking earlier, with the officers at the other crime scene—the NewsAction location. That's what some of their witnesses were saying about the killer, too. That he sounded like he was faking his voice."

"That's right," Delveccio said. "Several of them mentioned it."

Sergio glanced at the INN entrance. "Has anybody looked at the INN security camera footage yet?"

"Not yet, sir."

"Okay." The detective eyed the other nearby businesses. INN's neighbors were a drycleaner, an electronics shop, a low-rent jewelry story, and a tattoo parlor. Across the street stood a rusty ATM, surrounded by fast food trash. The bank machine looked like it hadn't been used in a decade. "These shops and offices will have security cameras, too," Sergio said. "Ask them if we can review their video footage."

"We did that." Delveccio pointed at the drycleaners next door. "The ones that said yes didn't have anything useful—only internal cameras, nothing aimed at the street. The drycleaner has an external camera that might have caught the killer walking up or exiting, but the manager said we had to get permission from the owner to see the security recording. When we called, the owner said he wants a warrant for the footage first."

FOURTH ESTATE

"A warrant?" Sergio frowned. "What's he doing, running a drug ring over there? It's a drycleaner, for Pete's sake."

"He says he wants to avoid a lawsuit. Some of those First Amendment guys were here earlier and they started scaring everybody. Some clown named Brimstone, I think."

Sergio scowled, putting his hand in his suitcoat pocket, and pulling out the business card of the self-proclaimed auditor he'd met outside the police station. He held the card in front of him and read it out loud. "Henson Brimley, Patriot. Sunshine State Audits." He shook his head as he read on. "Independent journalists representing the Fourth Estate, exercising our constitutional rights and fighting tyrants." Sighing, he stuffed the card back into his pocket. "This Brimley guy is some piece of work."

Delveccio nodded. "We've... put in a request with Downtown to start working on the warrant, Detective."

Kerri looked at Sergio. "They have security cameras with sound over at NewsAction. Maybe they captured his voice on audio."

Sergio tapped his phone and lifted it to his ear. "How do you know about the NewsAction security system, Kerri?"

"Reporters float around a lot these days, Detective." She folded the blood-stained towel and clasped her hands around it. "I worked at NewsAction before I came to INN. Lasya and I both did. Miranda and Jasper used to be married, and she created INN after they split."

Sergio sat back on his heels, nodding.

And now they're both dead.

"Is your roommate still at NewsAction?" he asked.

The young reporter shook her head. "She went to work for Florida Real Time News. They're more flexible with work schedules—that's why Lasya can get away whenever she wants. Miranda was old school, wanting all of her employees to come to the office every day. Even field reporters."

Exhaling, Sergio nodded again.

That's why we have all these witnesses.

"Okay." He turned to Delveccio. "Get the audio and video recordings from here and take it to Detective Sanderson downtown. I'll contact the NewsAction site and have someone pull their security system recordings. Maybe Carly can have someone start screening them."

"Uh, we tried that, sir. I was about to tell you, the INN system is on-site only, and the dead woman had the only access. One of their tech guys called the security company and they've got someone heading over here, but they said it could be a couple of hours before he can get into the system and retrieve what we need."

"Well, keep me posted. I want to see that footage as soon as possible." Standing, Sergio rubbed his chin. "The killer faked his voice to make it sound lower than it was, but we don't know why he killed Miranda Suarez or Jasper Menendez-Holswain."

"Why would a killer do that?" Kerri asked. "Fake their voice?"

FOURTH ESTATE

"To hide something." Sergio frowned. "Or to stand out. Everybody recalled that about this guy, right? So maybe the killer wanted us to remember that for some reason. If the officers at the other scene radioed here and said—" A jolt went through him. "Oh, crap. We're supposed to be staying off the radio with that stuff! Direct orders from Lieutenant Davis."

Delveccio put his hands up. "Hey, we are, Detective—now. But we didn't have those instructions when we first got out here. That's when we were talking to the other site."

Sergio put a hand to his face.

So, every reporter in town could have that information now—aside from the ones we have here. That's going to really complicate things for Carly.

We need to instruct all the witnesses not to talk to anyone but us.

But sharing the information helped establish an important link. And the witnesses are reporters, anyway—probably with friends at other news agencies, like Kerri said. So, what's the point?

He stifled a groan.

Freaking Davis. Adding a layer of rules that are just going to slow us down.

Pushing that particular distraction from his thoughts, Sergio refocused on the task at hand.

Maybe I can text the other site. Then we still share information without—

"Oh!" A woman behind him shouted.

Sergio wheeled around, looking in the direction where the sound came from.

Just outside of the INN doorway, Avarie Fox stood with her head in her hands, staring into the office. As Sergio went to go to her, she stumbled backwards, her mouth hanging open and her face turning pale.

He broke into a run.

CHAPTER 21

As Sergio raced away from her, Kerri stood up. The EMT dug through several drawers of the ambulance, his back to her as he gathered water bottles and towels.

Holding her breath, Kerri gently placed her used towel on the vehicle's bumper and stepped away.

If somebody is bent on killing news people today, this might be a good time to take a week off.

After a few paces, she turned and headed down the street, stuffing her copy of the police report into her pocket as she walked away from the INN offices. Her trembling fingers found the front hem of her Rolling Stones t-shirt, rolling it up and down as she directed herself toward the yellow line of police tape—and the uniformed officer there.

Just be cool, girl. You got this.

A small crowd had gathered on the other side of the yellow ribbon—just civilians, from what she could assess; no one taking notes or trying to get others to speak to them, and therefore no reporters.

That's perfect. Get across that line and blend in—and then slip away. This is no time to let anyone think you're a member of the media. For all you know, the killer is lurking right there in the crowd, waiting for the next chance to attack a news agency and kill the employees.

She grabbed her stomach.

Did Lasya say she was going in to Florida Real Time today? I don't remember. She said they were having a meeting... was that in person or by Zoom?

She could be in trouble.

Kerri's pulse throbbed, a lump forming in her throat as she neared the police tape. She clenched the black material of her shirt in her sweaty fingers.

I have to find out where she is, and if she went to the office, she needs to get out of there.

* * * * *

Avarie put a hand towards the stucco wall of the INN office as she slipped to the ground. Rolling over to her knees, she lowered her head and gagged.

"Hey." Sergio reached her, putting a hand on her shoulder. "You okay?"

"Mmm." She nodded. "I think I'll live."

Sergio patted her on the back, smiling. "I told you to stay in the car."

"Good call. Maybe I should listen to you next time." She turned over and sat on the sidewalk, wiping the corner of her mouth.

FOURTH ESTATE

"So?" Sergio asked. "What happened?"

She pointed. Sergio followed her gesture. In the INN doorway, two of the coroner's assistants lifted the bloody body of Miranda Suarez onto a gurney. As the coroner covered her with a sheet, the assistants wheeled the blood-soaked corpse out of the building.

"Look." Avarie wiped her lips and chin with the back of her hand, blinking away a tear. "Look what he did to her."

Sergio stood up and went to the gurney. "Hold it." He put a hand to the sheet and peeled it back.

The entire bottom half of the woman's face was missing, like some wild animal had gotten ahold of it. Her eyes stared upward, wide and still, unmoving except for the slight jostling of the gurney. Everything below the eyes was a massive gash of ripped flesh, like so much hamburger thrown at a wall.

The gray-haired coroner looked at Sergio. "I've never seen anything like this, Detective. He shot her so many times, the head has almost been severed from the body." Taking a handkerchief from the pocket of his lab coat, the medical examiner removed his glasses and wiped the lenses. "This looks like a case of absolute overkill. It's unbridled rage."

Frowning, Sergio put a hand to his abdomen and lowered the sheet back over the dead woman's face. "Delveccio, do we know the condition of the body at NewsAction?"

"No. Not yet."

"Who's running that investigation?" Sergio asked.

"Mark Harriman was assigned originally. Detective Roberts relieved him a little while ago."

Sergio winced.

Roberts? They called him in from night shift?

"Okay." He nodded to Officer Delveccio. "Thanks."

Sergio took his phone out and texted the older detective. *"Take a picture of your DB and send it to me."* Then he slipped his phone back into his pocket and got Avarie to her feet.

Roberts and Sergio had worked several cases together during the brief period before Sergio got assigned to his first partner, Franklin. Back then, Roberts had the occasional alcoholic beverage at lunch—and sometimes before breakfast—but it didn't seem to affect his work much. Sometimes Sergio thought it did. A few months ago, Roberts got assigned to work nights, and the word around the precinct was that it had been done to quietly help the senior detective avoid the temptation of bars and restaurants, and so he could attend AA meetings in the daytime.

Sergio's phone pinged in his pocket. Roberts' reply had come quickly. *"Ok."* A moment later the image arrived, followed by the older detective's sole comment. *"Sicko."*

And Roberts was right. The image on Sergio's phone could almost have been Miranda Suarez again, but with shorter hair. Jasper Menendez-Holswain's mouth and jaw had been

FOURTH ESTATE

blasted by so many gunshots, it seemed like the lower half of his head was missing.

Delveccio leaned over Sergio's arm, eyeing the image. "Your killer's trying to make a point." Glancing over both shoulders, he lowered his voice. "What do you think it is?"

"They were news people," Sergio said. "One ran a gossip rag and the other ran a sensationalist scandal sheet. The killer shot them both in the mouth. He was telling them to shut up."

"Well, they're not doing any talking now."

Sergio nodded.

They sure aren't. Who else does this maniac have a grudge against?

* * * * *

As Kerri Milner lifted the police tape, she lowered her head and slipped underneath.

There. Now, get ahold of Lasya.

She reached for her hip pocket, walking between the onlookers.

"Hey!" A male voice pierced the small crowd. "You, there! Stop."

Bristling, Kerri kept her eyes straight ahead, her neck and shoulders tensing.

"You, Miss! With the brown hair and the Rolling Stones shirt, stop! Police business!"

Kerri's hand crossed her torso, partially blocking the black t-shirt's lettering from view.

Keep going. That cop's just gonna ask more questions, and if you hang around that murder scene, you could end up just as dead as Miranda.

She emerged from the crowd and headed to the far sidewalk, not looking back.

"Stop her! Stop that young woman!"

Kerri increased her pace, resisting the urge to run. A few feet from the corner, she tugged her phone from her pocket and called Lasya.

Answer, Lasya. Answer, answer, answer.

Visions of Miranda's bloody face came rushing back, and how the assailant fired the gun right next to her. The blast made Kerri's ears ring as her boss dropped to the floor like a rock. Then the madman leaned over her and put the gun to Miranda's mouth, firing again.

And again.

And again...

When the weapon was empty, the odd-looking stranger stood up and gave one last look at the horrified faces in the newsroom, and the shrieking brunette in the black Rolling Stones t-shirt, curled up in the corner by the front door. As the smell of gun powder filled the room, the killer simply walked out of the INN office like nothing had happened.

The images overwhelmed Kerri now, causing the sidewalk to rock back and forth in her sight. Her mouth filled with saliva as her stomach churned and nausea welled up inside her.

Later. Deal with it later.

Forget all that right now. It's not helping.

Get away from here and get ahold of Lasya. That's what you need to do.

That's all you need to do.

The images persisted, filling her thoughts with the blast of the gunshots, and the shock of how warm the blood droplets were when they landed on

FOURTH ESTATE

Kerri's face. How Miranda's limp body dropped to the floor, so fast and so unnaturally. It wasn't like the movies, where the actress falls gracefully in an arc, maintaining her perfect hair and makeup. Miranda's arms went slack and she slumped like a cloth doll. Her head smacked the floor with a grotesque *whack*; her hair spilled over her bloody face in a curly brown mess. One arm went out at her side; the other bent backwards underneath of her. And unlike in the movies, Miranda's wounds quickly formed a large, dark red puddle around her on the floor.

The horrid replay in her head made Kerri's churning stomach insist on giving up her breakfast, so she bent over and let it happen.

Coughing, she put her hands on her knees and tried to refocus. She was a block away from INN, but not far enough. Her car was back at work, but Kerri could double back for it—if the crowd was still present.

Maybe even snap a few pics, in case the killer is among the spectators somewhere.

She stood up, spitting one last time for good measure, hoping to rid her mouth of the foul taste.

A hand landed hard on her shoulder. "Turn around!"

Kerri's insides jolted. Unable to breathe, she slowly turned and looked over her shoulder.

The officer at the crime scene tape had caught up to her.

"Okay, Miss. You're coming with me."
"What?" Kerri frowned. "Why?"
"You're a material witness to a murder, that's why."

"I told them everything," Kerri said. "They said I could go."

The officer cocked his head. "Who said that?"

"The police detective in charge. Sergio something." She dug in her pocket, producing his business card. "This guy, see? He's a Tampa police detective."

The officer stared at her.

"They have my statement, my phone number, and all my contact info!" Kerri pulled the copy of the preliminary statement from her pocket and waved it in front of the officer. "What else do you need? He said I could go!"

Plucking the paper from her hand, the officer looked it over.

Kerri shifted her weight from one foot to the other, holding her breath as the officer's eyes wandered over the form. It was only a preliminary interview, and Detective Martin had specifically stated that he wanted her to hang around so he could talk more with her, but Kerri didn't care. She wanted out, away from the news office that had become a murder scene. And she wanted to find Lasya before any more people died at the hands of this insane killer.

The officer lowered the paper and stared at Kerri.

She swallowed hard, trying not to tremble.

Come on, come on, come on…

"Okay." He handed the report back to her. "Thank you."

FOURTH ESTATE

"You're welcome." Kerri turned and headed down the street again.

Turn at the first corner and make a run for it before he talks to Sergio and finds out I lied. That murder scene is too dangerous for news people right now.

The whole city might be too dangerous for news people right now.

Panting, she put a hand to her forehead.

Circling back for the car might be too risky, too. Have an Uber pick you up at the front gates of the University of Tampa. That'll be as safe as it gets.

And call Lasya!

She called her roommate, but got no answer. A twinge of fear rippled through her abdomen.

I hope she's okay.

Kerri kept moving, calling over and over. Lasya didn't answer.

At the front gates of the university, Kerri stopped walking and looked down the road. The Florida Real Time offices were only about ten blocks away.

The killer already visited two news agencies today. Ten blocks is really close, if he wanted to visit a third one.

Clenching her teeth, she burst into a run, her heart racing.

Don't be in the office today, Lasya!

* * * * *

Sergio walked out of the INN newsroom and went outside. In the bright midday light, he turned his face to the sky, closing his eyes and letting the warmth of the sun wash over him.

A call to the downtown brass had allowed Harriman to be assigned to the INN scene, and he would be arriving shortly. Harriman had been on site at the NewsAction murder and might be able to notice any additional similarities.

The medical examiner was procuring all the information he believed would be necessary to do his initial report. CSI was marking the items they felt could be impactful for evidence; soon they would start the process of collecting and photographing it all. A dozen uniformed officers were still inside the INN newsroom, gathering statements from the remaining staff. Sergio had requested patrol cars be dispatched to locate and bring in the few employees that had not been present. All the murder scene needed now was continued management. Mark Harriman could do that—with updates sent to Carly and Deshawn for direction.

Now the real work could begin.

The detective squatted outside on the sidewalk, rubbing the stubble on his chin.

What happened to drive someone to do this? Was this the beginning of a rampage, the middle of it, or the end?

He reviewed the witness statements in his head, mostly the one from Kerri Milner, letting the scene unfold in his imagination as he stared into the INN entryway.

Miranda and Kerri were standing there, two people, both seemingly innocent, about to become victims of a maniac killer. Miranda would die; Kerri might be psychologically scarred for life.

Why?

FOURTH ESTATE

What did the killer gain from killing Miranda Suarez and Jasper Menendez-Holswain like that? And why would he let Kerri Milner just walk away?

The answer will make sense to the killer, but so far it doesn't make any sense to me.

Avarie walked over to Sergio, carrying a paper cup of coffee in one hand and holding the other hand to her forehead, blocking the fierce sunlight. She lowered the cup to him. "What happens now, Detective?"

Sergio kept his gaze on the doorway of the murder scene, taking the coffee and setting it on the sidewalk. "Now we do cop work. Ninety percent of solving a homicide is thinking."

Avarie moved beside him, following his line of sight to the bloody office floor.

"The stranger comes in," Sergio said. "He doesn't immediately appear to be a threat, so nobody reacts like he is. Most of the INN employees already know about the NewsAction murder, but Suarez has them all in the newsroom, burning up the phone lines, trying to get the story. So, they aren't looking out here, at their own front door." He glanced at Avarie. "Why would they? Nobody declared war on news agencies. Not that they knew of, anyway. Their statements say they're all working, making calls... All but Kerri Milner. She comes in late. According to her co-workers, Kerri never watches the news, so she has no idea who the guy in the red jacket is. He's just a guy blocking the exit when she goes to leave."

He studied the INN office space that was visible from outside. "When Kerri sees the killer, she asks him to move. He doesn't react to her. When he finally does speak, Kerri thinks the guy's disguising his voice. Then, Miranda Suarez comes out." Sergio stood, walking toward the entry. "Now, Suarez sees this guy. She should know he's the killer because the other reporters said she'd been watching the NewsAction replay on her office TV. But apparently she's so flustered about her team not getting the story, she doesn't put two and two together."

Avarie looked at him. "How do you know that?"

"I don't." Sergio frowned, pointing into the INN office and drawing a trail in the air with his finger. "Suarez tells the guy to go away because she doesn't have time for him. She doesn't jump back in fear because she sees her ex-husband's killer standing in front of her. Does she know him? Like, did Suarez pay someone to have her ex-husband murdered, and the hired killer shows up here because the deal went south somehow? According to Kerri, Suarez doesn't *act* like she knows the guy at all. Kerri actually has to grab Suarez by the arm before her boss understands something's wrong—and even then, Kerri still doesn't know what's up. She just thinks the guy is acting strange and might be dangerous. Kerri's three feet from the door and she doesn't try to run outside. It's only when the guy says he has information on the NewsAction story that Suarez decides to gives him any real notice at all. And by the time Suarez does pay attention to the guy, it's too late."

Sergio sighed, putting his hand on the wall. "The employees here don't pay attention to what's happening at the front door. The guy doesn't look

FOURTH ESTATE

like a threat to any of them. They don't scream, they don't run away. They scurry around their newsroom, trying to get the inside track on a killer who's twenty feet away—a guy who practically broadcasts his presence by wearing the same distinctive outfit to two murders in one day—and then he shoots Miranda Suarez in front of two dozen witnesses."

Folding his arms, he looked down. "But he doesn't kill Kerri Milner, just the boss. Here and at NewsAction, he only took out the owner. He let Kerri live—a witness that could potentially identify him, or see where he goes, what he drives away in… And this guy just strolls out the door like he was buying a Coke at a convenience store."

Avarie looked toward the street, where police cars blocked any traffic from coming by. "The killer acts like… like he doesn't care?"

"Yeah, but I think it's more like…" Sergio chewed his lip. "It's more of a statement. This guy acts like he accomplished what he came here to do." The detective tugged his sweat-stained collar, sending some air over his neck and chest. "He's done with this part. Now he's on to the next part—whatever that is."

Avarie put her hand to her mouth. "Another news agency?"

"That'd be my guess," Sergio said. "We need to get all the news agencies in town alerted—which means I need to waste more time calling downtown so the antichrist can give me permission first."

* * * * *

Kerri Milner rounded the corner and sprinted down the sidewalk, sweating and gasping for air as she reached the entry of Florida Real Time News. Fear and adrenaline surged through her as she heaved open the door and raced inside. "Lasya! Lasya Kumar!"

The desk in the reception area was empty. Kerri darted past it and into the corridor, shouting her roommate's name.

She raced past rows of empty desks in the newsroom.

Where is everybody?

A long, panel window looking into the wood-paneled Florida Real Time conference room allowed Kerri to see inside. A small cluster of people had crowded into a corner, facing toward the window, their attention appearing to be focused on the conference room's closed door.

There we go. They're all in a meeting.
Hurry! Find Lasya!

As Kerri rushed toward the wooden door, she caught a glimpse of someone moving in front of the group.

The employees' faces appeared scared.

What are they scared of? What's going on?

Gasping, she threw herself back a step, her eyes going wide. The Florida Real Time employees were looking at a large man standing just inside the conference room door.

Kerri dropped to the floor below the window of the conference room, her pulse pounding.

The man wore a green paper hospital mask over his face and was dressed in a baseball cap, sunglasses, and a red windbreaker.

CHAPTER 22

Sergio paced back and forth on the hot sidewalk, one hand to his brow, the other holding his phone to his ear, waiting for someone downtown to find Lieutenant Davis.

"He's probably holding a press conference." Sergio scowled. "Self-promotion is what he's best at."

The phone line crackled in his ear. "Sergio?" It was Carly's voice.

He smiled. "Hey."

"How are you holding up?" she asked.

"Me? I'm fine." His smile widened and he patted his chest. "This is my element—catching the bad guys. But I have to admit, things aren't as fun without you along for the ride. What about on your end? How are you enjoying desk work downtown?"

"It's… different. I feel like I should be at the scene. Deshawn visited crime scenes a lot."

Sergio waved a hand. "That'll happen, just not this time. You're needed there."

"Yeah…" Carly lowered her voice. "Davis is hampering things. He might have been right about keeping the media in the dark initially, but now… it's like he's trying to stay the course just because that's what he decided earlier. They could really help us. One look at the internet and it's obvious they all know anyway. The stories are everywhere—and the speculation is running wild."

"Well…" Sergio chuckled. "People like Lieutenant Davis get to work downtown because they can't make good decisions. That's just how the downtown staff is."

"Oh yeah?" Carly's voice grew cold. "If I get promoted, I'll be downtown."

Sergio's jaw dropped. "You—uh… You'll be the exception, of course."

"Of course. Hey, it looks like they tracked down the Lieutenant, so I'd better get back to coordinating cases. I'll put you on hold."

"Okay." He clutched his phone to his ear. "Hey, Carly—"

"Yes?"

He wanted to say more. He wanted to ask about other things, like what her plan was with Kyle.

He held his breath, trying to find the right words.

No. This isn't the time.

"Uh... Nothing." Sergio looked down the street, shoving a hand in his pocket. "It'll keep. I'll, uh, talk to you later."

I hope.

"Okay," Carly said. "Hold for the Lieutenant."

* * * * *

Lasya Kumar trembled as she stood frozen in the corner of the Florida Real Time conference room, her eyes fixed on the large gun held by a man in a red windbreaker. She and her fellow employees had been corralled into the room when the intruder came into their offices and brandished his weapon. Now, they stood silent, packed into one corner, afraid to move.

"Where's the owner?" the man shouted.

Lasya's eyes darted to the door of the adjoining room, where Jamaal Ainer kept his office.

The owner-editor's cluttered desk was piled high with stacks of file folders, as were large swaths of his office floor. The dozen or so filing cabinets lining the wall were stuffed to overflowing. Rising from the middle of the pile on the desk was Jamaal's computer, and somewhere under the paper rubble was his land-line phone. The perimeter of Ainer's unkept office was adorned with pictures of the rail-thin news editor receiving awards from various local and national celebrities, most of them resting in dusty frames that hung crooked on the wood-panel walls.

The killer peered at Lasya, then glanced over his shoulder to Jamaal's office. "Here? Is this the owner's office?"

Several of her co-workers nodded.

The man lumbered toward the office, keeping his gun pointed at his hostages. "Where is he?"

Lasya shifted her weight from one foot to the other, watching the intruder. She recognized him from the NewsAction videos bombarding the internet, and the shocking murder he'd perpetrated against Jasper Menendez-Holswain.

She forced herself to breathe.

The killer spoke in a voice that seemed falsely low. It sent shivers down her spine when she heard about it on the internet; in person, it pumped frost through her veins.

"He—he's not here," one of the co-workers said. "The owner—he's gone. He was here earlier, but he left."

The killer looked toward the employees. "Give him this message for me."

He raised the gun and fired into Jamaal's office, sending up bits of paper and leather chair as blast after blast filled the air.

The employees screamed and ducked, some covering their heads, some diving to the floor. Others crawled under the conference room table.

The bullets ripped holes in the office walls, the filing cabinets, the framed pictures, and the rear exit. The back door bounced open, spilling sunshine into the office as a bullet hit Jamaal's computer, exploding it and sending it crashing to the ground.

The killer's gun clicked. He stood still, his face to Jamaal's desk, his gun at his side. A glass-framed photo of Lasya's boss and the mayor rocked sideways once or twice, then slipped from the wood paneling and hit the floor, shattering.

FOURTH ESTATE

Lasya lifted her head.

The man in the red windbreaker turned to face her. "Get up." He glanced around. "All of you—get up. Now!"

Knees shaking, Lasya got to her feet, keeping her hands over her head and her gaze on the floor.

"Get out." The gunman pointed toward the rear exit door, hanging open in their boss' smoke-filled office. "Go!" He shouted, waving the gun.

The reporter in front of her raced forward, turning into Jamaal's office and sprinting out the back door. Others followed, keeping their heads down and rushing outside.

Lasya did the same, her heart pounding the entire time, certain that the killer would open fire and shoot them all in the back as they ran away.

* * * * *

On the other side of the conference room wall, Kerri Milner sat quivering, unable to move. The gunshots had barely cleared the air when she heard the madman order all of the employees out the back door.

Now she sat alone in the Florida Real Time office, with no earthly idea what to do, less than twenty feet from a deranged killer.

She lifted her head, peering toward the front entry.

Maybe I can crawl over there and escape.

Crashes came from the other side of the conference room wall. Pictures broke and stacks of papers were tossed. The gunman grunted, upending a filing cabinet and spilling its contents everywhere.

Or maybe I should find somewhere to hide.

She glanced to her left. The Florida Real Time restrooms were only a few feet away.

Kerri swallowed hard, the madman apparently intent on trashing Jamaal Ainer's entire office.

Crawl to the bathroom while he's making noise. You can climb onto the toilet tank and get out the ventilation window.

The noises on the other side of the wall continued. Trembling, Kerri lowered her face to the floor and held her breath, inching toward the ladies' room.

* * * * *

"No, Sergio." Lieutenant Davis growled into the phone line. "I told you—we keep the press out of this, and we keep control. This department doesn't need another black eye."

Sergio frowned, gripping his phone. "You'll have nothing but black eyes if you don't let the media help on this. They already know anyway. I told you, both the murders are all over the internet."

"You have your orders, Detective."

Sergio huffed. "Lieutenant, the guy's walking around in a pretty identifiable outfit. If we just let people know about it, somebody's bound to see him out there. They can tell us where he is, and we can pick him up."

"As I said, radio silence. Run everything through us. Is there anything else?"

Sergio squeezed his eyes shut, heat rising on his neck. "Sir, you're making this twice as hard as it has to be."

FOURTH ESTATE

"Maybe that's the new level we need to operate at. Get used to it, Detective Martin. Do your job."

The call ended. Grimacing, Sergio shoved his phone into his pocket and looked around. "Where's that reporter—Kerri Milner? Let's see if she can leak some stuff for us."

Delveccio scanned a clipboard, raising his chin. "Looks like she's gone, Detective. It says here that you cut her loose."

"What!" Sergio threw his hands out at his sides. "Why would I do that? We still have all the other witnesses here."

"Sorry." The officer shrugged. "We're all swamped. Somebody lost track."

Wiping his hands over his face, Sergio exhaled sharply. "Okay. We have a room full of reporters." He peered into the INN office. "Maybe one of them will leak for us."

"Should you do that?" Avarie stepped forward. "Disobey a direct order?"

"I don't have any—" He stopped himself, his mouth hanging open. Taking a breath, he softened his tone. "I… was going to say I don't have any choice. I guess that's not true."

"Whether it's true or not, it isn't your decision to make." Avarie stepped in front of him, looking up into his eyes. "You have bosses for a reason. They're the ones that have to make the tough calls, not you. Maybe Lieutenant Davis is right. You can't control the press. If everyone runs their crime scene information through downtown, it could help keep the public from panicking."

Sergio looked down, rubbing his chin stubble. "I don't know. Maybe."

Smiling, Avarie crossed her arms. "You know, we never had that breakfast you promised me. A food break might be in order."

He shook his head. "I don't have time for a break."

"You have your phone. The crime scene can't survive without you for a few minutes?" The consultant chuckled. "Consider it a strategy session. We'll talk about the case—or what's actually bugging you."

"Nothing's bugging me," Sergio grumbled. "I'm fine."

"No, you're angry. You have been all day." Avarie put her hands on her hips. "That, or you're the world's second biggest jerk—and I don't think that's the case. Now, let's go."

"Second biggest?" Sergio cocked his head. "Who's the biggest, then?"

She grabbed his arm, pulling him toward the car. "I'll tell you—over a taco."

* * * * *

Carly knocked on Lieutenant Davis' partially-closed door, pushing it open to peer inside. The Lieutenant sat at his desk, reading a folder, with Mellish behind him.

"Sir," she said. "I have another update."

Sighing, Davis sat back in his chair. "I have one for you, too. We have another murder."

Carly stepped forward, her stomach clenching.

Another one? Three, in one day?

FOURTH ESTATE

"This morning." Davis shook his head. "A clerk in a law office was killed. Two of the three lawyers who work at the firm were present when it happened. They gave the responding officer a description that matches the guy at NewsAction and INN—heavyset guy, red windbreaker, sunglasses, ball cap, paper mask." The Lieutenant slammed the folder onto the desk. "We pulled all available resources when the NewsAction murder hit, so this didn't get processed up to us until now."

"A legal clerk," Carly said. "And two news agency owners. What's the connection?"

Mellish stepped away from the desk, sighing as he sat down in one of the interview chairs. "Aside from the killer, we don't know of any connection."

"Then, we're missing something." She looked at the lieutenant. "Obviously."

Davis put his elbow on the desk and leaned his chin on his hand. "Obviously."

"Maybe…" Carly held her hands at her sides, watching the lieutenant's expression. "…it's time to let the media in on this, as Sergio suggested. We're pulling resources to help the case load, and things are slipping through the cracks. The media could help us."

The lieutenant leaned back in his chair, his eyes on his computer. "Thank you for the input, Detective, but we'll maintain the status quo. That will be all."

"But sir—"

Davis slammed his hand on the desk. "Sergio Martin is not going to be the one who decides how these investigations get conducted!" The lieutenant

DAN ALATORRE

glared at her, steeling his voice. "You have a lot of pots simmering on the stove, Carly. Be careful one doesn't boil over."

* * * * *

Heart pounding, Kerri crawled across the cold, hard floor, the restroom door now just inches away. Beads of perspiration dotted her brow. She moved only when the madman with the gun threw something else in Jamaal's office so his actions would obscure any sounds she made.

Reaching a hand up, she placed her trembling fingers on the doorknob, her pulse throbbing in her neck and ears.

Get in, get to the window, get gone.

A drop of sweat rolled down her forehead and dripped off the tip of her nose. Panting, she gripped the knob and gave it a twist.

Nothing happened.

Moaning, she gripped the doorknob tighter and tried again.

The metal slipped through her fingers. Kerri grimaced.

Let's get this done, girl!

He's going to come out of that office sooner or later. Don't be here when he does.

Kerri pushed herself upward to her knees and grabbed the knob with both hands. Gritting her teeth, she twisted the metal as hard as she could.

The knob turned. The door opened.

She exhaled, relief flooding over her as she put her hands to the floor, making herself less visible from Jamaal's office as she crept over the bathroom door threshold.

FOURTH ESTATE

The waistline of her jeans jerked backwards, stopping her. A jolt of fear flashed through her insides.

"Well, well, well. What have we here?" The killer's voice boomed through the office. He dragged Kerri backwards a few feet and flipped her over, looming above the petite reporter. "Going somewhere?"

DAN ALATORRE

CHAPTER 23

Sergio exhaled a long, slow breath, leaning back as he drove toward the nearby series of strip malls and the various food establishments among them.

Turning sideways in her seat, Avarie tucked a leg under herself and placed both hands on her shin, peering at him. "I know Lieutenant Davis bothers you. What you don't know is… He bothers me, too."

Sergio gave her a sideways glance. "He hired you."

She snorted. "Davis? No. A guy like that doesn't hire consultants—he thinks he already has all the answers. His ego won't let him take help from someone who's not a cop, much less from someone he thinks is an inexperienced young girl."

As he approached a stoplight, Sergio slowed his vehicle.

"I'm a professional consultant," Avarie said. "I specialize in helping law enforcement. In Florida alone, I single-handedly helped the police departments in Lakeland and St. Petersburg—and I have the Neilson polls to prove it. But I know the lieutenant doesn't respect me. He probably wanted a different consulting firm—maybe some friend of his, that he could control—but the Chief hired me. So, here I am, having to prove myself to a guy who almost has an interest in me not succeeding—if I fail, he can say he was right to want a different firm. But I'll get Tampa PD looking good in the eyes of the public, because that's my job and I'm good at it. Even when I do, I know it still won't be enough for a guy like that."

When the light changed, Sergio drove to the crowded parking lot of an old strip mall. The business on the end had a faded neon sign that said Enrique's Tacos—with the "A" burned out, and a line coming out the door. Carly and Sergio had eaten there many times over the years, jokingly referring to it as T-COS instead of by its actual name.

He glanced at Avarie. "Seems like you know the lieutenant pretty well."

"I know his type," she said. "I took a lot of psychology classes in college."

Sergio took the closest parking spot he could find—almost a block away—and shut off the car. "Can you look into your psychology crystal ball and see why Davis dislikes me so much?"

"I don't need psychology for that," Avarie said. "It's pretty easy. The lieutenant ascended to his position by following the rules. He sees you as a problem because you disdain the rules—and that threatens his mode of existence. Luckily for you, bad actors with oversized egos tend to create their own demise, so you just need to outlast Lieutenant Davis until he does just that." She undid her seat belt and lifted her purse from the floor, glancing toward the run-down looking restaurant. "Is this where we're eating?"

"We can go somewhere else," Sergio said, "but this place is the best. I… actually didn't take you for the taco type."

"When are you going to trust me? I'm the taco type, the burger type, the hot wings type… But I'm also the sanitary eating establishment type." She opened her door and got out.

"There's a place with a salad bar down the street, little sister." Sergio leaned over to talk to her as Avarie stood by the vehicle. "You'll be able to dine safely there."

"How about this?" She put one hand on her hip, the other on the open car door, leaning over. Her straight blonde hair fell around her face, framing it with golden strands. "I trust you, so we'll eat here."

"You sure?" Sergio asked. "I wouldn't want you to mess up that pretty blouse."

"Oh yeah?" Avarie stood up. "We'll see which one of us ends up wearing salsa. Messiest shirt pays for lunch." She pushed the door shut.

Smiling, Sergio opened his door and followed the consultant into the tiny restaurant.

* * * * *

Sergio ordered his and Avarie's lunch from the black-haired teenager at the busy T-COS counter, then located a booth by the widow to sit in.

Avarie slid herself across the old vinyl cushion and unrolled the paper napkin that held her flatware. She arranged the utensils on the table, glancing at her lunch companion. "So? What happens next in the investigation?" She placed her napkin in her lap.

"Normally, we'd try to figure out who the killer is," Sergio said. "Here, that's partly done. We have what appears to be the same guy, committing two murders at two different crime scenes, less than an hour apart. We need to look at all the evidence try to figure out the identity of the fat man in the red windbreaker. My guess is, the drycleaner video cameras caught the killer walking away or climbing into his car, talking to an accomplice—something. That'll give us a lot. Carly can request cell phone activity from all the service providers, too, so when we find a suspect, we'll have his own phone helping tell us he was there."

Avarie raised her eyebrows, nodding. "You make it sound easy."

"Oh, no. Not at all. There are a lot of ways for a killer to mess up when he commits a murder, and there are a lot of ways for the police to mess up the evidence. New cops, rookies—they're all trying to help, and I can't do it all, but mistakes happen. It's a lot of detail, and it's time consuming." He checked the time on his phone. "This could turn into a pretty long day for you."

FOURTH ESTATE

"For us. I'm glued to your hip, remember?" Avarie glanced at Sergio's phone, then returned her gaze to his eyes. "What would you be missing out on? What do detectives usually do in the evening?"

He chuckled. "A lot of them just go home and get drunk."

"Oh, count me in." She sat back in her seat. "After the INN crime scene, I could use a stiff drink. Or three."

Sergio folded his arms on top of the table. "I might have to check your ID first, little sister. How old are you, anyway?"

"Twenty-seven."

"Twenty-seven?" His jaw dropped. "Holy cow, you're still a baby."

Avarie looked away, waving a hand at him. "All you old guys say that."

"Old?" Sergio recoiled. "I'm not old."

"You're older than me."

He shook his head. "That doesn't make me old."

"No?" Avarie leaned forward. "Are you closer to forty or twenty?"

"Forty, but—"

"Then you're old."

Sergio opened his mouth to reply, but held his tongue as the teen from the counter arrived at the table. She took a red plastic basket from her tray and set it down in front of Avarie, followed by a gigantic plastic cup of ice water. A massive taco stuck up from the middle of the basket, surrounded by a pile of tortilla chips that spilled over onto the table.

The teenager placed an identical basket and cup in front of Sergio. "Do y'all need anything else, Mr. Martin?"

"I think we're good, Maria. Thank you."

"Mmm." Avarie leaned over her food and closed her eyes. "This smells delicious."

"That's very nice of you, ma'am," Maria said. "I'll tell Dad."

As the teenager walked back to the counter, Avarie turned to Sergio. "You must come here a lot."

"Not as much as I'd like." He plucked a small tub of guacamole from his basket and set it on the table, reaching for the bottle of hot sauce. "The owners are Enrique and Linda Garcia. They're my mom's neighbors. I ate here all the time as a kid. Maria is their youngest daughter. I went to grade school with her mom."

Looking at her lunch companion, Avarie placed her elbow on the table and rested her chin on the back of her hand. "Being a cop is a really personal thing to you, isn't it?"

"Isn't everyone's job personal to them?" Sergio picked up a broken piece of tortilla and tossed it into his mouth.

"No. I'd say Lieutenant Davis likes what his job does for him, not actually what his job is."

"Hmm." He munched his chip. "More psychology stuff."

Avarie shrugged. "It comes with the job."

"You know…" Sergio put his hand to his mouth and cleared his throat. "I wanted to ask you something. There's no Sonntag at Sonntag and Fox, is there?"

FOURTH ESTATE

"Nope." Avarie sighed. "Sonntag and Fox is basically just me. For some reason, the extra name added credibility when I sent out proposals. Like I had an old guy partner somewhere, with lots of experience, that's overseeing things and showing me the ropes. Prospective clients are more comfortable thinking that's the case, so I let them." She took a chip from her basket and put it to her lips. "How'd you guess my secret?"

"You said you did the St. Pete and Lakeland police departments single handed. And the guy with you in Lieutenant Davis' office this morning didn't act like a boss. But you did."

"Impressive." Avarie smiled. "You're a good detective, Detective."

Sergio nodded. "And you're a smart lady, little sister."

His phone rang, vibrating as it laid on the table. The words Tampa PD Main Line appeared on the screen. Sergio grabbed the phone. "Hey."

"Big news," Carly said. "We got a warrant emailed to the owner of the drycleaners, and Delveccio reviewed the footage. It shows the killer getting into a white Mercedes GLS—that's a big SUV. No info on the owner. The plate wasn't visible in the images."

Sergio got up from the table, clutching the phone. "The killer might have obscured the tag, but there can't be too many white Mercedes SUVs in town. Can we ask the DMV to run a county-wide list for us?"

"I just did," Carly said. "Including rental vehicles. When we get the list, we can start narrowing down the possible suspects. As soon as that pool is small enough, I'll request the black box data from the manufacturer so we can see where the cars have been all day."

"And hopefully where it is right now." He gestured for Avarie to get up and follow him.

"Don't get your hopes up," Carly said. "The black box data requires another warrant, and that's going to take a little longer. Some guy named Brimley has been filing a bunch of 'right to privacy' lawsuits on that kind of stuff and posting videos about it all over the internet. Judges and car manufacturers don't like bad press."

Sergio winced. "Brimley the auditor. My new friend."

"What?"

"Nothing." He headed for the door. "We're on our way. Thanks for getting this stuff so fast."

"Hey, we're a great team. Always were."

Her words soothed him, putting his mind at ease. Carly always knew just what to say.

As he exited the building, Sergio's phone pinged with a text. He looked at the screen.

"Kerri Milner has invited you to a livestream event."

"What is it?" Avarie asked.

"I'm not sure." Standing in the T-COS parking lot, Sergio clicked the link, opening a livestream video on a social media service. Kerri Milner's name appeared at the bottom of the image, like a news chyron, indicating that the recording was being done from her phone and one of her social media accounts.

FOURTH ESTATE

The video faded in and out of focus, shaking as it did.

"We're live," a woman said, her voice trembling. The camera was pointed toward a messy desk inside a business office of some sort. Wood paneled walls held shattered pictures.

"Give me that." A man's voice came from off screen, speaking gruff and low.

The camera jostled, going dark before displaying Kerri Milner in the corner of the office, hunched over and trembling.

The lens swung around to reveal a man in a red windbreaker and sunglasses, a paper surgical mask over his face and a baseball cap on his head.

Sergio's insides jolted.

"I have... an announcement." The man on the screen inhaled hard, the paper mask sucking in and out of his mouth with each breath as he walked around the destroyed desk and office. "Today, justice is being done. The courts have failed to do their job because they are lazy and unscrupulous, as is the citizenry that elects them. Therefore, the entire system must be held accountable, and those who have taken part will be punished accordingly."

He moved the camera around as he walked, going out of the little office and into a larger room.

Behind him on the screen, an exit door opened. Kerri Milner sprinted outside, disappearing as the door slammed shut behind her.

"Four people have died by my hand today," the killer said. "But it is obvious that, until more perish, the lethargic people of this city will not demand change. Therefore..." He stopped moving, holding the camera steady, sweat dripping down the side of his face. His voice grew louder. "It will be necessary to increase my number of victims."

He moved the camera closer, his face filling the screen.

"I will kill more people today, and more tomorrow, and each day after that, until I feel justice is done. Men, women… and of course, children." His eyes scrunched up, as if he were smiling under the paper mask. "Maybe I'll kill four more today. I think I'm starting to like it."

The image went dark again, then fluorescent ceiling lights passed across the screen. A door appeared in the distance, growing larger as the madman moved toward it.

"Do I have your attention now?" The killer giggled, staring directly into the camera lens. "Get ready, Tampa. Here I come."

CHAPTER 24

Racing out of the T-COS parking lot, Sergio called Carly's cell phone number from his car. Across from him, Avarie tightened her seat belt as the sedan swerved into the road.

Carly answered on the first ring.

"You'll never guess what I just saw." Sergio said.

"If you mean a murderer announcing he's going on an even bigger killing spree, I saw it." Carly huffed. "The whole world did. The words 'Get ready, Tampa. Here I come' are already making headlines across the internet. And who is the fourth victim? I only know about three."

"I don't know." Pulse pounding, Sergio gripped the steering wheel, speeding back to the INN site. "But our witness was in that video—Kerri Milner. She was in the killer's livestream. I saw her."

He frowned, clenching his jaw. "That poor kid must be scared to death. We need to locate her and find out where that livestream was done."

"Clues," Carly said. "If you can't reach her, we need everybody to look for clues in the video. But… Kerri Milner is a witness? Let's think about that. She was in the killer's presence twice—that we know of—and escaped unharmed both times. She might be involved. Do we know where she was when the Law office murder happened?"

Sergio shook his head. "She… Carly, Kerri Milner looked pretty scared when I spoke with her. That was only a few minutes after the Suarez murder. She looked shell-shocked."

"Maybe she's a good actress. Or a psychopath, like the guy she's working with."

"I…" Sergio winced. He hadn't really given thought to the idea that Kerri might be involved somehow. "I don't think she's a part of this thing, partner."

"No?" Carly snorted. "Are you willing to stake your life on that? We have her statement, right? Her contact information is on it. Maybe you should call her and see what she says now."

Nodding, Sergio exhaled. "Okay. I'll get her number from Delveccio and buzz you back in a few."

* * * * *

Carly refreshed her computer screen to replay the livestream event she'd just witnessed. She leaned close to the monitor, twirling a strand of hair between her fingers and letting it brush across her lips. "What's in here?" she whispered. "Give me something."

FOURTH ESTATE

The jerky video showed the destroyed office, papers strewn everywhere.

It's an older building. Wood paneling hasn't been done in construction for fifty years.

Other details met her eye.

Filing cabinets. Paper file folders. It's not very modernized—although we still use a lot of paper around here, so… If this is an active business, it's one that has people getting information on paper—or they used to do that, and the owner hasn't gotten rid of the old files.

Her eyes darted around the screen. Carly paused the video again and again to focus on the visible images.

Overall, the video is dark. So, the interior office lights either didn't work or they had been turned off. Out of business, maybe?

Her gaze landed on the exit door in what appeared to be the owner's office.

That's an odd feature, too. An exit door in the suite of the owner? Nobody would do that these days.

This business is in a repurposed building. A renovation, or a low-rent place that they moved into and didn't update.

That means money problems. Did the owner owe the killer money?

Over the closeup shots of the killer, framed pictures were visible—some on the walls, some on the floor.

She zoomed in, but the image got too grainy to show who was in the prints.

Where is this? Where is this?

It's local. Not more than an hour's drive from INN, or Kerri Milner wouldn't be there.

Carly sat up in her chair.

Why is she there at all?

If Kerri Milner wasn't in on this, why would a scared witness to a murder intentionally go to where the killer was?

Because she didn't know he'd be there. She went there for another reason.

She exhaled, the thoughts swirling in her head.

And if I were a news reporter who knew two news agency owners had been murdered in one morning, I'd be thinking another news agency was next. Reporters talk. Milner probably knew people at the place in the video.

But the other news agencies wouldn't know about the INN murder yet. I'd want to warn any friends who worked at other news outlets. Maybe I have a boyfriend working there. Maybe I knew the owner.

Carly frowned.

But if I'm Kerri Milner, why didn't I just call them? Or text? People Kerri's age practically live on their phones.

Deshawn approached her desk, carrying a file. "Carly, the lieutenant wants an update in thirty minutes, and there's a ton of new information hitting the internet…"

Carly's focus stayed on the screen as she considered Kerri Milner's actions in her head.

Maybe she did call them. Or, maybe she tried to.

FOURTH ESTATE

"Talk to me, Carly," Deshawn said. "What are you thinking?"

Carly peered up at the sergeant. "She would have called them. Kerri Milner wouldn't have gone to a place she thought was dangerous."

He rubbed his chin. "She might have. She's a reporter. Maybe she wanted a scoop."

"She already had a scoop," Carly said. "She was standing right next to someone who was murdered. She went there, to the place in that video, to warn them because they didn't answer her calls. Maybe they were in a staff meeting or something, but that seems pretty unlikely. We need to contact all the phone service providers and see which one has Kerri Milner's account. She probably placed calls to the location she ended up being at when the killer walked in. We need to request that her phone be put under surveillance."

The sergeant shook his head. "I'm not sure we need to do any of that. I was about to tell you, the internet is buzzing with people talking about what happened in that livestream video." He held up his phone, displaying a disheveled man in a parking lot, talking with a woman. "Looks like it was Florida Real Time Network that got shot up by our perp, and the FRT reporters are flocking to every social media site known to mankind. The owner is getting ready to make a press conference."

Carly stood up. "We need to get over there. Who's the owner of FRT?"

"Jamaal Ainer. But we don't go, remember? We delegate."

"Yeah. Yeah." She moved back to the desk chair, putting her hands in her hair. "Oh, this is rough. Okay, we need somebody good—and I mean good—to get over there."

"We'll send a unit," Deshawn said. "Have them talk to Ainer while running their body cams. You'll see it all, like you were there."

"Okay." She lowered herself back into her seat. "That's...more efficient. Thanks."

The phone on her desk buzzed, followed by the duty officer's voice. "Incoming call for you, Detective Sanderson. He says he's Jamaal Ainer from the Florida Real Time news network."

* * * * *

Sergio phoned the Tampa PD headquarters. "This is Detective Sergio Martin. I need you to connect me with Officer Delveccio, please. He's on site at the INN case."

"One moment, Detective."

As the phone rang, Sergio steered his car around the midday traffic, rushing back to the murder site.

"Wait." Sergio glanced at Avarie and pulled his phone away from his ear. "I don't need Delveccio to give me Kerri Milner's number. I have it. She sent me the link to the livestream from her phone."

He ended the call and tapped the screen, opening his recent calls and selecting the last inbound number.

"Yeah. I have it right here." Driving with one hand, he selected the number. "This girl's got some answering to do."

He maneuvered his car to the side of the road as the phone rang. "Come on, Kerri. Answer."

"Is it a set up?" Avarie put a hand to her mouth. "Oh, my gosh—is Kerri Milner helping to kill them?" Leaning back in her seat, a gasp escaped the consultant's lips. "I only caught a glimpse of her when you two were talking. She seemed so nice."

"She also seemed scared out of her mind. If she's not involved, she's having an extremely bad day." As the phone rang again, Sergio frowned. "Answer, Kerri…"

On the fourth ring, the call connected. Rustling came over the line.

"Hello?"

A hollowness flashed through Sergio's insides.

The voice on the other end of the call was male, with a gruff tone that sounded artificially low, as if the speaker was trying to make himself appear to have a deeper voice than he really did.

DAN ALATORRE

CHAPTER 25

As Sergio's mouth hung open, the phone went silent. He looked at the screen
Call ended.
"What happened?" Avarie asked. "Did Kerri answer?"
His thoughts racing, Sergio slowly shook his head. "She… didn't—he did. The killer." He moved his gaze to Avarie. "I think the murderer has Kerri's phone."
"What!" Avarie gasped.
"Wait, that's right. Kerri sent me the livestream link, but she gave him the phone at the start of the recording. Then she ran outside. Remember?"
"So where is she now?"
"Good question." He rubbed his chest. "Safe, I hope."

DAN ALATORRE

And not involved in these murders.

And not dead in a hallway somewhere, the next victim of this madman.

Holding the phone up, he selected the same number, his thumb hovering over the send button. Sergio pursed his lips. "I'm going to try him again."

* * * * *

Carly held the phone to her ear with her shoulder and clutched her pencil. "Mr. Ainer, why do you think the killer shot up your office? He didn't do that at the first two newsrooms he visited."

"No," Jamaal said. "There, he merely committed murders. I assume he trashed my place because I wasn't there—lucky for me. He killed the owners of the other news agencies when he found them."

"Do you have any idea who the killer could be?" She grabbed a notepad from the top of her borrowed desk, taking down the news agency owner's words as fast as she could. "You've seen the physical appearance. Have you done a story on anybody who would match that description?"

"We do dozens of stories every day. There's no way to keep track of any particular—"

"Sir, this would be different. Killers rarely start a spree of homicides without a few indications first. Has anyone called your office and made threats?"

"Yes," Ainer said. "Almost every person I've profiled for the last ten years has threatened me in one form or another. That's our business, Detective—speaking truth to power. And those in power don't like to be challenged."

FOURTH ESTATE

She nodded, rubbing her forehead. "Okay. Well, can I ask a favor? Your people are posting their story about being held at gunpoint by a madman that's still at large. I'd like to ask you to have them dial it back until they give statements to our officers."

"Of course."

A wave of relief washed over the detective. "Thank you."

"I mean, you can ask." Ainer chuckled. "I won't be requesting they do any such thing. I called to see what you're doing to catch this madman. I could have been killed, and two dear friends *were* killed. I'm not stopping my people from talking. I'm encouraging them to get the story out and find this guy."

"Sir," Carly said, "creating a groundswell of gossip and fear isn't helpful to the community."

"You mean it's not helpful to you, Detective. It's quite helpful to my interests. FRT hasn't seen this many clicks since Terrence Big Time got caught stepping out on his wife with Diamond Darrow."

She sat back in her desk, her shoulders slumping. "Mr. Ainer—"

"Please, call me Jamaal. And call me anytime. But please, at the moment, I must go. I have a press conference awaiting me."

"That's exactly what I'm talking about. That sort of thing is hampering our investigation."

"I completely understand," Ainer said. "You have to do your job and I have to do mine. So, goodbye for now, Detective Sanderson. I'll be sure to mention your lack of progress in my press conference."

The call ended.

"Crap." Carly tossed her pencil to the desk top. "He's all about the coverage and not about getting the killer."

"Why would he be?" Deshawn folded his arms across his chest. "I bet that killer is sending a lot of eyeballs to view Ainer's news site. The longer this plays out, the more revenue Florida Real Time makes."

Sighing, Carly shook her head. "That's a happy thought."

"I'm just saying, his interests and our interests are not the same."

"Then we need to persuade him to see things our way." She rubbed her chin. "How can we do that? Arrest the little scumbag as a suspect and get him off the street and away from a camera?"

"No." Chuckling, Deshawn pulled his chair up to hers and sat down. "Next idea."

"Okay, so..." Carly pulled a strand of her hair between her fingers, twirling it against her cheek.

We're playing defense with this guy. How do we get on offense?

She glanced at the sergeant. "How about we dispatch a small army of officers to his location and tie all of his employees up—along with Mr. Jamaal Ainer—by requesting additional witness statements until we have enough information to find our murderer? That could take a whole day. Maybe two. And they certainly have information we need, so it's not like retaliation."

Deshawn unfurled an arm and pointed a finger at her. "That's more like it."

FOURTH ESTATE

"What's the status on that law office murder?" Carly asked. "Have we spoken with the owner?"

Reaching across to his desk, Deshawn grabbed his mouse and clicked a tab, opening a preliminary interview report. "It says here that our people talked with her this morning. The owner is Tanika Stafford. She was shooting a video out by the airport at the time of the murder." He looked at Carly. "We can pull up the body cam footage of her interview if you want to review it."

Carly exhaled slowly, her eyes on her computer, brushing the strand of hair over her chin. "Two people are dead because they were connected to the killer somehow," she whispered. "Two more would be dead if they'd have been where the killer thought they'd be. That's important. We... we..." Glancing at the sergeant, she let her hair fall from her fingers. "Why would the killer think Tanika Stafford would be in her law office this morning? If he wanted to kill four different people, at four different locations, in one day, that requires planning. He had to know their schedules. Why didn't he know Stafford would be away doing a video?"

Deshawn shrugged. "According to the report our officers filed, the video shoot was a last-minute thing. Stafford's law partner confirmed that."

"Stafford was first on the killer's list," Carly said. "A list he planned and thought about. The order is important to him."

Dropping his hand to the sides of his chair, Deshawn drummed his seat cushion with his fingertips. "What do you think Stafford's significance was? Could she have been the most important name on the killer's list, or was she the starter as he was building up to a grand finale?"

"This had to be planned. That means the killer had to know her schedule, or he knew her routine." Carly's words rolled off her tongue as her mind raced. "Same with the others. Only, the murderer didn't know about Tanika Stafford's last-minute schedule change."

Scenario after scenario swirled in her mind.

The extreme nature of the killing suggests a personal connection. What connects a lawyer and a bunch of news agencies?

No...

The question is: What connects a lawyer and a bunch of trashy, tabloid-style news agencies?

A jolt went through her.

A scandal. One that requires a lawyer.

She sat upright, turning to Deshawn. "We're looking for a heavy black man who drives a Mercedes SUV *and* was in the tabloids *and* was represented by Tanika Stafford." Carly clapped her hands together. "If we tell all that to her, Stafford should know exactly who that is."

CHAPTER 26

An officer walked toward Carly's desk, gripping a notepad. "We reached that lawyer for you—Tanny Stafford. She's agreed to come in and talk, so we're sending a patrol unit over to pick her up, as you requested." He lowered his voice and glanced over his shoulder. "The lieutenant is wondering if that last part was necessary. Stafford's profile has been climbing in the community lately."

"Was it necessary to send a patrol car? Yes." Carly looked up from her computer. "But only if we want her interview done quickly, to possibly save lives. Besides, a ride in a cop car is fun."

Lieutenant Davis came out of his office, carrying a coffee cup. "You've been working with Sergio too long, Detective Sanderson. His fondness for sarcastic remarks is rubbing off on you."

"Actually, Lieutenant..." Carly leaned back and slid an arm over the back of her chair. "The truth is, riding in an actual cop car isn't something everyday people do. Having a high-profile attorney retrieved in one does two things. It expresses urgency, which is completely appropriate. And it lets her know in a subtle way that anyone involved in this will be in the back of a cop car soon. The same conversation, done here or done while sitting in her law office, behind her big desk, has a very different feel, and sends a very different message."

Davis smiled. "I stand corrected. You're thinking like a sergeant now—or maybe a lieutenant." He raised his cup. "Kudos. Maybe some of that will rub off on your partner."

* * * * *

Frowning, Sergio sat in his car on the side of the road, calling Kerri's number again and again. Each time, the call went straight to her voicemail.

"You've reached Kerri Milner of the INN news Network..."

On the last attempt, he got a different message, from her service provider's electronic voice.

"Mailbox full."

Exhaling, he squeezed his steering wheel in his fists and leaned forward on both arms. "I can't believe it! The killer has Kerri's phone, and I can't do anything!"

He sat up and dialed TPD headquarters. "I need a trace put on a phone number. Our killer could still have it in his possession."

FOURTH ESTATE

The admin clerk took down the information. "Okay. We should have that up and running in a few hours."

"A few hours?" Sergio's jaw dropped.

"Phone trace requests take time, Detective."

"We don't *have* time!" he shouted. "People are dying! I need that trace yesterday!"

As he ended the call, he started the car and put it in gear.

"Where are we going now?" Avarie asked.

"Back to the INN crime scene." Sergio dropped his phone into a cupholder. "There might be something we missed, and even if there isn't, we can follow up on any new evidence and start—"

His phone rang. Steering with one hand, he grabbed the phone with the other. "This is Detective Martin."

A young woman's voice came over the line. "I'm calling you from a friend's phone, so don't try to track it. I'm handing it back to her when we end this call and buying a burner phone."

"Kerri?" Sergio asked. He slowed the vehicle again and looked for another place to pull over.

"I, um… Yes, that's correct, Detective." Kerri's voice was nearly a whisper, but she didn't seem nervous. "I just wanted to call to… I wanted to tell you that I'm not involved in these murders, but I am leaving town."

"That's not a good idea." Sergio shook his head. "People will assume you're guilty."

"Check Insta. They already do." She sighed. "Anyway, I don't really care. I watched my boss die today. I… I'm not going to be next."

"Kerri, you're a material witness to a murder. We can protect you."

"The Tampa PD isn't looking super competent on that front right now, Detective. Florida Real Time is all over the internet telling everyone how screwed up you guys are."

"I could have you detained."

"You'll have to find me first," she said. "How about you find the killer instead?"

"Come help me do that." Sergio kept his voice calm and even, trying to sound reassuring. "You may know more than you think."

"Not at the risk of my own neck. I'm getting on a bus and getting out of Florida until that psycho is behind bars." A rustling of static came over the line. "Sorry, Detective. You seem like a good guy, but you can't keep me safe."

Sergio drove his car onto a half-empty parking lot, keeping the phone to his ear. "Kerri, listen to me. We can keep you safe. There's a lot we can do. What if..."

The sound in the phone's earpiece faded. Sergio glanced at the screen.

Call ended.

"Crap." He dropped the phone back into the cupholder and put his hand to his chin.

"Think she's involved now?" Avarie asked.

"No." Sergio shook his head. He drove around the lot and made a U-turn, pulling back onto the street. "Carly might think Kerri's involved, but I don't." He sighed. "That said... I could be wrong."

FOURTH ESTATE

Taking his phone from the cupholder, he made another call and pressed the speakerphone button.

"Hello. Detective Sergio Martin for Corporal Maizey McEnany, please." He held the phone away from his face and checked the time.

"Hello?" a woman said. "Sergio?"

"Hey, Mac." Sergio smiled. "I need a favor."

"I don't have any tickets to the game," the corporal said.

"I need to borrow one of your deputies to surveil the Greyhound bus station. A material witness in a murder case is trying to flee the state. Female brunette, medium length hair, slender build, mid-twenties. Approximately five foot six inches tall. She's probably trying to travel with a friend about the same age."

"When is she travelling?"

Sergio narrowed his eyes in the bright sunlight, peering out at the street. "Today, and probably soon. She may try to use a fake ID, but her legal name is Kerri Milner. No real identifiable marks, but she likes audio books so she might be wearing ear buds. Can you pick her up and hold her until I can send someone over?"

"You got it," Mac said. "I'll keep you posted."

"Thanks." Sergio nodded. "I owe you one."

"You owe me more than one, but I'll go easy on you since your department is getting slammed all over the internet." She chuckled. "I'll talk to you later."

As Sergio ended the call, Avarie looked at him.

"How do you know Kerri will be at the Greyhound station?" she asked.

"She said she's getting out of Florida, and she said she's taking a bus." He shrugged. "That sounds like Greyhound to me."

Avarie looked out the window, putting her hands out to her sides. "Well, then how do you know she's not there right now? She might even be on a bus already."

Sergio shook his head. "Greyhound stations announce train arrivals and departures all the time, over the lobby speakers, and they update constantly. I didn't hear any of that when I was on the phone with her. And I didn't hear the kind of rumbling and road noise that would indicate she was already on a moving bus. But..." He put a hand to his chin, his fingers sliding over his beard stubble. "I like the way she thinks. Kerri probably could have flown somewhere. A bus is a slow way to travel, and I don't think Kerri Milner wants to show up at any actual location very soon. Being on a long bus trip solves that problem for a day or two, maybe longer."

"And you figured there'd be two of them, because if you go all the way to your friend's place of business to warn her, you don't leave her behind."

"That's right." He smiled. "You'd make a good detective, little sister."

As they arrived back at the INN site, Avarie took out her phone and opened a search engine. Sergio peered across the car at the screen as Avarie scrolled through dozens of videos about the morning's three killings, compliments of Florida Real Time. Jamaal Ainer's employees interviewed each other, speculated about the connections, and offered every type of conspiracy theory and gossip to the internet—with Jamaal himself acting as the ringmaster of the circus.

The interviews ran the emotional spectrum, too. Some of the reporters mentioned how happy they were to have survived the brief kidnapping ordeal at the hands of someone who had murdered several others that day, and who had apparently arrived at FRT to do the same thing. Others broke down and cried, recalling how scared they were as the madman forced them at gunpoint to drop their phones, herding them into the FRT conference room where they feared they might be killed.

By then, they had seen the NewsAction video. Some of the FRT staff had even been on the livestream call, waiting to ask questions, when they electronically witnessed Jasper Menendez-Holswain's execution.

Avarie let her hands drop to her lap, still holding her phone, as the videos rolled from one FRT employee interview to another, in an unending river of drama and hype. She looked at Sergio. "How does a dead lawyer tie in to a couple of news agency owners being offed?"

Sergio shook his head. "She was a legal clerk, not a lawyer—and I don't know how it ties in."

"The killer says he's gonna murder a bunch of people…" She held up her phone. "But he let all the employees of FRT go—and Kerri Milner, too. How's that work?"

"Nope. I don't have the answer to that, either." He looked out the window, to the crime scene, and the bustling group of uniformed officers and crime scene investigators milling around. "Not yet, anyway." He turned back to her. "But I will."

Avarie closed her eyes, exhaling a long, slow breath as she eased her head onto the headrest. "Detective work is hard."

"That's why we make the big bucks," Sergio said. "Oh, wait. We don't."

She opened one eye, peeking at him. "When we were here earlier—I mean, when you asked me to stay in the car... I watched some videos of you. That First Amendment guy and his friends really made you look bad."

Sergio shrugged. "I kinda figured he'd get around to that, the little worm. That's his thing, his claim to fame. He picks fights to get views, and sometimes a cop screws up and the city has to write a check. What a scam." He tapped the steering wheel, looking at her. "Do I want to see it?"

"Nooo, no, no." Avarie's eyes widened. "Definitely not."

"Terrific."

"But I saw the original," she said. "I was there when it happened. I was at the station with Lieutenant Davis, watching the feed on the internal office channel. He and I both saw how cool you were to those guys."

Sergio snorted. "You'd think one of you would put out a statement saying so—since you're both trying to clean up the department's image and all."

"When?" Avarie said. "I've been with you all day."

"The lieutenant hasn't—and he knows all those local TV news reporters by name. He could easily have said something in my defense by now, since he's so worried about the department's image." Frowning, Sergio opened his door. "Come on, I've got a crime scene to investigate."

DAN ALATORRE

CHAPTER 27

Carly sat at her borrowed desk, with attorney Tanika "Tanny" Stafford, founding partner of the Stafford-Love law firm. The computer in front of them played a livestreaming news conference hosted by Jamaal Ainer and his news team from the parking lot of their business. Police cars and yellow tape restrained them from actually being on the property, but did little to keep their many camera lenses from zooming in whenever an officer walked out with a box of evidence.

A curvy blonde held a FRT microphone to Ainer's face, asking him questions so he could go on sprawling rants.

"Newsrooms used to be fortified," Ainer said, "but that has obviously laxed—like it has at banks and credit unions…" The gaunt newsman walked back and forth in front of the FRT building, the camera panning with him as he moved. "These days, a business might rely on video surveillance in an attempt to protect themselves—and law enforcement, of course. But both of those let us down, in a tragic way that has cost lives." He sighed, wiping a non-existent tear from his eye. "Everyone watching knows of some business that has no security at all, trusting the members of the public to remain civil. But as we have seen today, the false veneer of safety has been ripped away. Some lunatic can walk into any business in Tampa and kill everyone in the place, which is exactly what happened at two other news agencies this morning."

"Tragic," the blonde reporter said.

"Security costs money." Ainer held his hands out at his sides. "We were phasing it out anyway—along with this entire location. Why? Because like all businesses are asking themselves, why do we need a central physical location? Everybody works from home now, so we can ditch the lease and save some cash. I'm no different. All I need is a studio I can use for segment updates when we post videos."

The reporter nodded. "Like NewsAction did."

"Yes, like NewsAction did—and a lot of other places." Ainer lowered his head. "My dear friend Jasper wasn't the only innovator in our business. A high-quality green screen can give viewers the impression that a reporter is in our office when they're really on a sailboat in the middle of Tampa Bay."

Carly sat back and looked at the lawyer at her desk. "This is what we're dealing with."

FOURTH ESTATE

Tanny Stafford nodded, her eyes remaining on the livestream unfurling on the computer screen.

Stafford was attractive in ways most lawyers weren't. She was classically pretty, with long, well-styled dark hair and a terrific figure. Her hazel eyes and high cheek bones were the stuff that TV cameras—and possibly juries—absolutely loved.

Carly had spent a little time before Stafford's arrival watching her most recent Tik Tok videos, a combination of confidence, competence, good looks and charm, packaged to deliver what would otherwise be a flat message about some mundane aspect of the criminal law code.

But that seemed to be Tanny Stafford's unique appeal. She made the dull process of hiring a lawyer actually look interesting. Her Hollywood good looks made potential clients feel as if they were hiring someone from central casting, sure to get them off the hook before the final commercial break of the hour. Her posts received thousands of views and hundreds of comments—and not just from lonely male fans eager to engage with the beautiful attorney. Actual conversations took place on Stafford's social media platforms, where she explained important aspects of the legal system using simple, plain English.

She had worked for another law firm for a few years before starting her own, and two years after that, she took on a partner and hired several employees. Stafford-Love was born. But business really took off when the founding partner upgraded her wardrobe, makeup, and hairstyle, and took to social media. She didn't go sexy because she didn't have to; Tanny Stafford's looks and charm made her innately sexy. Her demeanor made her seem sweet, but also allowed the subtle feistiness to come through, letting viewers know she could fight when it was necessary. She was a star in the making, without appearing to know it—and if she did know, Tanny Stafford appeared to remain genuinely humble about it.

That modesty was another thing that separated her from most lawyers.

Stafford turned away from the computer and crossed her tan, well-toned legs, waving a hand at the circus on the screen. "Jamaal Ainer is an internet sensation wannabe. I don't think people take him or his so-called network too seriously."

Carly turned the video off. "Let's get down to why we asked you to be here. I think you know who our murder suspect is. Why haven't you come forward?"

"I gave a statement to your officer, earlier." Stafford looked at Carly, her long dark locks falling elegantly over the lapels of her cream-colored suitcoat. "I'm bound by no legal authority to volunteer to help in your investigation."

"No, you're not." Carly sat back and dropped her pencil onto her notepad. "But you might have been killed this morning. It could be in your best interest to help get the murderer behind bars. I mean… He might try again."

"Which is why I was considering taking a short leave of absence. A trip to the Bahamas, or to New York, possibly." She straightened the hem of her form-fitting skirt, lifting her hazel eyes to the detective.

The iciness of the formal lawyer had disappeared.

Stafford leaned forward, lowering her voice. "I'm quite distraught over Kaliope's death, Detective Sanderson." She blinked, pushing back the shiny wateriness that was trying to force its way into her eyes. "Kali and I went to high school together. She was my friend."

Sitting upright, the lawyer clutched her Dolce & Gabbana handbag to her lap. "But a woman in my business has to appear tough at all times, doesn't she? Yours, too, I'm sure. Even when the skies open and the storm is pelting us with barrels of crap, we have to pretend we have it all under control, don't we?"

Carly took a deep breath and let it out slowly, letting the impact of the lawyer's words wash over her.

Tanny Stafford didn't know the half of it.

It wasn't just the testosterone-fueled workplace, or the non-stop line of societal miscreants that paraded through the doors of the police station every day. It was the school schedule and the homework, the missed soccer games and the last-minute costumes for the school play. It was the late hours and coming home to a husband that wasn't there anymore, even when he was. It was trying to put a nutritious meal on the table at a decent hour, coordinating her mother's schedule so the boys would actually get to school on time or get home from school at all, and trying to be a soft shoulder for them after some girl on the playground giggled at a muffed kickball at-bat.

Carly's efforts in her work life ensured a peaceful existence for everyone else. And no matter how much of her last drop of strained, exhausted effort she wrung out into any given day at the office, the bad guys kept coming, like the waves of the Gulf of Mexico washing onto the white, sugar-sand of Clearwater Beach.

And every morning, no matter how exhausted she was, Carly climbed out of bed to do it again.

"Have you watched any of Jamaal's other videos?" Tanny Stafford's voice brought Carly back to the police station and her temporary seat at the sergeant's desk. The lawyer held up her phone, where a video of the FRT owner-editor was playing. "He's urging everyone in town to leave immediately, especially news reporters and lawyers."

"Funny, a moment ago I thought we agreed Jamaal wasn't credible." Carly reached for her computer mouse. "If you don't mind, let's just review the video recording from your office this morning and see what jumps out at us, shall we?"

Lieutenant Davis emerged from his office. "Is that... it is!" Grinning, he bolted toward Carly's desk. "Tanika Stafford. How nice to meet you in person. I'm a big fan."

Carly recoiled.

Fan? She might look like a Hollywood movie star, but she isn't one.

Davis reached out and took the lawyer's hand, pausing for a moment as if he might bend over and kiss it. For her part, Tanny Stafford remained in her chair.

He smiled wider. "What brings you down here?"

"Detective Sanderson," Tanny said. "She thought I might be of some assistance."

Carly gestured to the computer. "We were about to watch the video from her office, Lieutenant. If you'd like to sit in."

As if you didn't already know that.

"Yes." Davis looked around. "Yes, I'd like that very much." He grabbed a chair and pulled it alongside the curvaceous lawyer.

As Lieutenant Davis made smarmy small talk with Tanny Stafford, Carly opened her case file folder and clicked the video surveillance recording from the Stafford-Love law firm.

The portly African-American killer ambled into the firm's reception area, his face obscured by his ball cap, face mask, and sunglasses. But those features connected him to the other crime scenes, as did the red windbreaker.

He stood by the door, in the morning sunshine, not moving for a moment. Kaliope Hernandez addresses him.

A few moments later, he walked toward her desk.

"You don't need to watch this next part, Ms. Stafford." Davis glared at Carly. "Why don't we pause the recording for a second, Detective?"

Carly stopped the playback, her eyes focused on the intruder.

What am I really seeing in this video?

She started the recording over.

The man walked into the reception area and stopped.

He's acting like... like he's not sure why he's there. He's nervous.

The comments from Kaliope's co-workers flooded through Carly's mind.

"I heard him say he had a message to deliver to Tanny Stafford. Then... he shot Kali."

"I was right there when he started firing. It was like it was all happening in slow motion."

The software on the law clerk's desktop computer showed that Kaliope Hernandez had opened a window to make an appointment, but not a new client tab.

He must have said he was an existing client, then.

Carly peered at Tanny Stafford.

Why aren't you being more helpful? Why would you view helping me as somehow not beneficial to you?

What are you hiding, counselor?

Lieutenant Davis cleared his throat. "Ms. Stafford, is all this too..." He stood, buttoning his suitcoat. "Would you like some coffee, perhaps?"

"Tea, please." Stafford slowly lifted her eyes to him. "If you have it."

"Yes, absolutely." He held his hand out. "Please, come with me. We can watch the video again when you're ready."

Carly bit her tongue.

Was she not ready? What did she think she was coming down here for?

FOURTH ESTATE

As the shapely lawyer rose gracefully from her chair and sashayed toward the break room—the lieutenant practically falling all over himself along the way—Carly turned back to her work and restarted the video.

Deshawn leaned over from his desk. "That was something to see."

"What was?" Carly scowled. "The video, or the lieutenant drooling all over Tanny Stafford?"

"Both." He chuckled, scooting his chair closer. "She's become a big campaign donor of late. Davis is always trying to get in good with the moneyed class." He folded his arms and rested them on the edge of the desk. "What did you see here? I've watched the recording a dozen times."

"I have, too." Carly sighed. "But I'm trying to clear my head and watch it like I'm seeing it for the first time. It's been a few hours, but I thought I saw something."

"Like what?"

"I'm not sure." She glanced toward the break room. "The lieutenant broke my train of thought."

Pulling a strand of hair between her fingers, Carly leaned away from the screen. The man in the windbreaker lumbered toward Kaliope Hernandez and the reception desk.

"There." Carly stopped the playback. "Look at this interaction, before he really engages with her. What's wrong there?"

"His movements," Deshawn said. "It's an awkward encounter. In a room with someone and not talking. It's like he was in an elevator."

"I think he walks funny." Carly pointed to the screen, her fingertip landing on the man's upper body. "And look at those legs. They're too skinny for that body." She looked at the sergeant. "It's like in high school, when I used to help my dad dress up as Santa for the neighborhood Christmas party. He'd stuff a pillow under the Santa coat, but he never stuffed the legs."

"So..." Deshawn stroked his chin. "This isn't real. I mean... it's a disguise."

"Right." Carly nodded. "It's meant to throw us off the trail. We've been looking for a fat guy with skinny legs. We should have been looking for a more normal-looking guy. Maybe even a skinny guy. That's why Tanny didn't know who it was."

"That was certainly part of my rationale, Detective."

Tanny Stafford stood at the doorway to the break room, gazing at the man in the video.

Carly swallowed hard, putting her hand on the mouse. "Ms. Stafford, I didn't..."

The lawyer shook her head, coming forward. "Like you said, whoever that is, they wanted me dead this morning—and probably still do."

Carly nodded, the lawyer's logic finally dawning on the detective.

"You didn't recognize the man as a client," Carly said, "so you thought his presence at your office might be random. Now that you realize you don't know anyone like that, with a large upper body and skinny legs—and now that you understand it's a disguise you've been watching all day—it's occurring to you that this killer could be anyone.

FOURTH ESTATE

Glad to see you're finally coming around. But most people in your situation would be scared. You aren't. So, I think you're still holding something back."

"Detective..." The lieutenant cleared his throat. "There's no call for..."

"What game are we playing here ma'am?" Carly narrowed her eyes. "A man comes to your office this morning to murder you, and you barely react. And then you're indifferent to the people trying to help you."

Davis stepped forward. "I'm sorry, Ms. Stafford."

The lawyer held her hand up to Davis, silencing him as she moved toward Carly. "Detective, I'm a criminal defense attorney, mostly for drug dealers. That means all day, every day, I'm surrounded by people that your side has accused—people who may have killed someone when a deal went bad. People who enforce their territory through physical violence. And my job is to pick apart what the police did, where they made their mistakes, exposing their biases—and occasionally, their incompetence. I put police officers on the stand and tear them to shreds. That doesn't exactly make me the type to flinch at a video—and it certainly doesn't foster a cordial relationship with you or your responding officers. So when it came time to give a statement, you might imagine the Tampa PD seemed less than thrilled to be talking to me—and I was equally perturbed to be talking to them."

"I understand your job, and I understand mine." Carly got up from the desk. "But we're both after the same thing—justice. Right? So, any differences we might have, any past squabbles or discomfort—all that needs to be set aside..." Carly raised her voice, pointing to the computer screen, where the man in the red windbreaker stood frozen, his gun pointed at Kali Hernandez "...before that unhinged maniac decides to come back for you and finish the job he started this morning!"

The lawyer gasped.

"All right." Davis put his hands up. "That's enough." He scowled at Carly. "That was completely uncalled for, Detective. You will apologize to Ms. Stafford at once."

"No, she's right." Stafford nodded absently, stepping behind her chair. "Maybe I've been acting... foolish." She put her hands on the backrest, her gaze drifting to the image on the computer screen. "If someone does want to kill me... I should help you make sure it doesn't happen."

CHAPTER 28

"IT'S... A TENSE TIME." LIEUTENANT DAVIS TUGGED AT HIS COLLAR. "...for everyone involved." He glanced toward his office. "Uh, Ms. Stafford, why don't we conduct the rest of your interview somewhere more private? Detective Sanderson has a lot on her plate." He looked at Deshawn. "Sergeant Marshall, would you be so kind as to join us?"

"Of course, Lieutenant," Deshawn said. "Let me get a notepad and I'll be right there."

As Lieutenant Davis ushered his guest away, Carly sat down and grabbed her mouse, scowling at her computer.

Deshawn leaned over, whispering. "Try to remember this is still an interview for you."

"Yeah, that's what I keep thinking—after the fact." She sighed. "I'm probably already toast."

The sergeant picked up a notepad from his desk. "Davis isn't the only one on the committee. Solving this case will go a long way with the higher ups. Focus on what's important—and do me a favor."

Carly pulled her attention from the computer and peered up at him.

"Anything you wanted to ask that attorney…" He held up his phone. "Just text it to me. I'll ask it for you."

Carly leaned over and hugged her friend. "Do a better job of it than I just did."

Deshawn patted her on the back. "I'll do it the way you always do things as a detective around here, and the way you'll do things as a sergeant—top notch." He gave her shoulder a final pat and turned to the hallway, disappearing into Lieutenant Davis' office.

Carly returned her focus to her case, pulling up the videos from NewsAction and INN, as well as the video received from the drycleaner, to study each one again.

The noises of the busy police station faded away as she reviewed each recording in depth, and each participant in it. Years of police work had taught her that witnesses have an overall, initial reaction to what they see during an event—but they also have multiple, smaller reactions to it as well. Civilians can become confused when asked to recall details of what happened, opting to focus on the big picture to try to get it right. But in a situation where things are moving fast, like a murder, people can misconstrue the order that things happened in. As information in a video gets reviewed over and over, minor details can fade for a witness, while other details can become more prominent—and draw their focus away from aspects that might still be relevant.

Carly's goal as a detective was always to come in afterward and attempt to see all of the information with fresh eyes. A dozen separate incidents might happen during a short video of a crime, but each happened for a reason—action and reaction. The killer does something over here; the victim reacts over there. Why? What went through the victim's mind when the killer did what he did? The answer sometimes proved to be pertinent.

So, even if she had already watched a video half a dozen times, Carly tried to pause and refresh her mindset, viewing it the seventh time as if it were new to her, and attempting to notice and react to each of the recording's many details as if she were seeing them all for the first time. She tried to let all the initial reactions to those details come back again, and she took conscious note of them, as many as she could, because they happened for a reason.

Carly leaned close to the screen again as the killer entered the Stafford-Love reception area and stared at Kaliope Hernandez.

In this recording, the killer moves slowly. Why?

It's a small office, and they've been at the same location for the firm's entire life. If he's actually a client, then he's been there before. There are only a few rooms, so he'd know his way around. Why hesitate?

Why stand there wasting time in the lobby when each passing second increases the chance of you being seen and remembered—which will end up getting you caught?

Why would anyone risk that?

She put her elbow on the desk and rested her chin in her hand. Each recorded second in the video yielded its own potentially vital bits of information.

You had a reason. What was it?

Did you want to be seen? You want your disguise to send us somewhere other than to where you are. That's going to happen anyway, because it's all on video. You knew that.

You've been there before, so did you know the best camera image of you would be in the middle of the room? But you stood by the door. So you wanted to be seen broadly but not with too many specifics.

You wanted to be seen, but you only wanted to be seen in a certain way.

She nodded, her eyes on the screen.

That's smart.

She scribbled a note on her notepad.

We have a smart killer.

But then, why did you hesitate again? What was that about?

And why didn't you speak more? Because you were faking the voice. It was obvious to everyone who heard it, so you kept it to a minimum. That was smart, too. So you're definitely a smart guy.

Okay, then why did you hesitate so many times in that reception area? That wasn't smart.

Not because you were showing off for the camera. You knew we had your likeness because you knew there were security cameras. Your first delay gave us the images of you that we needed. But you got in front of Kaliope Hernandez… and then you waited.

Why would a smart person drag things out like that?

"Detective Sanderson?" A uniformed officer approached Carly. "Interdepartmental Relations asked me to bring you this, ma'am." He held up a pink sheet of paper. "The St. Petersburg PD called. A little while ago, a retired judge, Frederico Pallindas, was gunned down on the Vinoy golf course. The description of the killer matches your guy—red windbreaker, baseball cap, the works."

Carly sat upright. "The fourth victim. Was there any other connection? Did Kaliope Hernandez clerk for him or something?" She took the paper from the officer, reading over it as fast as she could.

"Nothing that we know of yet, ma'am." The officer hooked his thumbs into his belt. "The witnesses say Pallindas was on the practice green, and the killer drove up in a golf cart and said something—maybe asked the judge a question, nobody's sure. When the judge turned around to answer, the killer blasted him half a dozen times at almost point-blank range, then took off. The first shot drops the judge, then the killer leans out of the cart and empties the gun into his chest. A couple of other players ran over and tried to chase him, but the killer had too much of a head start. He drove away and disappeared into the back woods. According to one witness statement, the killer then ditched the golf cart and drove away in a white SUV that was parked on a service road on the far side of the woods. That's about all they can tell us."

Carly put her hand to her head, reading the report. "No license plate number? Nobody overheard what he said?"

The officer shrugged. "I guess if somebody starts shooting on a golf course, you dive into a sand trap and don't stick your head up again until after the smoke clears." He looked at the pink paper. "Their report was sparse on details. We'll keep digging."

"Well, their report gave us one important detail." She read from the paper. "According to this, 'The coroner states that all of the killer's shots were in the approximate area of the judge's heart.' This freaking guy is making a heck of a statement." Carly shoved the report onto her desk and sat back, rubbing her eyes. "I just wish I knew what it was."

* * * * *

Sergeant Marshall entered the lieutenant's office and closed the door behind him, sliding into the seat next to Tanny Stafford. Lieutenant Davis leaned back in his chair and folded his hands across his abdomen. Officer Mellish stood off to the side, just behind the lawyer and the sergeant, scrolling on his phone.

"Sergeant," Davis said, "if you'd proceed with Ms. Stafford's interview, please."

Nodding, Deshawn scooted forward in his chair, holding his notepad out, his pencil ready. "Ma'am, what arrangements have you made at your law office since this morning's unfortunate incident?"

Stafford leaned forward and set her purse on the lieutenant's desk. "Well, we were closed today, obviously, and we'll be closed tomorrow."

"Mm-hmm," Deshawn said. "You have a schedule, though. Appointments with clients, meetings…"

"Yes. My law partner Francie—uh, that's Francine Love—and our associate Benjamin Freed called all of today's appointments and rescheduled them. Tomorrow's, too. And we notified the courts to have our schedules pushed back."

"Court…" Deshawn glanced up at her, then turned to the Lieutenant. "Court appearances would be public information."

The attorney nodded. "Yes, that's right."

Davis sat forward in his chair. "Ms. Stafford, it's possible the killer could have checked the dockets to see if you'd be in court this morning."

"And if a criminal defense attorney isn't in court," Deshawn said, "it's a fair assumption that you're in your office."

"Well, yes…" She shrugged. "But I might also be doing an off-site deposition in a hotel room somewhere, or filing a motion downtown with the clerk of courts, or maybe even inspecting the crime scene where one of my clients was alleged to have partaken in some sort of criminal activity."

"Yes, ma'am." Deshawn made a note on his pad. "You'd know those types of things, of course. So would another lawyer, and law clerks… But a typical person off the street wouldn't know about those kinds of activities. That narrows the field of possible suspects. Now, you weren't at the firm when the killer entered."

"That's right," Stafford said. "I was away shooting a video."

* * * * *

Frowning, Carly clicked the mouse and moved from the recording of Kaliope Hernandez to the security footage from the drycleaner. There, the killer moved into the camera's view from the white Mercedes SUV and advanced quickly to the news agency door.

Carly gasped.

Holding her breath, she backed up the video a few seconds and watched it a second time. Again, the killer moved quickly to the news agency door.

You aren't limping.

She slammed her hand down on the desk. "You aren't limping!"

A few members of the admin staff looked up from their work, glaring at her. Carly grimaced, waving at them as she returned to her work.

She moved the mouse around, her heart racing.

What else is different? Keep telling me things, killer man. Keep it up, smart guy. You aren't as smart as you think you are—and you aren't fat, like you want us to think. You don't limp. What else? Keep up the charade, you...

She stopped the drycleaner video again and backed it up, letting it play at regular speed.

"You aren't hesitating," she said. "Not outside. Out there, you're moving fast. You only hesitate when you're inside."

Did you do that at every murder scene you went to?

FOURTH ESTATE

Pulse pounding, Carly clutched the mouse and opened the folder of NewsAction videos, clicking each one as fast as she could.

The confrontation in the conference room didn't have much movement once the killer was present. In the footage from the security video viewing the hallway outside the NewsAction conference room, the killer walked stiffly, like he had a limp.

Carly sat back in her chair.

What other camera footage do we have from NewsAction?

She scanned the video files. "NewsAction - Sidewalk Camera In Front of Office."

In it, the killer showed no limp. In the video from the hallway, the killer pushed past a male employee in a flowered shirt, and walked toward the conference room—again, with no limp.

Carly shook her head, writing on the pad.

You turn that limp on and off, don't you?

Because it's not a real limp. You're doing it for the cameras. For us.

"You're faking it, you little snake." Carly smiled, whispering to the killer on the computer screen. "You fraud. You are trying to put us onto a client of Tanny Stafford's who is overweight and has a limp. In that disguise, you might even be a woman. That would explain the faked deep voice."

But then why did Tanny deny having any such client? Your ruse doesn't work if there's no client to match it to.

Carly grabbed her phone and texted the question to Deshawn, then set it down and returned to the videos.

What else?

* * * * *

Deshawn's phone buzzed in his pocket. He reached for it, keeping his eyes on Tanny Stafford. "When did you first learn about the video shoot, ma'am?"

"Oh, Parnell called last night." Stafford tilted her nose up and peered at the sergeant's notepad as he wrote. "That's Parnell Leicester. He's a videographer. He does all my commercials and video shoots." She glanced at lieutenant Davis. "He said he had a last-minute cancellation and asked if I'd be available to go in the morning. He's very busy, so I said yes."

Deshawn read Carly's text. He shifted in his chair and held up his pad as if the question had been written there. "Now, ma'am, in your initial statement to our officers, you said that you didn't have any client that resembled the man in the video—Kaliope Hernandez's killer. Is that right? And our officer says you didn't act particularly upset when you found out about your high school friend's death."

"Sergeant, understand my position." The lawyer's face was rigid. "First, I don't have a client that resembles the man in the video. But as I said before, I'm an attorney with a rough clientele. I have to be able to partition my emotions or I can't do my job. Every day, I see horrendous images that my clients are accused of. To be effective for my clients, I need to be able to restrain myself from the reaction a typical person might have. I can feel it, but I can't show it. That's what I did when your officer informed me about Kali. In retrospect, it was a mistake, because it sent the wrong message, but I assure you I am quite human. I cried about Kali. I just didn't do it publicly. The same goes for my reaction to learning that someone attempted to kill me this morning. Francie will tell you how many times I threw up, if you'd like—because I did, quite a few times. That's not easy news to digest."

"No ma'am," Deshawn said. "I know it's not."

"Second, and maybe more importantly… as a criminal defense lawyer, I can't be seen as throwing my clients to the police after losing for them in court. It's bad for business. I assumed the murder of my law clerk was a mistake. I wanted to believe I represented people who were not the kind to come try to kill me afterward. I was in a bit of denial about the business I'm in—until this morning, anyway. I suppose I've allowed myself to be in denial overall, really, about what I do. Defending our worst criminals… It's a job that has to be done if the American system is going to work, but… it leaves scars."

The room fell silent, the beautiful attorney staring down at her hands, and the three law enforcement men around her apparently having no words for the realization she had just come to.

"Let's…" Deshawn lifted his notepad again. "Let's move back to our earlier discussion, if you're up to it, ma'am." He peered at Stafford. "The last-minute video shoot, in the morning—does your videographer do that often? Call suddenly with cancellations?"

"Occasionally." She took a long slow breath. "Not often—and not for mornings, usually. Parnell prefers to record me in the evening. He says the light softens the skin tones. And as I said, he's very busy, so I took the opportunity."

Deshawn made another note on the pad. "Ever go for a drink afterward?"

"Parnell is a friend, Sergeant." Stafford gave an icy look to the lieutenant. "Is this particular line of questioning absolutely necessary?"

Davis sat up, his mouth dropping.

"Ma'am..." Deshawn lowered his hands to his lap. "Someone planned on killing you today. We need to establish the nature of your relationships." He softened his tone. "I know some of these questions are awkward. It's not meant to embarrass you."

Stafford nodded, looking down. "Sometimes, a drink. Sometimes dinner." She swallowed hard, her eyes gazing toward the floor. "That's not public knowledge. Parnell and I are known as friends, but... My husband doesn't care for Parnell."

"Yes, ma'am. And... have you ever been with Mr. Leicester for anything other than a drink or a dinner?"

She bristled. "Is this relevant?"

"It might be."

Tanny moved her gaze to the ceiling, clasping her hands in front of her. "I suppose what you're getting at is, are Parnell and I... have we been... intimate?" She squeezed her eyes shut.

"We've been having an affair for just over two years. We meet a few times a week, either at his apartment on Bayshore Boulevard or sometimes in a hotel downtown."

Deshawn nodded. "What about business functions, or social gatherings? Would you and Mr. Leicester, say… intentionally try to run into each other at parties thrown by Tampa socialites and members of the political class? Things like that?"

The lawyer sighed. "Yes. To meet as often as we did, we scheduled ourselves to run into each other quite a lot. I suppose in hindsight we weren't very creative, Sergeant."

"Ma'am, you understand, this information might be vital to the investigation. It can widen or narrow the pool of people with a motive. Husband. Videographer. Law partner."

"Law partner?" Stafford's eyes widened. "Francie would never—"

"Ma'am, by any chance…" Deshawn put his hand to his chin. "…the hotel rooms that you and Mr. Leicester used for your occasional downtown meet-ups—did you ever charge any of those to your law firm as a business expense? List them as needed for a deposition—things like that?"

Her cheeks reddening, Tanny Stafford's voice fell to a whisper. "Yes."

"Then the business partner has a motive," Deshawn said. "And so does the videographer's wife."

Massaging one hand with the other, Stafford shook her head, her smooth skin and high cheek bones glowing a bright shade of crimson. "Parnell Leicester isn't married."

"Then that's one less suspect." The sergeant flipped his notepad shut. "Call me if you think of more."

Stafford stood up, reaching for her purse.

"And ma'am..." Deshawn rose from his chair. "I'd like the video footage you and Mr. Leicester took today. Could you request that from him, and have them sent to me as soon as possible?"

The crimson in the lawyer's cheeks deepened. "We... didn't record the commercial, Sergeant. When we got to the location this morning, it was already getting unseasonably warm. We tried a few shots, but I was perspiring, so we ended the shoot early and... went to his apartment."

"Yes, ma'am." Deshawn cleared his throat. "Still, any videos that you and Mr. Leicester made this morning could be helpful to the investigation. I can get a warrant for them, but if you'd turn them over voluntarily, it'd be much faster. I think you'd agree, that's better for everyone."

Stafford righted herself, clutching her handbag to her waist. "Sergeant, I hope you can understand me being specific here. I am a lawyer, after all." Her tone was terse and forthright, delivered without passion, as if she were standing in a court room discussing the order in which to introduce evidence. "Parnell and I shot some brief footage in a field near the airport. It turned out to be unusable. We also... made a number of recordings at his apartment afterward—one in particular that is of an extremely private nature, with his assistant Jasmina Petrov. No one other than the three consenting adults in that video need to see it." She looked at the lieutenant, then to Deshawn. "Other than that one, I will be happy to provide the recordings from the shoot by the airport and the innocuous ones we made at the apartment. Nothing more. Will that be acceptable, Sergeant?"

"Yes, yes. Of course." Deshawn waved a hand. "That will be fine for now, ma'am."

The flesh tones eased their way back to the lawyer's face. "Thank you for understanding."

"After the, uh… meeting, did the three of you leave together?"

"Parnell had another appointment, so he and Jasmina left about an hour before I did. I took a shower and slept in for a while. Video shoots can take several hours, so I knew I wouldn't be missed at work, and I needed a rest. Is there anything else?"

Deshawn reached into his pocket for a business card.

No wonder you were less than forthcoming when you gave your initial statement this morning.

"I'll need the contact information for the assistant." He pressed his card into her hand. "So we can verify your whereabouts. Mr. Leicester can provide the details of the second appointment, for us to follow up on. That should establish everyone as being where you say they were this morning."

"Then, good day, gentleman." She stepped toward the exit, chin held high.

Mellish lowered his phone and stepped aside, opening the door for her. Tanny Stafford walked out of the lieutenant's office and strutted down the hallway toward the elevators, leaving the three men blushing in her wake.

CHAPTER 29

AT THE SERGEANTS' DESK, CARLY LEANED closer to the computer, brushing her hair across her lips. "Come on, you fraud. Tell me something else."

The video from INN showed the same thing—the killer walking with a limp and hesitating once inside the building.

She studied the interaction between the people on the screen.

Sergio was right. The reporter doesn't act like she knows who the guy is. Neither does Miranda Suarez.

Carly clicked on the Stafford-Love video again and played it from the beginning, but paused it after only a few seconds.

It's extra creepy, knowing he's a killer and then seeing him walk in and then just stand there and stare at Kaliope Hernandez. Maybe he was trying to creep her out.

Carly moved her fingers back and forth, brushing the strand of hair across her lips.

No... I'm sure the killer creeped her out, but only because he hesitated and didn't respond to her. He's focused on something else—the murder he's about to commit.

So why stand around? You've planned this all out. You know the office because you've been there before. Why would you stand around in the reception area like that?

Because... you're afraid to do it. You've never killed before.

She replayed the footage again, eyeing his demeanor.

You aren't full of rage. Are you scared? You're nervous when you enter the Stafford-Love office, aren't you?

That means this is a big deal to you because you know it's wrong.

Did you build this big moment up, but now that it's go time, you almost can't go through with it? Is that why you're hesitating? There's no going back after murder. You know that, don't you?

She exhaled, staring at the screen.

Then you shoot Kaliope Hernandez until the gun is empty. So what was that?

And why did you hesitate again later, at your next murder scene?

She opened the Stafford-Love video again. The law firm's clerk interacted with the man in front of her.

FOURTH ESTATE

She engages, at first. She's doing her job. Your odd behavior makes her change how she interacts. Her back stiffens. She leans away from you. It's a give and take, an action-reaction thing happening.

But now we know you're acting. The costume, the limp—that's for the cameras.

When you decided you were going to kill her, the interaction changes. You changed. She doesn't know she's going to die, but you do—and you acted differently.

What did you do?

Carly moved her mouse over the time bar at the bottom of the video, backing the recording up a few seconds and pausing as the killer hesitated the second time.

You see her face, don't you? Kaliope's face. You see it. That's why you're hesitating.

You can see the fear on your victim's face, and you intentionally slowed down. You dragged out that moment.

Carly exhaled hard, gritting her teeth as she stared at the killer on the screen. "You hesitated the first time out of fear, but you hesitated the second time because you saw the reaction it got—and you liked it, didn't you?"

You enjoyed the look on Kaliope Hernandez's face, so you used that tactic again in the NewsAction conference room because it was powerful. You discovered a new feeling today. That's why you forced the reporter to record you at Florida Real Time, your next planned murder scene. You like the cameras and the attention they brought, but you got an unexpected rush from all those faces being so scared of you.

Her phone rang—Sergio. She grabbed it and put it to her ear. "Hey."

"Hey, yourself," he said. "What new stuff do you have for me?"

"Too much and not enough. I'm working on a theory." Carly frowned. "But why are you asking me what I have for you? I thought you were supposed to be feeding me stuff from the crime scene."

He groaned. "I think we got most of what we were gonna get out of this site in the first few hours. What's your theory?"

"Well, there's more than one. Let me ask you something…" She glanced at her notes. "I feel like I've been watching these recordings for days, okay? But something just came to me. I think this killer is new to murder. And until he killed Kaliope Hernandez, he didn't know how much he enjoyed killing. He got a rush from watching her be scared in front of him."

"Dude." Sergio said. "If he's enjoying this, it makes him a lot more dangerous."

Carly nodded. "Secondly, the killer unloaded his gun into Hernandez and the others. That doesn't add up, to me. In the first one, a crime of passion, sure—but he goes on to do it again at NewsAction and again at INN, and that's more than an hour later. By then, the out-of-control passion part would be gone, I'd hope, but he unloads his gun into Jasper Menendez-Holswain and then does the same thing to Miranda Suarez. So I think he's making a statement each time."

"Sure. One bullet gives you the murder you want. Emptying the gun announces it much louder."

Carly pursed her lips, pressing the phone to her ear. "He shoots the news people in the mouth… Like, the news people talked too much, so to speak—they did stories about him that he didn't like."

"Another statement," Sergio said. "It's showmanship, in a grotesque way."

"Well… I'm also thinking the guy in the video is disguised to look like someone else. Those news stories were about the guy we are supposed to think this is."

"Huh. Okay…"

She got up from the desk. "It's a costume, like a shell—no, a setup—for a shell man." Pacing back and forth in the sergeant's area, Carly waved her hand. "In reality, whoever we're supposed to believe we're watching, that guy might not even be angry."

"Ehhh, I disagree with you there. If it's a shell guy, then the shell has to be angry when we get to him—otherwise, the stagecraft doesn't sell." Sergio's voice broke up as static came over the line. "Think about it. When we track down the shell guy, we have to believe he's angry enough to kill all of these people. If it's really a setup, it doesn't work without that."

"So, the real killer already figured that part out." She sighed, putting her hand to her brow. "Where does this end? Is he playing us? What does he want?"

"Good question." Sergio huffed. "He shot the law clerk in the forehead, right? What does that tell you?"

Carly stared down at her notes. "Hernandez was a proxy for Tanny Stafford, right? If the killer isn't playing a second game with us, then it's another statement. He shot the clerk as a stand-in for the lawyer, and he shot her... in her brain?"

"Because he didn't like what she thought?"

"Because in his opinion, she wasn't smart enough." Carly snapped her fingers. "That's it! I bet she lost his case. Then, if it ties in with the other two murders, the case she lost made the news." Yanking the chair from the desk, Carly dropped down into her seat. She grabbed the mouse and opened a search engine. "What client of hers was in the news?"

"She's a criminal defense lawyer who represents a lot of drug dealers. All of her clients are in the news at some point."

"Okay," Carly said. "Then we need to cross reference her client list with the biggest stories that INN and NewsAction did. We can leave out the Hollywood celebrities and the politicians. This guy's local but he's probably only famous for the crime Tanny Stafford represented him for."

"A criminal, average height, unknown weight, unknown crime." Sergio snorted. "That won't be too many people."

"He drives a white Mercedes." Carly shoved the mouse aside and flipped through her notepad, searching for an empty page. "That should narrow it down a little."

"Yeah, no drug dealers drive those."

FOURTH ESTATE

Up the hall, Mellish burst out of Lieutenant Davis' office and rushed toward her. "Are you watching this?"

"What?" Carly looked up from the computer. "What are you talking about?"

"We have our guy." Mellish held up his phone. "Jamaal Ainer is livestreaming. He says he knows who the killer is and will reveal the identity live at nine P.M."

DAN ALATORRE

CHAPTER 30

Carly set her phone down and got the internet link from Mellish for Jamaal Ainer's FRT livestream event, entering it into the computer. As the Tampa PD screen went gray, a spinning hourglass appeared. Frowning, she sent the link to her partner and hit the speakerphone button. "I don't have a visual yet, Sergio. It's still buffering."

"Wow," he said. "A lot of people must be trying to watch."

Shaking his head, Mellish stared at his phone. "Almost a hundred thousand, and climbing fast—and it's barely started. Ainer is telling everyone to leave town."

Carly sighed. "Terrific."

The Florida Real Time owner-editor came into view on Carly's computer, holding a microphone to his face as he strolled back and forth in front of the camera and several bright lights. He dressed in a gray suit with a white shirt opened almost to his navel, wearing a thick gold chain around his neck with the word "Jamaal" on it in half-inch high letters. The FRT headquarters was visible in the background, as it was before, but now a small row of bleachers had been erected, along with several wooden stools in front of them—as well as microphone stands.

"Sergio." Carly looked at her phone. "Are you connected yet?"

"Yeah," he said. "And I don't like what I'm seeing."

Jamaal strutted toward the camera, his sparkly necklace bouncing around his throat and his voice nearly at a shout. "Again, I say, if you have had any interaction with this man, I suggest you leave Tampa. Maybe even leave Florida. It's only a matter of time before he strikes again. He came for me, but I was lucky. You might not be."

Grimacing, Carly peered at Mellish. "Has he mentioned the killer's name yet?"

The officer shook his head. "No, not yet. He keeps saying he'll announce it at nine P.M."

"And in between now and then," Sergio said, "he'll work the whole city up into a panic. Has this clown gone insane? What does he think he's doing?"

Carly put a hand to her forehead. "He's getting ratings, that's what."

The viewer count at the bottom of the livestream rolled past 200,000 and didn't slow down. Onscreen, Jamaal pointed to the FRT newsroom behind him. "Earlier today, twenty members of my staff were held hostage by an armed maniac—and we now believe we know who it is. At nine P.M. this evening, only on Florida Real Time News, I'm going to name the individual responsible for today's heinous murders, and I will reach out to that individual to see if he will talk to us. It is my belief that, at nine P.M., the Tampa killer will explain why he's doing this, but more importantly, maybe we can help this troubled soul and end the carnage our police seem unable to stop. Watch our livestream at nine P.M. tonight. You're not gonna want to miss it. But right now, a special event."

Ainer walked toward the stools. Several of his employees had taken seats there and were adjusting their microphones. Behind them, other employees ushered people into the bleachers.

* * * * *

In his parked car, Sergio turned to Avarie. "I can't believe what I'm seeing. Who does things like that?"

His companion sighed, looking away. "The news media does—the vaunted Fourth Estate. Don't worry about humanity, just get the clicks."

On screen, Jamaal Ainer pointed to the empty stools on his makeshift stage. "Now, a special treat. In just a few minutes, we'll be speaking with some of the family members who have been tragically affected by the mad killer running loose on our streets. The young son and teenage daughter of victim Miranda Suarez will be here. Lia Lenthrow, the girlfriend of victim Jasper Menendez-Holswain will be here. And Joe Hernandez, the husband of the murderer's first victim, Kaliope Hernandez. They'll all be joining us right here, so don't go anywhere."

The camera panned away, showing a young woman leading the victims' friends and relatives out to the chairs. Beyond them, a bodybuilder stood in a black t-shirt with the word "Security" on it, in front of a trailer with a star on the door and the name Jamaal Ainer.

Avarie shook her head. "This guy sure isn't doing anybody any favors. Those family members shouldn't be exploited like that."

Clenching his jaw, Sergio shoved the phone into his cupholder. "The faster we find the killer, the faster this Hollywood wannabe's sideshow ends."

* * * * *

Deshawn approached Carly's desk, his phone in his hand. It pinged with an incoming text from Tanny Stafford. *"Parnell records everything digitally. He is sending the videos to you now, with a simultaneous copy to me, in a group text. I will verify the contents for you as they come in."*

Nodding, the sergeant texted a reply. *"That will be fine for now. Thank you."*

Carly glanced at him. "What have you got?"

"Nothing solid yet," Deshawn said. "Stafford and her videographer were having an affair. They were at his place around the time of the first murder. Then, he took off and she took a shower and decided to sleep in for a while. There was a third party present, so their stories should check out, but I asked for the videos he shot today, just in case. He's sending those now. I'll keep you posted on anything

FOURTH ESTATE

I find." He glanced at Carly's computer. "What's the plan for this Ainer jerk?"

Sergio's voice came over the speakerphone. "Dude, could this circus clown possibly have the right information?"

She looked at the computer screen. "I don't know, but someone from Tampa PD needs to talk to him—now." Carly peered up at the sergeant. "And I don't mean a low-level uniformed officer, either. This guy's latest stunt has the potential to send this case out of control."

Deshawn looked at Carly and nodded. "Go."

"Sergio." Carly jumped up from her chair. "I'm gonna go talk to Ainer in person."

"I'll meet you there," he said.

As she rushed from the desk, she called out to Deshawn over her shoulder. "Can you press Lieutenant Davis again on using the media? We could really use their help right now. They might be able to swing things back our way."

The lieutenant stepped out of his office, blocking her path. "That's hardly necessary, Detective. As you say, the media is fully aware of this story. It's all over the internet and the local TV station, too."

Carly shook her head. "Sir, if we get on TV, maybe with a hot line number, we could probably stem the tide of what's surely going to be an uproar."

"Lieutenant." Mellish held his phone up. "Jamaal Ainer has a hot line for tips that goes straight to Florida Real Time News. It's on the screen now. He says he'll be taking calls."

The lieutenant looked at Carly. "See? Handled." He turned back to his office.

Pursing her lips, Carly put her hands on her hips. "It might be getting handled, it might not be, but it's definitely not being run through Tampa PD." She looked down, shaking her head as she took a breath. "Lieutenant, the general public isn't necessarily going to call useful information to a number on a livestream event. If we get our own number out there, they might."

Deshawn nodded. "At least they'll be calling us and not the ringleader of a media circus."

Lieutenant Davis walked back to his office doorway. "We are getting calls downstairs right now, Detective. I have people working through them and sorting them."

Carly stepped back, her jaw dropping. "I'm the lead on this. Why was I not informed?"

"Believe it or not," Davis growled, "you aren't the top person in this department. It took us a little while to get the operation up and running. You've done call-center work before. It doesn't happen in a flash. The killer's image has been everywhere all day, and the public is calling us."

She peered down the hall toward the admin staff. Each desk was filled with an officer answering call after call. Carly turned her attention back to the lieutenant. "Have any of the people calling in said they know who the killer is?"

"I'm sure we've gotten a hundred of those by now." He snorted. "Who knows how many of them are legitimate. People will call in and swear their trash man is the killer."

FOURTH ESTATE

"But we chase those down, right? And then we find out who the real bad guy is."

"With what staff, Detective?" Davis threw his hands out at his sides. "We're spread thin as it is!"

"So…" She rubbed her chin, turning back toward the administrative staff. "We've got people right now saying they know who this person is, and nobody's telling me."

"Okay, hold on, Detective." Frowning, Davis went to his desk and picked up a printout. "Here it is. Here's the data." He rifled through the pages. "This one says it's the mayor. This one says it's somebody named Terrence Big Time. The next one says it's their neighbor, a doctor named Zumendi." He lowered the report, glaring at her. "See? There's no basis to move forward here. Go see your circus ringleader and let us focus on sorting the leads."

"Yes, sir." Heat rose to Carly's cheeks. "Lieutenant, can we at least have somebody from admin request a warrant to track every phone number that our officers log into the database for this case?"

Davis looked at her out of the corner of his eye. "We could, but…"

"Then let's do it," Carly said. "There won't be too many, and we're going to need one of them eventually. By the time we know which number we need, we won't have the luxury of spending hours or days getting the warrant to track it." She looked into his eyes. "Doing it now might seem a little excessive, but it could save another life—and get the Department back on the public's good side for your forward thinking, sir."

A hint of a smile tugged at the corners of the lieutenant's mouth. "Good call. I'll see to it."

Rushing toward the elevators, Carly yanked open her purse and checked for her car keys.

"Carly." Deshawn said. "Keep an eye on the clock."

"What? Why?" She pressed the elevator call button and turned around.

"Don't you have a dinner to get to?" the sergeant asked.

"Dinner?" Carly furrowed her brow. "When I'm knee deep in—oh, crap."

She put a hand to her forehead.

Kyle.

"I'll, uh…" Carly dug into her purse and pulled out her keys. "I'll—I'll stop and talk to Jamaal Ainer on the way to the restaurant. It won't take very long."

Deshawn shook his head. "At least text your dinner appointment to let him know you're not coming."

"No, no. I'll be there." She squeezed her eyes shut and waved her hands. Behind her, the elevator pinged. "I just have to… It'll be fine. The meeting with Ainer won't take long. I'll make dinner."

Deshawn rolled his eyes.

"I can make it." Carly said, turning and stepping into the elevator. As she pressed the button for the lobby, she glanced at Deshawn.

He shook his head again.

As the steel doors slid across the elevator's entry, Carly leaned over and shouted through the shrinking gap. "I can!"

FOURTH ESTATE

* * * * *

Deshawn's phone pinged with an incoming text from an unknown number, grouped with the number of Tanny Stafford.

"Sergeant, here are today's videos. Parnell Leicester Photography."

A moment later, the phone pinged again with the first of the large files.

* * * * *

As Sergio swung his car around slower-moving traffic, his phone rang in the cupholder. The name "McEnany HCSO" appeared on the screen. As he picked up the phone, Sergio glanced at Avarie. "Do me a favor. Check Kerri Milner's social media pages. See if she's posted anything in the past few hours."

Avarie nodded, tapping her phone and opening a search engine.

"Mac." Sergio put the phone on speaker and dropped it back into the cupholder. "What's the word from the Hillsborough County Sheriff's office vis-à-vis the bus station?"

"Your girl's a no-show so far," Maizey said. "How long do you want me to keep my personnel there?"

"Well…" Sergio grinned. "Unless I miss my guess, you staked the place out yourself to have an afternoon off."

"You know me so well. But the question stands. Eventually, I need to go home—alone, sadly."

Nodding, Sergio put a hand to his chin stubble. "Mac, I'd say if she's not there by about ten

P.M., she's not coming. I hate to guess wrong on this, but I know I don't have an unlimited budget with you."

"Fair enough," the corporal said. "I'll wrap at ten."

"Thanks. I owe you one."

"You owe me a dozen. Maybe one day you'll start paying them back. Dinner would be a good start. Say, at my place, later tonight? What time will you wrap up for the day? We could rekindle some old times."

Sergio picked up his phone. "Here's a counteroffer. When we take down the killer, I'll make sure you and a few of your people are front and center, sharing the spotlight with Tampa PD. How's that?"

"Not as fun as dinner would be, but I guess it'll have to do."

Chuckling, Sergio ended the call and put the phone back in the cupholder.

Avarie peered at him. "Why did you have the sheriff's office watch for Kerri Milner at the bus station? Why didn't you have one of your own people do it?"

"Well…" Sergio shrugged. "The lieutenant says we're short staffed. Besides, if Davis doesn't know about it…"

"He can't pull the person off." Avarie nodded. "You don't trust Lieutenant Davis?"

"Not as far as I could throw him." He grinned at her. "I'm still not sure I trust you."

Shaking her head, the PR rep returned her gaze to her phone. "Well, thanks for that. Between the two of us, you're the only one who's almost gotten us killed." She smiled, looking at him from the corner of her eye. "But the day's not over yet."

* * * * *

As Carly raced down the spiral concrete platforms of the Tampa PD parking garage, she shoved an earbud into her ear and called Sergio's phone.

"Hey, partner," he answered. "You're on speaker with me and the PR consultant, Avarie Fox."

Carly's tires squealed as she made the last turn and sped toward the garage exit. "How far out are you from the FRT offices?"

"Uh…" He glanced at his GPS. "Maybe five minutes, plus or minus some traffic."

"Okay." Carly pulled onto the street. "Find me when you get there. I want us to present ourselves with as much of a show of force as possible when we confront Jamaal Ainer."

Her phone beeped in her ear with another call. The screen said "Home."

"Crap." Carly winced. "Sergio, it's the boys calling. I'd better take this. Something could be wrong."

"Do it," Sergio said. "I'll see you at FRT."

She ended the call with Sergio and clicked over. "Hello?"

"Mommy!" Her youngest, the effervescent ten-year-old Isaac, was on the line.

Carly smiled as she drove her car into traffic. Isaac had outgrown the word Mommy years ago, but enjoyed using it for effect whenever Carly worked late or if Grandma picked the boys up from school.

"Hi, sweetie. What's up? Mommy's pretty busy."

I need to rush this without looking like I'm rushing it.

"I have the hic—hiccups," Isaac said, interrupting himself with a hiccup. "Ethan keeps trying to sc—scare me so they'll go away."

"I am not!" her older son shouted from somewhere in the background.

The phone rustled with static. Carly put a finger to her earbud. "Where are you? Outside?"

"Ye—yes." Isaac giggled. "Are you c—coming home soon?" He broke into a laugh, obviously unable to control his abdominal spasms. "Can I have a c—cookie? Grandma says they'll make the hic—cups go away."

Carly shook her head. Every one of her mother's home cures, from the flu to the hiccups, seemed to involve candy or some other sweet treat. "Sweetie, I can't talk long right now, but how about trying a carrot? I heard those cure hiccups."

"A carrot? I'd rather ha—have the hiccups." He giggled again.

"Okay, well... Don't play outside too late. Is Ethan still close by? Can he come over and say hi before I go?"

"He's playing basketball now. At Alejandro's house."

Carly sighed. The distance of two houses was apparently too far for Ethan to traverse to say hello to his mother.

But he'd apologize later, when she crept into his bedroom and kissed him goodnight. Then, he'd wake up and give her a hug. Ethan was smart but more sensitive—and more brooding at times, now that he was almost a teenager—than Isaac.

More like his mother.

He tried not to show how her frequent absences affected him, but she knew. She also liked his way of asking to call his father at bedtime to ask "man questions" like how to tell if a girl likes you. Secrets are hard to keep in a small household, and harder when you wear them on your pre-teen sleeve despite your best efforts.

A small lump formed in Carly's throat. "What about Grandma? Is she around?"

"She had to go to her sp—spin class. Mr. Steiner's watching us 'til she gets b—back."

"Okay." Carly frowned.

Mom didn't tell them I wasn't coming home to have dinner with them. She's hiding the dinner with Kyle from the boys.

* * * * *

Avarie shook her head as she scrolled through Kerri Milner's social media accounts. "I don't think she left town. Look at this." She held up her phone. "Several of her accounts were private, but a few were public. None of them showed anything for today. But when the FRT livestream panned the growing collection of onlookers at their event, a few familiar faces appeared in the crowd. I took a screen shot."

Sergio glanced at the phone. Kerri Milner was clearly visible in the crowd, standing next to a dark-haired young woman of roughly the same age.

"Looks like Kerri Milner to me," Sergio said. "And that's gotta be her roommate Lasya, next to her."

Avarie nodded. "I think so, too."

"She was pretending." Sergio slapped the steering wheel, grinning. "She is so smart. Well, good for her—and good for us. Maybe we can pick Kerri and Lasya up when we get to FRT. Those two know more about the murderer's identity than just about anyone else, potentially. They could be a huge help. I just wish we had a line on where the killer's going to be when Ainer calls him—if it's not a total scam, which it very likely is."

"You know…" Avarie narrowed her eyes. "The phone Kerri called you from was probably Lasya's. Should we try to call them?"

Sergio shook his head. "They won't answer. Kerri knows my number and probably told Lasya."

"True…" Avarie smiled. "But they don't know my number. And they're reporters. They're probably always getting tips from numbers they don't know."

"A tip like…"

"Like the name of the killer," Avarie said. "If I told them I could positively identify the killer to them *before* Jamaal Ainer does it at nine, they'd have a real scoop. They'd probably agree to meet with me—and you could be waiting in the bushes."

"They probably would, wouldn't they?" Sergio chuckled. "It's worth a shot."

CHAPTER 31

As Carly drove toward the FRT headquarters, she worked to end the call with her son. "Okay, sweet baby boy—I love you."

"I'm not a b—baby." Isaac's hiccups showed no sign of relenting.

Carly smiled. "You're not sweet, either."

"Yes, I am." He giggled. "You always s—say so."

"Yes, you are." Carly sighed. "I'm going to miss you guys until I get home, okay? Please tell your brother to come say hi to me. I need to get going."

"He's all the way down the street now."

She winced, an emptiness filling her insides.

He wasn't all the way down the street when I called.

"Mommy, will you be home in time to t— tuck us in?"

"I'll..." Carly scrunched up her face. She hated to disappoint her children, but she did her best not to lie to them, either. She walked the parental fine line of obfuscation to protect their young feelings, trading immediate disappointment for an apology later, and hoping it didn't add up to resentment. "I'll be home late. But I'll see you tomorrow."

"For breakfast?"

"Uh... Probably for dinner. Let me run now, okay?"

"Only *probably* for dinner? Not for sure?"

"No, for sure," Carly said. "If I can. And I might come home in the middle of the day to take a shower, or... I don't know. But I love you guys. Now, let me get going, okay?"

"O—okay."

* * * * *

Sergio parked his car as close to the FRT location as possible, which wasn't close at all. The streets were packed with cars and news vans from local TV stations, interwoven with a steady stream of curious pedestrians, all flocking toward the televised circus show happening in the parking lot across the street from the murder scene.

Avarie entered Kerri Milner's number into her phone, pressing the send button as she looked at Sergio. "Look around for a place to have the meeting."

FRT had erected tall poles with flood lights, illuminating their show a hundred yards away. Jamaal Ainer walked back and forth in front of the crowd, his voice booming over an outdoor public address system as he evoked cheers and jeers from his audience. A demand for justice got applause; a disparaging comment about police ineptitude yielded a roar of derision. Cameras were mounted everywhere, compliments of the local news personnel; people in the crowd held up their phones and sent their own version of the livestream out to their various social media platforms.

Sergio glanced around. The parking lot was surrounded on three sides by old buildings, with walkways and alleys running in between. To the south, a row of hedges separated the makeshift sideshow from a small field filled with cars.

He rubbed his chin.

"That's gonna have to work." Sergio pointed to the hedge. "It's close enough to get Kerri and Lasya to come over, but not so close that anyone from FRT will see or hear what's going on. Between the bushes and the cars in that lot, I'll have enough cover to hide in." Looking at his accomplice, he lowered his voice. "If you're standing by yourself, you shouldn't appear to be any kind of threat to two adult women, and Kerri won't see me until I step out."

Avarie nodded, peering toward the row of bushes.

"Hello?" A woman's voice came over the phone line.

"Hello." Avarie held the phone away from her ear and increased the volume. "Is this the reporter, Kerri Milner?"

Sergio leaned in close to the consultant.

"I'm… a reporter," the woman said. "Who is this?"

Looking at Avarie, Sergio shook his head and mouthed the words, "That's not Kerri."

Avarie nodded, raising the tip of the phone to her lips. "I know the name of the killer Jamaal Ainer's going to reveal at nine P.M.—and I can give you that name right now."

Down the street, Ainer made a derisive comment over the PA, sending his live audience into an uproar. A moment later, the crowd noise came over Avarie's phone.

"You have my attention," the woman said.

"Good." Avarie swallowed hard. "Now, I'll give up the name, but I'll only give it to Kerri Milner, in person."

"Sorry, I can't do that."

Her eyes widening, Avarie glanced at Sergio. He gave her a thumbs up, nodding.

"Sure, you can." The consultant's voice was firm and even. "You're a reporter, and this is the scoop of a lifetime. Jamaal Ainer is hyping the big reveal of this name all over the internet, to millions and millions of people. You can release it first and make a real name for yourself. Now, I know you and Kerri are friends…"

Sergio winced.

Avarie clutched the phone with both hands. "I… I mean, I saw you together at the FRT live event. And Kerri mentioned you in the interview she did."

Rustling came over the line, followed by a different woman's voice. "The only interview I did

FOURTH ESTATE

was with a detective, and if you're with Tampa PD, I don't want to talk to you. Goodbye."

Sergio grabbed the phone from Avarie's hands. "Kerri! It's Detective Sergio Martin. Please—don't hang up."

"I hate to be rude, but I'm leaving now, Detective."

"Give me something, Kerri." Sergio gazed toward the stage, straining to spot Kerri among the crowd. "You were right there, next to the person who murdered your boss. Your roommate Lasya was held hostage by him. That means the two of you have more information than anyone else about this case. Your input could save lives or cost lives. Don't spend the rest of your life with the wrong decision on your conscience."

Kerri huffed into the phone. "I don't know any more than you do, and the only life I'm interested in saving is my own."

"That's not true, Kerri." He held the phone in front of himself, pursing his lips as he stared at it. "You're no coward. You went to FRT to warn your roommate. That takes real guts, especially after what you'd just been through. You would have left town if you were trying to save your own skin. You're at the FRT site because you want this guy behind bars as much as I do. I know it." He took a breath, softening his tone. "Now, help me. Please."

"If you saw me on the livestream, then the killer might have, too. So, thanks. I'd better leave now. No story is worth my life."

Sergio sat upright, his pulse pounding. "Pay me back, then." He gripped the phone. "What did you hope to accomplish by being present at the FRT livestream tonight? You have an angle. What is it?"

"You're smart, Detective. But I can't let *your* smarts end up getting *me* killed."

"What were you there for, Kerri? Just tell me that."

Another roar went up from the crowd across the way. Seconds later, Avarie's phone sent it into Sergio's car.

She's still here.

"The... microphones." Kerri's voice fell to a whisper. "Jamaal's mics are wireless, Detective. Any police scanner will pick up the frequency. From there you can track the other person's signal—okay?"

Sergio frowned, working it out. "You... were going to undercut the story. The signal takes you to the killer's location?"

"Yeah," she said. "And now, you can do that—if you get a scanner and the wireless signal isn't encrypted."

"And if it's encrypted?"

Kerri huffed again. "Then you're screwed. I can't do your job for you and mine, too, Detective."

Shaking his head, Sergio held the phone closer to his mouth. "You had a plan if it was encrypted, too, Kerri. Come on. Help me get this guy."

Down the street, another roar went up from the FRT crowd. Nothing came from Avarie's phone.

Sergio glanced at the screen.

Call ended.

Groaning, he handed Avarie's phone back to her.

"What's up?" she asked. "Is she leaving?"

He frowned, draping one hand across the steering wheel and raising the other hand to his head to massage his temple. "Part of me says yes, and part of me says no. She could be bluffing again. Kerri's acting like she's done with this story, but she's still a reporter. The story was too big for her to walk away from before, and I think it still is. If she stays at the FRT event, she probably hides now. That's a problem." He looked at his companion. "She did give me one piece of solid information, though. I need to get a scanner and some hardware sent down here."

As Sergio picked up his phone, Avarie looked toward the FRT crowd.

"If Kerri doesn't leave," she said, "what do you think her angle is now?"

Sergio shook his head. "Get some sort of scoop, I guess. She doesn't strike me as the kind of person who'll be content to wait until nine P.M. to get the same story as everybody else." He opened his door. "Let's get closer. Maybe we can figure out what she was up to."

* * * * *

As Carly approached the FRT site, the traffic slowed to a crawl, then to a standstill. She craned her neck, peering around the car in front of her. A long line of stopped cars stretched to the glass and steel horizon.

"Geez, it's like a Black Friday sale at the mall."

There are too many cars to get there quickly. Time for plan B.

Grabbing her phone, she opened a search engine and typed "Florida Real Time News." The website opened, and the video of the livestream played. Below Jamaal Ainer's on-air shenanigans, his tip line rolled across the screen.

Carly frowned.

Why does he need tips if he knows who the killer is?

Because he doesn't know?

From somewhere ahead of her, several loud blasts filled the air. Carly looked up to see fireworks rocketing skyward, leaving a trail of smoke and sparks. They blossomed into glittering chrysanthemums of red and gold, the booms of their explosions following a moment later.

On her phone screen, the same red and gold fireworks went up several seconds later, followed by the same delayed booms.

I sure wasn't wrong about Ainer wanting to put on a circus.

Time to put a stop to this crap.

She tapped the number on the screen and put the phone to her ear.

"Florida Real Time tip line," a young man said. "Drop a hot take for Jamaal Ainer."

Carly shook her head. "This is Detective Carly Sanderson of the Tampa Police Department. I need to talk to Jamaal Ainer."

"Mr. Ainer's a little busy right now, ma'am."

"Are you sure?" Carly undid her seat belt, letting it fly up and slap the holder. "Because I'm about to come over there and slap handcuffs on him in front of a hundred and fifty thousand viewers."

FOURTH ESTATE

The man chuckled. "The current livestream has over three hundred thousand viewers, ma'am."

"It'll be over three million if I drop your boss on the pavement and put him in irons with the cameras rolling." She threw open her door and leaped out, hustling toward the well-lit melee down the street. "And when he's picking asphalt out of his teeth with my knee in his back, I'll be sure to let him know you withheld my request beforehand. I guarantee Jamaal Ainer knows exactly who he's got taking the inbound calls right now. So, maybe you want to check with him before you pop off again, huh?"

"Uh... Hold, please."

Carly smiled. "Yeah, that's what I thought."

Jerk.

DAN ALATORRE

CHAPTER 32

Deshawn Marshall sat down at his desk, hooking a cord from his phone to his computer to transfer Parnell Leicester's videos files. Once transferred, he could log them into the case file, where he had created a secured folder for them, limiting access to himself, Carly, and Lieutenant Davis. Although Tanny Stafford had been generally cooperative, and as innocent as she implied the videos might be, if anyone had overheard rumors about her extramarital activities—whether inside the department or outside of it—any videos of her with Leicester could become a lucrative commodity among the gossip rags. Deshawn didn't want Tampa PD property being copied and sold out the back door by an unscrupulous co-worker who had access to the general case files.

He checked Carly's case file checklist. CSI was working the scenes; witnesses had been interviewed. The numerous other tasks had been assigned and were being followed up on.

Deshawn smiled.

She's thorough. She'll make a good sergeant.

He entered Leicester's information to check for any prior arrests and convictions, and while the computer searched, he clicked the secured folder and started the transfer of the video files. As the completion bar at the bottom of the screen moved from left to right, the sergeant sat back in his chair and shook his head.

That lawyer's playing with fire. "Private" videos have a way of becoming public these days. One bad argument with that videographer, or when the assistant decides she needs a pay raise but doesn't get it... Next thing you know, the private video gets leaked—and Tanny Stafford's career as a lawyer is finished.

So dangerous. Why would a respectable, accomplished person roll the dice like that?

But he knew the reasons.

For some women, the new man paid attention to her in ways that her husband or current boyfriend didn't anymore. Some grew apart from their partners. Some couples worked so much, they never saw each other. For a few married women, she felt like she was getting older, and a younger man finding her sexy had reignited her self-esteem; he simply made her feel good.

Others liked the risk. An extramarital affair was thrilling and dangerous and exciting, a turn-on for certain types whose lives had otherwise become mundane somehow. And if the bad boy was actually bad, so much the better. A bigger risk meant a bigger thrill.

Whatever the initial justification for marital infidelity, in the cases when it went horribly bad—when a body was in the morgue and a suspect was in the interrogation room—the police got involved, and the answers came. Tanny Stafford, a successful attorney and the founder of her own law firm, would have her reasons, too.

Hopefully, she won't end up in the morgue or the interrogation room.

"Excuse me, sergeant."

Deshawn looked up to see a tall, athletic lab technician standing in the hallway, holding a tablet computer. The visible portion of the young man's arms were decorated with tattoos, and his ears had several piercings in each one. A tiny, curved gold bar hung between his nostrils.

"Is Detective Sanderson around?" the brawny young man asked.

Deshawn shook his head. "She's in the field at the moment. What can I help you with, uh…"

"Max Fuentes." The technician extended a thick hand. "I work in the lab. Detective Sanderson asked me to review the videos from the murder scenes today, and I may have found something."

"Max Fuentes?" Deshawn rubbed his chin. "Yeah, you're Carlos Fuentes' kid. I remember now." He broke into a smile and shook hands with the technician, noting Max's big arm and firm grip. "I thought your dad wanted you to be a firefighter—

you sure have the build for it. Best job in the world, he said. I guess you disagreed."

Max shrugged. "Dad loves being a cop, but he thought being a firefighter would be a better fit for me. More science-y, I guess. It just... wasn't my thing."

"Cop life is definitely a calling," Deshawn said, "even if you're in the lab. Glad to have you on the team." He glanced at the tablet. "What did you want to show Carly?"

"Oh, sir, I found several interesting items." Grinning, the technician set the tablet on the desk and opened a video file. "This is this morning's FRT footage. That news office was a remodeled site, probably a former convenience store or small freight warehouse. The initial video was really dark, but I was able to improve the clarity by washing it through a synthetic digital enhancer. Now, you can plainly see there are height tape markings around the exit door in the owner's office." He looked at the sergeant. "That tells you the thief's height as he runs out the back with the cash from the register. Okay. Now, hold that thought."

The young man turned back to his tablet.

"Detective Sanderson asked me to review all the recordings and any related information I found, with a specific concentration on the way the killer walks, so I did. I think he's wearing shoes with lifts in them."

Deshawn cocked his head. "Lifts?"

"Yes, sir." Max opened a still-image file, displaying a cross section of a man's dress shoe. He pointed to the heel area. "Sometimes a short guy will buy special shoes that have a thicker heel and a hidden, raised lining inside the shoe. This can gain anywhere from three fourths of an inch to one inch for each of the two vertical enhancements. That can take a guy who's feeling inadequate at 5' 10" and make him six feet tall—when he's in the special shoes. But that's a big difference. A guy who's not used to the lifts would feel like he's wearing his mother's high heels—which is awkward for most men. He'd walk awkward until he had practiced it for a while." Max opened the file of the killer walking into the Stafford law firm lobby. "The gait of the killer in these videos is indicative of that same kind of awkwardness."

"So, he wasn't practiced at it." Deshawn nodded. "If he wore lifts, it was something new for him."

"He did okay outside and in hallways, where he could walk in a straight line. As soon as he had to move around in a tighter space, his walk got awkward. And Sergeant, when I reviewed the FRT video, the killer went back and forth in front of that exit door with the height tape on it. He initially appears to be roughly six feet tall." Max stood upright, grinning as he folded his arms across his thick chest. "Using computerized triangulation, we were able to pin his height to within a quarter of an inch."

Deshawn sat back in his chair, eyeing the video. "But if he's wearing lifts, like you think, he might be closer to five-ten. And we've been kicking around the disparity between his legs and upper body, like he's not heavy, as the videos would have us believe."

"I've seen some guys at the gym come in wearing bigger lifts, too." Max chuckled. "They stroll in after work and they're at six feet tall, but when they change into their workout gear, they're 5'8", tops."

"At 5'8'," Deshawn said, "the killer could even be a woman."

"Hmm. Maybe." Max scrunched up his face. "But a woman would usually be able to walk in heels better than what I saw on that video."

"What about his hands?" Lieutenant Davis asked, walking toward them. "Was the killer wearing gloves?"

"Uh…" Deshawn stood. "Nobody noticed."

"Nobody noticed?" The lieutenant scowled. "We have forty witness interviews and nobody noticed the killer's hands?"

"Sir, when a gun is pointed at you, it's hard for a civilian to focus on details like that."

Davis faced the technician. "We have the NewsAction recordings, from when they were livestreaming. What does that show?"

"It's hard to tell." Max opened the file, letting it play as the lieutenant peered over his shoulder. "It's a good recording, Lieutenant—high pixel count and quality equipment resolution. But the camera operators were obviously panicked. They were bouncing around and focusing on the killer's face, zooming in and out, which made the images blurry. And he was moving around a lot." As the video ended, Max sighed and shook his head. "It's possible he was wearing gloves. I'll take this back to the lab and do a frame-by-frame blowup."

Davis nodded, turning and walking back toward his office. "Work your computer magic and let us know as soon as you have something." He stopped at his office door, looking back at the technician. "But work fast. Lives may depend on it."

As Max departed, Deshawn scooted his chair forward and grabbed a pen and his mouse, clicking on a box on the upper left side of his computer screen. The video file transfer from Parnell Leicester had finished. He opened the box and selected a file.

The first video was essentially what the lawyer had described. Tanny Stafford stood before an open field, wearing a tight white blouse and a form-fitting charcoal gray skirt. A gust of wind pushed her long, dark hair across her face as she recited the lines of the commercial.

A man's voice came from offscreen. "Okay, cut. We'll try it again."

Deshawn nodded.

That must be Leicester.

As Stafford adjusted the lavalier microphone on her shirt collar, a commercial airliner entered the picture in the distance.

"Okay, hold," Leicester said. The camera jostled. "We have a jet wanting to share your spot, babe."

Tanny laughed, brushing her hair from her eyes. "How's my blouse? Too bright in this light?"

"Did you bring another one?"

"No." She looked down, tugging at the material. "I wasn't thinking."

"Then we'll make it work."

As the noise of the jet faded, Leicester adjusted the framing of the shot, zooming closer to Stafford. "Hey, you're sweating."

"I'm roasting." She grimaced. "It's way more humid this morning than I was expecting."

"No worries. I'll pull the camera back a little. We can crop it in editing."

Stafford rolled her sleeves up and smoothed out her skirt. "Okay. Ready?"

"Whenever you are, gorgeous."

About twenty seconds in, she muffed her lines. As she laughed, the camera cut out.

The subsequent videos were more of the same; three attempts, three failures. More wind, more botched lines, and one bout of uncontrollable laughter from Ms. Stafford, apparently over her inability to read Leicester's handwriting on the cue cards. Each video segment had a time and date stamp, showing they were taken within a few minutes of each other.

During the pair's next effort, the videographer's phone rang.

"Sorry," Leicester said. "That's Jasmina. I'd better take this."

The camera stayed in position as Stafford shifted from one foot to the other, dabbing at her forehead. "We might have to bag this, Parnell. I'm drenched. I'll need a freaking shower before I can go in to the office."

"Well, love…" He stepped in front of the camera, putting his arms around the shapely lawyer.

FOURTH ESTATE

"As luck would have it, Jasmina says she's finished processing the Kensington wedding video."

Leicester's black t-shirt and blue jeans hid any signs of perspiration, but Stafford's hair was much flatter than when they'd started, and her blouse seemed to be showing some slight staining around the collar.

The videographer kissed his model. "I could ask Jasmina to come meet us at my place for a bit of breakfast… and some horizontal refreshment. What do you say?"

Fanning herself, Stafford walked toward the camera, swinging her hips and smiling. "I'd say that may have been your plan all along, Mr. Leicester."

The video cut off.

Two short clips followed, taken in what was likely Leicester's apartment. In the first, the two women stood on a balcony, leaning on the railing, their backs to the camera and the wind blowing their hair. Beyond them, the waters of Tampa Bay shimmered in the morning light. The second video featured Stafford sitting upright on a bed, still in the attire from the prior shoot, with one leg tucked under her as she posed for the camera. She fluffed her hair and made pouty lips as the camera jostled. A curvy blonde woman in shorts and a t-shirt passed by, visible only from the neck down at first, but then reappearing onscreen a moment later to take her place beside the lawyer on the bed.

"Right." Leicester's voice came from off-camera. "One moment while I adjust the light." The video got darker, then lighter. "Perfect, my lovelies. Let me just end this shot and I'll start a new one without all the lens adjustments—and then, let the games begin."

The video ended as Deshawn made a few notes. He leaned back, setting down his pen. Only one video remained, and not much new information had come to light.

He stretched, glancing at the time display on his computer, then to the break room, where fresh coffee awaited.

Exhaling with a quiet groan, the sergeant clicked on the remaining, unviewed file.

I'll coffee up after I finish this one.

* * * * *

As Carly made her way through the clutter of cars and observers working their way toward Jamaal Ainer's circus, she tried to gently nudge each earbud a little further into her ears to prevent them from falling out. Ahead, Ainer's amplified voice echoed off the surrounding buildings.

Carly broke through the river of moving people to see the parking lot across from the FRT site and its host, center stage. A portly young man walked toward Jamaal, carrying a phone. As he neared the ringleader, the microphone picked up his voice, sending it over the PA system.

"Tampa PD for you, boss."

"Whoa." Ainer smirked. "I'd better take this." The gathering of onlookers laughed as he walked to a monitor, his fat necklace shimmering in the bright lights. "Hello? Police?" He raised his voice an octave, mimicking the tone of an old lady. "Police, have you found the killer yet?"

FOURTH ESTATE

Ainer's words were audible to Carly via the PA a fraction of a second before they came over the phone line. She clenched her teeth, rushing forward through the outskirts of the mob. "This is Carly Sanderson. I'm a detective with Tampa PD. If you know who the killer is, you need to tell me. Otherwise, you could be obstructing justice. I'll bring you in, Jamaal."

The crowd booed.

"Goodness!" Ainer did an exaggerated, fake swoon, putting his hand to his brow and fanning himself. When he finished, he turned to his audience and scowled. "That would make a great story, Detective. We'll be all over the headlines together."

"Just tell me what you know," Carly said, "and nobody has to go to jail and spend a few days eating county cuisine. I don't know if you've ever been locked up before but it's not pretty."

Ainer put a hand on his hip, shoving the microphone to his lips. "Are you trying to intimidate me, officer? I don't frighten easily."

Carly moved through the mob. The closer she tried to get to the stage, the thicker the rabble got—and the more obvious it became that the woman trying to push past them was the antagonist of the evening's host.

Sideways looks became glares, then turned into scowls and comments, growing louder and angrier with each step. About ten feet from the edge of the parking lot where Jamaal Ainer was holding court, the wall of fans separated for her no more.

A few people moved away from Carly, forming a small circle and surrounding her.

* * * * *

When the arrest and conviction report finished, Deshawn opened it. Parnell Leicester had a number of incidents, but none recently. The list showed armed robbery, several complaints of assault, and two for domestic abuse. There were restraining orders from girlfriends and domestic abuse charges.

Deshawn shook his head.

Maybe he graduated to murder and there was nobody alive to complain. I wonder how much of this Tanny Stafford knows about. Seems like a lawyer might check out a guy's background.

Maybe she did know. That might explain some of her odd behaviors. I bet she did.

She probably represented him on some of this stuff. That's what appealed to her about him. He's good looking but he's dangerous, and that was exciting for her.

The sergeant returned to the videos, clicking on the last one. It opened on Leicester, standing next to a convertible Mercedes with the top down. The videographer reached into the back seat of the car and removed a tripod, holding his hand up and blocking the camera. "Careful with my equipment, babe. That camera's expensive."

The sergeant furrowed his brow.

The video files must have transferred out of order. This video was the first one they shot.

A glance at the video's time and date stamp confirmed the sergeant's suspicions. The computer was constantly updating the case files and accessing Leicester's prior convictions check, so the order in which the files transferred didn't really matter. All the video files from his phone were present.

"I can afford it," Stafford said onscreen, laughing. The camera zoomed in and out wildly. "Besides, you're always recording me. This is payback."

Leicester wagged his finger at her as he walked around the car, selecting the props for the shoot. "I record you because you're beautiful. The camera lens is much less forgiving to me."

"Where are we shooting today?"

"Just there." Leicester pointed across the grass, to an overgrown dirt trail. Tire tracks had worn away a pathway through the greenery, disappearing into a thick woods beyond. "A little ways down there. We'll have the light, and the softness of the grass. It should be good."

"Where?" Stafford asked, bouncing the camera. "Way down there? Why so far from the road?"

"It's out of view of any traffic," he said. "So we won't be disturbed."

The camera lowered, capturing the back seat and its contents—a few makeup cases, makeup brushes, lights, and a fader umbrella. The equipment sat on a gray blanket and several pillows, next to a red windbreaker.

Deshawn bolted upright, his heart pounding
What did I just see?

He grabbed the mouse and backed the video up. Again, the camera panned down, viewing the back seat of the convertible—and the red windbreaker there.

The sergeant put his hands to his head, his heart pounding.

Stafford can't account for Leicester's whereabouts that morning. He left the apartment an hour before she did.

Deshawn flung back the pages of his notepad, his eyes scouring his notes, searching for the page from Stafford's interview in the lieutenant's office.

He dragged his finger across the page of his handwriting.

Parnell had another appointment.

He and Jasmina (asst.) left about an hour before Stafford.

Stafford took a shower and slept in for a while.

Stafford: Video shoots can take several hours, knew she wouldn't be missed at work.

The sergeant's jaw hung open.

He had a windbreaker with him on a warm day, pillows to stuff it with so he'd look fat, and he was wearing blue jeans.

With the makeup kits, he could make his face look African-American. Under the hat, mask and sunglasses, who'd know? The rest of him was covered.

He stood up from the desk, the recorded words from the video conversation echoing in his head.

"Where?" Stafford asked, bouncing the camera. "Way down there? Why so far from the road?"

"It's out of view of any traffic," Leicester said. "So we won't be disturbed."

FOURTH ESTATE

The hairs stood up on the back of Deshawn's neck.

He did graduate to murder. He was going to kill Tanny Stafford.

But he got interrupted.

And when he got to Stafford's office, she wasn't there. She was still sleeping in at his place.

Deshawn grabbed his notepad and sprinted to the lieutenant's office.

DAN ALATORRE

CHAPTER 33

CARLY KEPT HER FOCUS ON THE STAGE—but kept her free hand on the butt of her service weapon, eyeing the angry mob forming around her. "Jamaal, I'm just saying, if somebody else dies while you're playing games, you could be considered an accessory after the fact."

The little circle grew closer and less friendly. Comments came from all around.

"Hey, this lady is the one on the phone with Jamaal."

"She's one of the cops who can't find the killer."

"She's here, ruining the show, instead of doing her job."

A man in a khaki vest, wearing a Go Pro camera strapped to his head, took a step toward her. "She's another useless freaking tyrant, wasting the taxpayer's money—that they confiscate at gunpoint." He scowled at her. "You should leave free citizens alone, pig."

"Detective," Jamaal said. "Your threat of charging me as an accessory after the fact—it simply won't hold up."

"It won't have to." She stopped looking at Jamaal and turned toward the angry group of people surrounding her, making direct eye contact with each one as she clutched her phone. "You still get to spend the night locked in a cage, Jamaal. Maybe with a gorilla who doesn't like what you do for a living. Or you can just talk to me and tell me who we should be chasing. It might avoid another senseless killing."

Ainer snorted. "I'm afraid I'll just have to roll the dice on that one, Detective. Bye now. See you at nine P.M."

The call ended.

Carly frowned, sliding her phone into her pocket.

You'll see me a lot sooner than that, jerk.

* * * * *

Lieutenant Davis frowned as he scanned Deshawn's notes. "I should never have let Carly run off to FRT," Davis said. "That was a waste of time. This videographer guy—what's his name? Leicester? He just became our number one suspect." Davis dropped the notepad to his desk and walked to the window. "What's the reason for Leicester to have all the elements associated with the crimes with him in his car? Especially the red jacket?"

FOURTH ESTATE

The sergeant nodded. "There could be a reason, but... Leicester sure looks right for this. A lot of the pieces fit."

Mellish appeared at the door. "You asked for me, sir?"

"Hmm?" Davis turned to his assistant. "Yes. Have someone check this Leicester against the website archives for NewsAction, INN and Florida Real Time—with FRT as the priority. See if there were any stories about him."

"Yes, Lieutenant," Mellish said.

Deshawn put one hand on his hip, rubbing his chin with the other. "Sir, if Leicester's our killer, it's possible that his plan is to take out the guy from FRT during the livestream. We need to track him down, wherever he is."

Davis nodded. "We need to get some personnel over to FRT."

"Carly's already there," Deshawn said. "So is Sergio. But I can tell you, if we are raiding the videographer's apartment, Carly should be the point person. You put her in charge of the investigation, so it's her job to coordinate with the extraction team."

"Fine." Davis strolled back to the window, shaking his head. "But I don't want Sergio left in charge at the Florida Real Time site. He still has the PR consultant with him, and Jamaal Ainer is absolutely lambasting us on the livestream. We don't need Avarie Fox getting persuaded by anything that charlatan has to say." He peered at his sergeant. "Who else is available?"

Deshawn shrugged. "Roberts called in. He wrapped his initial investigation and is turning it over to the CSIs. He's also seen some of the videos FRT is running. He's not happy about what he's seeing. He thinks FRT might start showcasing witnesses from the murder sites, and he's not comfortable with that." He shook his head. "You have to admit, for this killer, that might be like waving a red flag under the bull's nose."

"Okay." Davis nodded. "Put Roberts in charge at FRT. That frees Carly up to run point with SWAT."

"SWAT? For an extraction in a high-rise apartment?"

"We're short on personnel, Sergeant, and this might be our killer. We go with what we have, and SWAT is available."

Deshawn frowned.

SWAT gets bigger coverage from the local news, too. I'm sure that didn't cross your mind.

He looked at Davis. "What about Sergio?"

The lieutenant moved back to the window. "While the consultant is with him, we need to keep Detective Martin away from the firing line. Have him stay at the FRT event and follow up with whatever he can find there." He peered at Deshawn. "Even if we're off the mark with this videographer, Jamaal Ainer is still likely to be the killer's next target."

* * * * *

The cluster of angry people around Carly moved closer, their comments getting louder and harsher. People held up their phones, to record or livestream whatever happened next.

"Pigs in blankets," a man with a megaphone called out. "Fry 'em like bacon."

FOURTH ESTATE

Another person yelled from the back. "All cops are dirty."

The man with the Go Pro stepped forward, glaring at Carly. "Sic semper tyrannis." He grinned. "Death to tyrants."

"Hey, it's Henson Brimley, the First Amendment auditor guy!" Sergio broke through the crowd, smiling at the man in the Go Pro. "Henson Brimley, Patriot—right? I thought I recognized you, Henson." He glanced at Carly, then turned his attention back to the auditor. "Hey, Henson Brimley, we all know the real tyrants are the dishonest media like that guy." He hooked a thumb toward the clearing, where Jamaal Ainer stood.

Brimley scowled. "Yeah."

"And you, too, Henson Brimley." Sergio smiled. "But I gotta go. Bye, Henson Brimley." He looked at Carly. "Come on, let's go."

As Sergio turned toward the mass of people, Carly fell in behind him. Brimley's mouth hung open.

"What was that?" Carly asked. "Why'd you say his name so much?"

"That bozo and his squad record everything," Sergio said. "He likes to start crap with cops, then edit the footage to make us look bad. But he can't do that with something that's got his real name spoken in it every two seconds."

At the edge of the crowd, a young woman in business clothes stood, hands on her hips, looking at Sergio.

Carly peered at the woman. "You must be the PR consultant."

"That's right." Sergio gestured from Avarie to his partner, and back again. "Carly, meet Avarie Fox, the consultant I'm babysitting, compliments of Lieutenant Beelzebub."

"*You're* babysitting?" Avarie rolled her eyes. "Funny, I felt like *I've* been the one babysitting today. Nice to meet you, Detective Sanderson."

As the women shook hands, Carly's phone rang. She pulled it from her pocket and answered.

"Carly," Deshawn said, "Tanny Stafford's videographer, Parnell Leicester, inadvertently recorded himself this morning with a red windbreaker and a makeup kit. That was just before the murder of Kaliope Hernandez. He has a fat record, too—armed robbery, domestic abuse, the works. Leicester had plenty of time to go from his video shoot with Tanny Stafford to the Stafford-Love law offices where he killed Hernandez. Lieutenant Davis thinks Leicester is our perp, and he's authorizing you to coordinate with SWAT to do the extraction and bring him in."

Carly chewed her lip.

SWAT? That's overkill. Lieutenant Davis must have a late-night news conference lined up with one of the friendly TV anchors.

But we only have a red jacket and a makeup kit? That's it?

"Sarge... that sounds thin."

"I disagree," Deshawn said. "Leicester was with the intended victim less than an hour before he walked into her place of business to kill her, asking for her by name and killing her receptionist because Stafford wasn't there. And he just happens to have the same kind of red jacket with him? Leicester didn't know Tanny Stafford stayed behind to take a nap, Carly. I think he initially planned on gunning her down during their video shoot, so he would have it recorded. When that didn't work out, he decided to do it at her office, where there'd be cameras and an audience—just like at the other murders."

She pursed her lips.

It's still thin.

But we can't ignore it and end up being wrong, either. In that scenario, people die.

"Okay." Nodding, Carly took a breath. "You sold me. What's his address?"

"2143 Bayshore, unit 13415. But we don't know if he's there."

"I'll call Tanny Stafford," Carly said. "She'll know where he is. But we'll start heading toward Bayshore right now."

"Uh, Carly—just you. Roberts is taking over at FRT. Sergio is to remain on site there and follow up with any leads. Get moving, and contact the SWAT commander on duty."

She ended the call and looked at her partner.

"What's the plan?" Sergio asked.

As Carly pulled out her car keys, she lowered her eyes. Sergio would hate being left behind on mop-up detail. Her stomach felt like a brick had been dropped into it. "I'm going to apprehend the lead suspect. You're to remain here."

"What?" Sergio threw his hands out at his sides. "Why?"

She pursed her lips. "Davis… wants it that way."

"Of course," Sergio said. "The antichrist strikes again. But you're the lead investigator. You can have me reassigned. It's your call."

She stopped and looked at him. "Yeah. That makes it my call. So, stay here and follow up on any leads, like I asked you to. Roberts will be here shortly with some backup officers. He'll be the primary."

The words hurt for Carly to say, and their effect was immediate and obvious to their recipient.

Sergio lowered his head, nodding. "Oh." Glancing up, his eyes met hers. "Okay, well… go get the bad guy, dude."

She forced a smile, nodding as she turned toward her car.

The decision might have technically been Carly's, to leave Sergio on an unimportant assignment while the action happened elsewhere, but it also wasn't her place to try to override the lieutenant. Not today, when she was still an acting Sergeant.

Whatever Davis' reasons, she needed to move fast. There wasn't time to argue.

And Sergio needed to follow orders, even if it meant leaving the department's best person on the sidelines.

As Carly made it to her vehicle, she reassured herself that sergeants had to make decisions like that all the time, and not everyone would be happy with the choice that got made. A dangerous assignment could make an officer a hero or it could end up getting an officer killed. That was the job, and everybody who joined the force knew the rules.

FOURTH ESTATE

She wanted Sergio by her side as much as he wanted to be there. It had been that way for almost five years. As Deshawn said, she felt strange without him next to her.

But she also realized the potential danger of the assignment, and a part of her didn't want Sergio there. Things could go wrong, and Sergio had a flair for heroic actions.

His presence could cause me to hesitate. That means he'd be a distraction, and I can't have a distraction during the apprehension of a killer.

Right?

She opened her car door, knowing that she was lying to herself the way she had just lied to Sergio. It wasn't really her call. It was the lieutenant's. But it's the call she would have made anyway.

Too much had already happened today. She wanted her man to come home safe.

* * * * *

Avarie looked at Sergio. "You okay?"

He stared at the ground. "Yeah."

Nodding, she clasped her hands behind herself and kicked a pebble across the uneven asphalt. "Wanna talk about it?"

"About how my partner just threw me under the bus and practically demoted me? Not really." Sergio peered off into the distance. "And Roberts is going to be the lead detective here? Geez."

Exhaling a long, slow breath, Avarie looked around. "I think I saw a taco truck over there somewhere." She pointed to the far side of the crowd. "Why don't we go grab a bite to eat?"

"I'm... not really hungry," Sergio said.

"Yes, you are. You said you skipped breakfast, and we had to ditch our lunch before we took two bites. I'm hungry, so you must be starving. Come on. Buy me a taco."

She reached out and took his arm, pulling him toward the far side of the parking lot.

"You can buy me one," Sergio said. "You're the one with the expense account."

* * * * *

As Carly made her way out through the onslaught of vehicles that were still trying to get in to FRT's livestream event, she called Tanny Stafford's number.

She figured out the same thing Deshawn and Lieutenant Davis just figured out. She had to.

That's why she acted so funny earlier, at the station. All day, Stafford's been wondering if her boyfriend is a murderer. Probably as soon as she saw that red windbreaker in the videos everyone's been showing online, she recognized it as Parnell Leicester's.

"Hello?"

"Ms. Stafford," Carly said, "it's Detective Sanderson. Where is Parnell Leicester?"

"Why?"

Carly bristled. "Let's not play games anymore, ma'am. You can do the math for this morning's timeline, the same as I can. Parnell's not one of your criminal defense clients—yet. Now, where is he?"

The traffic parted, and Carly increased her speed.

FOURTH ESTATE

"He…" Stafford's voice wavered. "He's at his apartment on south Bayshore. We just spoke. He asked me to meet him. I was just on my way out."

"Don't go into that apartment before I get to you." Carly frowned. "There's a pizza place at the intersection of Bayshore and Interbay. Do you know it?"

"Yes," Tanny said.

Carly nodded. "Wait for me there."

"Why, Detective?" Stafford's voice sounded strained, as if she had been crying, or was about to. "Parnell can't be the killer, he just can't. He wouldn't. He—he could have murdered me during the video shoot this morning. We were all alone. Why didn't he?"

Carly gripped the steering wheel.

Because he likes an audience. Because he enjoys the thrill of fear in his victim's eyes. Because killing you alone isn't good enough now…

And because he didn't know you were going to sleep in after your shower.

The detective swallowed hard. "Just… don't meet with him until I get there."

DAN ALATORRE

CHAPTER 34

At the taco truck, Avarie pulled out her credit card to pay for two tacos. Sergio stood a few feet away, near an empty picnic table, his hands in his pockets.

The consultant walked away from the window, holding a slip of paper. "We're number seventy-three. They said it'll be a few minutes."

Nodding, Sergio looked away.

"Oh, don't be such a baby." Avarie took his arm. "Pouting doesn't fit with the dashing, heroic guy I read about in your file."

"Yeah, it's just..." He inhaled deeply and let it out in a huff. "I always knew Lieutenant Davis was working the angles to get at me. And I helped him, too—I know that. I'd go outside the lines... But today I realized that Carly's promotion puts her in a position where Davis can manipulate her into working on me, too. He'll make her chisel the ground out from under me, a little at a time."

And then there's the whole Kyle situation that's still unresolved. I feel like I might be getting pushed away in every aspect of Carly's life.

Avarie leaned close, tugging on his arm. "I think you're forgetting why I'm here. I'm looking to improve the department. That means helping to improve the people in it. My advice is, be better tomorrow than you were today. Then, Davis will never be able to chisel enough ground out from under you to make a difference."

Sergio snorted. "That's easy for you to say."

"Think so?" She stepped back, putting her hands on her hips. "I know Lieutenant Davis doesn't respect me. The Tampa PD is under a budget crunch, right? So, I had to agree to work for peanuts to get this job—but I did it because it's building my résumé and my business. And I'll keep working cheap for jerks like Davis until my résumé is built. Then I'll be able to earn a decent living and move up in the world—and I'll keep moving up. And someday people like him will respect me because the quality of my work will prove that they should."

"Davis." Sergio shook his head. "The antichrist. He screwed both of us on this assignment. At least you'll be done with him soon. I'm stuck with that scheming jerk until he finally figures out a way to get me fired."

In the distance, Jamaal Ainer worked the crowd, going close to them and enticing a few people to come onstage and render their opinions of the situation. Massive monitors, more than ten feet tall and fifteen feet wide, had been erected on each side of his stage. The PA system broadcast his inflammatory comments over the parking lot, and the internet would send them all over the world.

Ainer walked along the edge of his audience, toying with his flashy necklace, microphone in hand. He goaded people into agreeing that the Tampa PD was inept because they had been unable to stop a killing spree.

It had been less than twelve hours.

Sergio winced. "Then there's that freaking guy, playing up this mess for his own benefit. He's another Davis. They're everywhere." He leaned on the picnic table with both hands, hanging his head.

"You're right," Avarie said. "They are. But there are ways of getting the Davises of the world."

Sergio peered up at her.

"One time," Avarie said, "I was doing a presentation for the sheriff and his staff in a small, north Florida county. This was to improve the image of the department, which was really bad at the time—and still is, by the way. That asshole sheriff should have hired me."

Sergio chuckled.

"Anyway…" She waved the little paper, walking along the side of the empty picnic table. "I was using my phone as a recorder, laying it on the table to take notes for me while I did my presentation, and I'd check it afterwards to see how I did. You know—did I say 'um' a lot, or talk too fast… Well, when I finished the pitch, the sheriff completely blew me off. He just said, 'No, thank you, ma'am,' and he had one of his people open the door for me to leave. So, I gathered my computer bag and my presentation stuff and I went to my car. I was really embarrassed, too. Usually, they ask questions or take a few minutes with me before saying no. Not this guy, with his 'No, thank you, ma'am.' So I was all red-cheeked, walking out to my car. But in the parking lot, I realized I'd left my purse and phone inside. Now, the last thing I wanted to do was go back in there, but I said, be a professional. You did a good presentation, and you're working hard to improve, so don't be embarrassed. So I stood myself up and went back in and got my things."

A hint of a smile tugged at her lips. "I was driving away and I needed to make a phone call, and I picked up the phone—and it was still recording. I forgot to turn it off. So, I played it. My presentation was there, and the sheriff's 'No, thank you, ma'am,' but when I left the room, the sheriff said he wasn't about to take advice from some little girl who looked like she was barely out of high school. Not, my price was too high. Not, her references didn't hold up or that I didn't have enough experience. I lost the job because of my looks."

Sergio shook his head. "That's... Yeah, that's rough."

"I can't say it surprised me—the sheriff hadn't been very receptive—but... it was still a shock, to hear someone say that about me out loud. But I learned something—and for my next presentation, I took Darryl. He's the guy you saw in this morning's conference. He's middle aged, got the gray hair around the temples, wears a nice suit... I closed my next deal, at my asking price."

"Sorry that sheriff did that to you." He stood, letting his hands fall to his sides.

"Thanks," Avarie said. "The point is, I didn't let a Davis outmaneuver me more than once. So, don't you."

Sergio grinned at his companion. Avarie was smart—he already knew that—but he didn't know the kind of crafty fighter she was. He admired it.

He put a foot up on the picnic table's bench and rested his hand on his knee. "You know, maybe you and I can—"

Behind him, a gasp went up from the crowd. Avarie's jaw dropped.

Sergio turned around. On the big screen, First Amendment auditor Henson Brimley was onstage with Jamaal Ainer, his hands at Ainer's neck.

"Oh, crap. Brimley's lost it." Sergio pointed at Avarie. "Stay here."

He raced across the parking lot toward the crowd, his eyes on the massive video monitor. As he waded into the crowd, some of Ainer's staff pried the two men apart and shoved Brimley off the stage.

Ainer's cameras followed the deranged auditor. Brimley grinned, walking away toward his own team of cameramen. His companion with the megaphone shouted taunts at the stage as they retreated.

"Not so fast, Brimley!" Sergio shoved his way through the mob. "I might be taking you in this time."

"What!" The auditor turned to Sergio. "That jackal called the flag a diaper for him to wipe his butt on."

The floodlights swung over Jamaal's fleeing attacker, searching for and finally finding him as he and his lackeys waded through the thick crowd.

Sergio was able to squeeze through the last rows of the pack of people, getting next to Brimley. "Still, assault is over the line. If Ainer wants to press charges, I've gotta arrest you."

Brimley stuffed his hands into his pockets, his face turning red. "You—you tyrant!"

"Oh, stop," Sergio said. "You know better. You say it at the end of all your stupid videos—plead your side in court, not on the field."

Ainer's cameras zoomed in on Sergio, the ringmaster's voice booming over the madness. "Finally, the Tampa police are able to apprehend a suspect! But only when one is practically hand delivered to them."

Sergio and Brimley flashed onto the gigantic monitors located at each side of the stage. The crowd erupted in laughter.

A microphone appeared an inch from Sergio's face, held by one of Ainer's minions.

Avarie grabbed the mic. "The detective has no comment at this time except to ask if Mr. Ainer would like to press charges."

On stage, Ainer shook his head. "No. No, officer, I won't press charges—as long as the attacker and his group leave right now. But I do think we may have to shut things down for a while."

The crowd booed.

"I'm sorry, but if the police in this town can't keep a simple gathering safe, maybe we shouldn't continue."

Comments erupted from the mob.

"Don't let them scare you, Ainer!"

"Fight the good fight!"

Ainer smiled. "I hear you, friends. I hear you. How about this?" He looked around. "I need to take a short break. I'll be back for the grand finale, the interview with the killer. Until then, watch some of the interviews we did earlier with my staff."

He walked off the stage and disappeared into his trailer. The large security guard moved back in front of the door with the star on it, his arms folded across his chest.

Sergio shook his head. "Guess you get to walk, Brimley—but I'd do it now."

Brimley straightened his vest. "Pushing the agenda of the tyrant, eh, piggy?"

"Okay," Avarie said. "Just go already."

Cocking his head, Sergio turned to the consultant. "I thought I asked you to stay put."

"You did." She shrugged. "I'm not a dog." A smile crept across her face.

Sighing, Sergio smiled back. "No, you're a free, sovereign citizen, right? Watch that you don't get hurt, okay? That's the one deal I made with Davis. Now, come on, let's get out of this mob and get back to our tacos."

DAN ALATORRE

CHAPTER 35

When Carly arrived at the pizza parlor, Tanny Stafford was clearly visible sitting in a booth by herself, a paper coffee cup in front of her. The lawyer kneaded her hands, glancing around as Carly entered the establishment.

"Thank you for coming, Ms. Stafford." Carly slid into the booth, taking the seat across the table from Tanny. "I have a uniformed officer on the way to meet us. I'd like you to stay here with him until I contact you."

Stafford frowned. "I'm telling you, this is a mistake, Detective. Parnell didn't…" The lawyer glanced around, lowering her voice. "He didn't kill anyone."

"I'd like you to be right, because I know you care about him" Carly said. "But I'd like you to be alive, too. Consider this a precautionary measure, for your safety." A Tampa police patrol car pulled into the parking lot and a uniformed officer stepped out, walking briskly toward the front doors. Carly looked at Stafford. "This isn't going to take long, ma'am. We'll know everything we need to know in an hour or so."

The officer walked up to the table.

"Officer Keats…" Sliding out of the booth, Carly gestured to the attorney. "This is Tanny Stafford. We think her life may be in danger. You're to stay here with her until I give you the all clear."

"Yes, ma'am, Detective."

The lawyer shook her head. "This is ridiculous."

"Ms. Stafford…" Carly leaned over to the lawyer. "I'm sorry for this inconvenience. Let us protect you while we check Parnell out. I'll only be an hour or so, then we'll know a lot more."

"And after that?" Tanny looked at Carly, her voice wavering. "You people think Parnell Leicester, a man I've known and cared about for years, is—is… a murderer. Well, I say you're wrong, Detective. But if you are wrong, then where is the killer? He could be outside right now, waiting in the parking lot." Frowning, she lifted her coffee cup to her lips. "What's to stop him from walking right through that door like you did and killing me here?"

"Me." Officer Keats patted his service weapon and sat down in the booth. "And a few of my co-workers that are stationed outside."

Stafford looked at the officer, her coffee cup shaking in her hands.

FOURTH ESTATE

Carly took the cup from the lawyer and set it on the table. "You'll be safe here, ma'am. Let's start with that."

* * * * *

At the food truck picnic table, Sergio took a bite of his taco, shattering the shell and sending a small avalanche of ground beef over his chin and fingers. "Mmm. Tasty." He nodded at Avarie. "But not as good as Enrique's at T-COS."

"How would you know? None of that bite got in your mouth." Avarie plucked a napkin from the plastic and chrome holder, dragging it across Sergio's chin.

He chuckled, glancing toward Jamaal Ainer's trailer at the back of the stage. A man walked out from behind it and rushed through the shadows, wearing a raincoat and a floppy hat pulled down over his head. He climbed into a large sedan a few feet away and started the engine.

Avarie gasped. "Is that who I think it is?"

"Maybe." Sergio set his taco down, taking a step toward the trailer. "Looks like Jamaal Ainer decided to leave after all—if that was him. He's been promising these people a show, but I couldn't see the face of whoever that was exiting the trailer."

Avarie followed behind the detective. "Ainer's not dumb enough to go meet the killer in person for that interview, is he?"

"This guy is dumb enough to do anything for ratings. Let's see if that trailer has a back door."

They reached the side of the trailer as the sedan inched onto the street and into the mass of slow-moving traffic. Crouching, Sergio crept around the back of the rectangular structure. Jamaal's bodybuilder security guard stood in front, facing the stage, where FRT personnel interviewed the victims' family members on the livestream.

The back of the trailer was parked under some scrub oaks and was surrounded on three sides by scattered, overgrown bushes, casting it in near-darkness despite the bright stage lights a few feet away. Between the hanging limbs and leafy overgrowth, a rear door was barely visible on the back of the trailer. The only light came from inside.

Sergio grabbed the handle of the back door and yanked it open. "Anybody home?" He leaned inside. "Jamaal?"

Ainer's trailer was little more than a long, thin box, with a shower and makeup table at one end and an unmade bed at the other. Other than that, it was empty inside.

Sergio eased the door shut, peeking through the brush at the large sedan's taillights. The vehicle crawled along with the snail-like congestion, headed north.

"We have an opportunity here." Sergio dug into his pocket and pulled out his car keys, holding them out to Avarie.

"Aren't you supposed to stay here with Roberts?" she asked.

"Carly said follow up on any leads. This is a lead. And now that I've been all over Jamaal's big TV monitors with Brimley, I'm sure Kerri Milner knows I'm here. So, she and her friend have either left or gone into hiding. That makes the sedan our only lead, and I'm pursuing it, as instructed." He

FOURTH ESTATE

grinned at Avarie and twirled his keys in a circle. "Are you in or out?"

"Oh, I am *so* in." She snatched the keys from him. "What do you need me to do?"

"This is Perkins Avenue, headed north." Sergio pointed toward the street Jamaal was driving on. "Take my car and go west, to Heron Lane. It's about three blocks, but it won't be clogged with traffic—that's mostly coming from the interstate. Go north from there and call me. When I find you, we'll slip in behind Jamaal and see where he goes."

"Are you going to be able to keep up with him on foot?"

Sergio nodded. "Jamaal won't get far in this mess. You saw the traffic when we came in. It's only gotten worse since he's been talking about livestreaming an interview with the killer. I'll be able to move as fast as him for the next ten minutes." He pushed through the brush, turning to Avarie. "But probably not longer than that, so get going."

* * * * *

Carly pulled in to the Bayshore Towers Apartments, putting down her window and waving at a SWAT team member on the side of the street. "Detective Sanderson, Tampa PD. Where's your commander?"

The young officer pointed to a large man with a crew cut, holding a clipboard and addressing a small group of SWAT team members dressed in all black.

The detective parked her car and walked up to the SWAT leader, holding her hand out.

"Commander? Carly Sanderson, detective with Tampa PD. What do we have so far?"

The commander shook her hand and nodded toward the apartment building. "Pretty straightforward, Detective. The subject's unit has one main entry from the hallway, with an emergency fire door at the rear. I've stationed personnel on each end of the subject's hallway and one in the stairwell, three in the lobby and one at each corner of the parking lot. If he's here, he's surrounded."

She glanced around the small parking lot. "What about the car? A Mercedes convertible. It's supposed to have some pretty incriminating evidence in it."

"We're searching for it now," the Commander said. "The residents' parking garage is spread over the first five levels of the building, and it's full to capacity. Our people are going through it floor by floor."

"Okay. Let me know as soon as they locate it." Carly looked up at the high-rise. "Tanny Stafford says our suspect is upstairs, waiting to meet up with her—or he may be waiting to kill her. Ready to go knock on Parnell Leicester's door and find out which it is?"

"Just waiting for your go-ahead, Detective." He smiled, holding up a Kevlar vest. "Shall we dress for the party?"

Carly slipped into the bulletproof jacket as the commander put on his own. The borrowed garment was awkward-fitting, extending from her shoulders to her crotch but protecting nothing else, allowing for a combination of security and mobility.

FOURTH ESTATE

More protection would cause the wearer to be less able to move, thereby potentially compromising their overall safety; more maneuverability meant the vital organs would be less than adequately protected. A hit to the kill zones—the torso—was defended, but an arm or leg could still be sacrificed by someone wearing a Kevlar vest. A head or neck shot would almost certainly result in death as well, but such shots were difficult for an assailant to hit with a bullet because although they were unprotected by the vest, they were also comparatively smaller targets. SWAT team members typically wore helmets on operations, but almost no other Tampa PD personnel had them as standard gear.

She slapped the Velcro straps into place above each hip and under her arms. "Let's go."

The elevator ride to Leicester's floor was quiet. Carly stood next to the commander, with three heavily armed SWAT members behind them.

"If what the lawyer told you is accurate," the commander said, "this should be a simple knock and talk."

Carly nodded, a knot growing in her abdomen.

Nothing about knocking on a potential killer's door was ever simple. Suspects ran. They fought. They jumped from fourth-floor balconies or held family members hostage. Some tried to sic a dog on the entering officers; others were passed out on the couch, limp and unconscious in a haze of drugs, on their way to death.

There was no way to know if the door Carly knocked on would explode outward with bullet holes or if Leicester would cordially open his residence with a cocktail in his hand and cordially invite the officers to have a seat on his living room sofa.

The elevator doors opened. Carly's stomach tightened as she looked out.

The corridor leading to Leicester's apartment was well appointed in its décor. Plush beige carpeting rolled out under white wainscoted walls and understated colonial-style wallpaper. A small chandelier dotted the high ceiling every twenty feet or so. But aside from its upscale decorations, the corridor was also empty—except for a black-clad SWAT team member at the elevator door, and another down at the far end of the hallway, their large rifles clutched diagonally across their chests.

"You are clear to the subject's door, Commander," the closest team member said.

Carly followed the commander out of the elevator, her pulse throbbing. Leicester was a good guy, according to Stafford—but girlfriends were often wrong about the secret lives their illicit lovers maintained, and sometimes they were willfully blind. Parnell Leicester was the secret lover to a married woman, and he 100% knew it. That meant he was up for breaking rules.

Who knows how far that impulse has taken him?

It wouldn't be the first time the façade of a normal-looking "person of interest" had unraveled to expose something far more dangerous than anyone had previously imagined.

FOURTH ESTATE

The commander stopped at Leicester's unit. Carly pulled her service weapon and held it to her side as she verified the apartment number.

"This is it," she whispered. "On my signal."

As his junior members stepped away from the door and pressed themselves to the wall, Carly moved to one side of the entry and stretched her fist out to knock.

The unit seemed quiet inside; no TV or music was audible to Carly from the hallway.

She glanced at the SWAT Commander, mouthing, "Ready?"

He nodded.

Carly held her breath, her heart pulsing in her ears as she moved her hand out over the door.

Anything can happen, so be ready.
Here we go.

She rapped her knuckles firmly against the door. "Parnell Leicester! Tampa Police! Open up!"

Silence.

No footsteps, no fumbling around, no noise at all.

Carly leaned in close.

If anything bad is going to go down, right now is when it would happen.

She held out her hand to knock again.

DAN ALATORRE

CHAPTER 36

SERGIO WINCED AS HE TROTTED ALONG the dark sidewalk, his side aching with a looming cramp. Sweat rolled down the sides of his head.

How do I end up always being the one running after someone?

Panting, he maintained a line of site on Jamaal Ainer's sedan as it moved northward. The vehicle was getting farther and farther away with each passing block.

After a few more streets, traffic is going to free up. Jamaal will be able to move faster, and I'll lose him.

He wiped an arm across his wet brow, glancing at the upcoming intersections, trying to see any sign of Avarie and his car.

Come on, little sister. Where are you?

* * * * *

Carly made a tight fist and held her breath again, preparing to knock on Parnell Leicester's door a second time.

Sometimes the silence on the other side of a door meant the suspect was passed out on the couch or asleep in their bed. Sometimes it meant they were carefully loading a gun and preparing to unleash a torrent of bullets.

She rapped sharply on the door and pulled her hand away, gripping her gun. "Police! Open up! Parnell Leicester, if you're in there, this is your last chance!"

No noise came from the other side.

The SWAT members lowered their rifles an inch.

"No," Carly hissed. "Stay on the alert. This isn't over yet."

The door lock rustled.

Carly tensed, raising her weapon. The SWAT members pointed their rifles at the residence.

The sound of metal on metal came to her ears, followed by a light thump inside the door.

Carly bit her lip.

That's the deadbolt unlocking. He's going to open the door.

Peacefully, I hope.

She swallowed hard, forcing her voice to remain firm and even. "Parnell Leicester, this is the police. Open the door, keep your hands where I can see them, and take two steps back."

The door swung open. Parnell Leicester stood barefoot in a robe, his hands in the air and his mouth hanging open. "What? What is it? What's happened?"

The SWAT team rushed past him, rifles pointed as they swept through the room.

"Is anyone else in the apartment?" the SWAT commander shouted.

"What?" Parnell squeezed his eyes shut, cowering. He clutched his robe to his shirtless chest. "No. I mean, yes. I'm... working. What's going on?"

Carly put her hand to the videographer's shoulder and guided him to the wall. "Who's here? Where are they?"

"In the... in the bedroom," Parnell whimpered. "In the back. What's going on?"

Two of the SWAT members disappeared around a corner.

Parnell breathed hard, trembling as his gaze darted around his residence. "What's happening? Is this because of the video? I'm licensed. I have permits to record here."

Carly frowned. "What video?"

What's he filming in here?

"All clear, Commander," a SWAT member called out. "The situation is..." He broke into a chuckle. "Everything's under control. We're coming out."

The SWAT member emerged from the bedroom accompanying a short, elderly woman with sparse gray hair, and a heavy, elderly man. Both were barefoot and apparently nude under robes that matched the one Leicester was wearing. The SWAT member shook his head as he guided the duo toward the doorway.

Carly glared at Leicester. "Would you care to explain what's going on here?"

"This—this isn't illegal." The videographer pulled his robe tighter. "They hired me to make a personal video for their own private usage. I have the consent forms, and they get the only copy."

Carly leaned forward, squinting at the old woman. "Are you... Councilwoman Perry?"

"Detective Sanderson." The woman nodded. "Nice to see you again. This is Claude. He is not a prostitute. He is..." She patted the old man's hand. "A dear, dear friend of mine."

The old man smiled at Carly. "Ma'am."

Carly turned away, her hand on her stomach. "Mr. Leicester, please—explain this to me."

Leicester shifted his weight from one foot to the other. "Well, the councilwoman enjoys an active lifestyle, and she enjoys having some of her private encounters recorded. Kind of like her own personal film series, if you will."

"Series?" Carly winced. "Oh, boy. But... but why are *you* undressed, Mr. Leicester?"

He shrugged. "When Ms. Perry brings a gentleman friend along for one of her sessions, he may find that he is unable to, uh, to... to rise to the occasion. And so she will ask me to serve as a kind of a stunt double."

Exhaling sharply, Carly nodded.

The SWAT Commander frowned. "Are you sure this isn't illegal?"

"I don't know," Carly said. "Call vice and let them check it out. Meanwhile, the apartment's clear, but we still have to conduct an interrogation." She looked at Leicester. "Where were you for the hour before the shooting at the Stafford-Love law firm?"

Wh—why, you know where I was. I sent your sergeant the video evidence with a time and date stamp. Tanny confirmed—I was with her, right here. She and my assistant, Jasmina Petrov."

"What about after that?" Carly asked. "Stafford said you left. Where were you? After you wrapped your session with Tanny and Jasmina, where did you go?"

"I—"

"Parnell was with us," Councilwoman Perry said. "With Claude and I. We had a scheduled session at my home in south Tampa this morning. The three of us were just getting ready to start when we saw the reports about the shooting. That's why we're here now. We were all too upset to continue this morning after learning about how that poor woman was killed in cold blood. It was all over the news."

Carly nodded. "Yes, it was."

The Commander's radio squawked. "We've located the vehicle. The top is down and the jacket is here."

Carly glanced at the Commander. "Ask them to send me a video of what they can see from outside the car. Tell them not to enter the car or reach in."

"What car?" Parnell asked. "My car?"

"The videos you sent to my sergeant showed a red windbreaker in your car," Carly said. "The same kind of windbreaker the killer wore. We... the videos you sent indicated you had enough time, unaccounted for by the videos, to get to the Stafford-Love office."

Carly's phone rang with a Facetime call. She answered to see the face of a SWAT member in the parking garage. He pointed his camera toward the back seat of Leicester's car, where the red windbreaker rested.

"That? That's the jacket?" Leicester chuckled. "Have him pick it up, Detective."

"You don't have to give us permission," she said.

"It's okay. Pick it up."

Carly held the phone to her mouth. "Mr. Leicester says it's okay to pick up the windbreaker. Go ahead."

The SWAT member reached into the car and lifted the jacket. One side was red. The other was patterned in a black and white checkerboard.

Carly winced. "Okay, thanks. You can put Mr. Leicester's windbreaker down now."

The videographer scowled. "You thought I murdered Tanny's receptionist? And that I planned to kill Tanny, too?"

"We… needed to investigate." Carly lowered her head. "To rule you out."

"To rule me out. Uh-huh."

The councilwoman stepped forward, the bottom of her robe swirling around her knees. "I'm sorry, but there's no way, Detective. My house is twenty minutes from here at that time of day."

"Yeah, it is." Carly sighed. "I know the Councilwoman's house. It would take at least twenty minutes to get from here to there, so if Mr. Leicester was with the two of you, there's no way he had enough time to leave here, drive to the Stafford-Love office, kill Kaliope Hernandez, and drive back to your home in south Tampa for your session." Pursing her lips, she held her hands out at her sides. "This was all a big mistake. My apologies to all of you. Mr. Leicester, Councilwoman Perry, Mister, uh… Claude. I'm very sorry to have disturbed your evening."

Leicester turned his nose up. "You'll be hearing from my attorney."

"Tanny Stafford, right? Yeah, I bet I will." Carly walked toward the videographer. "Which is fine by me—I admit my mistakes. You, on the other hand, will have to explain…" She looked at the councilwoman and Claude in their robes. "…all of this. I'm guessing Tanny thinks she has an exclusive deal with you—or, with you and your assistant."

Carly walked toward the exit, with the SWAT commander following her. "Detective, what on earth?"

She shook her head. "We blew it, Commander. Plain and simple. Somebody jumped the gun. That happens when there's a madman out there who's killed three people in one day. And I'm back to square one, which means—"

She froze, her jaw hanging open.

"Detective?" The commander asked. "Are you alright?"

"Three people in one day." Carly's voice was a whisper. "He said he was going on a spree." She peered at the commander. "Didn't the killer say something like that?"

"Yes."

"But he stopped." She put her hand to her forehead, walking back into the apartment. "The killer was supposed to be out there shooting up the town. Maybe four more today—that's what he said." She faced the others. "That's why the whole police department's on edge. But he's not doing it. He hasn't killed anyone since this morning."

The commander frowned. "Maybe you just haven't found the newest victims yet."

"Oh, no, no, no, Commander." Carly shook her head. "Not this guy. He plays to the screen. TV, internet—our killer likes an audience. A big one. No, he's stopped. The only question is, why?" She looked across the room, the downtown Tampa skyline looming in the distance. "And I think I might even know."

The commander snorted. "Make sure your intel is better than a red jacket this time, Detective."

"Oh, it is," Carly said. "In fact—"

Her phone rang with an incoming call. The screen lit up with the words "Jamaal Ainer, FRT News."

"Speak of the devil," Carly said.

* * * * *

Sergio leaned against a tree, sweat dripping from his nose and chin. Ainer's sedan was about three blocks ahead of him, but it was still visible in the traffic. Gasping, Sergio raised his head and glanced to the next intersection. There was no sign of Avarie or his car.

She should have been here by now.

FOURTH ESTATE

A car horn honked beside him. "Hey, Detective!" Avarie waved at Sergio from the driver's side of his car, crawling along in the traffic.

He shook his head, reaching for the passenger door. "Where've you been? My grandmother drives faster than you."

"She probably has a better car than this one." Avarie craned her neck and peered over the steering wheel. "Is Ainer still up there?"

"About three blocks up." Sergio nodded, wiping his brow. "If it's him. But for now, it's a lead, so I'll take that gamble. Traffic's gonna thin out when he gets to Himes Avenue, so stay as close as you can. We don't want to lose him."

"I'll go as fast as the traffic lets me."

Sergio tapped his heels on the floor of the car, his eyes trained on the sedan.

From Himes, he can get to the interstate. If we aren't close when that happens, he's gone.

* * * * *

Carly put her phone to her ear. "Nice to hear from you, Jamaal. Of course, I'm only saying that to be polite."

Ainer chuckled. "Ever the diplomat, Detective Sanderson. And here I called in good faith. How disappointing that your little excursion into Parnell Leicester's apartment didn't turn anything up."

Carly's jaw dropped.

How would he know that already?

"Cute jacket, though," Jamaal said. "Not my style—I don't care for checkerboard prints—but who

DAN ALATORRE

knows? It might look good under the bright lights and cameras."

She gripped the phone, pressing it to her ear. "How do you know all this? Did you hack the body cameras of the SWAT team?"

"Let's just say I was provided a tip from someone who may have had knowledge. A very reliable tip."

Carly frowned.

Too reliable. We've either been hacked or he has a spy in the department. This whole investigation could be compromised.

"You're really stretching the limits of the law, Jamaal."

"I don't disagree," he said. "But the Supreme Court has ruled that it's only illegal for me to access classified information. It's not illegal for me to publish that information when it's given to me. The people have a right to know. Thanks to people like me, they do."

She gritted her teeth.

He's working with someone inside the department. That's the only way he could have this information so fast.

And he's probably announcing our latest foul-up all over the internet.

Crap!

Carly paced back and forth outside of Leicester's apartment. "What do you want?"

"Nothing," Jamaal said. "If you had walked in on the killer just now, I'd have a terrific scoop that I could use to make another big splash all over the internet." He sighed. "But as we both know, the killer wasn't in Leicester's apartment. And as you indicated, my access to such timely information might be pushing things a bit. I want to stay on the right side of the law. It's hard to sell advertising from a jail cell."

Carly huffed. "I'll translate that to mean you realized that getting locked up would keep your face off the internet for too long, and that would hurt your business model."

A jolt went through her abdomen.

If Leicester's not the killer, then I need to get back to the FRT site.

She turned to the SWAT Commander and cupped her hand over the phone. "Can you wrap this up for me? I need to be somewhere else."

The Commander scowled. "Go ahead. What's one more of your messes for us to clean up?"

Carly raced down the hallway toward the elevator, pressing the phone back to her ear. "How about this, Jamaal? Tell me what you have, and I'll forget about your questionable access to our internal information. But that stuff stops, and I mean now."

"Such a tough negotiator, Detective Sanderson—even when you have an empty hand." Jamaal chuckled. "It's thin, but… Your killer was a heavyset black man in a red windbreaker, a ball cap, and sunglasses—remember?"

At the elevator, Carly pressed the call button and put her hand on her hip. "Go on."

"Our tip line accumulated several leads that might interest you. Turns out, there's a local man who walks two miles around his neighborhood every day—basically dressed in the same attire as your suspect. A bunch of his neighbors have been contacting us, all reported the same thing. He walks funny because of a skiing accident he suffered recently, and his walks are part of his physical therapy."

"Names." Carly hissed. "Now."

"I'll text them to you when we end the call, I promise. Now, I have a show to do, and you have an investigation to run. Does this tip even things out between us?"

"Maybe. Why didn't the neighbors contact the police? Did your internal hacker jam our lines?"

"No, but what an interesting premise. Anyway, I'm sure some of the neighbors did call you. It's our job to get them to call us, too—and we give them an added incentive. We can put them all over the internet and make stars out of them. Everyone loves their fifteen minutes, Detective."

Carly gasped. "If you put them on the internet, the killer can see them and come after them!"

"My, that could be a problem, couldn't it?" Jamaal chuckled. "But what a ratings bonanza for me. I suppose you'll just have to catch the killer before he can get to any of them."

"Who did they identify, Jamaal?" Carly shouted, her pulse throbbing. She pounded the elevator call button again and again. "What's the killer's name?"

"Call the neighbors, Detective. They'll tell you. But don't take too long."

Carly slammed her hand against the steel door of the elevator. "This isn't a game!"

"Of course it is." Jamaal snorted. "The sooner you understand that, the sooner you'll catch your killer."

DAN ALATORRE

CHAPTER 37

The traffic on Himes Avenue thinned, as Sergio had predicted. Jamaal's sedan made its way onto the interstate and headed north. The driver kept the vehicle's speed slightly under the speed limit and made no sudden lane changes.

As Sergio and Avarie followed, a light rain dotted the windshield of the detective's car. Avarie turned on the wipers. "What are your thoughts on Kerri Milner?"

"She's a reporter." Sergio put an elbow on the door and rubbed his chin. "I can't see her just walking away from the biggest story of her life. She'll try to cover it somehow."

"Maybe," Avarie said, "Or… she's part of this thing." She glanced at Sergio. "Your partner thinks Kerri could be working with the killer. It explains how she was able to get away from the

Suarez murder and get over to FRT. Being at both places while the killer is present? That's a heck of a coincidence."

"Yeah, but there are only a handful of those gossip rags in town. The killer was going to them all, and her friend worked at the next closest one. And I talked to Kerri Milner after the Miranda Suarez murder. She was shaken up. She was white as a sheet."

"She could still have been in on it." Oncoming headlights illuminated Avarie's face in the dark car. "Maybe she never saw a murder close up before. Maybe before this morning, it was all talk, and seeing it in real life was a shock to her. It sure shocked me."

Jamaal's sedan turned off at the last Tampa exit and drove due east, slowing at a faded sign at the front of a road that appeared to be half gravel, half potholes. A faded sign at the corner read "Breezeway Mobile Home Park. 2BR Rentals, $125 Week. 1 Small Pet OK." Fifty yards further stood a run-down convenience store with a flickering light shining down over a small, dirty parking lot.

Jamaal's car turned, kicking up a light cloud of dust as he drove down the trailer park's entryway. Avarie slowed Sergio's vehicle.

"No, keep going." Sergio put a hand on the dashboard. "Pull into that little store."

As Jamaal's taillights bounced away into the darkness, Sergio opened a search engine on his phone and located his position on a mapping website.

"This road is a loop." He glanced toward the entrance to the mobile home park. "The only way in or out is that gravel drive. Pop the trunk."

Avarie pressed a button on the lower dashboard as Sergio undid his seat belt and opened the car door. He moved to the rear of the vehicle. Avarie shut the engine off and followed him.

In the light of the trunk, Sergio removed the magazine from his service weapon and checked the number of rounds, then replaced it and shoved the gun back into his holster. "I'm going to see where Jamaal's car went. You stay here. If I'm not back in… let's say an hour, then you call Carly and have her send in the Cavalry." He picked up a Kevlar vest and strapped it over his white dress shirt.

Avarie peered over his shoulder. "What do you think is going to happen in there?"

"Well…" Sergio dug through his trunk and pulled out a navy-blue sweatshirt. He slipped it over his head and pulled it down over the vest, covering all but the very top of his shirt collar. Grabbing a second Kevlar jacket, he placed it over the sweatshirt. "If Jamaal still intends to host the killer at nine P.M. for a livestream broadcast, that doesn't leave a lot of time."

Avarie swallowed hard, clutching the car keys to her chest. "You think the killer is back there somewhere?"

"That would be my guess. So stay here. Sit in the back seat of the car—and keep low." He shut the trunk lid and glanced at the flickering streetlight overhead. "This is a bad neighborhood but there should be enough light here to keep you from getting abducted for the sixty minutes."

"Sure. I can score some crack cocaine while I'm waiting."

"Detectives don't get to pick the locations of our job sites, little sister. We just go there and get the bad guys."

She nodded, looking at him. "Be careful."

"You, too." Sergio smiled, adjusting his vest. He tucked his shirt collar down into the blue sweatshirt, hiding it. "I'll be back soon."

She took a step toward the driver's door, then turned and threw her arms around Sergio, squeezing him tight. "Don't go getting shot or anything, okay?"

He patted her on the back. "I'll do my best."

She squeezed him harder. "Promise."

"I promise." He held his hands out at his sides for a moment, uncertain of what to do, then gently returned her embrace, letting the warmth of her young body calm him.

Avarie released him and moved away, looking down. "I… I don't know why I did that." She wiped her cheek, sniffling. "I'm sorry."

"It's okay. I get it." Sergio leaned over and peered up at her. "Things just got real, right? Hypothetical stats in a report turned into a person, with flesh and bones and things they have to do tomorrow. Someone you got to know, and maybe like—and that makes all those reports you create seem a little different now. I get it."

"Of course I like you." She looked away, wiping her cheek again. "You'd be hard not to like."

"Tell that to Lieutenant Davis when you get a chance." He hooked a thumb over his shoulder, walking backwards toward the gravel road. "I have to get going or there may not be anything to find in there."

"Okay." Avarie brought the car keys back up to her chest and squeezed them with both hands. "Be careful. Remember your promise."

DAN ALATORRE

CHAPTER 38

CARLY SPRINTED ACROSS THE PARKING LOT, THROWING open her car door and jumping behind the wheel. Her tires squealed as her vehicle sped over the asphalt.

Ainer's playing a game that's going to end up getting even more people killed. He needs to be stopped, freedom of the press or not.

She slapped at the steering wheel, going around a corner and gunning the engine as she raced toward the FRT site.

I'd better update Deshawn and the Lieutenant, too. They should hear about the screwup at Leicester's apartment from me before someone else tells them.

Carly winced.

That's going to hurt. Davis will want to pull me back into the office.

She stared at her phone.

But I have to tell them. I'm in charge. It needs to come from me.

Then I'll work on Davis to let me go back to FRT. Even he'll have to admit I'll do a better job than Roberts—and that will matter to the media, so that will matter to the Lieutenant.

It'll work. It has to work.

* * * * *

Sergio trotted along the mobile home park's gravel road, searching for Jamaal's sedan in the fading light. Perspiration dripped from his forehead as he passed by the run-down trailers. Panting, he wiped his brow with the sleeve of the blue sweatshirt.

Hey dummy, remember to put a dark-colored t-shirt in the car so you don't roast to death the next time you're doing surveillance.

The detective glanced around. Most of the residences in the Breezeway Mobile Home Park were under large, overgrown trees and were in varying states of decay. Some were rusty. Some sat on uneven foundations or had sagging roofs. A few had no windows at all; others had piles of assorted potted plants lining a weed-filled perimeter and the butt of a box air conditioner sticking out of a living room window, humming and grinding as water dripped from the back and stained the siding below. A formerly white mobile home squatted under a scrub oak, turning a mossy shade of green. Trash and other debris filled many of the tiny spaces that served as the residents' front yards.

A few of the trailers had lights on inside, but only a few. The others were either unrented or the occupant had yet to return home for the night. Not many cars were visible anywhere in the park, either, and those that were present had dents and faded paint or were rusty and decades old.

As Sergio neared the back of the park, Jamaal's shiny new sedan came into view. The mobile home it was parked in front of was one of the cleaner ones in the little neighborhood, and the closest to a busy road behind the park, on the other side of a high wooden fence. Trees and gangly brush almost shielded the residence from view, but a light inside made it as visible as Sergio needed.

He crouched, wiping the sweat from his brow with his shoulder as he inched along the gravel road.

Here we go.

What's up inside there, Jamaal?

Stopping behind a bush, the detective peered into the living room of the trailer.

Warped wood paneling hung from the walls, pulling away in places. A stained lampshade rested atop a 1970s-style Mediterranean lamp. A faded green couch sat against one wall, across from a burnt-orange chair with holes in the corners.

But no one appeared to be inside.

Sergio surveyed the surrounding area. No one was walking a dog or jogging. The nearest trailer flickered inside with the light of a TV set.

He lowered his head and continued inching toward Jamaal's mobile home, stepping across the sparse grass to the big sedan. A quick look through the vehicle's window showed it to be empty, so he moved on. At the trailer, Sergio pressed himself to the vinyl siding under the biggest window and lifted his head to peek inside.

The small room revealed nothing more than it had before.

Sergio took a deep breath and let it out slowly.

Jamaal has to be here somewhere.
Where did he go?

He scanned the thinning lawn. The light from inside the trailer illuminated tire tracks in the grass, going around toward the back yard. Sergio turned and followed them.

* * * * *

As Carly swerved through the streets, racing back to the FRT site, she called the names and phone numbers of Jamaal's witnesses. Each person she spoke with provided the same name to her: Doctor Jackson Zumendi.

If Jamaal is going to host a livestream with the killer, I need to get back to FRT as soon as possible. That's where Jamaal will be, so that's the best chance at getting to the killer.

As she pressed the accelerator to the floor, her phone rang. Carly pulled her hand away from the wheel long enough to hit the green button. "Hello?"

"Sanderson!" Lieutenant Davis shouted. "What kind of shoddy, misguided investigation are you running out there?"

She cringed.

"I just got off the phone with the SWAT commander," Davis growled. "Not only did you leave a mess for him to clean up, but the entire operation was botched right from the beginning."

FOURTH ESTATE

Carly swallowed hard. "Mistakes were made, sir…"

She stopped herself.

But I was acting on information provided to me from downtown. And I understood it was you who requested SWAT's involvement.

That wouldn't fly. Davis wouldn't want her laying the blame at other people's feet, even if those feet belonged to him. *Especially* if those feet belonged to him.

So what do I say?

She clenched her jaw.

Nothing. Deflect and move on.

Tell him about the new information Jamaal gave you, then hard sell him on letting you continue with your plan.

"Sir," Carly said, "we are pursuing all leads. That one didn't pan out. I can apologize to SWAT later, but right now we have a big connection. Jamaal Ainer called me, and he said—"

"No, no, no, Detective." Davis huffed. "I don't want to hear anything else about that media clown."

Carly frowned. "Lieutenant, Ainer knew we came up empty at Leicester's apartment almost before we did. He's got access to our data. But most importantly, he provided leads on the identity of the killer. I spoke to three of them, and they all said the man they saw on TV was Doctor Jackson Zumendi, their neighbor in Culbreath Isles."

"Detective—"

"Sir, if we can get to the FRT site before Jamaal's livestream interview at nine, we have a good chance of apprehending the killer. I suggest we scramble a team and move on our new suspect's house in Culbreath Isles while a second team surveils the livestream at FRT. I'm headed to FRT now."

"No," Davis said. "You're headed here, to the office. I never should have let you try to run this from the field. The wheels are coming off your entire investigation."

Carly's shoulders slumped. "Sir, I called the witnesses myself. They all independently identified Doctor Zumendi."

"Ainer could have set you up with fake names. Did you think of that? They're probably his employees' phones, as they help him manufacture another story—and another embarrassment for the department. And he might be baiting you into sending a squad of officers to his livestream interview just to make us look bad when the killer isn't even there!"

"But, sir…"

"No buts." Davis' voice grew firm. "Earlier, everyone identified Parnell Leicester, right? And look how that turned out. No, Detective. I'm not sending an army of cops to one of Tampa's most prestigious addresses and embarrassing this department more than you've already done today. Come back to the office. We'll contact the leads and verify their information, then we'll have someone attempt to contact your new suspect. What's your ETA?"

Carly grimaced.

But I've already done that! We need to move on Doctor Zumendi and FRT right now!

FOURTH ESTATE

The Lieutenant lowered his voice. "Don't turn into another Sergio, Carly. You're better than that. He's your partner, not your alter ego—that's why you're up for a promotion and he's not. Now, come in and run this thing the proper way."

Carly slowed her vehicle, letting the Lieutenant's words sink in.

Maybe he's right. It's more like Sergio to run after everything at top speed. I'm usually the voice of reason. I was already wrong once...

So why does it feel like if I go to headquarters, I'll be wrong again? It could be a huge mistake!

Sighing, she let it go. Orders were orders. She would return to the office and run the investigation from a desk, the way the Lieutenant wanted it done.

"I'm... about five minutes away," Carly said. "I'll be right there."

* * * * *

Avery knelt on the floor in back of Sergio's car, her elbows resting on the seat as she checked the time for the fourth occasion in ten minutes. Drumming the seat, she lifted her head to peek out the back window, grumbling to herself. "Are you gonna take the whole hour?"

She glanced at the time on her phone again and exhaled sharply, rubbing her abdomen. Groaning, she lowered her head and tucked herself into a ball, biting her fingernails.

The streetlight over the convenience store parking lot flickered like it was auditioning for a bad horror movie. Avarie shifted on the floor, the warm, humid night air making her feel sticky and uncomfortable. Fighting the urge to shudder, she tipped her head up and peeked out of the window again.

Sergio, please come back soon.

"Hey, there." A disheveled man walked toward the car. "I thought I seen something in this car."

Avarie tensed. The stench of body odor and stale beer wafted through the open window.

The semi-toothless stranger put his weathered hand on the car door. "Help out a veteran with a few bucks?" His face was overly tan, etched with deep lines and covered by a long, straggly beard. Greasy hair hung around his head; dirty, threadbare rags covered his thin frame. "I ain't eaten in two days." He leaned toward her. "I won't buy drugs or beer with it."

Avarie moved herself onto the back seat, trying not to inhale the foul odors coming off the stranger. She lifted her purse from the floor and dug into her wallet. "Sure. I'll help you."

"Thank you kindly, ma'am." The stranger reached out with trembling fingers. Avarie took a few bills from her wallet and extended her hand.

Her fingers trembled, too.

An uneasy feeling washed over her. She stretched her hand outward, but leaned her body back and away from the man.

He nodded. "Much appreciated..." He reached closer, his dirt-stained fingers brushing against the money.

His hand stayed there, the bills lifting upward in a gentle breeze, his eyes fixed on her.

"Okay," Avarie said. "Take it."

The man's breath grew harder, his hands shaking.

Avarie's pulse quickened. "Take it. Go get something to eat."

His hand darted past the money, latching onto Avarie's wallet and snatching it from her lap. The stranger recoiled, hauling her wallet out the window as he scurried a few feet away from the car.

Gasping, Avarie jerked backwards. The stranger dug through her wallet, taking out all the cash. He turned around and disappeared into the darkness behind the convenience store, dropping the wallet as he ran.

"Great." Avarie huffed, opening the car door and sliding out. She walked across the dirty asphalt, glancing around the parking lot of the decrepit business to find her wallet. The headlights of an approaching car illuminated the leather billfold perched among some broken glass and a wet stain. She reached down, picking the wallet up with two fingers as brown liquid dripped from its corners. "Yeah, that's just great."

* * * * *

Sergio slinked along the side of the trailer, holding his breath. A sagging, wood-frame garage stood at the back of the mobile home property, close to the rear fence where the trees and brush were the thickest and the noise from the busy road was the loudest. A flashlight beam bounced around inside the garage walls.

"Come on." Jamaal's voice came from inside the wooden structure. "Walk."

A large African-American man stumbled from the garage, his hands behind his back and his eyes covered with a blindfold. Duct tape covered his mouth.

Jamaal emerged behind him, holding a shotgun.

"Move it," Jamaal said in a hushed tone. He poked his hostage in the back with the shotgun.

The man exhaled sharply through his nostrils, his head hanging. He sagged forward, lumbering through the weeds as he made his way toward the rear of the trailer home. A groan escaped his massive chest.

"Keep moving." Jamaal prodded him again. "It's almost over."

The kidnapper and his hostage climbed a small wooden staircase that led inside the run-down mobile home. Scuffling noises came through the windows, and a light came on above Sergio's head.

The detective ducked, pressing himself to the trailer wall.

"Just relax and get comfortable, Doc," Jamaal said.

Sergio raised his head a few inches and peered into the trailer.

Jamaal lowered himself into a leather chair behind a shiny, Scandinavian-style desk, his hostage tied with ropes to a chair in front of him.

The interior of this part of the trailer looked new. Fresh paint, clean carpet, bright new lights. A computer rested on top of the desk, along with several microphones on small stands.

FOURTH ESTATE

The bound man groaned again, sagging against his restraints. His frame was robust, but he looked weak in the bright light. His shirt was stained with dirt and sweat; his brown skin was smeared with grime.

Jamaal held up a phone and tapped the screen. "Good." He glanced at his hostage. "We're right on time."

Standing, the news man walked across the little studio to a closet and removed a blue baseball cap, sunglasses, a paper face mask, and a red windbreaker.

Sergio crouched again, putting a hand to his chin stubble.

What am I witnessing? Do we have our killer, or do we have one heck of a publicity stunt? That shotgun tells me Jamaal is either forcing a confession, or...

Or I don't know what.

But he told everyone he was going to interview the killer on a livestream. That means his hostage is the killer, or is supposed to be. But it sure doesn't look that way to me.

Sergio put his hand on the butt of his service firearm.

Guess it doesn't matter. I need to break up this tea party before something worse happens and we—

There was a bang from the front of the mobile home. Heavy footsteps came from the other side of Jamaal's trailer studio, along with the voice of a woman.

"Let me go!"

A jolt went through Sergio.

That's Avarie.

He looked inside as the studio door flew open. Avarie fell forward, crashing to the floor as Detective Roberts stood in the doorway, waving a gun.

"Look what I found," Roberts sneered.

"Who's that?" Jamaal jumped up from the desk. "Why did you bring her here? We have a plan!"

Roberts chuckled, bending down and grabbing Avarie by the hair. He lifted her head.

"Ow!" Avarie shouted.

"So, you don't know who this is, Jamaal?" Roberts asked.

"No, I don't. And I don't want to know." Jamaal glared at Roberts. "We have a schedule to keep. What are you thinking, bringing a stranger in here like this?"

"This girl is a consultant to the Tampa PD," Roberts said. "I spotted her walking around in the parking lot of that crappy convenience store near the front of the park." He looked at Avarie. "Not that I could miss her. She looked a bit out of place for the neighborhood, all dressed up in those nice clothes."

The fat detective stepped to the window, raising his gun. Outside, Sergio lowered his head into the shadows.

"This girl was assigned to be working with Tampa PD personnel," Roberts said. "Specifically, she was assigned to work with Sergio Martin this morning. If she's here, he's here—somewhere."

"What do we do?" Jamaal's voice was strained. "It's almost time for the interview."

FOURTH ESTATE

"Oh, I think I know how to handle Detective Martin." Roberts walked away from the window. "Believe me, when it comes to Sergio the showboat, I know exactly what to do."

The fat Detective stepped to where Avarie still lay on the floor, putting his foot on her back and pointing his gun at her.

DAN ALATORRE

CHAPTER 39

CARLY SPRINTED FROM THE TAMPA PD PARKING LOT to the front doors.

You can run the investigation from a desk. Just follow the leads and follow the evidence.

She hurried across the lobby to the elevators.

Trust your people in the field. Build a solid case, like making links in a chain. Each step is connected to the other, in a...

She gasped.

It's links in a chain. The murders are all connected like links in a chain.

The killer got arrested for something, so he needed a lawyer. He got convicted by a judge. The news agencies ran his story. But since he got convicted, he decided to take revenge on everyone who played a role.

He's eliminating everyone who failed him—all the links in the chain.

As the elevator doors opened, Carly's heart pounded.

So, what are the next links?

Deshawn stood in the hallway talking to Max Fuentes from the lab. The young technician looked up. "Detective Sanderson." He grinned at Carly and held up his tablet. "I may have something for you."

As Carly opened her mouth to reply, Lieutenant Davis barged out of his office. "Welcome back to work, Detective." He folded his arms across his chest and glared at Carly. "I'd like a word with you in my office."

She shook her head, brushing by him and heading for the sergeants' desks. "There's no time for that right now, Lieutenant." She glanced at Deshawn. "I figured out what's going on."

The lieutenant recoiled. "Excuse me?"

Sergeant Marshall and the lab tech followed Carly to her desk.

"The murderer is taking revenge." Carly sat down and woke up the computer. "Each victim is a link in a chain from some prior conviction he had."

Davis put his hand to his forehead. "Detective Sanderson, two hours ago you said this was all a setup to point us at the wrong man..."

She held her hand up to Davis as she continued speaking to Deshawn and Max Fuentes. "A conviction means an arrest, a defense lawyer, and a trial. Today, our guy killed a defense lawyer, a judge, and the heads of the news agencies that ran with his story—all the links in the chain. But he promised to kill more people, so what comes after the judge? What's the next link?"

The lab technician gasped. "That could mean the jurors from the trial are at risk, a parole officer, maybe an appeals judge…"

"Yep." Carly nodded, typing on the computer. "Anyone who played a part. They're all links in the chain."

She sat back and put her hand on the computer monitor, turning the screen toward her sergeant.

"I got a tip from Jamaal Ainer," Carly said. "The names and phone numbers of three witnesses. Each one of them identified Doctor Jackson Zumendi, of 494 West St. Croix Drive in Culbreath Isles, in Tampa. He drives a white Mercedes GLS, an SUV, license ITK-771."

Frowning, Lieutenant Davis walked up to her desk.

"Sergeant…" Carly smiled at Davis. "Would you be so kind as to read the participants in Doctor Zumendi's arrest file, please?"

Deshawn leaned close to the screen. "Doctor Jackson Zumendi. Arrested in a domestic dispute, defended by Tanika Stafford of Stafford Love law firm, Judge Frederico Pallindas presiding." He stood up. "I remember that case. It was all over the…"

"All over the news." Carly nodded. "Mainly, it was all over NewsAction, INN, and Florida Real Time News—Jamaal Ainers outfit. But all three slaughtered this guy."

Deshawn exhaled a long, slow breath. "The killer visited every one of those places today."

"And he promised more?" Fuentes said. "Holy cow."

At the end of the hall, a door banged open. Cass Clemmons, the Chief of police, walked toward them, carrying a briefcase. "I've been asked to give Mayor Mills an update, folks. What's the situation with this murderer?"

Davis cleared his throat and stepped forward. "I was just assessing that, sir. I've concluded that all of today's victims were figures from the arrest of Doctor Zumendi a while back. I was about to rally a team to go to the doctor's home in Culbreath Isles as well as the FRT livestream site."

Carly shook her head.

You concluded? When was that? After I concluded the same thing and you rejected it?

"Very good, Don." The chief nodded to the group. "Stay after it, people. Let's get this guy."

"Yes, Chief," Deshawn said. "We will."

As Chief Clemmons departed, Lieutenant Davis turned to Carly.

She smiled. "Sir, should I rally a team to go to the doctor's home in Culbreath Isles as well as the FRT livestream site?"

"Yes." The lieutenant adjusted his collar and looked away. "Yes, that would be good."

He disappeared back into his office.

Carly turned to the lab technician. "Max?"

Fuentes whipped around to face her. "Yes, ma'am?"

"Well, first, chill out." She chuckled. "Call me Carly. When I came up here a second ago, you said you had something for me."

FOURTH ESTATE

"Oh. Yes, ma'am—uh… Yes, Carly." He lifted his tablet and showed it to her. "You asked me to review all of the recordings from this morning's murder sites and any related information I found. But while I was doing that, I was also following the FRT livestream event and its surrounding activities." He tapped the screen, displaying a video of First Amendment auditor Henson Brimley and Sergio, on the Sunshine State Audits website.

"Yeah, well…" Carly scrunched up her face. "Things like that are going to happen. Some of these so-called auditors are more like professional agitators. They try to goad a cop into making a mistake on video, then their lawyers file a civil rights lawsuit in the hopes of landing a big payday. Sometimes cities will have to settle for fifty or a hundred grand, but even the minor stuff can draw ten or twenty thousand dollars. That's a lot of cash for a few hours' work."

"Yes, ma'am." The lab tech scrolled through a few more videos. "But I thought you should know, the guys from Sunshine State Audits have been online almost nonstop ever since they got kicked out of the FRT event. From more recent posts, I think they're following Jamaal Ainer somewhere."

"Following?" Carly bolted upright. "He's not at the FRT livestream anymore?"

"He… might be." Max swiped his finger across the tablet screen. "He left the stage to take a break a while ago and hasn't come back since."

Deshawn frowned, crossing his arms. "Carly, that doesn't sound like the Jamaal Ainer we've been watching all afternoon."

"It sure doesn't." Carly glanced at the time display on the computer. "He's only a few minutes away from his big interview with the killer. Where would he run off to?"

CHAPTER 40

Roberts leaned forward, pressing his foot into Avarie's back.

"Ow!" Avarie pounded the floor. "Get off me, you fat pig."

He snorted. "Pig? You sound like one of those First Amendment idiots." Roberts turned to the window, raising his voice. "Come on, Sergio! Show yourself, or I'll kill this girl. I know you're out there."

Crouching by the window, Sergio clenched his jaw.

Show myself. Then what? You take me hostage and kill us both?

"I swear, I'll do it." Roberts reached into his suitcoat pocket and pulled out a flask. "I'll put a bullet right through her pretty little head. Now, come on out. I know you can hear me." The fat detective opened the container and took a big sip, glancing around.

Sergio fanned a mosquito away from his face, slowly raising his gun to the window.

That moron might actually shoot her. Maybe I can get a shot off at Roberts first, but through this glass, there's no way to know where it'll go. If I miss, he might go ahead and kill Avarie. One of these guys has already committed several murders today, so what's one more to them?

Roberts leaned on Avarie again, sending a squeal through the room.

"Boy, don't you test me!" he shouted. "I'll kill her, Sergio, but I won't do it fast. I'll blast her nose off and then put two rounds into her gut and let her bleed out. Now, show yourself!"

Sergio exhaled, gripping his gun.

Crap. No time to call in the cavalry...

He frowned.

Crap.

"Okay." Sergio stood, raising his hands over his head. "Hold your fire, Roberts. I'm coming in."

"Good boy." Roberts took another swig from his flask and tucked it into his pocket. "I can see the front door from here. Come in that way, hands raised, with your gun hanging from your left pinkie finger. Have the magazine in your right hand—and boy, the slide on that weapon had better be locked all the way to the rear, so everybody can see it's completely unloaded."

"Yeah, yeah." Sergio trudged to the entrance, unloading his weapon as instructed.

FOURTH ESTATE

Roberts can't just blast me through the door. That doesn't fit with all the planning that went into today's scheme.

So, go on in there. An opportunity will present itself. Be ready when it does.

He slipped the trigger guard over his left pinkie finger and twisted the tarnished doorknob to the trailer.

Taking a deep breath, he pushed the door open.

"Over here." Roberts waved the gun. "Get in this room. And keep those hands up."

Sergio walked into the studio, his hands raised.

"Put your gun and the magazine on that desk and step away," Roberts said. "I'll have that bulletproof vest, too."

"It's not gonna fit you." Sergio placed his gun and the magazine on the desk and stepped back, undoing the Velcro straps and slipping his Kevlar vest down over his shoulders. "These are made for people, not pachyderms." He threw the vest at Roberts' head.

Scowling, the fat detective heaved the jacket to the corner behind him. "That's enough of your smart remarks, boy. I'm about to shut that big mouth of yours for good."

As Roberts picked up Sergio's gun, beads of sweat appeared on the fat man's brow. He slipped the confiscated weapon into his suitcoat pocket and aimed his gun back at Sergio. "Now, put your back against that closet, showboat, and don't move. Don't you even breathe too fast." He nudged Avarie with the toe of his shoe. "And you, girlie. Stay low and get your butt over there by your buddy."

Groaning, the consultant crawled toward the closet, her hair falling over her ears and exposing her earbuds. She sat down, huffing as her back pressed against the flimsy wood-panel door.

Sergio looked at her.

Earbuds. Of course, she's wearing her earbuds.

He looked at her. "Can't you ever just stay put like I ask you?"

Avarie narrowed her eyes, looking up at him. "Well, I didn't the first two times, so why did you think I would this time? Besides, in my defense, he pulled a gun on me."

Nodding, Sergio frowned. "Yeah. You were probably trying to get a better signal for your phone. Stay in the car, I said. Stay down."

"I wasn't on my phone. I was looking for my wallet."

"Hey," Roberts said. "Pipe down."

"It's a simple thing." Sergio glared at her. "Stay in the car. Don't call people. Don't put your earbuds in. Stay alert, because it's a bad neighborhood. But did you listen? When a cop gives you an order, you're supposed to follow it." He pulled his phone from his pocket. "It was a dangerous situation. You shouldn't be calling people on your phone!"

Avarie's mouth hung open.

"When I tell you to do something," Sergio shouted, "it's always the opposite with you. Always the opposite! Why can't you pay attention?" He winked at her with his right eye, so the others in the room couldn't see.

Roberts raised his voice. "I said shut up."

"See the mess we're in because of you?" Sergio waved his phone at Avarie. "Are you paying attention now?"

She nodded slowly. "Yeah. Yeah, I think I get the idea."

"Shut up! Both of you!" Roberts' face turned red. "Give me that phone." Stepping forward, he pointed his gun at Sergio. "Now."

With Roberts' weapon leveled at his torso, Sergio extended his hand to give his phone to his captor.

"Wait. No." Roberts stepped back. "You might be up to something." He narrowed his eyes. "Put it on the desk. And boy—you move as slow as molasses in winter."

Ainer paced back and forth by the window, wringing his hands. "Hurry up! It's almost time."

"Do what you gotta do to be ready for your broadcast." Roberts glared at the FRT owner. "Set up your stupid computer or whatever. I'm dealing with another one of your unforeseen circumstances."

Sergio leaned over and eased his phone onto the corner of the desk. "Is that okay?"

Roberts nodded. "That's fine—smart ass."

Putting his hands in the air again, Sergio stepped back to the closet. He scowled at Avarie. "Did you understand the instructions? Or was it too complicated?"

"No," she said. "I understood perfectly."

Maintaining his surly expression, Sergio nodded. "Then do what the man said."

"Humility." Roberts grinned. "I like that. It's a new look on you, showboat."

"It sure is." Avarie placed her phone facedown on the desk. "Sergio's been ordering me around all day."

"Is that right?" Roberts chuckled. "Well, showboat here always had a thing for the ladies. I didn't know it was a dominance thing, though."

She stepped back to the closet, looking at Sergio as she pushed a strand of hair past her ear. The earbuds were visible. She let the hair drop back and turned back to Roberts. "Yeah, Sergio's been absolutely impossible. A real tyrant."

"Huh." Roberts grinned, pointing his gun at Sergio. "Well, I have a feeling he won't be pushing you or anyone else around much longer."

CHAPTER 41

As Carly ran Doctor Zumendi's Mercedes through the DMV database, her phone rang on the desk. She tapped it, answering on speaker without looking away from the computer. "Detective Sanderson here."

Sergio's voice came over the speakerphone.

"Keep complaining," Sergio said. "See where that gets you. My partner Carly was never dumb enough to say anything like that. But maybe she just always understood what I was up to."

"Maybe," a woman said, "Carly just didn't know what you were up to, Sergio."

Carly stopped typing and looked at the phone. The screen read, "Avarie Fox, Sonntag and Fox Consulting."

At the desk next to her, Deshawn and Max looked up from their work.

Carly lowered her hands from the keyboard.

That must be Avarie. What's going on?

"Carly's smart," Sergio said. "She always knew what I was up to."

Avarie laughed. "You'd better hope she's smart. No wonder you're so worried about messing up this case."

"Shut up," a man shouted in the background. "Both of you!"

Deshawn pushed his chair across to Carly's desk. "What've you got?"

Shrugging, Carly picked up her phone, holding it close to her lips.

What's going on? Do I say something? It's not like Sergio to talk to a woman like that.

Actually… They're both talking kind of strangely.

Carly opened her mouth to speak.

"Hold it!" Max jumped up and put his hand on Carly's phone, easing it down to the desk. "I think they may be talking to you, Carly. Covertly. Let's listen for a second."

* * * * *

"There we go." Ainer looked at his computer screen in the run-down trailer. "Yes… yes. It's all working." He smiled, looking at Roberts. "My interview with the doctor—I mean, my interview with the killer—is going out to the whole world, and it looks fantastic."

Sergio viewed the monitor from an angle. Ainer was on a split-screen with a man in a red windbreaker, complete with the ball cap, sunglasses, and paper face mask. Under that image, several other windows were open, streaming the content from news agencies and other websites. One of them was the Sunshine State Audits page, where Sergio's confrontation with Brimley at the FRT site was on replay.

Sergio glanced from the monitor to the man tied to the chair. The frame and body type of the hostage didn't match the man on the screen. Neither did the head shape. They were close, but not the same. Even in his slumped down position, the hostage was visibly shorter than Ainer, too.

He peered at Ainer as the media man rubbed his hands together and giggled, his eyes on the computer screen.

Ainer's hostage is a dupe, set up to take the rap for the murders. The interview was pre-recorded, so Ainer could be interviewing almost anyone. It's all a frame.

Ainer jumped up from behind the desk. "This is working better than I anticipated. We're already over a million active viewers. We could get to ten million, maybe twenty. It's all working perfectly!" The FRT chairman moved next to Roberts, eyeing Sergio and Avarie as he lowered his voice. "What, uh… what do we do with them?"

Sergio raised his hand. "If I get a vote, I say you let your three hostages go. At least release me—the unarmed cop." He looked at the consultant next to him. "You can do whatever you want with Avarie."

"Thanks, Detective." Avarie frowned at him. "You're going to get us both killed in this crappy trailer, talking like that."

* * * * *

Carly's gaze went to Deshawn, then to Max. "You're right. They're obviously talking to me."

The sergeant nodded. "But what do we do about it?"

"We triangulate the phone signal," Carly said. "We trace it to wherever Avarie's phone is, and we move a SWAT team to that location."

"Yep." Deshawn moved back to his desk. "I'm on it."

"They're in a trailer." Max opened a tab on his tablet and started typing. "And there are three hostages."

Carly's heart pounded. "I heard two other voices, both male. So, we have at least two kidnappers holding them." She frowned, putting a hand to her forehead. "But it's not enough. The kidnappers are talking about killing the hostages." Her gaze moved to the phone. "We might only have a few minutes before we're too late."

CHAPTER 42

"SIMPLE," ROBERTS SAID. "WE KILL ALL THREE OF THEM."

"Wait." Ainer put his hand on the fat detective's elbow. "All three? What will that look like?"

Roberts shrugged, pulling his arm free. He pointed his gun toward Sergio and Avarie. "You were going to set up Zumendi as a suicide by cop after pumping him full of meth—he got all hopped up in this trailer, thought he was superman, and antagonized the police into turning him into Swiss cheese. But that takes time. I have a better idea. I kill Sergio and the girl with the murder weapon, then I kill Doctor Z with my gun. An anonymous call comes in to the police about a bunch of shooting in a trailer park, and I got here first. I stand outside, and as soon as I see the patrol cars coming down that long entrance road, I fire off a few rounds with both guns, toss the murder weapon in the window, and start the fire. I tell the cops there was a shootout, and the killer is dead—but he got two last victims first. It's almost what we originally planned."

Ainer put a hand to his mouth, biting his fingernails. "I don't know. The girl and the detective aren't connected to everything like the earlier murders were. It doesn't fit."

"Sure it does." Roberts chuckled. "You took out the attorney who defended Zumendi, and the online news agencies that trashed him, the judge that convicted him... As far as these two go, it doesn't matter. The cops got the killer—that's all they care about." He glanced at Avarie. "The girl's death is an unfortunate circumstance of Sergio's bravado. He's a showboat—everybody knows that. He rushed in and they ended up getting killed. Boo frigging hoo. She was just in the wrong place at the wrong time, like Kaliope Hernandez was when you went into the Stafford law firm. It happens. But the cops will be focused on the big prize—the killer is dead. That's what all the headlines will be."

Sergio shook his head. "Those rope marks around his wrists are going to tell a different story. They'll know he was abducted."

"Think so?" Roberts said. "After you three are dead, Jamaal takes his equipment out and I drop a match in this rickety old tinder box. Good luck finding a Fire Marshal who'll sift through the smoldering ashes of a trailer and find any intact skin at all, let alone cuts from some ropes on it."

He took a step toward the duo by the closet, raising his weapon.

"Now let's get this over with."

* * * * *

Carly picked up her phone. "Sergio, Avarie—it's Carly. I can hear you. Can you let me know if you can hear me?"

Deshawn looked at the detective and pursed his lips.

Staring at her phone, Carly held her breath.

"I hear the police," Avarie said. "I hear a siren. Carly heard your prayer, Sergio. I definitely hear the cops coming."

Carly exhaled, beaming at Deshawn and Max as she pumped her fists in the air. She turned back to the phone. "We're doing all we can, but we don't know where you are yet. Can you give me a clue?"

* * * * *

Roberts went to the window. "That's a load of bull. I don't hear anything." He scowled at Avarie. "She's bluffing."

"Am I?" she said. "Get your hearing checked, old man. The north Tampa Breezeway Mobile Home Park is going to be swarming with cops in a second."

"Then we kill them now!" Roberts aimed his gun at Avarie. "And little miss big mouth gets first honors."

"No!" Ainer grabbed the fat detective's arm, yanking it downward. "We need more time. The video runs for almost fifteen minutes. The download will take at least five. It'll run by itself after that, but if you start shooting, you could draw someone's attention before I'm ready to leave. We can't go yet."

"You can't," Roberts said. "I'm finishing my part of this and getting out of here."

On the computer screen, the Sunshine State Audits website replayed the incident where Brimley and his cohorts rushed the stage and grabbed Ainer around the neck—coming away with the showman's necklace and brandishing it like a prize.

Sergio looked at the FRT owner. "You'll need more than five minutes. You'd have to redo your whole interview with the killer—because everyone can see it was faked. Who'd you get to play the other person, anyway?"

"What?" Ainer's jaw dropped. "How? How can they tell it's faked?"

Sergio nodded at the computer screen. "Look."

Ainer rushed back to his chair and stared at the screen.

On the Sunshine State Audits site, Brimley held up the necklace. On the FRT screen, Ainer was wearing it.

"You blew it," Sergio said. "You're wearing the necklace after you lost it, and you invited a million viewers to be witnesses."

Ainer dropped back in his chair, his mouth hanging open.

"Pretty soon," Sergio said, "everyone will know your livestream interview was recorded. And once they know that, they'll know the timeline doesn't match. That kinda implicates you in the murders, Ainer."

FOURTH ESTATE

The FRT owner's hands dropped to the sides of the chair. "I... I don't..." He looked at Roberts. "What do we do?"

"We kill these two!" Roberts shifted his weight from one foot to the other, breathing hard. "Then we figure the rest out. The plan can still work, Jamaal, but we can't let Sergio and the girl live after what they've seen." He pulled out his flask and took a swig. "Nobody knows they were here. We—we kill them and move the bodies to a safe site. Then we torch this trailer, just like we planned. It'll still work."

Sergio shook his head, his eyes fixed on the news man. "Jamaal, Tampa PD knows I'm here with you. You probably had a plan to avoid blame for all the other murders, but killing me—now—lands you in the electric chair."

Ainer raised his eyes to Sergio. "No, your... your office spreadsheet—it shows you're at FRT. With Roberts."

"Not anymore." Sergio smiled. "Check Avarie's phone."

"What?" Ainer reached across the desk.

"The plan will still work!" Roberts aimed his gun at Avarie. "It has to work!"

Ainer flipped over the phone. The screen displayed an active call, and the words "Carly Sanderson, Tampa PD."

"No!" Ainer shouted. "No! They've been listening the whole time?"

"Hang up, you moron!" Roberts grabbed the phone from Ainer's hand and threw it to the floor. He took his weapon in both hands and pointed it back at Avarie. "And I'll see you in Hell. Both of you."

"No!" She cringed, raising her hands. "Don't!"

"Sorry, girlie." He cocked the weapon. "But I'm not sorry."

Sergio jumped in front of Avarie as the gun fired.

Pain slammed through Sergio's chest and mouth, his ears ringing. He crashed to the floor as his chest and shoulder erupted like they were on fire.

Tiny red dots illuminated the wall behind Ainer and Roberts, like a cluster of mosquitoes carrying miniature Christmas lights.

"What's that?" The news man's voice quivered as he looked at the incandescent dots. "What's happening?"

"That's... SWAT." Frowning, Roberts looked down at his rotund torso. Half a dozen of the red beams hovered on his chest. "Those are the laser sights from their rifles." The fat detective sighed, raising his hands. "The girl was right. The police were on the way. They've got us."

Ainer squeezed his eyes shut and dropped to his knees, hanging his head.

Groaning, Sergio tried to lift himself from the floor. The ceiling and walls swung back and forth, his eyes fuzzing up with splotches of green and yellow. Warm liquid filled his mouth, spilling over his lips as he coughed.

A man's voice on a megaphone boomed through the trailer. "This is the authorities. Put your guns down and put your hands in the air!"

FOURTH ESTATE

Cursing, Roberts dropped his weapon.

The door flew open and several armed men rushed inside. They were dressed in plain clothes, carrying shotguns and hunting rifles, each with a laser sight attached.

"What?" Roberts eyes went wide. "Who are you?"

A man in a vest, with a Go Pro on his head, slammed Roberts into the wall and handcuffed him.

"You can't do this!" Roberts scowled. "I'm a cop! Under what authority do you think you can—"

"The U.S. Constitution, tyrant." Henson Brimley forced the fat detective around, leaning into his face. "I'm a sovereign citizen. That's the only authority I need."

Avarie knelt by Sergio's side, cradling his head as her eyes filled with tears. "You—are you…" She swallowed hard, blood seeping over her fingers. "Hang on, okay, Sergio?" The words caught in her throat. "Just… hang on." She looked up at the auditor. "We need an ambulance."

Brimley nodded. "The police scanner says an ambulance is on the way, and the cops are pulling up now. About time. Me and the boys have been in those bushes out back for twenty minutes." He gestured to his megaphone operator as his teammates corralled Roberts and Ainer out the door. "Help that man, Red. He's a rare thing—a good cop."

Sergio's head hummed. The pain in his chest grew softer.

As Red pressed a folded cloth to Sergio's upper chest, he put two fingers to the detective's bloody neck.

"Weak pulse," Red said. "Very weak." He shook his head, sighing. "Talk to him, ma'am. Make him... comfortable, if you can. He doesn't have long."

Sergio put his hand on Avarie's arm, trying to speak.

"They have an ambulance coming." She blinked back a tear. "Save your strength, okay? It will be here soon."

As the SWAT team entered the trailer and took over the scene, another wave of pain surged through the injured detective. Sergio forced his mouth open and lifted his head. "Tell... Carly..."

He sagged back to the floor as he choked on blood.

Avarie brushed his hair from his forehead, sniffling. "I will," she whispered. "I'll tell her something for you."

The ceiling grew dim. Sergio squeezed the consultant's arm. "Tell her..."

"Whatever you want." Tears fell from Avarie's cheeks, landing on her new friend's shoulder. "Say it. You tell me, and I'll tell her."

His lips moved, his words indecipherable. He let out a long, slow breath.

Avarie clutched his limp hand, tears filling her eyes. "You're a good man, Sergio Martin." She sniffled again, the words barely coming. "And I'll tell your partner that you... that you were thinking of her when..." Avarie blinked hard, sending another wave of tears spilled over her cheeks. "That you were thinking of her. Okay?"

FOURTH ESTATE

Sergio didn't reply. He lay motionless on the floor of the run-down trailer, his eyes fixed and unmoving.

Avarie fell forward onto him, sobbing. "You broke your promise. You said you wouldn't get shot."

Sighing, Red patted Avarie on the back. "Come on, girl. He's gone. Come away. Ain't nothing you can do for him now."

One of his Sunshine State teammates lifted a police-band radio to his mouth. "Officer down. He has... he's passed. Repeat. The downed officer has passed away."

* * * * *

At the station, Carly yanked her radio from her hip. "Who?" she shouted. "Who was it? Which officer died?"

"Stand by," the auditor said. "Miss, what was his name?"

Avarie's voice came over the radio. "He was Sergio Martin. He... he was a Tampa police detective. And a friend."

"No!" Carly dropped her radio. "No, no, no, no, no." She clutched her stomach, doubling over. "Oh, no, no, no."

CHAPTER 43

The SWAT commander climbed into the back of his armored box truck and sat next to his heavily armed squad leader. Flashing lights from his vehicles and the responding ambulance bounced off the steel walls of the truck's interior. Frowning, the commander looked at the prisoner, a handcuffed Jamaal Ainer.

Perspiration from his mission dotted the Commander's forehead and neck. He rubbed the top of his buzz cut, looking Jamaal in the eye. "I don't know what you drugged Doctor Zumendi with, but the paramedics say he's going to recover. He managed to tell them that you two were friends. So why'd you want to pin a bunch of murders on him?"

The prisoner stared at the floor. His only movement was his chest moving in and out as he breathed, and his quivering hands as one moved over the other, kneading and massaging.

DAN ALATORRE

The commander leaned forward. "Mr. Ainer, if you tell me everything, and tell me now, we're willing to take the death penalty off the table. The detectives are worried you have other murders planned or in motion, and they want to stop any more carnage." He sat back on his seat, glaring at his prisoner. "Personally, I'd prefer to see you fry."

The audience of one remained quiet.

"It's a heck of a death, the electric chair." The commander stretched, sliding his hands down his thighs and over his knees. "A guy spends ten or fifteen years in a tiny concrete box that he'll never leave alive, staring at the concrete walls, twenty-four hours a day... Then one day the appeals wear out. They walk him down to the lower level and strap him to a chair." The commander shook his head. "The blast from the voltage is so harsh, the guy's convulsing and kicking, flailing around like a rag doll in a Doberman's mouth. And after a few minutes, if the first round didn't take—I mean, after he's messed his pants, and his hair's all been scorched off, and his skin is steaming and cracked like old paint... they wind up the hot plate and go again." He sighed, looking around the interior of the fortified steel vehicle. "Sometimes it takes two, maybe three times to get the job done. By then, the guy's eyeballs have boiled up inside and popped, spilling blood all down his cheeks, and he's smelling like an outhouse in August because he's sitting there in his own feces..."

The commander fixed his gaze on the prisoner. When spoken to a criminal who had yet to become familiar with the internal workings of the

FOURTH ESTATE

Florida prison system, his speech rarely went without achieving the desired effect.

Jamaal's breathing intensified, his knees shaking.

"Or," the commander said, "you can tell me what the detectives want to know—and avoid that terrible, terrible, ugly death."

The prisoner's head sunk low. His shackled hands rested between his knees, secured to the floor with a steel chain, quivering.

"You might as well tell your side of it," the commander said. "Your partner Roberts is in the truck next door, singing like a bird. The internet's ripping you to shreds over that faked interview. Talk. Help yourself. No sense in letting everything get pinned on you."

The news man's head sunk lower, his shoulders sagging. Slowly, his head bobbed up and down. "Okay. Let's do it."

The commander checked the audio recorder. It was on.

"Doctor Jackson Zumendi—he was your friend," the commander said. "Why were you trying to ruin his life by pinning these murders on him?"

Jamaal swallowed hard. "Yeah, he was my friend. Jackie and I have known each other since we were kids. Everything always went right for him. He was good at sports, popular with girls… He went to med school, started a successful practice, had prestige… All the doors always opened for Jackie. But me?" He looked up. "My best efforts never amounted to anything. The one thing that reached any notice was FRT—because my friend, Doctor

Jackie Zumendi, took pity on me and loaned me money to avoid bankruptcy while I stole employee after employee from competitors, trying to get over the hump. And until about six months ago, FRT was still sinking under the waves. Meanwhile, Jackie was being interviewed on television for his thoughts on some new drug, or a special medical procedure. It was too much. He kept being more and more successful and I kept languishing in the shadows. I… hated him for it."

The commander sat silent, the recorder catching every word the news man uttered.

"Then…" Jamaal shrugged. "I saw a way to take it all away from him." He looked at the commander.

The murderer sat upright, the color returning to his face. "FRT had done a story about a domestic abuse situation. This lady called the cops on her husband, and the cops took the guy away that very night. He almost lost everything—his job, his house, his kids… It was all being taken away because he was sitting in jail, unable to pay a lawyer to defend him. Then, one of the child services investigators was interviewing a neighbor and she found out it was all a lie. The wife admitted to a friend that she'd made it all up. So here was this guy, totally innocent, and he was close to losing everything. If the wife hadn't opened her mouth…"

Jamaal smiled, a sparkle coming to his eyes. "That's when it came to me. I could stage a domestic abuse claim against my friend Jackie, and the rest would take care of itself—with help from FRT, of course. My news agency could play the story up, every step of the way. Prestigious doctor, accused of abuse, then a leaked story about alleged drug use, prescription fraud, insurance fraud, overbilling clients for tests that were never run… It was all alleged, of course, and always from an anonymous source who, as we say in the news business, was close to the situation. All I needed was a partner—a woman who could play Jackie for a sucker." Jamaal smiled broader. "My career has put me next to a lot of shady, good-looking young women who could do what I needed done—with the promise of a handsome monetary payoff down the road. The whole thing only took about six months. My shill got a job at Jackie's hospital, made sure she was always scheduled when he'd be working, flirted a little, but always acted like he was so smart and so interesting—which he was—but no one's immune to flattery, especially when a beautiful woman is saying it. And… and we were on our way. Pretty soon, she was staying at his house on a regular basis. She only went to her own apartment once a week to pick up the mail. When six months had passed, she started lodging the domestic calls, and the cops did what they always do in those cases. They believed her. FRT was right there, every time, splashing it all over the headlines. The other news agencies picked up the story, but with FRT leading the parade. The prestigious Doctor Jackson Zumendi got pilloried, week after week, month after month, until he was destroyed in the public eye. It was… delicious."

A giggle escaped his lips. He turned away as the smile faded, his eyes moving over the rigid steel walls surrounding him. "After that…" He shrugged, his voice growing softer. "Well, everybody would conclude that Jackie had lost it. The final chapter in the saga was, he went on a murder rampage, taking revenge on the system that had persecuted him. Case closed, end of story."

"But your partner," the commander said, "The woman—she was going to go down just like the other victims—right?"

"Not quite. It was a car accident, where she wasn't wearing a seat belt." Jamaal chuckled. "A thousand people die like that every month. That's almost forty each day. Nobody would even give it a second thought. Terri Anne Lafferty. She died three days ago, near the port. Broken neck."

The commander took a deep breath and let it out slowly. "We found the clothing on the desk—the windbreaker and the hat and all. It's covered in blood splatter and gunshot residue. Then there's the makeup kit we found in the closet of your little studio here, and your special 'lift' shoes. I have a feeling that's all going to match the crime scene evidence."

"It does." Jamaal sighed, shaking his head. "You know, since this story started, our ratings have climbed through the roof. Right now, we're number one. I... I was so close to pulling the whole thing off."

"You were." The commander nodded. "So, just to sum up... You did the killings, blamed Zumendi, and Detective Roberts ran defense. Is that about it?"

Jamaal sighed. "Roberts had access to the Tampa PD database. He told me where the cops were looking, so we could avoid being sniffed out. And he'd delete reports or move files so nobody would connect the dots."

The commander sat back. "The dots, as in, the chain of events that all had to happen before the killing could get started."

"Yes, the chain of events." Lifting his hands, Jamaal rattled the steel links that secured him to the floor. "Links in the chain."

DAN ALATORRE

CHAPTER 44

Carly forced herself upright. She tried to take a deep breath, hoping the urge to vomit would subside, but couldn't get the air to go into her lungs.

Her head throbbing, she looked at the law enforcement professionals around her. Their words to her were a buzz; noise, among other noises.

She squeezed her eyes shut, trying to focus. "What?"

Deshawn stepped to her desk. "Carly, listen to me. SWAT has the mobile home site under control. They're bringing in all those Sunshine State goofballs, too. Jamaal Ainer and Detective Roberts were behind the murders, and SWAT has them in custody. It's all under control, so why don't you—"

"Good." Carly panted. She glanced around. "That's all good. We should… uh, we…"

"The site's secure," Deshawn said. "CSI has been dispatched. Take a minute and... and get some water. You've had a shock." He put his hand under her arm. "I'm sorry, Carly. I know how tight you and Sergio were. Come on. Take a break. I'll go with you."

"We..." Carly stood, putting her hand to her brow. "We, uh... the vehicles. We—"

Max nodded. "It's okay, ma'am. We requested a tow service to bring in the suspects' vehicles."

"Okay." She stepped away from the desk. "Yes, please do that."

"Carly," Deshawn whispered. "You don't need to do this. You don't need to pretend. Take a break."

She shook her head. "I... I have to be strong. I need to... to..."

"You don't." Deshawn looked at her. "Not at a time like this. You can be human."

Taking a deep breath, Carly peered at Deshawn and swallowed hard. "Sergeant, will you take over the investigation for a few minutes please?"

"Of course," he said. "For as long as you need."

"Thank you." She walked to the ladies' room, opened the door, and stepped inside. Reaching the sinks, Carly placed her hands on the countertop and lowered her head.

The emotions welled up inside her again, crushing her insides with pain and anger and guilt. The tears came like the drops of an afternoon Florida rain, falling slowly at first, then building and building

FOURTH ESTATE

until it grew into a storm and had released its energy out onto the world.

Carly put a hand to the wall by the long mirror and closed her eyes, unable to look into the reflective glass.

"You killed him." She sobbed. "You ordered Sergio to stay at the FRT site, and that got him killed. It was your call, so it's your fault."

* * * * *

Deshawn stood with his hands on his hips, halfway between the workspace and the ladies' room, pursing his lips.

"Update, Sergeant." Max waved a hand, looking up from his tablet. "The SWAT commander reports that he got a full confession from Ainer."

Putting a hand to his forehead, Deshawn walked toward the lab tech. "What about Roberts?"

"Nothing yet." Max scrolled through the report. "According to the commander, Roberts is doing his impression of a clam. Apparently, he hasn't said a word except to ask for a lawyer. But we don't need it if Ainer admitted to the murders."

Exhaling, the sergeant shook his head. "Don't worry, Roberts' tongue will loosen up after he figures out that Jamaal would have killed him, too. That guy wanted no loose ends. But why did he do all this in the first place? That's what bothers me."

"Jealousy," Max said. "The commander's notes say Ainer was obsessed with Doctor Zumendi. He kept comparing himself to his friend, who was always doing better, and it ate him up." He lowered the tablet, peering at the sergeant. "What a shame. Ainer was obviously a very smart guy. Imagine if he'd have used the FRT news agency for something good, instead of making it a scandal rag. Who knows what might have happened."

Deshawn shook his head. "For whatever reason, Ainer apparently just didn't have that in him."

* * * * *

The ladies' room door flew open. Carly stormed to her desk, grabbing her keys and purse. "I'm going to Tampa General Hospital."

Deshawn recoiled. "Hold on a second. You're doing what?"

Her cheeks burning, Carly turned and headed toward the elevators at the other end of the hallway. "I'm going to Tampa General. The investigation is all but mopped up. I'll do the paperwork tomorrow."

"Carly," Deshawn said. "No. You've had a shock. We all have. Take a few minutes."

"No!" She wheeled around, tears brimming at the corners of her eyes. "Not now. I can't, Deshawn. You said I should delegate? I'm delegating." She pointed her finger at her desk. "You take over the wrap up. Tell the EMTs at the mobile home park to take Sergio's body to Tampa General Hospital for the postmortem. I'll…" Her voice wavered. "I'll meet him there."

"Okay, Carly." Deshawn nodded. "Whatever you want. It's your call."

"I forced Sergio to stay at FRT, Deshawn." She looked the sergeant in the eye. "My decision is the reason he's dead. The whole world watched it on the internet, so the least I can do is face his mother and sister when they come for the body. I won't make them go to the morgue." She lowered her voice, her gaze going to the floor. "I put him on that assignment. I got him killed. The least I can do is face his mother and sister myself when they find out."

Turning away, Carly pressed the elevator call button and closed her eyes.

It was my call.

DAN ALATORRE

CHAPTER 45

As the elevator descended, Carly's service radio squelched. She sighed, reaching down and clicking it off.

I delegated. I'm done with that crap for the night.

She took out her phone and powered it off as well.

The elevator arrived at the lobby, her insides growing emptier and emptier. She walked across the spacious tile floor as if she were in a daze, reaching the parking garage and driving toward Tampa General Hospital without focus.

My friend, partner and lover are... gone.

The pain welled up inside her again. Thoughts of what she would tell his mother—and the ensuing emotional scene—filled her head, only to be pushed out by images of Sergio. Laughing at one of her lame jokes. Playing in the yard with her boys...

And then the image of his mother reappeared in Carly's mind, with his sister.

And the cycle started again.

She inhaled deeply, trying to shake it off.

Cry later. Right now, be strong for his family. He would want that.

Past tense.

From now on, the man she had come to care about and trust like no other, would no longer be referred to in the present, because she had caused him to no longer be alive.

You took Sergio from his mother and sister, and you took him from yourself.

Her chest ached. Blackness flooded through her insides.

He's gone, and you're the reason.

There would be no more fun mornings, playing around as they dressed for work. There would be no more late-night dinners after a case, eating hot wings as he joked about their boss or their workmates. No more looking across a desk as she filed reports and seeing him looking back at her.

She remembered the first time she ever met him.

"Detective Sanderson? Hi, I'm Sergio Martin. Sorry I'm late. I misunderstood. I thought they said 'Carl,' so I was watching for the big hairy guy from ballistics."

He was young and handsome, sporting the trademark smile she would come to enjoy on a daily basis, and the sense of humor.

FOURTH ESTATE

But he had become more than a friend and partner. Carly's thoughts filled with the images from the first time she thought about kissing her partner, one night after they'd gone for a drink after work.

Sergio had regaled her with a story about being at an outdoor party the year after he graduated high school. While there, he had run into a few girls who he recognized as being a year or two behind him in school. He gave them a friendly wave from across the lawn, and one of them meandered over by herself—after a few pokes and prods from her friends. Pleasantries were exchanged, and then she blurted out that she'd had the biggest crush on Sergio in school. She said she had really liked watching him play sports… and had always wanted to kiss him.

Carly had anticipated the end of the tale—that Sergio bedded the young lady—but his story took an interesting turn. He said he smiled his best smile at her and asked her to come to the side of the house, where he gently took her face in his hands and gave her a long, slow, soft kiss.

He eased his lips away from hers, telling her how beautiful she was and that he wished she had told him her feelings back in high school.

Afterward, the girl went back to her friends. Sergio's pals teased him that he let the fish off the hook instead of reeling her in, but he disagreed. She wanted a kiss, he said. Doing more would have ruined a happy fantasy she'd kept all those years.

That night, Carly imagined the girl, working up her courage, gazing at Sergio's square jaw and full lips… and imagined herself in the girl's place.

As the memory faded, her insides emptied again. The traffic light ahead turned red. Carly stopped her car, lowering her head to the steering wheel.

That's all gone now.

He's gone. He's gone. He's gone.

She lifted her head, the tall façade of Tampa General Hospital filling the horizon.

"Okay, that's enough, Carly." She sniffled, wiping the back of her hand under her nose. "You need to be strong now. Sergio's mother and sister deserve that. Be a professional."

The light turned green. Carly took her foot from the brake and sat there, gripping the steering wheel, her foot hovering over the gas pedal.

She would walk into the emergency entrance and approach the admitting nurse at the desk, the way she had done many times before. She would get the room number of the individual she had come to see. She'd walk to the elevator and arrive at the proper floor and walk down the long white corridor. And then she would enter the room where Sergio's body laid.

And her life would forever change.

Swallowing hard, she pressed the gas pedal and headed to the hospital entrance.

CHAPTER 46

Carly slowed her pace as she neared the room number the admitting nurse had given her.

She had never hesitated before, in all the times she had to view a corpse and explain to the loved ones what had happened. She hated it, but she never hesitated. It was part of the job.

But this time, it was more than that.

She clutched her hands, dreading walking into the room.

Behind her, the elevator bell dinged. The doors opened and Sergio's mother and sister stepped out.

Carly grimaced.

Oh, no.

She wasn't ready.

Taking a deep breath, she turned to walk toward them, but her feet wouldn't move.

"Where is he?" Sergio's mother shouted. "Where is my boy?" She walked toward the room, her face red, looking at each room number.

Carly's heart sunk.

Mina held onto her mother's arm. "It's down the hall. This way." She peered at Carly. "Oh, I didn't expect to see you here. Which—"

A burst of laughter came from inside one of the hospital rooms.

"How do you explain that?" a man said.

"Well," another said, "he never was any good at the medical side of things."

Another round of laughter spilled into the hallway.

"At least he didn't pass out!"

Carly sighed. Someone was getting good news in a hospital room, and their friends and family were enjoying it with them.

She wished it was her.

"Where is my boy?" Sergio's mother said.

Carly turned to the women. "I'm sorry, Mrs. Martin. I…"

Sergio's mother turned to his sister. "What room did they say?"

Mina pointed to a nearby door. "Five twenty-one, Mama. It's the next one down." She rolled her eyes, smiling at Carly. "Hi, Detective Sanderson."

Carly recoiled. "What?"

Sergio's voice came from inside the room. "Hey, I saved your life, little sister. You owe me dinner, at least. I'm starving."

"There." His mother frowned. "There is that idiot son of mine!" She pushed past Carly and entered the room.

Her jaw hanging open, Carly staggered in behind her.

Sergio sat on the side of the hospital bed, his shirt off. Avarie leaned over and gave him a kiss. "Thank you for saving my life."

The room was filled with people. Doctors, nurses, several men in plain clothes. Carly sagged into the wall.

What is happening?

"Idiota!" Sergio's mother stormed to his bedside, smacking him on the arm. "Why you don't return my calls? Your sister was hurt!"

"What?" Sergio flinched, raising his arm. A large bruise was visible on his collarbone. "I've been trying to call you both all day!" He looked at his sister. "Mina texted me and said *you* were hurt, Mom. I tried to call you back a hundred times to find out what was going on."

"No. You didn't call me." Mrs. Martin smacked him again, holding up her phone. "I don't have any messages from you today! None!"

Sergio grabbed her phone. "That's because your phone is turned off!"

His mother looked at the phone, her face falling. "What? How is that?"

Sergio glanced at his sister. "Maybe you could tell me what happened."

Mina shook her head. "It was nothing. I twisted my ankle, and Mama insisted we come in and get it checked out." She lifted her foot, wiggling it.

"See? I'm fine. But she insisted on taking my phone and powering it off until I healed—whenever that is. We only knew to come because your sergeant called us on her land line."

"I bring Mina for an x-ray because my son buys us the good insurance." She turned to Sergio, scowling. "And I turned off the phone because it gives off radiation. But you still should have called!"

Sergio faced Carly, smiling. "Will you help me with this?"

"You..." Carly put her hands to her abdomen. "You're alive."

"For the moment. Maybe you can arrest my mom before that situation changes." He picked up his phone and held it up to his mother. "Look. It says right here, 'Come to Tampa General ASAP. Mama is trouble.' See? *Mama* is in trouble. I thought you had a heart attack."

"No," his mother said. "You read it wrong. It says, 'Come to Tampa General ASAP. Mama. There is trouble.' You can't read?"

Sergio laughed. "That is not what it says!"

"Why would you think your mother has a heart attack?" Mrs. Martin frowned, taking her phone. "Why do you wish bad things for me? It's a sin!"

Shaking his head, Sergio looked at his partner. "Help me, would you?"

"You're alive." Carly dropped her hands to her sides. "You're alive!"

She raced to Sergio, throwing her arms around him.

FOURTH ESTATE

"Hey!" He winced. "Take it easy. I may have a broken collar bone."

"No." A doctor walked toward the bed, carrying an x-ray print. "There's no fracture. Just a bad bruise. You'll be able to go home in a few minutes."

Carly looked at Sergio. "They said you were dead. On the radio—I heard it…"

"Oh, that was my man Red's fault, ma'am." Henson Brimley stepped forward, his Go Pro headband in his hands. "He's one of my auditors. Made the wrong call there." He shrugged. "Sorry. He must not have been paying enough attention during our militia's medical training."

Avarie nodded. "They updated the erroneous report a few minutes later. I guess you didn't get the news."

"No, I didn't." She looked at Sergio, tears in her eyes, her arms still wrapped around his neck. "I was… I thought…" She closed her eyes, burying her face in his naked shoulder.

Sergio patted her on the back. "I'm okay, I promise."

"Your reporter friend was there, too," Brimley said. "At the trailer—that Milner gal. Taking all kinds of pictures. She said to tell you she's sorry she baited you into going to FRT, but she had a feeling if she followed you, she'd get a good story."

"Sneaky." Sergio chuckled. "She might have what it takes to be the head of her own news agency one day."

Avarie looked at Carly and pointed to Sergio's bruised collarbone. "Detective Roberts shot

Sergio when we were trapped at the mobile home park, but Sergio was wearing a bullet proof vest…"

"A second one," Sergio said.

"Right. A second one." Avarie nodded. "And the bullet knocked him down, but…"

"I hit my head on the floor," Sergio said. "When I did, I bit my tongue and somehow gave myself a bloody nose. I must have gotten a concussion from the impact, because I kinda passed out."

"No. No concussion." The doctor peered at Sergio's medical chart. "You're a little dehydrated and your blood sugar level is very low. That's the culprit." He snapped shut his metal clipboard. "What have you had to eat today?"

Sergio scrunched up his face. "Uh… nothing."

"Mm-hmm." The doctor turned toward the door. "Eat something, Detective. We need these rooms for people who are actually sick."

As the doctor left, Avarie chuckled. "Anyway, with all that blood, and him passing out, the auditor guy came over and checked his pulse. He said Sergio was dead. Then, the EMTs got there and they said he wasn't."

"Again, sorry to scare everybody." Brimley lowered his head. "Red's in a lot of hot water for that one."

"Oh, I can't believe you're not dead." Carly hugged Sergio again. "I mean, I'm glad you're not dead." She pulled away, frowning. "And what was that when I came in here?" She smacked Sergio on the arm. "I thought you were dead. I come in here and you're—you're in here making out with the consultant! What was that all about?" Heat rose to Carly's cheeks. "Is that what you two have been up to all day? Why were you kissing her?"

Sergio rubbed his arm. "I wasn't."

"We must have different definitions of kissing, then." Carly stood, placing her hands on her hips.

"She was saying thank you." Sergio shrugged. "It wasn't like I asked her. Or like I even enjoyed it."

"Hey!" Avarie said.

"Well, I enjoyed it, but—Carly, it wasn't that kind of thing! She was happy because I saved her life. You heard her."

"You know what? Never mind." Carly turned and stormed to the door. "I don't want to know. Today's been one thing after another, and I'm done. It's been too much today. So if you'll excuse me…" She left the room, her cheeks on fire.

* * * * *

As the people in the room chuckled, Avarie shook her head. "Is your partner aways like this?"

"Almost never," Sergio said. "But then she never walked in on me kissing a—hey, I need to go." He jumped up from the bed and grabbed his shirt.

"Go." Avarie waved. "We'll have dinner another time—all three of us. After she calms down. My treat."

"That could be a while." He raced out the door, the room bursting into laughter again.

* * * * *

Officer Mellish sat at his desk just outside Lieutenant Davis' office, updating the evening's reports. The phone rang at the Lieutenant's desk, so Mellish punched the extension and answered it. "Lieutenant Davis' desk, Officer Jordan Mellish speaking."

"Jordan?" Chief Clemmons asked. "Where's Don?"

Mellish glanced at the restroom doors. "He's unavailable at the moment, sir. Is there something I can help you with?"

"Oh, nothing important. I just finished up with Mayor Mills. He's very happy about the way the case wrapped up, and he happened to mention an old unsolved case—Sarah Tarrington, from about ten years ago. The mayor thought Sarah was the first victim, and I thought she was the second one. Not a big deal, but we were going back and forth, and I couldn't find it in the system…"

"I can check that for you, sir." Mellish put Chief Clemmons on speakerphone and got up, going to a row of metal filing cabinets. "Some of that older stuff was never computerized." He scanned the drawer labels and moved to the one marked T-U, opening it. A mass of beige folders presented themselves, jammed to overflowing with papers.

Lieutenant Davis stormed down the hallway, pausing at his office door. "This night has been a disaster." Davis shook his head. "No matter what I try, I can't win."

Mellish looked up from his files. "Sir?"

"I told you," Davis said. "Using this consultant was my best chance to get rid of Sergio,

FOURTH ESTATE

and I'm blowing it. I wanted that girl glued to Sergio's hip night and day, and instead of screwing up, he's looking like a hero. Now, how am I going to undo that?"

Mellish looked at his phone and held his hand up. "Lieutenant—"

"Don't you understand?" Davis paced back and forth. "Sergio Martin is making a laughingstock out of me, and I'm going to run him off." He looked at Mellish. "Can we change the reports for tonight? Can we say he disobeyed an order? There has to be something."

The officer pointed to his desk. "Lieutenant, please don't say—"

"I'll say whatever I have to! I'll make it up if necessary—since Sergio didn't screw up." Davis put a hand to his brow. "There has to be a way to hang this guy out to dry. I just—"

Mellish shook his head. "Sir!"

"What?" Davis grimaced. "What do you want?"

"The chief." Mellish pointed to the phone on his desk. "He's on speakerphone."

Davis stared at the phone, the blood draining out of his face. His jaw dropped. "Sp… speaker?"

The Chief cleared his throat. "Lieutenant Davis…"

"Sir, I…" Davis put a hand to his mouth. "Uh… Chief Clemmons, I, uh…" He went to the desk, leaning close to the phone. "I hope you didn't misunderstand me, in what I said just now. What I meant was that Detective Martin is a fine officer, and, uh…"

"Oh, I understood you perfectly, Lieutenant." The chief's voice was gruff. "In fact, I've been considering your job performance for quite a while. It's time we looked at a different assignment for you."

Davis panted. "A... a different assignment, sir?"

"Yes," the chief said. "The parking meter division has been looking for a supervisor. That might be better suited for your talents than overseeing the detective squad."

"But, sir..."

"Or I could just fire you. Hostile workplace, misappropriation of funds, attempting to falsify reports. Totally your choice."

Davis swallowed hard. "I've actually been..." He lowered his head and closed his eyes. "Chief, I think that sounds like... like an exceptional... What I mean to say is, I'd be very... uh, very interested..." His voice faded. "I've... actually wanted to transfer to the parking meter division for quite some time, sir."

His head hit the desk.

"That's what I thought," the chief said. "Put in a transfer request—tonight. I don't want you anywhere near the detectives again. Is that clear?"

"Yes, Chief."

"Good. I'll expect to see you at the motor pool for the parking meter division's scooters in the morning. It's oil change day. Don't be late."

The call ended.

Davis staggered into his office and closed the door.

FOURTH ESTATE

Deshawn walked up to Mellish, looking at him and smiling. "It was your idea to put that consultant with Sergio in the field, wasn't it? Letting her see him push the limits."

Mellish shrugged. "It's what he does best. Doing a duty tour and meeting with department heads would almost certainly result in Sergio making a comment that would get him into hot water. Chasing bad guys is what he's best at. Keeping her with him in the field was the only way to keep Sergio out of trouble."

Deshawn cocked his head. "Even if he bent some rules?"

"Especially then." Mellish lifted a faded folder from the drawer and shut the filing cabinet.

Lieutenant Davis opened his office door and stepped out, his face gray.

Mellish placed the case file next to his computer. "Seeing the reason behind why a rule might need to be bent, and seeing Sergio making that decision in real time, with limited information…" He faced the sergeant. "That would be very hard for a consultant to dismiss. If Averie Fox was truly interested in improving the department in the eyes of the community, Detective Martin would almost certainly end up being the star of her report."

"You snake." Davis scowled at his former assistant. "You undercut me."

"Yeah. I learned from the best." Mellish put his hands in his pockets and walked away. "Maybe I'll see you around the parking meters, Don."

* * * * *

In the hallway of Tampa General Hospital, Sergio trotted after his partner. "Please stop. Please?"

Carly kept walking.

As she approached the elevators, the doors opened. Carly got in, with Sergio making it just as the doors shut.

She turned her nose up. "Don't bother explaining yourself. I don't care."

Sergio chewed his lip.

Yes, you do. Only a woman who cares a lot would be this upset.

He held his breath, uncertain of what to do.

The elevators stopped at the fourth floor. Another man got on, reading the news on a tablet. After a moment, the man chuckled. "Check it out," he said. "One of our state senators wants to end Daylight Savings Time."

Sergio kept his eyes on Carly; she kept her eyes on the elevator display.

"I'm all for that," the man said. "Daylight Savings Time is awful."

The elevator stopped on the third floor. The man tucked his tablet under his arm and departed.

As the elevator commenced its downward journey, Sergio shifted his weight from one foot to the other. "You know, that's not a bad idea—getting rid of Daylight Savings Time. I mean, in December, I'd go over to mow my mom's lawn at noon, and I'd be worried it was gonna be dark before I finished."

Carly stared at the elevator display, offering no response

"When it switches," Sergio said, "I keep thinking it's later than it is. I wake up and the clock says four in the morning, and I'm like, well... It's really five, right? Getting up at five's not too insane. But then I'll fall asleep at seven in the evening. It's totally messed up."

His partner's face remained frozen.

"I bet pets get confused, too. They can't tell time, so all they know is, it's dark and my humans haven't fed me yet."

A hint of a smile tugged at the corners of Carly's mouth.

Sergio grinned. "But I think if we just got rid of Daylight Savings Time all together, everybody would adjust. What we need is, some kind of a holiday to replace it. Like something with fireworks. What do you think?"

Carly looked at her phone. "I like fireworks."

A massive grin stretched across Sergio's face.

"So," he said, "twice a year we'd have a big fireworks thing and some kind of special meal. And then, it's a holiday and everybody loves it."

"Like, remember those days that used to suck?" Carly said. "We fixed that."

"Pheasant, maybe." Sergio rubbed his chin. "It sounds nice and it's one of the most underrepresented meats in holiday dining. Heck, I'd even go for pork chops. Maybe with French fries."

Carly chuckled. "I want party food. Nachos. Chili cheese fries would work, too."

"Besides," Sergio said, "I'm under the impression that if we hadn't made turkey the official Thanksgiving meal, we would eat turkey a heck of a lot more often. We screwed that up. I like turkey, but unless I get a turkey sub for lunch, I only have turkey once a year."

The elevator doors opened. Carly walked out, heading toward the parking garage. "You should write that senator. Voice your support."

"I think I will. Or—were you kidding?"

She smiled. "Maybe."

"Huh." He shrugged. "I think I will anyway."

As she made her way into the parking facility, he followed behind.

"Are you free for dinner?" Sergio asked. "I'm kinda hungry now. And the doctor said—"

Carly wheeled around, glaring at him. "Don't ever do that again."

"Dude, I promise." Sergio held his hands up. "You are the only woman I kiss from now on. Except for my mom."

"Not that crap." Carly stepped toward him, jabbing her finger into his chest. "I mean… Don't ever… let me think you died." Her expression softened, her words catching in her throat. "I hated thinking I'd lost you. My whole body ached. It was the worst. I can't… Don't ever…" She wrapped her arms around him. "Just don't, okay?"

He nodded. "I promise."

She pressed her lips to his, the warmth radiating through him. When she pulled away, she put her head on his shoulder and let out a long, slow breath. Sergio stroked her hair, peering at the back of her head. "Is it safe to assume you missed your dinner with Kyle?"

"I texted him and cancelled." Carly lifted her eyes to meet Sergio's "He had his chance. I've moved on."

An even bigger smile stretched across Sergio's face.

"Come on." Carly took his hand. "I know a diner that serves awesome pork chops."

They walked together across the parking garage, holding hands as they headed to her vehicle.

"Then," Carly said, "some of the dealerships are open late. We can do some car shopping."

THE END

Carly and Sergio will return in
DOUBLE BLIND BOOK 5

FIVE SPARROWS

The body of a seventh-grade student is found in the woods near the exclusive school she attended. It could be a suicide, or it could be a murder; Carly and Sergio are called to investigate. Security recordings might show the killer, but those have gone missing and the administration wants everything kept quiet to preserve the institution's reputation. But someone is quietly pointing the detectives toward secret societies that allegedly don't exist at the school, and the bullying that allegedly takes place on campus. The most powerful group, a small clan of girls called The Sparrows, was recruiting the deceased girl, but none of the sparrows are talking—and their influential parents are threatening lawsuits if any of their precious young darlings are implicated.

**Find out when and where you can enjoy this new book by joining my Readers Club at www.DanAlatorrer.com
as well as getting the inside scoop on other stuff before anyone else.**

And if you liked Fourth Estate, please pop over to Amazon and Goodreads to say so. Just a few words from you helps other readers find a new book they'll love.

A NOTE FROM THE AUTHOR

Dear Reader,

I hope you enjoyed Fourth Estate. I always enjoy the banter between Carly and Sergio, and it's fun to put them in a new, different situation where it seems like they can't get out, and then try to figure out… How to get them out!

Readers always ask what's next for their favorite characters. Some of them want to see more of these newer characters, like Avarie and Max, and some want to see old friends like Big Brass, Tyree; and Abbie… Others want to see new and different villains. I think I'll be able to accomplish all of that in the next book of the series.

Remember, YOU are the reason that I will explore the future of these characters! So, tell me what you liked, what you loved, what you hated… I'd love to hear from you. You can write me at www.DanAlatorre.com under the "Contact Me" button.

Finally, I need a favor. If you'd be so kind, I'd love

a review of Fourth Estate. Love it or hate it, I'd really enjoy your feedback. Your honest review will help readers who like what you like to find my stories, and help those with other tastes to not pick up a book they won't enjoy.

Thanks a bunch for reading Fourth Estate and spending time with me. It's an honor to know you enjoy my stories.

In gratitude,
Dan Alatorre

ABOUT THE AUTHOR

Dan Alatorre has published more than 50 titles in over a dozen languages. His unique page turners will make you scream, chuckle or shed tears—sometimes on the same page. His novels always contain unexpected twists and turns, and his amazing characters will stay with you forever.

Readers agree, making his thrillers #1 on bestseller lists across the globe.

You'll find heart stopping chills in the medical thriller series The Gamma Sequence, intense crime drama in the thriller series Double Blind, action-adventure in the sci-fi mystery The Navigators, a gripping roller coaster ride in the paranormal mystery A Place Of Shadows, an atypical comedy-romance story in the hilarious and very sexy The Italian Assistant, spine-tingling chills in the short story horror anthology series Dark Passages, and much more.

Prior to becoming a bestselling author, Dan achieved President's Circle with two different Fortune 500 companies. He resides in the Tampa, Florida, area with his wife and daughter.

To join his Readers Club and learn about new books and special offers before the general public, go to DanAlatorre.com and click the link!

DAN ALATORRE

FOURTH ESTATE

OTHER BOOKS BY DAN ALATORRE

NOVELS
Jett Thacker Mysteries
Tiffany Lynn Is Missing, *a psychological thriller*
Killer In The Dark, *Jett Thacker book 2*

The Gamma Sequence Medical Thriller Series
The Gamma Sequence, *a medical thriller*
Rogue Elements, *The Gamma Sequence, book 2*
Terminal Sequence, *The Gamma Sequence, book 3*
The Keepers, *The Gamma Sequence, book 4*
Dark Hour, *The Gamma Sequence, book 5*

Double Blind Murder Mystery Series
Double Blind, *a murder mystery*
Primary Target, *Double Blind book 2*
Third Degree, *Double Blind book 3*
Fourth Estate, *Double Blind book 4*

OTHER THRILLER NOVELS
A Place Of Shadows, *a paranormal mystery*
The Navigators, *a time travel thriller*

OTHER BOOKS
The Water Castle, *a fantasy romance novel*
The Italian Assistant, *a very funny, very sexy romance novel*

Dan Alatorre Short Story Horror Anthologies
Dark Passages
Dark Voodoo
Dark Intent
Dark Thoughts

DAN ALATORRE

Short Story Horror Anthologies With Other Authors
The Box Under The Bed
Dark Visions
Nightmareland
Spellbound
Wings and Fire
Shadowland

Family Humor
Savvy Stories
The Terrible Twos
The Long Cutie
The Short Years
There's No Such Thing As A Quick Trip To Buy-Mart
Night of the Colonoscopy
Santa Maybe
A Day for Hope

Illustrated Children's Books
Laguna the Lonely Mermaid
The Adventures of Pinchy Crab
The Princess and the Dolphin
Stinky Toe!

Children's Early Reader Books
The Zombunny
Zombunny 2: Night of the Scary Creatures
Zombunny 3: Quest for Battle Space

Writing Instruction
A if for Action
B is for Backstory
C is for Character
D is for Dialogue
E is for Emotion
F is for Fast Pace

FOURTH ESTATE

DAN ALATORRE

Made in the USA
Coppell, TX
05 July 2023